~ *The* ~
Ringmaster's
Daughter

CARLY SCHABOWSKI

~ *The* ~
Ringmaster's
Daughter

GRAND CENTRAL
PUBLISHING

NEW YORK   BOSTON

Copyright © 2020 by Storyfire Ltd.
Written by Carly Schabowski

Reading group guide copyright © 2021 by Carly Schabowski and
Hachette Book Group, Inc.

Cover design by Sarah Whittaker
Cover photos: night sky by Deyan Georgiev/Shutterstock; planes © Matt Gibson/
Shutterstock; circus tent © RMMPPhotography/Shutterstock
Cover copyright © 2021 by Hachette Book Group, Inc.

Grand Central Publishing
Hachette Book Group
1290 Avenue of the Americas, New York, NY 10104
grandcentralpublishing.com
twitter.com/grandcentralpub

Originally published in trade paperback by Bookouture, an imprint of
Storyfire Ltd., Carmelite House, 50 Victoria Embankment, London EC4Y 0DZ
First Grand Central Publishing edition: November 2021

Grand Central Publishing is a division of Hachette Book Group, Inc.
The Grand Central Publishing name and logo is a trademark of
Hachette Book Group, Inc.

The publisher is not responsible for websites (or their content)
that are not owned by the publisher.

The Hachette Speakers Bureau provides a wide range of authors for
speaking events. To find out more, go to www.hachettespeakersbureau.com
or call (866) 376-6591.

Library of Congress Cataloging-in-Publication Data has been applied for.

ISBN: 978-1-5387-5455-9 (trade paperback)

Printed in the United States of America

LSC-C

Printing 1, 2021

For my mother,
who always taught me that wondrous things could happen.

PART ONE: SUMMER

Between the dusk of a summer night
And the dawn of a summer day,
We caught at a mood as it passed in flight,

And we bade it stoop and stay.
And what with the dawn of night began
With the dusk of day was done;
For that is the way of woman and man,
When a hazard has made them one.

"Between the Dusk of a Summer Night," William Ernest Henley

CHAPTER ONE

Paris

The streets of Paris wound their way around Michel Bonnet as he walked to his small apartment in the 14th arrondissement. The evening sun was reluctant to descend, and the early summer heat clogged the air along with exhaust fumes, dust and garbage. The Seine was a deep green, and Michel stood on the bridge of Pont Neuf, watching it snake its way out of the city.

Small boats sluggishly cut a path through the water, as if it had thickened to soup, and people ambled along embankments, unaware of their watcher from above.

On one such embankment stood a husband and wife with their small daughter at their heels. Michel watched as the father picked up the child and held her high to see the river and beyond. Suddenly, the child waved, and Michel waved back until the family were out of sight. Michel leaned against the stone of the bridge, still warm from the day's heat, feeling the chill of the river reaching him from the depths beneath, as dragonflies hummed and skipped over the heavy water, cooling themselves.

The broad blue sky was streaked with thin clouds and held no promise of rain. Michel hitched his bag further up his shoulder and continued his journey home, every now and then wiping the sweat away from the back of his neck with his red handkerchief.

The warm winds stirred up the dust on the pavements into mini tornadoes that raced towards his shoes, encasing them with a thin layer of city soot, reminding Michel of summers spent in the countryside as a child, when he would chase the dust as it danced down tracks edged with neatly plowed soil and tall sunflowers. The winds stirred something in Michel too; a feeling akin to when his maman died, which had changed everything so deeply and quickly that Michel had still not realized the full force of it. Michel whispered to the wind to take his love to his mother, to say hello, and that he missed her. Yet the wind whipped by Michel, capturing only a few of his words, so that he was left wondering just what it was his maman would hear.

The city should have been busier this time of year—when schoolchildren usually clogged the pavements with their chatter and glee to be free for the summer, and tourists sat politely at cafés sipping iced drinks—yet the city was as dead as if August had come early and its occupants had sought holidays away from the oppressive heat. Michel noticed that the bars usually frequented by many a rich gentleman were empty, the lone bartender left to wipe away imaginary watermarks from the mahogany bar. Maître d's stood with waiters, talking, and shaking their heads at the lack of wealthy customers, whilst the awnings of red, blue and yellow fluttered relentlessly in the breeze above them.

The bombs that had fallen just four days earlier had sent a ripple of fear across the city and now shop windows were taped and boarded up, air raid shelters were being stocked with provisions, and all around there was quiet—too much quiet.

Sandbags had arrived quickly to shore up doorways, and every now and then the hum of a military aircraft would drone overhead, causing those left in Paris to turn their faces to the sky to see if it was all really about to happen—would the City of Light really be taken from them? Michel stopped now and watched as another plane flew low through the skies. Behind him, two waiters ceased polishing already clean glasses.

"I hear they crossed the River Meuse in only one day," one waiter said.

"They have webbed feet; it's no wonder they crossed that quickly," the other answered.

"Webbed feet?"

"How can they be human and get here so quickly? Must be webbed feet."

"You're mad."

"They say a school was hit, you know. They killed schoolchildren."

"They kill everyone. Children. Old people. Everyone. They don't care."

"There's still smoke in the sky from those buildings—almost like it can't escape Paris."

"It can't. We can't either."

Michel turned away from the expensive restaurants and towards home, where coffee shops were still busy as people huddled close to radios to listen to the latest news. Soon he turned down a small cobbled lane where shops and small cafés sat cramped together in harmony; the flowers from one hanging basket escaping and joining the next, tables and chairs so cluttered that you were not sure which café you were sitting at, yet no one cared. Men sat and drank thick tumblers of beer, and women wore red lipstick and drank house wine, all of them talking about the bombs, about the time they had left.

"If I'm going to go, I'm going with a beer in my hand and a full stomach," one man shouted to the people at the tables.

A joyous cheer rose up. "Best get the drinks in then!" another retorted.

Michel noticed a few familiar faces but continued on, before stopping outside Arnoud's boucherie, where the carcasses of cows and pigs hung from weighty hooks in a window that had been taped and secured, and where two stray dogs sat outside, waiting patiently for Arnoud to give them their daily scraps.

Michel patted one of the dogs on the head, but the animal took no notice, his eyes transfixed on the meaty shell of a cow. "Ah, not long now," he told the dogs. "Almost closing. I'll get mine first, then it will be your turn."

"Is that you, Michel?" Arnoud's roar sailed out to Michel from inside the shop.

Michel walked inside and pulled his money from his breast pocket; a thin roll, barely a weight at all.

"Ah, *bonjour*. Has it been a month already?" Arnoud asked.

"Not quite, but I got paid today." Michel handed over a few francs to cover the cost of some mutton and a couple of slices of ham.

"Is that all you can afford? That gypsy does not pay you enough."

"He is gone."

"I'm not surprised. I told you he would leave. Not one to stick around—you shouldn't either."

"You said the same thing last month."

"And I'll say it again. He treated you like an old blind woman; made you depend on him but left your purse almost empty. You have been taking care of those horses, training them, feeding them, and what does he pay you? A pittance, that's all. And now look. He's gone."

Arnoud's mustache twitched and he fell silent as the thick, shining blade sliced down into the ham, cutting it so thinly that Michel swore he could see through it. "And I'll keep saying it until you come to your senses."

Suddenly the back door flew open and Estelle, Arnoud's teenage daughter, appeared, her perfect young skin flushed from racing downstairs.

"Michel!" she greeted him, barely hiding her breathlessness.

Michel saw Arnoud turn to look at his daughter, shake his head, then move to wrap up the ham in paper.

"Estelle. How are you?" Michel asked.

"I'm fine, thank you. You know, as fine as I can be. Every day I must come back here to help my father, but I am fine."

"You torment me every day, when you are not at that art school," Arnoud said. "That one that costs me money, yet I see nothing in return."

"Oh, Papa." Estelle kissed Arnoud on the cheek. "One day it will."

"She's right, Arnoud. You just have to be patient," Michel said.

"See! Michel understands. And, Michel, I *am* patient. As patient as…" Estelle trailed off as she gazed out of the shop's large window. "As patient as those stray dogs!" She laughed. "I will wait just like them to get what I want."

Michel took his handkerchief from his pocket and wiped the back of his neck again.

"Estelle, go and do something useful. For a seventeen-year-old girl you are always under my feet, like a small child!"

Estelle ignored Arnoud. "Did you walk home again, Michel? Is that why you are so hot? I can get you water."

"No, no, I'm fine." Michel tucked his handkerchief away. "It's the weather, that's all."

"You know, you shouldn't have to walk all that way. It's not safe. What if a bomb had dropped right on top of you?"

"*Estelle*," Arnoud said wearily, "are you still here? I said, go and do something useful. Go and practice your art or help your mother prepare dinner—just, something."

"Did you see the planes, Michel? I sit and watch them. We were given a letter today at school, telling us that the Germans are getting closer to Paris every day—not just planes, but *actual German men*, with guns and tanks. Do you believe that, Michel? That they will come?"

"I didn't—I thought we could hold them off. But I think now we have no hope."

"Maman says they rape women. She says we should be thankful we are not Jewish."

"Estelle! Enough! Go and help your mother. Tell her to stop filling your head with rubbish."

"Yes, Papa." Estelle retreated, but just before she closed the door, Michel was sure she winked at him.

"I'm sorry, Michel. A handful, as you can see."

"She's just young," Michel said.

"Yes. Young. Young and stupid. I worry for her." Arnoud looked deflated.

"She'll soon settle down."

"What, like one of your horses, you mean?" Arnoud laughed. "I doubt it. She's wild, like you. No good having two wild ones together. I need to find her a nice boring man, like a librarian!"

Michel laughed along with Arnoud, and the dogs, sensing something had changed, tried their luck and poked their noses into the shop.

"Gah! Out! Not yet!" Arnoud shouted at the dogs, who slowly backed away. He then began to take the scraps of meat, gristle and bones from the tray and gather them into two bowls. "They drive me crazy, these dogs, every day wanting food. They're not even mine, and yet here I am feeding them when my customers are disappearing one by one."

"The cafés and restaurants are certainly quieter."

"People have come to their senses. Like you say, there is little hope—and you and I will be left here with the dogs and the scraps and my daughter who draws pictures."

"It's really going to happen, isn't it?"

"It is certain."

"Will you leave?"

"What? Leave all this?" Arnoud spread his arms wide. "My business is mine. I'd like to see them take it from me." He lowered his arms then stroked his mustache. "The way I see it, they still need food, no matter what. Those Boche love meat, sausages. Fat and lazy, the lot of them. All this about them being tall and strong—that's just now. Wait till they get here. You'll see, eating meat and drinking beer soon enough. They'll leave me be as long as I feed them."

"And Estelle?"

"I'm packing her off to her grandparents. She doesn't know it yet. Neither does the wife—she's going too!" He chuckled. "They are going this evening, down to the coast. They'll be safe there. And I'll be safe here."

"I hope you are right."

"But you, Michel—you should go. Trust me. They'll bomb and blitz the place first—show us who our new boss is. You don't want to be caught up in that, especially with no job. Nothing keeping you here. If I were you, I'd go."

Michel waited as Arnoud finished wrapping up his mutton and ham, and handed them over.

"*Merci*, Arnoud. I will see you soon."

"Ah, and maybe not, eh? Let's see. If I do not see you again, enjoy the meat, and find yourself a wife? A nice quiet one, not like my Estelle!"

Michel chuckled and for the first time ever shook Arnoud's hand. The man grasped Michel's shoulder and held on for a moment.

"Your mother would have been proud of you, Michel. Always an adventurer. Just like her."

Michel nodded and left Arnoud, who, having changed his mind, began filling the dogs' bowls with some of his finest cuts of meat.

Michel stopped again at the corner of Rue Crocé-Spinelli where Odette's café sat, the laughter and the chink of glasses reaching out to him, enticing him to come inside for *one beer, one chat, one laugh*, until he inevitably stumbled upstairs to his apartment in the early morning, his meager wage packet emptied by a friend he would never see again.

This evening, the way the sun hit the peeling white paintwork of the apartment block, and how it ignored the rusting of the wrought-iron railings, extracting the crimson peonies and violet alliums of the early planted window boxes, made Michel feel as though he were returning home to much more than his sparse apartment.

Michel saw his neighbor, Monsieur Bertrand, sitting on his balcony writing his daily notes into his diary, the space awash with color from his planters, and a pair of finches chattering and singing in their cage next to him. Michel knew that later this evening he would be sitting across from his friend, enjoying a rich glass of red, perhaps some warm bread and cheese, and together they would dissect their days, discuss a book or two, and perhaps reminisce about Michel's mother or Bertrand's late wife.

"Michel!" a high-pitched voice rang out.

Michel turned to see Odette herself, a curvaceous woman in a red wrap dress that made him think of a ripe apple. Her gray hair was escaping from its messy bun as if making a break from its owner.

"You stopped out front but did not say hello? What is this about? Is it because that young lady from the other night did not come back?"

"Madame Odette." Michel kissed both of her warm rouged cheeks, and caught the thick scent of flowery perfume combined with the potent glasses of wine she drank with her customers.

"Come now Michel, come inside. There are far prettier girls than she. Why, there is a young lady at the bar right now, with long brown hair and a happy face. Surely you would like to meet her and buy her a glass of my finest cognac?"

Michel laughed. "Madame, you do keep a detailed calendar!"

"I do?" Odette lit a cigarette.

"You always remember when I get paid."

"Oh! You have been paid?" Odette patted a few stray hairs back into her bun. "Why, I had no idea! But now that you have said so, come inside, see the lady."

"I have a prior engagement," he said with an air of importance, then looked up to Bertrand's balcony.

Odette followed his gaze. "That old brute! Well, you tell him he owes me still for losing at cards, and he will not have his morning coffee tomorrow without payment."

Michel smiled and watched as Odette huffily returned to the café, her large behind swaying importantly, yet he did notice that she threw one last glance at Bertrand before entering her lair.

He turned the key in the main door and climbed the small flight of stairs to his apartment. Before he could open his own front door, Monsieur Bertrand appeared.

"Michel! I have been waiting. Come. Come in!" Bertrand opened the door wide.

"I won't be long; I will just put this food away, have a wash—"

Bertrand cut him off with a shake of his head. "No. No. This is important, come!" Bertrand then disappeared into his own apartment.

Michel followed and found Bertrand in the kitchen, fussing over uncorking a bottle of Burgundy. Then he turned to Michel and instructed him to sit in the living room. Michel chose his usual horsehair-stuffed crimson chair near the bay window. He felt himself relax into the chair's deep embrace and leaned back to admire the floor-to-ceiling bookshelves that surrounded him, the thick scarlet, blue and gold Persian rugs underfoot, and the photographs of Bertrand's wife that adorned the walls and every available shelf. He coveted this apartment and wanted to be like Bertrand one day; well-read and traveled with bottles of the finest wines always in his kitchen.

Bertrand finally appeared and handed Michel a glass of the Burgundy—dense and aromatic. Michel did as Bertrand had taught him and sniffed the bouquet, which was woody and had a hint of chocolate, then took a sip, savoring the initial tang of alcohol followed by the notes of cherry on his tongue.

"Good?" Bertrand asked.

"Very. What's the occasion?"

Bertrand turned to the side table and switched on the radio, setting the volume low—the muffled voices became ghostly echoes.

"Tell me about your day," Bertrand began.

Michel shrugged. "There isn't much to say. I'm out of a job."

"Monsieur Abramowski...?"

"He left. Left a note—said he had to go. I don't blame him. If what everyone is saying is true, he was not safe here."

"But he paid you, yes?"

"Yes."

"Everything he owes you?"

"Almost."

"Ha! See? I told you he would con you."

"He took care of me. He gave me a job."

"I know."

"You are just bitter because he took your money at cards."

"One time, Michel! And I knew he was cheating."

Bertrand turned to the radio once more and nudged up the volume.

The newsreader's crackly voice permeated the apartment, his abrasive tones—urgent and authoritative—cutting through the rough airways, almost all the other stations having faded to white noise.

"Today, on the seventh day of June 1940, we can confirm that the German forces are nearing our capital. The government insist— Fight— Those who can, must leave— The German army have defeated our troops to the east—"

Bertrand fiddled with the radio, trying to tune it, but was met with more static.

He stood and ventured to the dark mahogany drinks cabinet only unlocked at Christmas, returning with two glasses filled to the brim with an amber liquid. "Brandy," Bertrand said. "It's good for the nerves. At least, that was what my mother said."

Michel drank deeply as Bertrand reached over and turned the dial until the radio fell silent once more.

"It's happening?" Michel asked, almost to himself.

"It's over. They are coming."

Michel drank the rest of his brandy and Bertrand stood, collected the cut-glass decanter, and emptied more of the numbing liquid into Michel's glass.

Michel held his glass to the light and looked into the brandy; his head already felt muffled. "What would Maman say if she were here?"

"She'd say leave." Bertrand sat back into the beige sofa. Its stuffing was escaping through a small hole and he pulled at it as he spoke.

"Would she? But where would I go?"

Bertrand shrugged. "What does it matter? All that matters is that we are not here when they come."

"But others will stay—Arnoud, Madame Odette. I should stay too."

"And where will you work?"

Michel shrugged.

"The Boche will not want a Frenchman looking after their horses. And even if they did, I would not permit you to help them."

"Do you have a cigarette?"

"Here. Take one."

Michel lit the cigarette and drew deeply, watching the smoke rise above him, curling all the way to the ceiling. "There are cobwebs up there, Bertrand. You need to dust better."

Bertrand looked up and laughed. Soon, Michel joined in.

"You see, we are no good, Michel. Here we sit in a place that any moment will be swarming with German pests, and we laugh about my poor housekeeping. We surely wouldn't last long here."

"So, what do you propose we do?" Michel allowed Bertrand to refill his brandy once more.

"We leave."

"When?"

"Tomorrow."

"And where shall we go?" Michel asked, a smile at his lips, feeling the alcohol numb his brain. It was like the games he used to play when he was little.

"Away, Michel, just away. You cannot stay here because there will be nothing here for you. Soon, there will be nothing here for any of us. They will take our jobs, our homes. They will take whatever they want."

"How can you be so sure?"

Bertrand leaned over and scuffed the back of Michel's head. "Is there anything in that brain of yours? Anything? You think it will all be the same as before? You weren't here the first time; no food, no jobs. So many dead, so many wounded. It will be the same again. You heard the bombs fall—you saw the fires."

Michel rubbed the back of his head.

"Checking if anything has fallen out, hey? Perhaps there's some common sense you can put back in."

"Arnoud says he won't leave."

"Arnoud is stupid."

"He's sending Estelle away to her grandparents."

"Ah! Arnoud is a smart man. He'd be smarter if he went with her, though. She still has eyes for you?"

Michel shrugged.

"Come now, don't be bashful. You like her too. I've seen the way you look at her."

"She's too young."

"Ah, yes. True. You prefer the mademoiselles at Odette's café. The ones with long legs and expensive tastes. No wonder you have no money!"

"They weren't all like that. There was Juliette, and Vivienne."

"And where are they now?"

"I don't know." Michel grinned then took a sip of his brandy.

"See! What a charmer. He says, 'I don't know.' You know—you got tired of them, bored. Of course you did. If I had looked like you at your age, I would get bored quickly too."

"It's not like that. Not all the time."

"My thoughts are getting jumbled with your nonsense. What was I saying? Yes, we leave. Tomorrow. And there's no more argument about it."

"So where will we go?"

"Your grand-mère, is she alive still?"

"Dead. Her neighbor, Monsieur Dubois, wrote to me and told me. That was…what, three years ago? I told you."

"I am old. My memory is failing."

"You are sixty."

"And that is old."

"Where did she live?"

"Saint-Émilion."

"Ah, yes. I remember now. That should do well enough."

"For what?"

"For us. To go there."

"But she's dead."

"But you know people there, no? This Monsieur Dubois. You spent summers there as a boy. I'm sure they can help us now."

"Bertrand, you're drunk."

"I am as sober as I am in the mornings. That's all I can say." He grinned.

"Saint-Émilion…" Michel mused. "You really think we should go?"

"Michel, the city is emptying faster than my brandy bottle. We have heard the rumble of guns, the bombs that dropped. Does this not scare you?"

"I am scared, but I'm scared to leave too. This is my home."

"And mine. And thousands of people's homes. We can come back. When it is over."

"You think it will be over one day?"

"Who knows? All I can say is, for now, let us go on a new adventure. The two of us together. That way you will not be scared to leave."

"I need to sleep."

"It's you who are drunk."

"A little. I need to sleep." Michel stood and felt the room spin. He wanted to tell Bertrand that he wasn't going anywhere, but his tongue felt too big for his mouth and wasps had moved into his brain—all he could hear was their constant, irritable buzzing.

"Go now." Bertrand guided Michel across to his apartment.

Michel spotted his bag on the floor and picked it up. "I have ham," he said with a grin.

"Good. Eat your ham, pack a few things, and I will see you tomorrow."

"Tomorrow…"

"Better to leave as soon as we can. Let's not dither any longer."

Michel nodded, his brain still sluggishly processing the warnings from the radio, from his friends, and from the fear on everyone's faces.

He managed to push the key into the lock and open the door just as Bertrand's own door sealed shut. He dropped his bag into the middle of the room; a room which was living area, bedroom and kitchen together. He opened his bag and took the ham and mutton from it. Heating up a small frying pan on one of the two gas burners, he cooked them whilst humming a tune his mother would sing when she used to make dinner.

As he prepared his food, he looked around his apartment—a lone chair sat by the window and a single bed with rumpled sheets was pushed against the far wall; a few books were scattered on the floor and a threadbare green rug lay at the end of the bed. It had not always looked like this; when his mother was alive it had been cozier, with more furniture, rugs, vases full of flowers and thick curtains at the windows. But all that was gone, sold first to pay for her funeral and then to pay off Michel's occasional gambling debts over the years.

The ham sizzled in the pan and spattered Michel's hand with hot fat, but he barely winced. He turned off the blue flame, and slid the ham and mutton onto a chipped cream plate, then sat with his meal on his scruffy pale blue chair and ate, looking out at the street he had known since he was a child. He could not imagine that his life could ever really be any different.

CHAPTER TWO

Au Revoir, Paris

Michel heard the knocking; his brain felt as though it were smacking into the side of his skull with each pound. He opened his eyes, his lids heavier than usual, and moved his neck, which was sore and stiff. It was then that he realized he had fallen asleep on his chair, the empty plate from his dinner smashed at his feet.

"Michel, for goodness' sake!" Bertrand's voice came from behind the front door.

Michel gingerly walked to the door and opened it, revealing an angry Bertrand, a traveling case and violin on the mat beside him. "Are you ready?"

"For what?" Michel said, his dry lips smacking as he spoke.

"We. Are. Leaving," Bertrand said slowly. "The. Germans. Are. Coming."

Suddenly Michel remembered the night before, the warning from Bertrand, the crackly radio presenter, and the brandy. "I can't go," he said, and put a hand to his head as if by doing so it would stop the incessant thud. "What time is it?"

"Two o'clock. I let you sleep whilst I chatted to Mathis from next door. He is going to Bordeaux but couldn't fit us in his car. He says everyone is trying the trains." Bertrand pushed his way into the apartment, grabbed Michel's knapsack and stuffed clothes into it. "Where's your book?"

"They're over there." Michel waved Bertrand towards the stack of books that littered the floor and sat back into the comforting embrace of his chair.

"*The* book, Michel! The one I gave you as a boy!"

"Over there." Michel waved him again in the general direction of the floor. He could hear Bertrand mumbling and swearing under his breath, then silence. After a while, there was more noise and something else; a smell that lifted Michel slightly.

"Coffee," Bertrand said. "Madame Odette was not happy with me, but you need her coffee; no other will do the trick. I had to pay off my debts to get this so you'd better drink it all."

Michel opened his eyes, not realizing that he had closed them again. "Was I asleep?" he asked, taking the coffee from Bertrand and sipping it slowly.

"Yes, whilst I packed. Here"—Bertrand threw his bag at his feet—"you are ready to go."

"Are you sure we should, Bertrand, really sure?"

"Look out there. Go on, look." Bertrand pointed to the window.

Michel peered out onto the street, the daylight brightening even the dullest grays of the buildings so that he had to shield his eyes a little. It was a few seconds before he realized what Bertrand meant, and then he saw. His neighbors were not just walking down the street, going to the shop or exercising their dogs; they were scurrying like small animals, bags on their backs, suitcases under each arm as they packed up their cars or bicycles. Other cars had arrived—family members—who helped tuck children into the back seats and more suitcases on top.

"You see?" Bertrand asked.

Michel nodded and drank his coffee in silence.

Michel and Monsieur Bertrand left their tiny apartment block at four o'clock in the afternoon. Bertrand carried his violin in its worn, battered black case, and a compact leather suitcase with brass clasps. Michel carried his small woven knapsack, which still smelled of horses from the stables—inside there were a few changes of clothes, an apple, a photograph of his mother, and the tatty copy of *Le Lotus Bleu* by Hergé, a children's book that Bertrand had gifted him years ago. He had checked his cupboards and his drawers, and felt a pang that there was little else worth taking with him.

His coat was too thick for this time of year, a dirty green coarse wool that weighed him down in the early summer heat, but Bertrand had insisted he wear it. It was his only coat, a big clumsy affair, and which he had no recollection of buying or being given.

Bertrand walked ahead, seemingly knowing exactly where they should run away to. Michel looked over his shoulder every few steps, watching as the already small apartment block became even smaller. Then they turned a corner and it had disappeared. *I will be home again, I will. The Germans will not come; Bertrand is surely mistaken*... Yet Michel noticed that Bertrand did not turn to take a last look at the home he had lived in his whole life.

Scores of people hurried along the pavements carrying suitcases; children were stuffed into pushchairs alongside bags, ornaments, a pet cat or dog; plates, cups and saucers were piled into old carts along with anything else that could fit. One old man carried his wiry gray terrier in his arms and nothing else, as if the dog was the only thing in his life worth saving. Michel watched as small children staggered behind their parents, half dragging sheet-wrapped bundles. Fathers had coats stuffed under their armpits, their hands clasping heavy, bulging cases, their faces red and sweating, whilst their wives shuffled along, wearing as many dresses as they could, their abundant necklaces and jeweled earrings catching the sunlight.

The sun welcomed the growing crowds with its sultry arms, causing them to sweat and grumble. Michel felt as though he were melting inside his coat, and stopped to remove it and tie it around his waist. He wiped his forehead and face, disturbing the dust that covered it, which was being churned up by the cars in their getaway.

He and Bertrand fell in behind the slow-moving traffic, side by side, their arms touching. Michel could hear the late afternoon chorus of sparrows as they swirled around the berried bushes of a nearby park, whilst pigeons, fat and sullen, pecked on the ground at rubbish and rotten fruit bursting from its skin.

Suddenly the procession stopped, and everyone looked to the sky as the distant hum of artillery fire peppered the air. "It's getting louder," Michel said.

"It's getting closer," Bertrand remarked, and lit a cigarette.

Michel looked past the Eiffel Tower, as if he would be able to see the soldiers fighting there.

"It's all right," Monsieur Bertrand said. "There's time. We've time."

They turned a corner and the boulevard was choked with cars, buses and trucks. Michel watched as an old woman was helped onto a milk truck, her bag thrown in behind her, whilst wealthier families packed their cars so full that their belongings obscured every window.

"How much further?" Michel asked.

"Not far. Not far."

At the next corner, Bertrand needed to stop. He opened his suitcase and took from it a silver flask, engraved with his initials. He drank deeply and offered it to Michel, who sniffed the thick burnt aroma of whisky and drank too whilst the clogged procession of vehicles moved past them. He handed the flask back to Bertrand and sat on a low stone wall, holding his small bag to his chest.

"Have you seen what I packed for you?" Bertrand asked.

"I did."

"I made sure it was in there."

"I know. Thank you."

"*Le Lotus Bleu*. Such a delightful book. The adventurer Tintin and his travels to Shanghai. Why do you like it so much, Michel? I have given you so many books over the years, yet this is the one you love the most."

"It helped me," Michel said. "You know it did. My stutter. I couldn't say words properly before this book, but I did as you told me and read it to the horses to practice; bit by bit, my voice became clearer."

"No. No." Bertrand drank once more from the flask and handed it to Michel. "What did it *mean* to you? What was it in this book that made you want to keep reading it over and over again?"

Michel drank again, welcoming the alcohol to ease his hangover from the night before, and watched as a mother and father walked past, their son and daughter following a few steps behind. The mother's eyes were red and puffy, the father squinting at the road ahead, his jaw clenched, dark stubble visible on his cheeks and chin. The daughter was crying as she scurried after her parents, yet the little boy was skipping, dragging his wooden toy duck on a string behind him and trying not to step on the cracks in the pavement. He waved at Michel, who waved back and watched the boy move out of sight.

"It felt like an adventure," Michel finally answered.

"Adventures are good."

"You have had so many."

"I have had none," Bertrand said. "This is my first one."

"But you always said you had traveled far, seen the world?"

"I did. With my wife. We read about it all in books. Every day, a book each. Then we would tell each other about it, as if we had visited those places—London with its Palace and Big Ben, or the mosques of Constantinople, or the deserts and tombs of Egypt. I saw it all with her. Then she died, and I was left in Paris. So there were no more adventures for me."

Michel thought of all the trinkets, the rich rugs and paintings in Bertrand's apartment that had seemed so exotic. "But the—"

"From the markets. We made our adventures feel as real as we could. My marriage was my biggest one."

"Except this one."

"Yes. Except this one." Bertrand put the flask back into his case. "*Allez!* Let's go." He stood.

They walked in companionable silence until they came to the Gare du Nord and stopped short of the doors. Hordes of people pushed and shoved against the entrance to the station. Michel saw a young girl drop her teddy bear and her mother not notice. She picked up the child and pushed through the crowds, ignoring the child's cries for the bear which was now being trampled. Michel made to move towards the bear—he had to rescue it, had to give it back to the girl—but he felt a tug on his arm.

"Come. We will try the Gare d'Austerlitz." Bertrand was already walking away, and Michel followed, every now and again checking behind him to see if anyone had saved the bear.

It seemed to Michel that others had turned from the station and were now following them. "Everyone is running away," he said.

"And why not? No point in staying." Bertrand shrugged, as if he were simply out for a morning stroll to retrieve his newspaper and sip a morning café au lait at Odette's.

"Aren't you sad to leave?" Michel suddenly asked. "It was your home for so long."

"It is a building, a room. I used to think that walls were important. But then Amélie died, and our only child died at two years old, and I realized my home left with them. So, I carry a few bits with me; some sheet music, a photograph or two. Nothing that important. My violin and my few treasures. That is all I need."

*

By early evening they came wearily to the Seine, which was ever more shrunken from the heat and flowed lethargically under the indigo sky. As they walked across the Pont d'Austerlitz, they found themselves again amongst a growing crowd of people, all walking towards the station. Michel looked at Bertrand, waiting to see if he would suggest they try somewhere else, but he did not and instead ushered Michel forward, falling in with the rest of the human traffic as the sun disappeared behind the glass terminus.

Inside, it was chaos. Masses of people stood, and sat, on every available surface. Michel turned to leave but found he couldn't, as more people had now pushed him into the waiting crowd. A woman reprimanded her son for opening their luggage to look for his toys, whilst her husband shoved his way over to a blank time-table, studying it as if the train times would appear any second.

The air inside was thick with heat and the aroma of unwashed bodies. Michel needed air and felt the cloying nearness of the anxious crowds too much. He turned again for the exit, but Bertrand grabbed his sleeve and pulled him instead towards the platforms, where more people waited for invisible trains. Bertrand gently squeezed a path through, Michel noticing the chatter as he followed.

"They'll come, won't they? They will, won't they, Phillipe?"

"Can we go home now, Papa?"

"Where's the kitten? Hold on to it. The train will be here soon. Just wait."

"Check the ticket again! Check it. It's for today, isn't it?"

They reached the end of the platform at the opening of the terminus, where Michel could see the endless tracks running out into the night. He sat down with his back against a post, holding his bag tightly to his chest, whilst Bertrand squatted atop his suitcase.

A bee, baffled by all the visitors and early summer heat, rolled on the floor, his tiny wings beating as quickly as Michel's heart. He held his hand flat so the bee could climb aboard his palm and sit for a while, until it finally felt able to hum away into the night.

Not far down the platform a tall, thin man with a heavy black mustache was arguing with a conductor. "We have tickets!" he screamed. "We have them! Where is the train?"

The conductor did not answer, and Michel could see the fear on his face as another voice entered the argument.

"We all have tickets! All of us. Why do you think we are here?"

"I'm sorry," the conductor mumbled. "I am sorry."

"No point in apologies. Just tell us when the trains will come!"

"I don't know. Soon, I think? Yes, soon. Any minute now." The conductor took out his pocket watch as if it would confirm the trains' arrival. "Yes, yes, soon. They'll all come soon."

His answer settled the mood slightly, and the mustached man went to sit with his family once more, whilst the conductor pushed past the seething walkway to his office.

The night-time shadows had fallen completely now, so Michel could no longer see the tracks, but the dark was bringing some quiet to the station as voices lowered, and babies ceased their howling. Michel could hear the coo of pigeons nesting in the rafters above him, and every now and then a feather fell with the sound of flapping wings.

Suddenly, from outside, a light stabbed at the now dark blue summer sky, a huge beam that sought its prey.

"Search planes," Bertrand grunted.

Others had noticed and looked to the sky too. Their voices rose again, and Michel heard a woman sobbing.

The mustached man started talking once more, this time to a short gentleman who sat alone but had an abundance of luggage. "They'll be here before the trains arrive," the mustached man said.

"You may be right," the short man replied.

"I left home two days ago. Two days! And we are still waiting. Why is no one helping us? Do they want us to die?"

"We won't die," the short man said. "The Germans will come, but we will not die. We will just have to live different lives—the lives that they want for us."

The mustached man scoffed and lit a cigarette. "You know it all, eh? You know what will happen? I've been a soldier before. I know what happens in war. I know what the Germans are like."

The mustached man's wife began to weep, holding her smallest child to her chest and letting her tears fall onto its golden hair.

The short man shook his head. "Maybe you're right. Maybe. But isn't it better to hope that we can survive?"

The mustached man turned away, and Michel saw the short man take his flat cap off; underneath he wore a kippah. The short man looked at Michel, smiled, then replaced his cap.

A baby woke and wailed, a high-pitched howl that made Michel want to hold his hands against his ears. Somewhere, a dog barked, and another child started to cry.

As if by magic, Bertrand's violin appeared in his hands, and he began to play a soft tune. At first, the melody was so quiet that it did not reach the ears of the waiting crowds, but as Bertrand played, the volume increased just enough for it to echo off the glass terminus.

Slowly, people turned to find the source of the music, and although they could not see Bertrand and his small wiry hands moving the bow across the strings with such care, they gradually stopped their worrying chatter.

Michel felt a surge of warmth in his chest as his friend played and soothed everyone's souls. He leaned his head back against the cool metal of the post and fell into a fitful sleep.

When he awoke, Bertrand was not by his side. Michel stood, yet found it almost impossible to move from his spot as most of the crowd were lying on the platform, trying to sleep. Just as he felt the panic rising in his throat, he caught sight of Bertrand, who was talking to the conductor. He saw the conductor say something; Bertrand nodded and the two shook hands, then the conductor placed his hand in his pocket and smiled at Bertrand.

Michel sat down and waited for his friend to return.

"Come," Bertrand whispered. "We are to go."

"Where?"

"Shhh. Keep your voice low and follow me."

Carefully, Bertrand and Michel stepped over the sleeping bodies, until they reached the end of the platform where the tracks led out into the night.

"Jump down," Bertrand instructed.

Michel jumped the two or so feet down to the tracks, then helped Bertrand.

"Where are we going?"

"To find a train. Where else?"

They walked for an hour, in a straight line, until they came to a large junction with tracks shooting off in six different directions.

"I need to sit," Bertrand said, and wiped his brow with a white cotton handkerchief.

Michel guided him towards the side of the tracks to a thicket of bushes and grass. "The conductor told you a train would come?"

"Yes. He did."

"Why wouldn't he tell anyone else?"

"Because it isn't really a train for people. And besides, I used to play pétanque with him. He knows me. It is a favor from a friend."

Michel sat on the damp grass and Bertrand opened his case quickly, then closed it again. He handed Michel a small paper-wrapped bundle. The paper was greasy under Michel's fingers. He unwrapped it to reveal a butter croissant and bit into it, remembering he had not eaten since the morning before.

"It will be light soon," Bertrand said.

"Where is your food?"

"I am not hungry." Bertrand waved his hand in the air then took a cigarette from his pocket and lit it, the smoke curling upwards into the ever-lightening sky. "Will you miss Paris, Michel?"

He rubbed the crumbs from his lips and balled the paper in his hand. "I think so. The horses, most definitely. Your apartment. Odette's café. But I think I'd quite like to see more of the countryside. Maman came from the country and she always told me how beautiful it was to walk through fields for hours, to see sunflowers growing wild, to play in the river with her friends."

"That's good." Bertrand smiled then clapped Michel on his back. "Give me the paper; I'll put it away."

Michel handed Bertrand the ball of paper and Bertrand opened his case to put it inside. He tried to close the case quickly, yet was too slow. "Why is your case empty?" Michel leaned over his friend and lifted the lid, revealing nothing more than the wrapper from his croissant and the silver flask.

"Ah..." Bertrand said.

"Bertrand—" As Michel spoke, he felt a rumble underneath him, and heard a clatter in the distance as a train approached.

"It's here!" Bertrand exclaimed, jumping up and pulling Michel with him. "You must be quick, Michel. The train will reduce its speed at this junction and will be slow enough for you to run alongside and jump aboard one of the wagons. Do not hesitate. This is your one chance!"

"Me? But you too?"

"No. No, not me."

Michel looked towards the junction and saw the dim lights of the train heading for them. "I don't understand."

Bertrand grabbed Michel by the shoulders and turned him to look at him. "I am old. I cannot leave—I had no intention to leave. But I had to get you away, to be safe. I promised your mother."

"But I don't want to leave you alone."

"Michel, you must. This is your adventure. You are a man now. No longer a stuttering boy who has only horses and an old neighbor for friends. You can be whoever you want to be! Now go! Quick! The train is coming."

Michel looked at his friend and then took him in his arms, smelling the spicy cologne and earthy tobacco smoke for the last time.

"Write to me. Tell me of your adventures so I can pretend I am having one too!" Bertrand quickly kissed Michel on both cheeks, then pushed him away.

The train slowed at the junction and Michel ran alongside. He could see a red cargo carriage, the door slightly ajar. The train was already beginning to pick up speed and Michel could hear Bertrand shouting at him. He ran, his legs feeling as though they would crumple beneath him, his bag slapping against his back. Soon he was there—*almost, two more strides*—then he reached out his arm and grabbed hold of the door and scrambled inside just as the train rounded the bend, its pace quickening. Michel sat down, his legs dangling outside the carriage, watching as Bertrand waved, growing smaller and smaller, his hat in his hand, his violin case at his side.

Michel did not cry, even though he wanted to. He felt exhausted and exhilarated all at the same time. He looked about the carriage to see what else was in there, but the compartment's darkness prevented it. So, he leaned back against the cold wood of the door frame, and as the train rocked gently from side to side, he felt himself drifting to sleep, the familiar, yet unexpected, musty scent of horses on the air.

CHAPTER THREE

Le Clandestin

The brightening dawn woke Michel and as he stirred, he smelled the rich musk of coffee coming from Bertrand's apartment. He opened his eyes, expecting to see the whitewashed ceiling of his bedroom streaked with spider cracks, but instead over him stood an exceedingly tall man in a purple suede suit with a cravat at his neck, and a short man no larger than a ten-year-old child, in brown checkered breeches and a waistcoat, his shirt matching the sunflower yellow of the tall man's cravat.

Michel wondered if he was still dreaming and did not move, expecting the vision above him to disappear. Yet, as the seconds passed by, nothing changed. The tall man stood erect, a fixed smile on his face, a piece of wood in his large hand, resting against his long leg. The smaller man drank from a chipped mug, his lips puckering from the bitter coffee or at the sight of Michel.

"Do you speak?" the giant asked.

"I do," Michel answered, stifling a laugh. This was certainly a dream.

"So, who are you?" the small man asked.

"Michel, Michel Bonnet."

The giant laughed and tapped the wood against his leg. There was something in the movement, the noise, which was so real to Michel, it wiped the sleep completely from his brain. He sat up and shuffled backwards until his spine rested against the wood of the carriage. The small man continued to sip at his coffee and gave the giant a long look, raising his eyebrow conspiratorially.

"I'm just trying to get away," Michel explained, raising his palms in surrender.

"And you chose us," the giant said.

"I didn't choose anyone, I just needed to get away."

Again, there was a look between the two, and Michel glanced at the partially open carriage door with the trees and track rushing by.

"I wouldn't do that if I were you," the small man said, following Michel's line of sight. "You'll be dragged underneath or break every bone in your body on the fall down. Either way, not a nice way to go."

"Who are you running from?" the giant asked.

"The same as everyone."

Perhaps only a minute passed, but it felt to Michel like an age. The clack, clack of the wheels was all he could hear, and in his mind was the image of being dragged underneath, onto the tracks.

Finally, the giant held his hand out to Michel. "Jean-Jacques," he said.

Michel took his hand and gently shook it.

The small man grabbed Jean's arm and turned him away. Michel could hear urgent whispers between them—"the boss... forbidden," then "it will be fine... trust me."

Jean turned back to Michel, a smile on his face, but the small man refused to look at him.

"Ignore him," Jean said. He sat down next to Michel, folding his long legs underneath him, resting his enormous hands on his knees, and with his tapered fingers he tapped his bony kneecaps in a jaunty rhythm. "Are you hungry?" he asked.

"A little..." Michel answered.

"Giordano, go and get us some breakfast. Come straight back."

"And what will I tell the others, eh? That we eat with the animals now?" Giordano turned around so quickly, his coffee leapt out of the mug and fell with a slop onto the wooden boards of the carriage.

"Tell them nothing. They won't care what you are doing. If anyone does ask, you tell them we are working on our act in the stock car."

"As if they would believe I'd spend my time in here! My suit would get dusty and smeared with dirt."

"Hush now. They don't pay as much attention to you as you think." Jean raised a hand to silence Giordano as his mouth opened, full of protestations. "Just a few pieces of bread, some cheese and some more coffee."

The soft lilt of Jean-Jacques' voice was at odds with his huge frame, and held some power over Giordano, who nodded and quickly departed, stirring up a swarm of dust motes with his heavy tread, which danced and swirled in the early morning light.

"Thank you," Michel said once they were alone.

Jean shrugged. "I have been where you are."

"Where are you going?" Michel asked.

"Wherever the train takes us."

"Who is us?"

"Our troupe. Do you not realize what train you have stowed away on?"

Michel looked at the crates, most of which were hammered shut, yet a few revealed small secrets: colorful material—perhaps a suit, a dress; some sequins spilled out from crates that had been badly closed. Suddenly, Michel heard a low rumble partially disguised by the screech of the wheels as they clattered onto a new track, taking them further away from Paris.

Michel looked at Jean, who smiled. "Can you not smell them? I am surprised they did not wake you earlier. Monsieur Aramis is an early riser and usually much louder than this."

"Monsieur Aramis?"

"The lion. You just heard him roar, did you not? Come now, do not tell me it is not obvious to you? The costumes, wild animals, a dwarf and a giant?"

"The circus. You're a circus."

"Aha, correct!" Jean-Jacques clapped his hands.

"Maman took me once. I think I was five—no, maybe six. It came to Saint-Émilion."

Jean-Jacques produced a packet of cigarettes and offered one to Michel.

Michel took one and Jean lit it for him with a gold lighter, engraved with the Ace of Spades.

"You like it?" Jean asked, giving Michel the lighter to take a closer look. "The first magician I ever met gave me this. He said it was lucky."

"And is it?"

"I like to think so. I'm still here, aren't I?" Jean grinned.

"There is a circus in Paris, the Cirque d'Hiver."

"Of course. Our competition, although we do not match them. They have more performers—the best—more animals. Hell, even their train is enormous! Their carriages stretch for miles. Not like this rickety six-trailer. Although, we did have more. Once."

Giordano reappeared carrying a plate of bread and cheese in one hand, and in the other a jug of coffee with small cups stuffed into the pockets of his breeches.

"You could help, you know," he snorted, as he struggled to close the carriage door behind him.

Jean stood and relieved him of the coffee and plate, and Giordano removed the cups and joined Michel on the floor, crossing his legs as Jean poured him some coffee.

"Did they ask anything?" Jean asked.

"No," Giordano said sulkily.

"They didn't notice your new suit and that you were taking your breakfast in here?"

"No."

"My friend," Jean laughed and slapped him on the back, which spilled the man's coffee once more, "you need to stop being so vain!"

"I'm not vain. I just like to look nice."

"We shouldn't quarrel; we have a guest. Michel, this is Giordano. He is moody and sulky, but he is also the best man you shall ever meet."

With the compliment, Giordano lifted his head and held out his small hand to Michel. "I am not moody. Nor sulky. The rest is correct."

"Eat." Jean passed Michel some bread and a slice of cheese.

The trio ate in silence for a few minutes, enjoying the crispness of the air that whistled through the half-open carriage door, smelling of wildflowers and now and again the scent of water, clean and fresh. As the carriage rocked gently from side to side, Michel felt calm, as if he were a child once more and his mother was rocking him to sleep.

"Where are you going?" Giordano suddenly asked, slurping his coffee.

"Saint-Émilion," Michel said. "My grandmother used to live there."

"And you come from where?" Giordano asked.

"Paris."

"Ah, Paris!" Jean leaned back against a stuffed woven sack. "I love Paris. The theater, the romance, the life on every corner!"

"You come from Paris too?" Michel asked.

"No. Not Paris. It was not really a home for me. I was the freak—I was the gossip."

"Me also," Giordano said. "But my home was in Italy, where the food and wine are far superior, but perhaps the thoughts are the same."

"Eh! Your food was inspired by the French! You would be nothing without it."

"You always say this, but how you think it could be true I can't imagine!"

"Come now, settle down, we have a guest. Although I wager that Michel, as a Frenchman, agrees with me. France is better."

Giordano's face reddened, and he looked to Michel like an overripe tomato about to burst its skins.

"Have you always been in the circus?" Michel asked, trying to defuse the argument.

"I was eighteen—no, nineteen," Giordano began.

"He asked *me*," Jean said. "But you can go first." He sat back once more against the stuffed sack and waved his hand languidly in the direction of Giordano, giving him permission to continue. Giordano swatted his friend's hand away, poured himself another cup of coffee and spoke.

"If you know Italy, it is shaped like the boot of a woman. I know this shape very well, not because it is my country but because my mother wore such boots and would kick me with them when I would tumble and fall as a child. My legs, as you see, are not like yours, but though my body is small, the rest of me is just like you—like everyone. But my mother, a woman who had five children—who were, as she said, *normal*—hated the way I looked, the way I moved and perhaps just who I was.

"Yet, do not despair for me just yet, Michel. I was loved. I was loved by my father and his mother, my grandmother, who gave me everything I needed. My grandmother was the one who saw the opportunity for me to become famous in the circus—what else would I do? My mother laughed. Of course she did, and told me a lion would eat me or an elephant would trample me into the ground. But I did not stop trying. I joined every show, every visiting troupe I could. I learned magic, how to spin plates, how to tame a lion. I learned it ready for the day when it would be my turn. I found my way to this circus like so many others. So many others just like you. By pure accident."

"Or perhaps by fate?" Jean said, and Giordano nodded.

Before Michel could ask either of them what they meant, the door to the carriage burst open, and in front of Michel stood a tall woman in a deep orange corset dress, peacock feathers adorning her long black hair, and—perhaps the strangest thing of all—a glistening curly beard covering her chin and above her top lip.

"Oh my! Who is this? A stowaway?" the woman cried.

She did not wait for an answer and strode quickly towards Michel, pulling his head into her bosom for an embrace.

"It is all right now," she said. "A stowaway. A poor boy. I shall take care of you."

"He is no boy!" Giordano laughed. "Young, yes. But a man nonetheless. You can't have him this time, Madame."

The woman let go of Michel, who was grateful to breathe air once more—her scent was flowery and spiced, with a hint of natural musk which made Michel's head swim and dip.

"What are you trying to say?" Madame screwed her eyes into tiny slits as she addressed Giordano, who stood and stretched as if nothing important was happening.

"I am trying to say that you collect things. And this time, you cannot have it."

"What? What do I collect?" she demanded.

"Oh now, let me think... my peacock feather I brought from Italy, the green gem presented to me on our last night in Venice, or perhaps," Giordano's eyes were wide, "the diamond pendant currently around your swollen neck, given to me by a fair aristocratic lady in Versailles as we waved goodbye!"

"How dare you! They are mine! Why would women give you— a man, and a small man at that—jewels and feathers? You are mad. That is what you are. Mad!"

With that, and before Giordano could take the necklace from her, she stormed off, a fit of tears streaming down her face, tracking through the thick rouge on her cheeks.

As soon as she departed, Jean-Jacques laughed. He laughed so much that he had to lie on the carriage floor and pound at the rough wooden boards.

Michel watched as dust filled the air with each of Jean's thumps, and looked to Giordano for explanation. But Giordano, far from being angry, was laughing too, tears streaming down his face; much like Madame's, but filled with mirth.

"I don't understand..." Michel began.

"They are mine; they are!" Giordano squealed. "But a long time ago I replaced the real stones with fakes. She has glass around her neck. But it amuses us every time, and every time she storms away we imagine this: she sits in her room, and then polishes her precious stones, and thinks she has won—but she has not!"

Jean controlled himself and sat up once more. "You think we're crazy, yes? Perhaps a little, Michel. We have been on the road together for some years now. We must entertain ourselves. A thief is thwarted but does not know it, giving us a great many tricks and games to play. No one is hurt. No, Madame is happy— she thinks she has nice, real treasures, stolen like a magpie in the night. And we"—he shrugged—"we have some fun, a laugh. What else can we do?"

Before Michel could answer, Jean held out a hand to pull him to his feet. "May as well meet the others. Madame Geneviève would have told them of your existence by now. No need to hide. We will take care of you."

As Michel followed the pair to the carriage door, he heard the muffled stamp of a hoof on the floor, the familiar snort and whinny of a spooked stallion preparing to take flight. But before he could move towards the sound, Jean had pulled Michel's arm through to the next carriage and with a quick sure hand closed the door behind them.

The carriage they entered was clouded with cigarette smoke that hung below the roof and made the daylight gray. Michel looked at the rows of blurred faces, talking, laughing, not noticing the new arrival.

Jean moved ahead down the aisle with purpose and Giordano followed. Michel hitched his bag over his shoulder and began to follow slowly, yet with each step taking in the faces around him. Here sat three identical young ladies—and yet no, one was male, he realized. All with short blonde hair, blue eyes and elfin features, they sat close as if they were stitched together, and looked and talked to no one but each other. Across from them was a woman with deep auburn hair and a beautiful open face, though there was a slight crease in her brow as she looked at Michel. Michel smiled at her as he passed, and the wrinkle disappeared. The woman smiled back and was ready to speak, when a voice from further down the carriage called out, "Odélie!" and she turned to see who had called her name.

Odélie. It was a nice name, Michel decided. A name that befitted a woman like her. Michel turned to glance at her again. She caught his eye and winked.

Michel saw that the next row held a man with a thick gray mustache and wire-rimmed spectacles. He had a brown sack at his feet and a monkey perched on his shoulder. He did not take his gaze away from the window, but the monkey regarded Michel with its coal-black eyes, then stuck out its tiny pink tongue.

Michel took the seat that Jean offered him, next to the window and opposite the bearded Madame Geneviève and Giordano. Jean sat next to Michel, his large frame pushing Michel close to the carriage wall.

"We have someone new then!" Madame Geneviève exclaimed, her voice high and rich like an opera singer.

"Not yet," Jean said. "I have to get approval first."

The woman pretended Jean had not spoken. "So, what is your talent?" she asked. "A magician? No. A musician? Oh, how I love someone who can play an instrument! Tell me, what is your talent?"

Seeing the glow of excitement in Madame Geneviève's eyes, Michel wanted to lie and tell her he did indeed play an instrument—the piano, or perhaps the accordion. But he feared being put to the test. "I have no talent, Madame."

"Oh, you are not to be believed, I'm sure!" Geneviève looked heartbroken.

Suddenly the monkey appeared and climbed onto Geneviève's shoulder.

"This is Gino. Say hello, Gino," she demanded.

The monkey stuck its tongue out at her and scampered back to its owner.

"Well, that's pure rudeness, Kacper, pure rudeness! You should teach him better manners!" Geneviève turned to reprimand the old man, who now held an accordion in his hands. With the wheezing soon came a flurry of notes, which silenced Geneviève and the rest of the carriage. Then, as if all the notes had now properly arranged themselves, a mellifluous jaunty tune emerged from the accordion with each push and pull. A fiddle joined in, then drumming hands, which kept a steady beat on the wood of the seat rests. Soon, the only person not joining in was Michel, as Geneviève sang, with Jean and Giordano accompanying her in somber baritones.

Michel relaxed back into his seat, letting the music envelop him. He looked out of the window, which was now spattered with raindrops, the sun still shining as though reluctant to let the rainclouds win. He watched the drops shiver as the wind blew over them, almost as if they were dancing to the music. He thought of Bertrand, of his apartment, of the life he had left behind. He traced a drop as it made its escape and ran away down the glass.

Jean-Jacques pulled him out of his reverie. "Here, take this." He handed him a glass of water and two sweet crackers that were flavored with lavender and orange, a taste of summer.

Kacper's accordion began to slow, and he allowed the fiddle to take over most of the work—a slow, melancholic tune that had everyone nodding quietly, as if they all knew the lyrics but no one dared sing them.

"It's about love and loss," Geneviève said, taking one of the sweet crackers from Michel. "It was a French ditty but has spread all over, in so many languages, that there is not now one rendition."

"I like it," Michel said.

"Good." Geneviève grinned. "I knew you would. I wouldn't trust a person who didn't."

Geneviève ceased talking as a large man in a red shirt open to his waist, revealing bulging hairy muscles, and tight black trousers covering toned thighs, entered the carriage and stopped in the aisle; his long, black, curled mustache twitching as if it were counting the seconds before he would speak.

"Serge." Jean finally acknowledged his presence.

"Who is that?" The man pointed at Michel.

"This? This is Michel."

"And why is he here? Does Werner know?"

"Not yet."

"You need to speak to him." Serge did not take his eyes off Michel.

"Why should I? I have no doubt you will relay the message before I have a chance." Jean said.

"You need to learn your place, Jean."

"I do?" Jean got to his feet, towering over Serge, who stood his ground.

"Tell him. Or I will." Serge turned from them both, his large thighs rubbing together with a swish-swish sound as he walked away.

Michel heard Serge speak once more, and he turned to look. Serge was talking to a slight man who swayed as they spoke.

"You owe me money," the slight man said.

"And you'll get it."

"When?"

"When the boss says so."

"I want it now."

Serge smiled at the man. "You'll get it when you get it."

"How about I just leave, eh? Everyone's scarpering. Why don't I? Who'll put your tents up? Feed the horses?"

"Then leave." Serge's smile was stuck in place.

"When I get what I'm owed." The slight man lit a cigarette, blew the smoke into Serge's face and laughed.

Serge grew bigger, outwards and upwards, and then pushed him hard against the carriage doors.

Within a second everyone had left their seats to either watch or stop the fight. Suddenly, the veil had lifted and the carriage held a drab collection of everyone the world no longer wanted; their colorful costumes hiding their fears, their voices too light, too high, masking who they truly were. The triplets so elfin and sweet now looked like scared, skinny orphans; Odélie, the woman with the auburn hair, seemed much older as she pushed her way towards the fight. Even the monkey was not funny and endearing anymore; he had transformed into a wild animal, jumping from seat to seat, afraid and excited, squealing and screeching at the melee.

In that moment Michel wanted to leave, yet he could not, as something or someone appeared, changing the kaleidoscope once more, back to the burning color of light and life, muffling the pitch of voices, silencing the caustic tongues. *She* had arrived.

At first, all Michel could see was the top of her head—raven-black shining hair that glowed in the muted light of the carriage. Her presence had stopped the fight and within moments people returned to their seats. Odélie's face, no longer contorted, was beautiful and young again. Gino the monkey was quiet, and the triplets were now back to being otherworldly. As the crowd dispelled, Michel saw more of the woman. Her forehead, smooth and a light olive tone, then her eyebrows, black as her hair and perfectly arched; underneath, her eyes were green, but not any green Michel had ever seen before. Emerald, he would have called them, but even that did not seem to do them justice. She spoke quick, quiet words to Serge, then surveyed the rest of the troupe. As she did, her eyes stopped for a moment and lingered on Michel's face. Serge swiped his head to see what she was looking at, and she smiled ever so slightly at Michel, then turned on her heel and beckoned Serge to follow.

"Who is that?" Michel asked.

"Who?" Jean did not look at Michel and instead shuffled a deck of cards with quick, expert hands.

"That woman."

"You should go and see him now," Giordano muttered to Jean, taking the cards from him.

Jean stood and walked in the direction of the next carriage, where the woman with the emerald eyes had taken Serge.

"Is it his wife? That woman?"

"Who? Serge's wife?" Geneviève smiled over at Michel. "Hardly!"

It felt to Michel that mere seconds passed before Jean reappeared, his face pale. "I'm sorry," he said.

Jean was suddenly pushed roughly aside as two strong arms lifted Michel from his seat. He heard Madame Geneviève gasp as he was dragged down the aisle, away from the frightened-looking giant and the solemn dwarf.

Once in the next carriage, a door was opened and the arms, which Michel had realized belonged to Serge, threw him into an opulently decorated parlor.

Michel scrambled up, steadying himself on a gilt-edged chair.

"A stowaway then?" a voice said.

Michel looked around the compartment to find the source of the voice; at the back of the carriage was a compact four-poster bed, thick purple curtains hung around it; nearby stood a rich mahogany writing desk and seat, then the chair Michel was leaning on, and across from that a sofa of the deepest reds and purples, strewn with heavy cushions colored burgundy and stitched with gold thread.

"You won't answer me? You come onto my train, infiltrate my troupe, and you won't answer me, *the ringmaster*?" The voice was loud, the person near.

It was then that Michel realized the voice was coming from the mound of pillows on the sofa. In fact, the voice *was* the mound of pillows. It moved and shifted towards Michel so he could see now that the sofa's occupant was dressed in a burgundy jacket and riding breeches, a white shirt unbuttoned to show a red potbelly. The speaker's face was lined with crimson spidery veins, and Michel was reminded of those clients of Odette's who drank her cheap wines and beers late into the night.

"I'm sorry," was all Michel could think of to say.

The man managed to heave himself into a sitting position. His black, twirled mustache rivaled Serge's for its luster and movement as he spoke. "And what are you sorry for?"

"For being on your train?"

"Are you asking me or telling me?" The man lit a pipe, and as he did the flame illuminated his face, showing Michel cool black eyes under heavy brows and the puffy skin of one who did not often get to bed before late. "You woke me from my nap. I do not enjoy being woken from my nap prematurely, do I, Serge?"

"No, you do not." Serge was leaning against the adjoining carriage door. "You certainly do not."

The ringmaster leaned towards a low side table where a cut-crystal decanter sat next to a matching tumbler. He poured a thick measure of brown liquid into the glass then knocked it back in one.

"Serge tells me you were fighting. Not only do I have a stowaway on my hands, I have one who is so confident that he thinks he can harass my troupe?"

"I didn't—" Michel began, and Serge reached over and grabbed his upper arm so tightly that Michel thought he would rip it off.

"No need to argue. I do not deal with stowaways. Or at least, I deal with them in only one way. Serge! See to it that our friend here finds his way home."

"Yes, Werner," Serge answered, and made to pull Michel from the cabin.

"Oh, and Serge?" the small, rotund ringmaster said. "Bring that Jean to me later. He has much to answer for."

Moments later, Michel was facing an open door between the two carriages. He saw the trees rushing by, could feel the air on his skin as Serge tipped his body towards the opening. Michel pushed his weight backwards, feeling the warmth of Serge against him. He tried to speak, tried to beg, but the wind caught in his throat. The trees were slowing now, the ground that was once a blur of gray and brown was now dirt, pebble-stones. The train's brakes squealed beneath them as they rounded a bend. Then Michel saw the trees grow closer, felt the wind once more as he sailed through the open door towards the sky; then to the ground, the pebbles, the stones and the dirt as the train click-clacked away from him, the giant and the dwarf watching from a window as their stowaway rolled in the dust and mud, down a bank and away from sight.

CHAPTER FOUR

La Campagne

As Michel lay on the warm, damp afternoon earth, he listened to the train as it headed away from him. He groaned and moved first to one side, then the next. He lifted one leg, then the other, repeating the movements with his arms. Nothing broken, nothing too badly damaged. His right side ached—it had taken the brunt of the landing—his palms were bloodied and grazed, his knees similarly ripped, but otherwise he was, in most respects, in one piece.

He stood and took in his surroundings—a small shelf of land above a steep green hillside, that below held a silvery snake of river between blots of verdant woods, brown roofs and plowed crisscrossed fields surrounding the plain, with a church spire announcing the village.

He stretched a little and managed to walk a few steps towards a tree. Leaning against it, he looked left, right and above to the train tracks, and then he spotted it—his bag. Carefully, he made his way over to it and hefted it onto his back. Although not heavy, the weight pulled at his shoulders and the muscles surrounding his bruised ribs, made him wince.

A narrow path littered with leaves and overgrown weeds led from the outcrop to the hill, and then down into the village. Michel followed it, watching each foot as he took a step, leaning his weight to where he could bear the bag better, so his ribs did not scream with pain.

It took him some time to reach the foot of the hill, where he found himself in a field of sunflowers that had yet to open. Their thick stems jutted from the ground in neat rows, and Michel, suddenly tired from the descent, lay amongst them to catch his breath and ease the pain a little.

He lay back, putting his bag under his head, and closed his eyes. The pain was not worse, but it was not better, and his side burned. He tried to imagine something else to shift his focus from the soreness, and found himself thinking of her face once more—the emerald eyes, heavily kohled, which in his mind's eye had looked at him with a questioning amusement, as if he were a new animal to play with—perhaps he would dance for her or sing, making her plump rouged lips turn upwards into a smile.

Michel opened his own eyes and watched the streak of clouds overhead, remembering how just a day or so before, he had stood on the bridge over the Seine, looking at the sky, wishing it would rain and dampen the heat of Paris. The clouds here danced and changed from moment to moment, first showing him a horse, then, as he watched it, transforming itself into a balloon, then into a cup, then disappearing altogether. He moved to sit; his shirt was stuck to his back and he could smell himself, a rich musk that would surely make the flowers wilt.

He could hear the hum of the grasshoppers that cooled themselves all around him, yet he never saw one. The caw of a lonely crow pierced the quiet countryside, and eventually Michel stood, heaving his bag onto the other shoulder, following the field towards the river.

He soon came to an uneven road of sorts and followed it to a low stone bridge, which led him into dense woodland of oaks and elms. He welcomed the shady embrace of the thick trees and, as their branches danced in the late afternoon breeze, he stopped and tried to catch their secret whisperings.

He is here. He has come. But soon he will be gone...

In a cluster of wild poppies that bobbed their delicate heads, Michel spotted two pairs of blue eyes watching him. He made to move towards them, but a hiss, then a meow, sent him a message that he was not welcome. Then he saw their tails gently waving in unison, like two snakes awaiting their prey, begging him to come closer. He sat on the bank of the river and observed them. When they curled up, wrapping their tails around themselves, he moved gently left, then right, watching their keen eyes follow him.

Suddenly, Michel removed his jacket, and leapt from the bank into the water, his nostrils filling with the heavy algae water that brought back a sudden memory of his youth. He sank down, his feet soon touching the slush of the riverbed, and he counted—one, two, three—and watched the air bubbles rise above him, popping on the shimmering surface. His lungs burned and his head ached, so he pushed himself upwards, towards the rippled distorted reality above, kicking hard and reaching until his fingertips broke through, then his arms, and finally his head and shoulders. He breathed in deeply, then, treading water, wiped his face and eyes with an arm. He blinked—once, twice—then started to swim to the bank. His eyes searched for the twin cats, and not seeing them, he felt strangely bereft; he was alone again.

With some effort, Michel pulled his waterlogged body onto the bank. Now free of the claustrophobic embrace of the river, he lay back, his arms stretched out from his sides, and closed his eyes. For a while, he watched the shapes on the underside of his eyelids merge and shift, like oil on water—there a dot, then a bright spark, then a face, eyes... a mouth he had imprinted on his mind. Michel's eyes snapped open again and for a moment he hoped she might be leaning over him, yet all he saw were the same shape-shifting clouds; all he heard was the murmuring river in his ears.

He rolled over and took a cigarette from his jacket pocket. He tried to light it with a match, but a drip from his arm extinguished it. He tried once more and, finding a spark, dragged deeply, lighting the end into a comforting orange glow.

From behind him he heard a rustle of grass, and he wondered whether the twin cats had come back to play. He made a clucking sound, one he had used to quiet nervous horses, encouraging them to come closer—*Trust me*, it sang, *I'll take care of you.*

Nothing appeared, and Michel was left with the sound of the leaves as they whispered to each other, remarking on their new visitor and wondering when he would leave. He wondered the same, and said aloud, "Soon. Soon I will go, the moment I know where I am going." The leaves repeated his message, allowing the wind to take it far and wide: *Michel has nowhere to go—someone must find him quickly.*

Michel waited until his clothes had dried enough, then left the charm of the riverbank and the chatter of the wood to meander into the small village nestled between the river and the hillside, covered with neat rows of vines that revealed the settlement's history of wine-making.

The village had no sign to welcome a weary visitor, no inn, no *pension*. Just a handful of thatched houses, a small café and the church, and in the small square a statue of the Virgin Mother. Michel looked at the statue. He had never seen such a tribute; she was not green and mottled like the outdoor statues in Paris; instead she shone in bronze, buffed and polished daily by a devoted hand.

He turned from the statue and settled upon the café, where a pair of old men sat and played backgammon, a black-and-white dog lying between them. Michel took the other table and waited.

Minutes ticked by on the church clock tower—five minutes, then ten, and finally fifteen before a middle-aged woman appeared, her apron stained by food and wine, her hair streaked with gray and curling at her shoulders.

"Who are you?" she asked.

"A visitor."

"We do not get visitors."

The two men stopped playing their game and looked at Michel. Even the resting dog raised her head for a moment.

"I am just passing through." Michel smiled at her.

The woman shook her head. "What do you want?"

"Water, please."

"Just water?" She laughed. "This is not a charity."

"And a small glass of Burgundy."

"Mmmhmmm," she murmured and walked away.

"No visitors here," one of the old men repeated to Michel, only four teeth showing in his gummy mouth. "It is a quiet village. Quieter now. Some people left; you know who." He tapped the side of his nose and winked. "Better they are gone."

"Better for who?" the other man chimed in, his busy eyebrows raised in question. "For you? You just do not like anyone."

"Not true!" the gummy man snapped. "I like French people. Good, proper, French *Catholic* people. Not them with their ways and their little hats and beards. Not to be trusted."

The proprietor returned with Michel's glass of red, which she slammed down onto the table, sloshing wine over the rim, and then demanded payment straight away. "No tabs. Not for strangers."

"There'll be more strangers soon," the eyebrow man laughed. "And here you all are thinking how lucky you are that they left. Now you will have the Germans instead. They will take your wine, your food—hell, they will even take your wives and daughters!"

"Can't be worse than the Jews." The gummy man stood and threw some coins onto the table so they clattered, and the dog growled.

"Pah! Away with you. Begone!" the eyebrow man cackled. "Always a sore loser, that one. Never mind him."

Michel nodded and sipped at the wine, expecting it to be bitter and heavy with ethanol, but it was pleasant and ripe on the tongue.

"It's good, isn't it?" the eyebrow man said. "Even our cheap wine is good. Not a bad place to live, if you ask me. What's your name?"

"Michel."

"Well, Michel, I am Lucien, and this here under the table is my dog Coquette. And our waitress who has shown you so much hospitality is Madame Guillaume. Do not mind her; she is angry with her husband for drinking too much last night. He is still in bed."

"Nice to meet you."

"And you. Always good to see a new face, eh, Coquette?" The dog sat up and looked at Michel. Then, as her master waved his hand, she trotted over to meet the visitor.

"She likes you," Lucien remarked, as Michel rubbed the old dog behind her ears.

"I like animals."

"It shows. So, what brings you to our little village of Vodable?"

"I'm not sure." Michel sat back in his chair and took a mouthful of wine whilst Coquette rested her head on his thigh. "I left Paris and I was thinking to visit Saint-Émilion, where my grand-mère lived, see if some friend of hers would perhaps give me a job for a while. But now I am not sure."

"What has made you unsure?" Lucien raised his glass in a toast.

"I don't know," Michel said, feeling the warmth of the alcohol swirl around his brain, making him suddenly tired. He yawned.

"Did you go off to fight when it all started? I wouldn't blame you for wanting to get away from that life now. A soldier's life is a sorrowful one—take it from me."

"No." Michel shook his head; tried to shake the tiredness away. "I couldn't. I broke my leg a few years back. It healed badly. One leg is a bit shorter than the other now."

"Better for you. If you had gone, you'd be mincemeat by now anyway. Is it true the Boche are in Paris?"

"They were arriving as I left."

"Not surprising. They're a quick bunch, looking for the next bit of land. Not sure why they need so much. I tell you, just as I told my wife, they'd be better being a little more French, a little more relaxed. Drink some wine instead of beer, eat proper food. The wife says they eat nothing but pork. Now and again a bit of bread. You think that's true?"

"I've heard similar things."

"You like this wine?"

"It's very good, though I shouldn't have bought it, really."

"What is money for if not for wine?"

Michel laughed and nodded.

"Where will you stay tonight?" Lucien asked, draining his own glass.

"I'm not sure."

"I tell you what. You come and stay with me, on my farm. I'll let you sample my own wine—much better than this—and you can pay me with stories of your travels. My wife will not mind... Well, if we get her some flowers, she won't mind so much, eh?" Lucien winked.

"Are you sure?"

"I've been married for forty years. Imagine that. Forty years—just me and her. No children. We welcome a friendly face from time to time; it gives us a little entertainment. Not much here—as you can see." Lucien indicated the quiet square.

"That's very generous of you."

"He who is generous will himself be blessed, for they share their food with the poor—so say the Proverbs. You know the Bible?"

"My mother taught me, but I can't say I'm devout."

"No matter to me! You see, so many people around here—take my gummy friend Armand from the square who you met earlier.

Says he is Catholic, says he is part of the Church, but you see how he is? Unfeeling towards anyone not like him. Not very Christian, is it? I say I've seen more Christian people in my life, proper Christians, who have never once stepped inside a church!"

"They say Hitler is Catholic."

"See! Proves my point exactly. Says one thing yet then goes and does another!"

Michel yawned again.

"You need food," Lucien said. "Come. We eat, we drink, and we tell some stories. What else is there to do around here?"

As he spoke, a gust of wind dragged a cloud of dirt around the statue and the Madame slammed the wooden window shutters, announcing the closure of the café, and thus the whole village. It was decided Michel would stay with Lucien.

Lucien did not live far, and Michel thought at first that he was being taken back into the woods and towards the river. "There were two cats there?" he told Lucien, pointing at the thick branches. "Two, identical. They had blue eyes, I think, or green, and they watched me. Sorry." He stopped. "I sound foolish. The wine, you see, and little food."

"You saw the twins," Lucien said.

"The twins?"

"My cats. Twins, as I said. Same litter, the same markings, and as villainous as each other. They come and purr by the fire for a while, but then, my friend, they plot and scheme to make my life difficult. One minute I go to sit down and one of them runs underneath my foot, so I fall! But I look over and there they sit, together, their tails moving in time with each other. I know they are laughing at me; I know! But my wife, she thinks I'm mad. One day, though, one day, she shall learn the truth!" Lucien's voice had taken on a distinct edge that set the dog Coquette howling along with her master. "See?" Lucien pointed at his dog. "She knows. She understands."

Michel wanted to tell him that he mistrusted cats too, but his tongue was thick and heavy, his mind swam with tiredness, and the pain in his ribs had returned, reminding him of the afternoon's adventures.

"Not far now," Lucien said. "This heat makes the strongest of men wilt."

"It is not just the heat."

"Then it is your journey."

A minute or two later, Lucien rounded the bend to reveal a tidy farmhouse with stables and barns to the rear, vegetable patches to the right, and to the left neat rows of vines that continued for a mile or so.

"A few vines?" Michel asked.

"Just a few."

Before they reached the green-painted front door, it was swung open by a squat woman with white hair, cheeks as rosy as apples, and eyes as blue as the sky. "Lucien!" she commanded. At her tone, Coquette ran to her and sat at her heel, giving a perfunctory lick to the woman's bare calves by way of apology. "Lucien!" she shouted once more.

"This, Michel, is my wife—my darling, darling wife, Isabelle." Lucien took the worn cap from his head and bowed deeply, as if visiting royalty.

"Get up, you old fool! He has been drinking again at the café. I can tell. Why did you let him drink?" she asked Michel.

"I didn't," he muttered.

Isabelle looked Michel over, head to toe. "You're not from here?"

"No."

"A city. Paris, Marseille?"

"Paris."

Suddenly, Isabelle's face softened. "Paris is my love. I should have married it and not this brute. Come. Come in, Michel. I'll get you some wine."

"And me?" Lucien asked.

"You have had quite enough."

Michel followed Isabelle into a warm kitchen, where pots and pans bubbled on the stove and the back door was open to let the last of the day's air seep inside as the sun began its lazy descent.

"Sit, sit," Isabelle demanded, indicating a chair at the wooden kitchen table.

"You see? They are here again! Causing havoc!" Lucien appeared in the kitchen, blood-red wine spilled down his shirt, a bottle in one hand, cork in the other, and the twin cats, pebble-colored, swarming around his ankles. "They did it on purpose."

Isabelle looked at her husband, tutted under her breath, then turned to Michel. "Wine? Yes? Lucien, pour him some wine. I am making dinner—just chicken, vegetables, nothing like your food in Paris. Tell me. What is it like there now, with everything?"

"With everything?" Michel asked.

"Take this." Lucien handed Michel a glass of deep red. "We'll try the white with dinner. But I want you to taste this. See how good it is compared to the café."

Michel sipped. "Wonderful."

"Cherries? Strawberries? What do you taste?"

Michel drank again, sniffed the wine. "Strawberries."

"Very good, very good." Lucien sat across from him, satisfied with his guest's palate.

"Hush now, Lucien. Michel wants to tell me about Paris. Is it true what they say? That the Germans are everywhere now? Taking what they want, even the women and children?" Isabelle asked, one hand on her heart.

"No, no, Madame. Not yet—they were not there when I left. They were coming, of course, but I don't know what they will do when they arrive."

"I do," Lucien said, and poured more of the red from a dense green bottle into Michel's glass.

"Ignore him. He went to war once—once! And he thinks it will be the same."

"It will be worse," Lucien said. "If we are to believe what has already happened, what is happening—it will be worse. They target people now; Jews, gypsies, the Poles, the educated, the dark-skinned—anyone they decide isn't German, just like that." Lucien snapped his fingers.

"I had heard—" Michel began.

"Quiet, now. Both of you. Lucien, get the white. Michel, eat this before we begin; you look pale." Isabelle placed a warm bread roll in front of Michel with a knob of crumbly cheese.

"You'll see," Lucien said, his Adam's apple bobbing up and down as he swallowed the last of his wine in one gulp, then stood and placed his coarse hands flat on the table. "You think I know nothing, but it is the opposite—I know too much."

Isabelle took the seat that Lucien had vacated. "Go and find the white," she repeated, her voice quieter.

"Is he right?" she asked Michel.

"I don't know. I hope he isn't." Michel thought of Bertrand, of Madame Odette.

"I went to Paris twice, you know. The galleries, the cafés, the restaurants—I was in love, Michel. Tell me they will not ruin it? Will it be German now? All their names—those strange names that are harsh on the tongue. Not civilized, not good enough for Paris."

"I don't think anyone would dare ruin Paris," Michel replied. "It is Paris. It will always be Paris."

The answer calmed Isabelle, who returned to stirring pans on the stovetop and checking the roasting chicken in the oven.

"White!" Lucien pronounced, and sat down again, placing the bottle in the middle of the table.

Michel sipped more slowly now and watched as Lucien drank one, then two glasses.

"Careful now, Lucien," Isabelle warned as she placed the hot food between them.

Michel ate as quickly as Lucien drank, wiping the chicken juice from his chin with the cream napkin that Isabelle handed him. As his stomach filled, his fork slowed, and Isabelle noticed.

"Tell me more about yourself, Michel. Where are you going?"

"None of our business." Lucien grinned at her.

Isabelle leaned back in her chair, taking a small glass of wine for herself. A contented look passed over her face that smoothed the lines on her brow. "Tell me more of Paris then."

"There is not much to tell, Madame. I worked as a horse trainer and then I had to leave. Just like most of Paris have, or will have by now, unless of course they thought they should stay..."

"I dare say no one would choose to stay." Isabelle shuddered and pulled her cardigan closer to her.

"Not everyone has somewhere to go," Lucien offered. "Where would we go, if they come here?"

"They won't come here. Why would they? What do we have that they would want?"

"They want whatever they can get their hands on. My wine. You know I have started to hoard my wine, my best bottles? Hidden them here and there so if they come, they won't find them!" Lucien laughed.

"Indeed, he has hidden them. Hidden them so well, in fact, that he cannot remember where half of them are!" Isabelle lightly cuffed the back of Lucien's head.

"How will you get to Saint-Émilion? The nearest train station is in the next town, but I think you may have to go back to Paris to get the connection." Lucien lit a pipe and sucked until the fragrant tobacco burned slowly.

"I can't go back. The stations were full of people trying to get away; packed like animals. I was lucky—a friend helped me to stow away."

"A stowaway? Ha! I love it. Just like I used to dream of doing as a child," Lucien said. "When I was bad, which was often, I would pretend to run away. Had a stick with my little handkerchief tied on the end, filled with a toy and a piece of bread. I had the idea to jump on a train and go somewhere new—see wild animals, explore jungles."

"A train wouldn't get you to the depths of Africa!" Isabelle laughed.

"I didn't know that then. It was a sense of adventure; that outside this little village there was a magical world just waiting for me."

"Did you ever succeed on your quest?" Michel asked.

"Never. I once got close to the train tracks and I waited for an hour or so, but nothing came, and I got bored and went home. Papa hadn't even noticed I had gone!"

"There were wild animals on the train I hid on." Michel leaned forward, as did Lucien and Isabelle. "I heard a roar—a lion. There were all sorts of people on there too—a giant, a dwarf, a monkey!"

"A monkey! Oh my!" Isabelle exclaimed.

"He was a tiny monkey; stuck his tongue out at me as I walked past him." Michel stuck his own tongue out at the pair, who fell about laughing.

"You are joking, of course," Lucien said.

"Not at all. Hand on heart, I am telling you the absolute truth. It was a circus troupe—they even had a bearded woman!"

"Ha! They should employ you, my dear." Lucien stroked Isabelle's chin where a few gray and white hairs stuck out.

Isabelle swatted his hand away. "You'll pay for that. I'm off to bed. You with your silliness."

"Ah, come now. I am sorry, my dear!" Lucien called after her. "She'll be fine, don't you worry. I'll buy her a gift tomorrow, and all will be well. She knows I am just joking."

Lucien poured the rest of the white wine into Michel's glass. "You told me of the circus people, the train you were on. There is a story I know from my childhood about a great magician, who they say is still alive today."

"That wouldn't be possible," Michel said, and smiled at Lucien, whose cheeks were a darker hue than the Burgundy he had drunk at the café.

"No! It is true. I saw him myself at a fair, and I tell you now it is true. Listen to me, Michel. His name was...wait, I forget his name, but he was a magician, a wonderful one. He was from Paris, they say, and he joined circuses or fairs and would entrance anyone who paid to see his tricks. Then, one day he fell in love with a beautiful young woman who worked at the same fair as him. They became lovers, but she was promised to a merchant who would give her a home and a title. The woman, rather than marry the merchant, threw herself from a bridge, and the magician, angered by his love being taken from him, traveled the world thwarting young love wherever it bloomed. They say he took a different form each time—that was his magic, to appear as someone else, so no one would ever be able to catch him."

"And you met him?" Michel asked, yawning, his eyes closing.

"I did."

"And?"

"And..." Lucien dropped his voice low, moved closer to Michel. Michel leaned in, awake now.

"He was...Isabelle's father!" Lucien cackled and slapped his knee with mirth.

Michel joined in, but mostly from politeness.

"Lucien!" Isabelle stood in the doorway, her hair in a net, her nightdress glowing white in the darkened room. "Enough. Bed."

Lucien nodded and followed his wife up the small staircase, Michel behind them. "Your room is there." Lucien pointed to a door across from theirs.

"Thank you. Goodnight, Lucien."

"Goodnight." Lucien turned to walk away, then said, "Michel, you know the story is true. Not that the magician was Isabelle's father—although he may have been—but it is true. If you fall in love, watch out for him. He is always there, waiting to take it away."

"Lucien!" Isabelle shouted.

"Ah, he should have taken this one away." Lucien grinned and closed their bedroom door.

Michel lay in bed, thinking that sleep would come quickly, yet when it did not, he lit the candle on the bedside table and lay back once more, thinking of Lucien's tale of the magician and the woman he had loved. The candle flickered as the light wind that came from the open window teased it, and Michel watched as the flame danced, taking on the silhouette of a woman that moved and swayed her hips as if entertaining a guest. The shadows on the wall jumped, danced and somersaulted, and Michel imagined them to be the circus troupe—*look there: the elongated shadow, that was Jean, and the smaller, grumpier, immovable shadow, that was Giordano.* Michel scanned the dancing shadows, looking for the one person he wished to see more than anyone. And there— suddenly, against the cracked plastered wall of the cottage, she flipped mid-air, turning and twisting. There she was. The woman from the train; her emerald eyes gleaming at him. Just as Michel smiled, the wind, sensing the change in mood, blew out the flame, encasing him in darkness.

The morning woke Michel with its sounds of the country; first the crow of the cockerel, sure and confident as he stood on top of the barn, close to the iron weathervane, and sang his morning tune, hoping that the females would hear him and wonder at his magnificent voice. Next came shouting and swearing from the farmyard as Lucien meandered to the toilet at the bottom of the garden, shooing chickens out of his way and the twin cats who, after a night of hunting, were curling themselves around their master's legs, asking to be fed before they would sleep the day away.

Michel lay in his bed, his face to the ceiling, which was covered with the finite tendril-webs of its resident spiders, and let the sounds of the morning wash over him. They were somewhat softer than he was used to in Paris. There, his morning wake-up call was the traffic, both human and vehicular, that arose before dawn had broken, as people shuffled and dragged themselves along the Parisian streets to jobs that required them to be up earlier than most. The baker, the butcher, the café owner—all were up early to prepare for the day's customers. Michel had always listened to that hustle for half an hour or so before he would rise, wash his face, and meet Bertrand for a coffee before heading to his own job. Now, Michel had nowhere to be, no friendly coffee to welcome him to the day, so he turned onto his side and fell again into a dreamless sleep, whilst the cockerel crowed above him and morning life stirred all around him.

When Michel woke once more it was because of a nose, wet and cold, pressed against his own, snuffling loudly as if it were checking that Michel was still breathing. He opened his eyes to be greeted by the sight of Coquette. Upon seeing his eyes open, she gave him an enthusiastic lick, welcoming him back to the world.

Michel laughed and shielded his face, which made her all the more determined to complete her mission of cleaning him.

"That's enough, leave him!" Lucien's voice rang out and she obeyed, trotting to her master's side, sitting close to his heel.

Michel sat up.

"She wake you?"

"I heard the cockerel."

"He is a noisy one. I'm surprised you found sleep again after that."

"I should be going." Michel climbed out of bed and tucked his shirt into his trousers, everything mussed and creased from his travels the day before.

"Take some bread and coffee before you go. Isabelle has it ready. Then be on your way. Try and flag yourself a car if you find someone going in that direction. And, if you can, try to stop at a town. I'll give you a few francs so you can take some lodgings; you do not want to find yourself outside at nightfall. Not these days."

Michel nodded his thanks and Lucien shook his hand. "Take care of yourself. Perhaps we will meet again?"

"Perhaps," Michel said.

"If you need anything, you know where we are now. Just in case no one helps you where you are going."

"I am forever in your debt, Lucien."

"Ha, begone with you! Kindness costs nothing. Remember that one. That, and always drink the best wine: anything else will make you ill!"

Michel said a quick goodbye to Isabelle after breakfasting on bread, pastries and thick rich coffee. She had prepared him a picnic of sorts, as if he were taking a lady for a quiet walk in the country, to spread a blanket under the shady arms of a tree, where they would eat and discuss a happy future together. Lucien tucked their address and some money into Michel's pocket. "Just in case you ever need us."

It was a quarter past nine by the time Michel found himself in the small village square once more, the church clock dully chiming whilst the woman from the café decked the two outdoor tables in their checkered cloths.

"You leaving already?" A chuckle.

Michel saw the gummy man—Armand—who Lucien had been playing backgammon with, sitting down at one of the café tables, book in hand.

"You'd better be. No visitors here, my friend. Unless of course you are a good Catholic?" The man waved the brown leather book in the air, and Michel saw the dull gold of a cross on the front. Armand chuckled again, then accepted his small cup of *café* from the Madame. "Only Catholics here, my friend! You see any of those others, you tell the Germans where they are hiding—do your duty, man! You are French. Remember that…"

The man's voice faded with each step Michel took, but he imagined that he would never stop—the words of hatred ringing out in the bare village square, bouncing off the quiet walls for no one to hear.

CHAPTER FIVE

Le Cirque Neumann

That night, in a field which sloped towards a valley of pine trees, Michel lay on his side, the earth warm from the day's heat, the grass prickly underneath his bare forearm. As the light faded, he ate a sandwich and a boiled egg from the pack Isabelle had given him that morning, his stomach growling as he bit into it. When he could no longer see, he took his winter coat and, wrapping it around him, lay down once more, falling asleep before he could worry about his fate.

Michel dreamt of the cats that had seen him jump into the river. Their eyes were no longer blue but the deepest black. In his dream he reached for the twinned eyes, trying to coax them near, trying to ask them what they wanted. *Saint-Émilion*, they whispered. *Saint-Émilion. Come to me*, they whispered.

And then he awoke.

He looked about him; all was calm. The grass was still and heavy under the early morning dew, the sky lightening with every moment—all was as it should be. Michel sat up and rubbed the sleep from his eyes. His clothes were damp, and he could feel the chill reaching his bones.

The dawn brought with it the sounds of waking crows, and blackbirds that squawked as they flew then dived for food, accompanied by the lighter trill of a sparrow or the coo of a wood pigeon. The wind had let up into a gentle breeze that now stirred the leaves into a soft murmur, and the long grass into whistles and squeaks.

Michel was hungry. Hungry and cold. He pulled his knees to his chest and listened to the morning chorus as it sang sweetly above him, wishing for Odette's café—for hot coffee and a warm croissant. He took some bread from Isabelle's parcel and ate it dry, ignoring the ham and cheese in the greaseproof paper—he had to ration the food.

From behind the rustle of leaves came a new sound—not new to Michel, for he had heard it before, but new to this field, full of blue and pink wildflowers that tipped their heads above the long grass, competing in their height as to who should be the prettiest, the brightest. It was the stomp he knew—a pawing almost, irritable and scared. He closed his eyes to help place it. *The clack of wheels, the loud voice of Madame Geneviève—yes!* He opened his eyes. The horse, the horse he'd heard on the train—the one he knew had wanted to get away—it was here. As soon as the thought entered his mind, from behind a thicket of blackberry bushes it appeared, a young Friesian stallion with a shining blue-black coat that shimmered with each movement in the daylight.

Michel stood and watched as the stallion cantered, then trotted and came to a stop a few yards away. It was tired; its nostrils flared and its flank was slick with sweat. The horse bent its head and sniffed at the damp morning grass before he began to pull and chew at it, as if he had not eaten for weeks.

Michel was in awe of him. The sheer height, perhaps seventeen hands or even more; the gloss of his coat and his strength was something to behold. Certainly Monsieur Abramowski had never had a stallion of this caliber. Michel edged closer, shuffling on his hindquarters, picking at blades of grass with his thumb and forefinger, as if he too were eating. Within a minute or so, he was a few feet away and could hear the rhythmic chomp and grind of the stallion's teeth as he ate. Suddenly, the stallion noticed him and raised his head. His ears bent back, with one hoof he pawed at the ground as if in warning for Michel not to come any nearer.

Michel began to hum a tune, a tune that he had mastered over the years; a soothing song that perhaps his mother had sung to him as a baby, but one which he had always used on horses to gain their trust.

At first the stallion had no interest, snorted at Michel, and took a few steps backwards. Michel sat on the ground and dipped his head, not making eye contact but continuing with his song. The horse soon dipped his own head once more, sensing no threat from Michel. Michel moved closer still, ripping some grass and holding it out in his palm, eventually nudging the stallion's nose. The horse gently ate the grass from Michel's hand, the hairs on the silky soft muzzle tickling his palm. He was bedecked in a bridle and reins of rich black leather and gold. No saddle meant no rider, and to Michel that meant this horse was in need of a new master.

The pair continued in this way for over half an hour, with Michel never ceasing his calming song, the stallion not ceasing in his goal to eat.

As the sun warmed Michel's back, he took a risk and laid his palm flat on the stallion's cheek, stroking it gently, whispering soft words in his ear. The horse welcomed Michel and sniffed at his shoulder, allowing Michel to rest his head on his cheek so the two of them would look to an observer to be in a lovers' embrace.

Michel slowly stood, all the while talking to the horse, now patting his neck, his flank. He gently took hold of the reins, and the stallion obliged as Michel led him to his sleeping spot, where he packed up his bag and slung it over his shoulder.

Michel led the horse slowly down the steep hill until he reached the thicket of trees. He found a rough stump, stood on it, and prepared to mount. At that moment, a deep cry pierced the air, causing the stallion to skitter in fright, ears back and eyes wide. Michel looked up to the hill where, comically, a short man in red breeches and a white shirt that flapped open ran headlong towards Michel, his arms in the air, his voice deep with authority. Michel climbed down from the stump and watched as the man, sweating, rotund, pink as a suckling pig and hairy as one too, came into view. The ringmaster, Werner.

"*Le voleur! Le voleur!*" the ringmaster sang, all the while his round thick belly moving side to side as he ran towards Michel.

Michel waited calmly and stroked the horse's neck.

"*Le voleur!*" The ringmaster was in front of Michel now. Out of breath, he leaned forward and rested his hands on his knees, drawing in air quickly. "*Le voleur,*" he gasped.

"I am no thief," Michel answered.

"My horse. You stole my horse! *Le voleur!*" The ringmaster stood now, hands on hips, breathing heavily, sweat dripping down his red face, soaking his twirled mustache.

"I did not know he belonged to anyone."

"What, you saw no bridle? You are blind?"

"I saw a scared horse. I calmed him," Michel said.

"You!" The ringmaster pointed a finger at Michel. "You! I recognize you! Coming onto my train and now stealing my new horse. I knew you were trouble the moment I laid eyes upon you!"

Michel raised his palms in surrender. "I was just trying to calm him. No more. It is what I do, I train horses."

Although short, the girth and strength of the ringmaster was plain to Michel; his forearms were taut and large, his neck wide; a man used to getting his way.

"I promise," Michel said. "I was just trying to calm him."

The ringmaster dropped his hand by his side, then with his other, wiped away the sweat that had pooled in his mustache. "Tell me," he said. "Tell me how you did that. Beau does not want to be tamed."

"I did not say he is tamed, but calmer; that is certain."

"And what would it take to tame him? For me to do it?"

"I am not sure that you can," Michel said.

"Who do you think you are, telling me what I can and cannot do? *Un beauf!* Eh! I can see from your clothes—poor, no refinement. You think you know more than me?"

"Not at all. All I know is horses; that's it."

"Listen to me. I *know* horses. I know acts, shows, animals. What I don't know is why a piss-poor lad is plaguing me!" the ringmaster spat.

Michel picked up his bag then held the reins out to Werner. "How long?"

"How long what?" Michel asked.

"To train him. How long?"

"A week or so."

"Too long." The ringmaster reached into his pocket and pulled out an ivory cigarette holder, into which he inserted a long, thin white smoke that he lit with a gold lighter.

"Less than a week if I am with him every day, and all night. He needs to feel safe—secure."

"You're not a performer, that's for sure—the cut of you, with your skinny arms. No use to me really. Not that I'd ever give you the chance anyway. But the horses—perhaps."

"I'd be grateful for the work."

"I'm not paying you. Not for this. Trust must be earned. Food. Lodging. You have five days to get Beau ready. That's it. No more."

"Five days."

"If you behave maybe I'll give you a few more days. If not—you remember Serge?" He grinned. "I'll tell you now, this is my circus, my troupe, my rules. You are here to sort the horses and that's it. You are not to annoy the performers; you are not to ask questions. I *tell you* what to do, and you do it. Understood?"

The ringmaster walked away. Then he stopped and turned. "You coming, then?" He beckoned.

Michel took the stallion's reins and followed this sour red sphere of a man, his thoughts immediately returning to the woman from the train.

"Your name?" Werner asked.

"Michel."

"There's a village not far from here. One of the farmers is a friend of mine and we are setting up in his fields as we speak."

Michel followed the line of Werner's extended arm and waited for him to say more, but he was silent during the walk that took them three more miles to a field which edged around a railway track, a disused train shed and dilapidated platform crumbling and sad in the near distance.

The red-and-white striped Big Top was already in place, dominating the field and, like a dancer performing on center stage, it begged to be looked at and admired. Michel felt drawn to it, his gaze only broken by the sight of Serge from the train, his muscles bulging from his white shirt as he leaned against a wooden post and talked to a woman with long legs.

"Over here," Werner said, indicating the static train and the wagons.

Michel followed, the horse at his shoulder, now and again snuffling at his shirt.

"Here. This is his." Werner drew open a wagon door and pulled down a ramp. The horse knew what to do and walked dutifully into his wooden home. "He's Beau, my newest. He's for me—a stallion for a stallion!" The ringmaster roared at his own joke, his belly sticking out as hard and ripe as a watermelon.

Werner gathered himself and pulled a pole across the open door. Michel saw Beau eye it as if it were a mere annoyance; it would not keep him inside if he wanted to leave.

"Next door, this is Claudette and Bisou." Werner patted the nose of a white mare who received the affection with a low whinny and a nuzzle at her master, and then the nose of the miniature pony, piebald and jittery. "Our star horses. Two carriages down, that's where we keep our working horses; not much to look at, but strong."

Michel dropped his bag on the ground and stroked Claudette's nose.

"We'll sort you a tent—a small one, mind. Have it put up here, next to the horses. Wait here. I'll send someone."

Michel watched as the ringmaster walked away, barking orders to men in brown trousers who wielded hammers and plunged pegs into the ground to secure the Big Top. Others were putting up smaller canvas tents and makeshift wooden stalls, and setting out large wooden poles atop which lanterns were hung, along with lengths of wires and bulbs to light the way through.

Michel turned back to the horses, who had now lost interest in their new visitor and pulled and tore at the hanging nets of hay. He sat on the edge of the wagon and waited.

From far off he saw the sway of a woman walking towards him. His mouth was suddenly dry. *Is it her?* He squinted in the bright light, then shielded his eyes, seeing, finally, that it was the woman with the auburn hair from the train, not the woman with the emerald eyes who had haunted his dreams.

"You are from the train, right?" she asked him.

Michel nodded.

"Werner giving you a chance, then? I'm not surprised, a strong man like you." She smiled at him and sat down, crossing her legs so that her skirt rode up just above her knee. She did not smooth it down.

"Want a smoke?" She shook one from a packet and handed it to Michel, allowing her to light it, her long red fingernails clicking at the lighter.

"It's Odélie, isn't it?" Michel asked.

"Since the day I was born. And you are Michel. Michel, the man who can tame wild beasts!"

"Only horses."

"All the same to me." Odélie rested her chin on a cupped hand, her elbow on her bare knee so that Michel had to look. "You'll like it here. Easy money, different people all the time. It's nice to have new faces, you know?"

A man in a white shirt and tan trousers walked past, his blond hair neat and smooth, his tanned arms holding a small black box.

"New wireless, Anton?" Odélie called out.

"It is." He stopped in front of them. "Who's this?"

"Michel," Odélie answered for him. "Our newest."

Anton dipped his head in a welcome.

"Can I borrow it later?"

"Not again. You broke my last one."

"I did not! I was listening to the music and then suddenly it just stopped working."

"More like you knocked it over!"

"Either way, Anton, it stopped. That's all."

"Buy your own."

"What do you listen to anyway? I've never heard it play anything nice."

"What's it to you? You're not to take it again, Odélie."

"And what would you do if I did?" She ground the cigarette out under her bright blue heels.

"Don't do it. I don't take anything of yours."

"You can have anything you want of mine!" Odélie winked at him, and Anton blushed and walked away.

As soon as he was out of sight, Odélie laughed and patted Michel on the knee. "Only a bit of fun. He gets all embarrassed at everything. You should see what he's like when we are in our costumes, all tight and our legs out! It's hilarious."

"What does he do?"

"Anton? He's trapeze. Strong, lean, beautiful to watch. But, like I said, shy and a bit of a loner. You'll not get him as your friend."

"I wasn't thinking of trying. The ringmaster says I'm to concentrate on my work and keep to myself."

"Werner? He says that to all the workers. Doesn't like them being too friendly with the talent—says it distracts us."

"And are *you* talent?"

"Is it not obvious?" Odélie stood and pirouetted in front of him. "I am the lead acrobat; Werner did not mention me? No, of course not. He's in love with the triplets at the moment and I, alas, am out of favor for now. But not for long. Have you met our triplets? Strange creatures."

"Michel! You're here! I thought it was not true. But here you are." The long figure of Jean-Jacques loomed in front of him and Odélie turned, a crease of annoyance on her brow.

Michel stood and allowed Jean to pull him into an embrace.

"I am so sorry for what happened—it was my fault."

"It really wasn't you."

"Ah, you are too kind." Jean-Jacques bowed as if asking Michel for a dance. "But I should have left you hidden. I had thought that perhaps a quiet word with Werner after his breakfast would have worked; but Serge beat me to it."

"You certainly know how to make an entrance, Jean." Odélie stalked away.

Michel watched as she went; the swing of her hips, the sway of her hair.

"Be careful there." Jean-Jacques followed his gaze. "She's a tough one."

"Werner said I was to have a tent?"

"Giordano is on his way with it."

"And you are here to help put it up?" Michel grinned.

"I'll supervise."

*

The following hours were spent with heavy grunts from Giordano, shouting and swearing. Finally, a small white canvas tent, dirty and stained around the skirt, was erected. As Michel hit the last wooden post into the soft soil, a bell rang out, softly at first, but growing louder and more insistent with each chime.

"Dinner!" Giordano yelled, and disappeared around the striped Big Top.

Michel laid down his sledgehammer and wiped the sweat from his brow with his arm.

"Hungry?" Jean asked.

They ambled along towards where Giordano had disappeared and found themselves at the back of a long line.

"Should have run with Giordano," Jean said.

Michel tried to look down the line for the glimpse of blue-black hair but could not find her amongst the throng.

"Odélie? She'll be up front with the triplets—they're young, see, so they get fed first."

"And the others?"

"Others?"

"You know... Serge, and Werner."

"Ah, Werner will have his delivered. Serge will be delivering it to him. Anyone else you're curious about?" Jean raised his eyebrow quizzically.

"No, that's everyone."

"Of course, Madame Geneviève, being the lady that she is, will dine with the other ladies. Like Frieda, for example, our trapeze artist. Extraordinary talent—something to see when she is flying through the air."

Michel looked at Jean. "I thought Anton was the trapeze act?"

"One half of it. You would have seen her on the train; green eyes, tall?"

"So...she and Anton?"

"Not Anton's, no. She's Werner's, so don't get any ideas about her. Trust me."

As the queue shortened, Michel could see crowded wood-slatted fold-out tables and chairs which were placed under a large awning. At one end was a larger wooden table, laden with blackened pots and pans that emitted curls of steam and were manned by a trio of cooks; kerchiefs tied around their necks, stained aprons around their portly bellies.

Michel took a plate, and a short cook with fat arms filled it with a thick stew and vegetables. He followed Jean and sat at a table with him, Giordano, and a thin man who ate with his face close to his plate, spooning in the food as if he was afraid it would soon be taken from him.

"This is Felix." Jean nodded towards the thin man. "Sets things up, carries things and such."

"Hello," Michel said.

Felix looked up. "Yes?"

"I'm Michel."

"Good. Eat your food, Michel."

"Not a big talker, is Felix!" Jean laughed. "Don't be offended."

Michel ate and listened to Giordano lament the lack of good food, and how, perhaps, he would have to return to Italy soon if things did not improve.

"Where are you from?" Michel attempted to engage Felix once more. "Your accent—I can't place it."

"I am Polish," Felix said.

"When did you come to France?"

Felix stopped eating and looked at Michel. "A while ago. Why?"

"I just wondered."

"Don't bother yourself with wondering. I am here and that is that." Felix stood, took his almost empty plate, and found another table to sit at.

"Don't mind him," Jean said. "Like I said, not one for talking."

Michel nodded and ate slowly, aware that now and again Felix looked over at him.

That night, Michel slept uneasily in a fold-out bed that dipped in the middle, the sound of horses breathing heavily nearby. He hovered on the edge of sleep, where dreams and reality merged; more than once he awoke to the sound of rustling, believing that it was Felix, there to challenge him or perhaps to tell him why he had looked so afraid.

Michel woke for good when it was still dark outside, and he was cold. He swung his legs out of bed and reached for the torch that Jean had given him. His winter coat was lying on his bag; he picked it up and wrapped himself in it. As he did, he heard voices outside. One voice, then another, low, murmuring. He cocked his head to the side to try and hear better, but the words were too muddled for him to make out what they were saying.

Michel crept out of the tent, the grass cool underfoot, and walked a few steps into the dark.

Then suddenly, he heard the crackle of static, another voice, then more static—it was Anton's radio. Just as he was about to turn away, he heard another voice, this time clear—it was Werner.

"What is it?" Werner asked.

A whisper from Anton.

"You know what I said!"

"It isn't that." Anton's voice was firm.

"Better not be. I told you you'd go. I told you. Do you think I lie?"

"No."

"No what?"

"No, sir. I don't think you lie."

"I'll not say it again..."

The voices trailed away to strong whispers. Then, quiet.

Michel picked his way back to his tent, and saw it was lit up from inside with a torch, a figure moving around like a shadow puppet behind the canvas. Drawing back the flap, he was confronted with his night-time visitor.

Odélie.

Her face and rouged lips glowed in the light of the torch she had placed on the ground; she perched on his small bed, smiling at him. "Where have you been?"

"I was looking—"

"For me?" she interrupted. "Come, sit with me."

Michel sat on the edge of the bed and stared at Odélie, her eyes bright, her lips glistening. He smiled at her. "Cigarette?" he asked, and took one from his trouser pocket.

"Let's share," she said, drawing in the smoke as he lit it for her.

Michel nodded and took the cigarette from her. "Is this allowed?"

"Sharing a cigarette? I think that's OK." She grinned and took the cigarette from his mouth.

As he blew the smoke out, she waited a second then kissed him, pushing herself against him so that he fell into the kiss and down onto the bed.

He pulled away. "We shouldn't. I'll get thrown out."

"You'll stay," Odélie said, leaning down. She turned off the small torch, and in the blackness, he heard her remove her clothes.

"You'll stay," she said again, as she lowered her naked weight on top of him.

Michel woke at dawn, feeling relaxed and warm. He opened his eyes and Odélie was gone, but the scent of her remained. He dressed quickly, washing his face at the two barrels of water that had been placed near the dug-out latrines.

He did not breakfast but grabbed a cup of coffee to take with him before collecting Beau and leading him to a nearby field, away from distraction.

Michel let Beau loose to roam and feed. He sat in the long grass and sipped at his coffee, watching him move—the twitch of his tail, the ears that moved back then forwards—always alert, never relaxed. It was the kind of summer morning that inspired slowness, when in Paris, women would hang out laundry, then sit with their neighbors and wait until it was dry; when Bertrand would roll up his sleeves, pack a picnic and beg Michel to take a day off, and together they would spend a day boating, reading and drinking wine. Here, slowness was all around him; bees buzzed lazily, still tired from their nighttime slumber, whilst birds dipped and chirped as they sought their breakfast. Even the camp behind him was slow to stir. Turning around, he saw people walking towards the breakfast tent; some sat, smoked and drank coffee outside their tents. He looked for Odélie, for Jean and for Frieda, yet he could not pick them out.

Returning his attention to Beau, he saw how the stallion's eyes still watched Michel, his muscles taut beneath the black sheen of his coat—ready to run, ready to disappear.

Michel knew how he felt—restless and scared. When his coffee was gone, he placed the cup on the ground and stood slowly, taking a few steps closer to Beau, every now and then crouching down slowly when Beau stared at him. The wind was gentle, weaving in between the blades of grass, causing it to ripple like water. It calmed Beau, and even Michel felt his heart slow, his limbs become lighter.

Suddenly, as if the two had spoken, Beau walked towards Michel, his head bowed, and nuzzled into Michel's chest.

Michel clipped a lunge rope onto his bridle, and bit by bit gave him length. With a whistle and a gentle tug on the rope,

Beau walked in a circle around Michel, then with a click of his tongue, and some more length to the rope, Beau began to trot.

"You'll need this!" a voice rang out.

Michel turned to see Werner at the fence, waving a large lunge whip in the air. Beau caught sight of the whip and whinnied. He stomped at the grass, his ears backwards, his nostrils flared.

"I don't use them," Michel said.

"Well, I do. Use it. Give him a quick flick and he'll soon learn."

"It's better my way. You asked me to train him."

"I did. I thought you knew what you were doing. Obviously, I was wrong. Take the whip."

Michel drew Beau close to him and patted his neck, whispering in his ear to calm him. Michel felt a sudden sharp sting on his arm. He looked to Werner who grinned at him, still holding the whip in the air.

"It's the only way to learn." Werner walked away, humming a tune as he did.

By late afternoon, Michel returned Beau to the carriage and opened his tent. There on the bed was the lunge whip. He knocked it to the ground and sat down. He lit a cigarette and thought of leaving. He could. He could just leave. Nothing was keeping him here. Werner was never going to be easy to work with. This was never going to work.

"You all right?" Jean walked into the tent. "Didn't see you at breakfast or lunch."

"I was training Beau."

"The way you say that doesn't sound too hopeful."

"It's not him that's the problem."

"So, who is?"

"Werner."

Jean sat next to him on the narrow bed. "With so many of us, there's always someone who is a problem. Giordano drives me mad most of the time."

"It's not that. It's clear he doesn't like me, so why give me a job? He gave me that." Michel nodded at the gift from Werner. "He says it's the only way to learn."

"Wants to whip you into shape." Jean took the whip in his hands. "Maybe I can use this on Giordano when he snores? Ah, come, Michel, put a smile on your face."

"There's something else."

"What? Me?"

"No, not you, Jean! Of course not. It was last night..."

"You and Odélie?"

Michel looked at Jean, his mouth agape.

"Word gets around quickly here. You're not in trouble, don't worry. Odélie had her eye on you on the train and didn't stop talking about you even after you were gone. Just be careful there—she's..."

"She's what?"

"Tricky, Michel. Tricky."

"It wasn't Odélie I was going to mention," Michel said, rubbing at the stubble on his chin.

"Oh, yes! Someone else?" Jean laughed. "Goodness, you work quickly."

"No, not that. Last night I heard Werner talking to Anton. He was just listening to the wireless, but Werner threatened him—said he would be thrown out! Just for listening to the radio? I can't see how it can work, my staying here—I don't know his rules, and even if I did, I am pretty sure I would willingly break them."

"When I was younger, I had an uncle, always shouting at something, always mad and thrashing about. Once, he got mad when the wind blew a tree over in the garden—he was mad at the wind, Michel! It was only when I was older that I realized he had had hard times as a child. The anger from that was still there."

"Is Werner your uncle by any chance?" Michel laughed.

"Not so! But you see what I mean? He is just a small angry man. Who knows what ails him? But he gives us work, food. No small thing these days. What else could we want?"

"Apart from the freedom to listen to the radio?"

"I see you have your humor back. Perhaps Werner simply did not enjoy the music?" Jean slapped him on the back. "Come, you are just tired and in need of food before rehearsals."

"Rehearsals?"

"Early evening. Dinner is always delayed until afterwards. You'll be needed at some point. Better to eat now. Come, Giordano has coffee, Madame Geneviève cake. And me, cigarettes."

Michel followed Jean to the Big Top, where a table had been set up outside; coffee, cakes, water and fruit piled on top.

"We used to get cheese." Giordano sat next to the table, his plate full, his eyes downcast. "But Werner says this is all we get now before rehearsals—says too much food makes us like slugs."

"More like he doesn't want to pay for the cheese," Madame Geneviève said, and handed Michel a slice of lemon sponge cake. "I made it."

"More like he can't afford to." Odélie appeared and sat next to Michel on an upturned wooden crate.

"I heard there was food?" Anton had his wireless tucked under his arm.

"You really think I would steal it?" Odélie asked him, pointing to the radio.

"You have before; I dare say you'd do it again."

"Play us something, Anton. Find some music," Jean urged.

"It's not for music. It's for the news."

"Well, then let's hear the news," Geneviève said.

"It's in German mostly. Or nothing. Just static."

Michel ate his cake and thought of the voices that had come from the radio the night before—all he knew was that the voices, whilst not clear, were certainly not German.

"Give it to me." Odélie took it from under his arm and twiddled with the dial until she found an echo of music, light and soft, with no words.

"Classical music, beautiful!" Madame Geneviève clapped her hands together.

Odélie handed Anton back the radio. "I'd rather have silence," she said.

"Shame we can't listen to some news reports." Felix wandered over and took a cup of coffee. "I'd like to hear."

"Should you be here?" Odélie asked. "Surely there's a stump to thump or something to build?"

"He's here." Felix pointed at Michel. "He's not a performer. If he's here then it's OK if I'm here, I figure."

"Quite! Everyone welcome. No one turned away." Geneviève smiled.

"I can go." Michel stood and wiped the cake crumbs from his hands on his trousers. "I've got to check on Beau anyway; stables to clean and all that."

"Stay awhile," Jean urged.

"No, really, it's fine. I'd rather just get on."

When Michel reached Beau's carriage, he saw the behind of someone crouched over, wearing a pair of black trousers.

"Can I help you?" Michel asked.

The figure stood and turned to face him. Frieda.

"I'm sorry. I hope you don't mind? I borrowed some tools, just a hammer and nails. I was thinking to sort Beau's door a little. You know, the pole won't stop him—he's run away so many times I've lost count."

"I can help," Michel said.

"You can?" She smiled at him then tucked a piece of hair behind her ear; it had escaped the blue cloth that held it back. "I look a mess, I know. Not very ladylike. Werner would burst a vein if he saw me, but then again, he nearly burst two when Beau scarpered yesterday." She held out the hammer to Michel. "You said you'll help?"

He took the hammer from her and tried to think of something to say, but he could conjure no words.

"I was planning to nail in some planks, you know—halfway up the door?"

"We'd need a hinge," Michel said, his voice quieter than he would have liked.

"A hinge? I'll go and ask one of the men to give me one. Maybe you nail the boards together whilst I'm gone?" She smiled again.

"I can do that."

"Good. Be back in a minute."

As soon as she was gone, Michel set to with the boards. *I can do that.* Is that what he had really said—is that all he could muster? Like a child. *I can do that.* What was wrong with him?

He took a nail and hammered it into the wood. It split and he had to try again. He suddenly thought of the butcher's daughter, Estelle, of the way he could talk to her with ease, even in front of her father. Then of Odélie, and of the women from Odette's café. He had said more to them—talked of music, of life. He had made jokes—yes, jokes! One woman—Adele, was it?—she had said he was funny.

He took another nail and splintered the wood again.

"Here, a hinge." Frieda held it over his shoulder.

He took it from her, his fingers touching hers, and felt the words fall away once more.

"I'll hold the nail in place. Maybe that will help?" She bent down in front of him and they worked silently for a few minutes, save from the knock of the hammer on each nail.

When they were done, Michel sat back.

"I should have asked the men, you know, to do this... that's what Werner would have done."

"But you didn't," Michel said.

She sat back too, her bottom on the ground, her legs pulled up so she could rest her forearms on her knees.

"I like Beau. I was the one who told Werner to buy him. No one wanted him, did he tell you that?"

Michel shook his head.

"He was going to be shot. They said he had too much spirit. But I liked him; I saw something in him that reminded me of someone. So, I got my way. And now it is my responsibility to keep him safe. That's why I didn't ask for help. He's mine. I want him safe."

"I'll keep him safe for you."

"I know you will. I can see it in your eyes."

"Can you bring Claudette to the tent?" Odélie appeared behind Michel, her voice loud and harsh.

"Claudette?"

"Yes. To the tent. Now. We are rehearsing."

"Sorry, he was helping me." Frieda stood.

"Werner wants us all."

"I'll finish this later," Michel said.

"Claudette? Michel! I need her now."

Michel turned to Odélie and went to Claudette, seeing the shadow of Frieda disappear out of the corner of his eye.

"What were you helping with?" Odélie asked as Michel fixed the bridle onto Claudette.

"A door for Beau."

"Just a door? Why was she doing it?"

"I don't know. She was here when I came back."

"Werner won't be happy."

Michel looked at her. "And who will tell him?"

Odélie grinned at him. "We all have secrets, don't we, Michel?"

"About last night…"

"What about it?" She smiled slyly at him. "I was fast asleep—I'm not sure what you were up to? Get her ready and bring her to the tent. Quickly now. No one wants to see Werner upset."

A few minutes later Michel led Claudette to the Big Top. He walked her around the outside until he saw Felix, leaning against a post, smoking a cigarette.

"Do I take her through the front?" Michel asked.

"You're so friendly with them, thought you'd know where to take her," Felix said.

Michel turned away and walked Claudette through the main entrance. In front of him lay a dusted circle ready for the performers, encircled by tiers of seats that workers were still banging nails into.

"Not here! Are you that stupid?" Werner walked towards him from the middle of the ring, a spotlight from above making his costume glitter. "Behind! Behind! You think that the audience want to *see you* with a horse?"

Michel turned Claudette, who, ruffled by all the shouting, pushed her nose against his cheek.

"It's OK, it's OK," Michel spoke calmly to her.

He walked her past Felix once more, who grinned at him, and found the back entrance to the part of the tent that held the performers away from sight of the audience's seats.

"I'll take her." Eliáš, the male triplet, took the reins from Michel.

"Odélie said Claudette was for her."

"And I will take her to her."

"Stand here, Michel." Jean came forward and ushered him behind a wooden stall. "Stand here and watch the rehearsal. You'll like it."

"Jean, you look magnificent," Michel exclaimed. Jean was dressed in a wig of white curls, his face painted white with red circles on his cheeks. A ruffled white neckerchief peeked out over a waistcoat of gold, framed by a jacket and pantaloons of scarlet velvet. His legs were clad in white tights and his giant feet in black patent shoes.

"I am a king—if just for a day, Michel. Giordano is my court jester. Giordano, where are you? Are you hiding again?"

Giordano appeared from behind a cut-out throne being carried by two men to the center of the ring.

"I look foolish!" Giordano cried.

"You look like a jester," Michel said, admiring the man's red, green and blue striped outfit, and stifling a laugh as he spotted the slippers that were upturned with bells on them.

"See? You think I am stupid."

"You are funny, my friend, and that is the point," Jean said, and placed his arm around Giordano's shoulders. "Now, Michel, wait here—watch and see some magic!"

Michel stood in the shadows and watched as the performers all met in the ring. The triplets were decked out in silvery white cotton leotards, their sequins catching the light. Werner held court, standing on an upturned box, his red overcoat unbuttoned, his top hat on the ground.

Odélie appeared, her body encased in the same silver-white as the triplets, her hair piled high and pinned with sequins that winked as they caught the light. She stretched and laughed with the others as Serge walked into the ring, a bag on his back, the shining tips of swords peeping out of the top.

"From there, you hold out one arm, and she will jump on behind you," Werner instructed Eliáš, who was clambering aboard Claudette bareback.

"I know. I've done it before," he said.

"No backchat! Go! Get on with it."

Eliáš rode Claudette around the ring to warm her up, her head pulled high, her strides short and clipped.

Michel stepped back, just one step, and tripped over something soft.

"Ouch!" A woman's voice.

Michel turned to apologize and there was Frieda.

"Sorry. I'm sorry."

She smiled at him. "It's all right."

"You look…" Michel lost his words.

Gone were the men's trousers and shirt; now she was in a navy-blue leotard bedecked with sequins and silver thread, her long legs encased in transparent tights.

"Better than my workman clothes? Not my best costume, this one, but it will do for rehearsals."

"Did I hurt you?"

"Only a little. It's nothing compared to the injuries I've had over the years. Trapeze isn't for the faint of heart."

"I don't doubt it."

"Are you going to watch?"

"I want to."

"Frieda! And you, why are you still here?" Werner stalked towards them. He grabbed hold of Frieda's arm, pulling her away from him. "You damage her foot, you damage my show!"

"It was an accident. It doesn't hurt. Not even a bruise, see?" She turned her ankle left, then right. "See?"

"Are you still here?" Werner looked at Michel.

"No. I'll go."

"Better get to it, then." Werner dragged Frieda across to the others, who all stared after Michel as he walked out.

The next morning, Michel woke tangled in his sheet, his forehead slick with sweat as if he had a fever. With the mercury steadily rising each day—it never stayed still long enough for someone to record the exact temperature—the inside of the tent was growing stuffy.

Michel went to see Beau and Claudette, who were lethargic and lay on the ground to cool themselves. He could not train Beau in this heat—he would have to wait until early evening.

He spent the day grooming the horses instead, picking their hoofs and checking them all over for summer ticks. He even read to them from his book, feeling strangely at home—as if he were back in Paris, back at his job, and soon would be dining with Bertrand.

He finished fixing the door to Beau's carriage and wished Frieda were there to help him once more, but she was not at breakfast nor at lunch—he wondered where she went when she disappeared.

"You look busy." Odélie wandered over and sat on the edge of the carriage as Michel was finishing brushing Beau's tail.

"Almost done."

"You need a break. This heat is unbearable."

Michel sat down next to her and took the water she offered him.

"See, I'm thinking of you. Don't you think I look nice?"

He looked at her, her sunshine-yellow dress and bare feet, the toenails painted red. "You look like summer."

"I try. You've been hiding today."

"It's too hot to train them; better to gain their trust—talk to them, groom them."

"They like that?"

"They do. It makes them feel safe, I think."

"You spend too much time with them."

"It's what I'm paid to do, or rather, not paid, not yet."

"Did you see me at rehearsals? That flip off Claudette's back was the best I've done for ages."

"I didn't get to stay."

"No matter. You think you'll be free this evening? Anton says he's found some music, finally. Me and a few others are having a drink and going to listen to it this evening."

"I'll try."

"Good." Odélie pushed herself off the carriage ledge. "I'll be waiting for you."

Just as the sun sluggishly took itself to bed and the caw of crows and tweets of birds grew louder as supper-time approached, Michel took the sweating Beau, Bisou and Claudette to the nearby river, where they could stand knee-deep and allow the cool water to lap around their legs.

Michel sat on the riverbank and watched the horses, his own feet dangling in the murky water. Now and again they wandered a few paces to churn up the water and cool their flanks. Finally, hot and tired, Michel undressed and climbed in too.

He ducked his head under—once, then twice—resurfacing each time to the delight of Claudette, who stamped her hoof, splashing him, then bent low to nuzzle his wet hair.

Beau let out a low whinny as Michel swam towards the opposite bank, but before he could turn to check on him, there was a loud splash, then short, quick ripples that caught Michel on the back of the neck. Beau whinnied once more; then a voice, a female voice, calmed him. *Odélie?*

Michel turned to look, but she was gone, swimming towards him under the water, a hazy warped shadow followed by a trail of bubbles that popped on the gentle ripples.

He found the soft soil of the river's bottom under his feet, the water up to his chin, and waited for her to resurface.

"Odélie?" he said.

Her slick hair was not auburn but jet black, her face smooth, her eyes kind. Frieda.

"You were expecting someone else?" she asked.

"Frieda," he said.

"You don't mind, do you? I saw you leading Beau and the others away. I thought I'd follow."

"I don't mind."

"He's harmless, you know."

"Beau?"

"Werner. I know he shouts and things, but just ignore it."

"It's sometimes hard to ignore."

Frieda ducked her head under the water, and when he saw her silhouette, he realized that she was naked as she swam away from him towards the bank. Then she turned and came back to him.

"Beau likes the water," she commented as she trod water. "It's good that you brought them here. Good for them to cool themselves in this heat."

"I fixed his door, his new one," Michel said.

"I saw. And I thank you on his behalf. And mine."

"He kicks at it."

"He thinks he wants to run away again, but really he doesn't know how good he has it."

"That's very philosophical."

Frieda's head bobbed a little, so her lips were underwater for a moment before she resurfaced and spurted water at him, then laughed. "I'm not sure I am that deep, Michel—not a philosopher. I'm nothing but an act, a performer. We don't think too much."

"I like the way you think," he offered, then watching her smile, he mirrored it.

Claudette snorted and pulled herself out of the water onto the bank. She drew herself along the trunk of a tree to scratch an itch. "It's almost time for them to be fed. Claudette always knows the time," Michel said.

"In that case, it is time for me to go too."

Frieda swam away from him, this time a slow crawl that made her hair fan out over the water and glisten in the evening light. She reached the bank then stood, her naked back and then her behind and long legs. She quickly dressed in her baggy black trousers and a mustard-colored shirt. As she tucked it into the waistband, she turned and grinned at Michel, then patted Claudette's neck and disappeared into a thicket of trees.

Michel swam the same route back as her. As he reached the bank, he heard a rustle and the crackle of leaves. He looked to the bushes that edged the riverbank and was remined of Lucien's cats from Vodable; how their eyes had watched him, their tails swishing in perfect unison—as if waiting to catch their prey.

Michel shook his head; he was tired, and his mind was full of Frieda. He climbed out of the water and dressed. Clicking his tongue, he motioned for Beau and Claudette to follow him.

Back at the camp, Werner was arguing with a local gendarme who was shouting at the ringmaster that he was not welcome in town.

Michel led the horses to their carriages and then doubled back towards the group encircling the two.

"I beg to differ," Werner said. "The Captain himself said we were welcome! I spoke with him. We have permission to use this land, permission to put on the show."

"He never said this to me."

"And why would he?"

"Things are a little different now, from before. You have to understand that."

"I see no Germans here."

"Not yet. Not quite."

"Are they coming?" Madame Geneviève wailed.

"No, Madame, no." The gendarme had beads of sweat on his brow. "But we are to exact certain rules now that Paris has fallen and the government is in the control of the Germans."

A collective gasp was heard throughout the group.

"You did not know?" the gendarme asked.

"No. So it is certain."

"Monsieur, yes. *Certainment*. France has fallen. We are to follow their rules now."

"Well...all I can tell you is I have permission." Werner produced some papers.

The gendarme looked perplexed for a moment, then said, "Let me see your identification."

Werner handed it over.

"Surname Neumann. German," he said.

"And French," Werner replied.

"But it is a German name, Neumann."

"Surely that does not matter now? In fact, I should think it would be a positive thing, now that we find ourselves in our new circumstances?"

The gendarme looked nervous and handed the papers back. "I'll check with the Captain. If he says so, I'll be back, and you will have to move on."

Werner turned away from him.

Michel followed Jean to his tent as the crowd dispersed.

"You think he'll come back?" Michel asked, as Giordano set up a small table and chairs and Jean began to shuffle a deck of cards.

"Probably, but Werner will take care of it."

"It's true, then. France is now German."

"For now." Jean dropped a card on the ground then picked it up. "Have you no hope? It won't last. Nothing lasts. Sit down. We need to talk of brighter things."

"I don't see how we can." Michel sat.

"How can we not? What are we to do? Talk of war, of what is happening, of what could happen? All we can do is sit here, enjoy each other's company and drink. What else can we do?"

"I don't know, but I feel we should be doing something."

"Well, we are playing *mouche*. You know it?"

"I do."

"Then I'll deal you a hand. Giordano, bring the drink."

Next to them, the triplets practiced their baton twirling, the lamplight catching on the silver-painted sticks of wood that they threw into the air, turned, then caught behind their backs. Kacper played on his accordion, Gino asleep on his lap. Others sat around drinking and talking, the workhands growing louder and louder as they drank too and played their own card games.

"You like it here, Michel?" Jean asked.

"It's different."

"Different in a good way?"

"I'm not sure yet—just different, I suppose. Werner...is he German?"

"Obviously," Jean said.

"I mean, I knew his name was. But his French is flawless."

"His mother was French," Giordano said. "Well...I'm not sure whether I believe that, mind you. But that's what he says."

"She was," Jean confirmed.

Giordano placed five coins on the table. "You in, Michel? You need to add your money."

"I'll loan it to you for now." Jean placed his and Michel's bets.

"May I join?" A man with red hair appeared, his gray-green eyes bloodshot.

"Michel, this is Hugo; Hugo, Michel. Hugo is our clown and makes the best génépy in France. What's your bet?"

"I have two bottles with me now. One to drink, one to bet." Hugo proffered two brown glass bottles of the herbal liqueur. Giordano took one and placed it under the table.

"Fine. Jean is dealing."

Jean dealt the cards, and each decided whether to stick or exchange.

"You are looking after the horses?" Hugo asked Michel as Jean deliberated over his cards.

"Yes."

"About time we got another hand around here. I had to clean their hooves. Damn near had my head kicked in by Beau."

"He's OK—just needs to calm down."

"Ha! Ask me, I say he needs to be put down!"

"Are you going to play or not?" Giordano asked Jean.

"I'm thinking. Fine. Give me one."

Michel stuck to his hand; Giordano excused himself to use the toilet.

"Are you taking your cards with you?" Jean asked.

"I don't trust you."

"I don't trust people either," Hugo said, drinking a full tumbler of génépy and immediately pouring more. "You know...why would you? I have family, you know, who have run away from the Boche—gone into hiding. They don't trust people."

"Hugo, you need to drink less."

"And you need to drink more!"

Just as Giordano reappeared, Michel caught a glimpse of Frieda, ducking into Werner's carriage on the train. As she opened the door, warm orange light filtered out, then she closed it behind her. She was gone.

"Don't even *look* at that one," Hugo said. "Not worth your time. German, too."

"Ah, hush. Now look"—Giordano stuck to his cards—"see: I win!"

The rest of them slapped their cards on the table.

"One more round," Hugo said. "I'll get another bottle."

*

The following days, Michel worked hard with Beau. By the third day Michel had him cantering calmly around the sanded floor in the Big Top whilst workers finished erecting the tiered seats.

"He's coming along well." Odélie, who was practicing nearby, applauded him once Beau was done.

"He is. But not fast enough. Werner is anxious he won't be ready for the show."

"Werner is always anxious about something."

"I should take Beau back. He needs a rest."

"I'll walk with you," she said, and hooked her arm in his.

As they walked, Michel heard the muffled roar of Aramis. "I still haven't seen the other animals yet."

"Not many to see. Aramis has no teeth now, so hardly a scary beast, but he roars and the children like seeing him. He is really just Werner's pet. He sits with him at night and talks to him and strokes him."

"So, no elephant then? A bear?"

"We had an elephant. Werner sold her a few months back. We had a llama—just one. We have Gino the monkey, of course, but he belongs to Kacper. Then, we still have two parrots and a snake that used to be Serge's pet."

They walked past Felix, who was telling two other workers that the opening to a smaller tent next to the Big Top needed pegging again. It would soon hold the Mysterious Madame Rosie and her fortune-telling powers.

"She'll be in the middle of telling some fool that danger will befall him unless he buys some useless charm, and then, boom, the tent falls down on top of them!" Felix said.

"Might make him buy more charms?" one of the workers joked.

"Any more of that and you'll be gone—don't think we can't get someone to replace you."

"That threat might have more power if we weren't owed a month's wages," the other man argued.

"We should go into town tonight." Odélie spoke over the men. "Have a drink before the craziness begins tomorrow."

"Sure," he said, not really listening. He had spotted Frieda walking arm in arm with Werner towards them, the ringmaster whispering something in her ear to make her laugh.

"I'll see you in a bit." Odélie kissed him on the cheek, just as Frieda looked over, her smile faltering.

CHAPTER SIX

Le Grand Spectacle

The sound of the train's engine woke Michel before the sun had yet risen properly in the sky. The horses stomped their hooves and whinnied, thinking that they were on the move again. Michel dressed quickly and went to Beau, whose new calm had been disturbed. The rumble of the engine stopped; then a clang and loud swearing.

Felix's oil-stained face and clothes appeared from the engine room. He jumped down and walked towards Michel.

"You'll have to get the horses out of here for now," he said, wiping his brow but smearing more grease into his skin than off it.

"What's wrong?"

"You deaf, or just stupid? Engine's broken. Not sure what's wrong. I need to fix it today and it isn't going to be quiet work."

"What is that godforsaken racket?" Werner clambered out of his private carriage, wrapped in a purple dressing gown with matching slippers. "You know it's opening night, right? And I need my sleep."

"Sorry boss, it's the engine again. I thought that after last time—you know, when we broke down—it would be sensible to take a look at it before we move on tomorrow. I didn't mean to wake anyone."

"I'm not bothered that you woke him at least." Werner quickly looked at Michel. "Lazy gadabout, that's what he is. Drinking with the performers. Think I don't know what goes on here? He's lucky if he lasts until tonight."

"Shall I keep going?" Felix raised his eyebrows.

"Yes, yes. I'm up now. You told him to move the horses? Don't want them spooked for tonight."

"I did."

"I am right here; you can talk to me," Michel said.

"I'm quite aware *you* are here." Werner turned to him. "Quite aware, *too* aware. I'm actually wondering *why* you are, and not getting these damned horses *off* the train!"

Werner stomped back to his carriage, his waddle almost comical as he parted the rising mist that hung over the tracks.

"Going to be a hot one, no doubt about that," Felix said. "You see mist like that in a morning, and it only means one thing."

"Where am I going to shelter the horses?" Michel asked as he led Beau down the ramp.

"See those trees and the river beyond? Best sit there with them today. Stay in the shade. Good for you to be out of the way, anyway, seeing as the boss has taken against you so strongly."

Michel did as Felix suggested, and tied the horses with loose ropes under the thick shade of the trees near the riverbank.

He sat with them, his feet dangling in the water, watching as the sun burned away the dewy fog, and realized that tonight would be his last with the circus. Beau nuzzled into his neck and he rubbed at his nose.

"It's all right for you," he said to Beau. "Look at you! He'd never get rid of a beauty like you."

Bisou the pony noted the attention Beau was getting and tried to push Michel's hand off Beau. "You jealous, eh? I don't blame you. You get forgotten because you are so small. But then again, sometimes it's better not to be noticed."

"You talking to yourself?"

Jean stepped into view, his large feet snapping twigs underfoot. "I brought you this—didn't see you at breakfast and Felix told me about your new camp for the day."

Michel took the coffee and warm roll from Jean. "Thank you. I wanted to come by, but I couldn't leave this lot."

"The workhorses are coming down in a bit too—four of them. Felix said he'll bring them. You OK, Michel? It's opening night and you look as though you didn't get a ticket!"

Michel sipped his coffee. "I don't fit in here, Jean. It's not for me."

"You're leaving?"

"Tomorrow morning. I'll see if I can find some work in the town."

"But why? You were getting on so well."

"Like I said, Jean, I just don't fit in—Werner has made that pretty clear."

For a minute or two, neither spoke, and the only sounds were those coming from the birds singing their morning song to each other and the slap, slap of river water that gently lapped against the brown dirt of the bank.

"Michel, have you noticed anything about us—anything strange?" Jean broke the silence and Claudette lifted her head, her strong teeth crunching grass.

"Am I supposed to have noticed something?"

"You mentioned, when you were on the train, that you know of the Cirque d'Hiver, in Paris. It's an amazing masterpiece. They have everything, you know—the best costumes, the best acts, elephants, birds of prey: everything. Have you been?"

Michel shook his head.

"No matter. My point is, think about what you have seen with us—we are hardly world-famous performers. We are nothing more than a bunch of street performers with worn costumes and a train that hardly ever works. We can't even put on a full circus show anymore, and have turned ourselves into a fair to distract everyone from the lack of talent, animals and magic. So, to say that you don't fit in is absurd. None of us fit in! That's the point!"

Michel smiled at Jean. "That's kind of you to say, Jean, but Werner, he wants me gone. Better to leave before I'm thrown out."

"Just wait until after tonight, Michel. You have worked hard with Beau."

"He's not finished training yet—he can behave when ridden now and isn't as flighty, but he's a far cry from dancing like Werner wants."

"And he'll see that. He's a reasonable man—really."

"Ha! That's the best joke you have ever told!" Michel laughed.

"No, really he is. He's always like this on the day of the show. Trust me. Just wait."

"You really do like him, don't you?" Michel asked.

"Most of the time. Sometimes I don't."

"But he's beastly to everyone."

"He likes perfection."

"Why do you excuse him so much? I've heard the way he talks to you too."

Before Jean could answer, Felix appeared, leading a cart-horse with each hand, and then following behind, Frieda with two more.

"They OK here?" Felix began grounding their lead ropes with a peg. "Brought some more pegs for these so they can move about. No good having them tied to a tree all day."

"They'll be fine, thank you, Felix."

"Giordano's looking for you, Jean," Felix said as he began to walk away. "Something about how your costume is always better than his and he's going to cut yours to his size."

"I need to go!" Jean leapt up and chased after Felix, yelling, "What else did he say?"

Michel saw that Frieda had not left. Instead she was running her hand down Claudette's rear leg before lifting it to inspect the hoof.

"Anything wrong?" Michel walked over to her.

"I thought I noticed her kicking it out in rehearsals. She injured it not long ago. I told Odélie but she said she rode fine. I just wanted to check though."

Michel crouched next to her—she smelled of lemons. He snatched a glance at her face as she inspected Claudette's hoof, her eyes quick, her lips pursed as she concentrated. A wisp of hair had escaped her red polka-dot headband and it took all his concentration not to tuck it behind her ear.

"See anything?" he asked, just so she would turn her face to his.

"Looks OK. I think I am just overprotective. Werner says I am like a mother without a baby sometimes—always wanting to care for something."

"Surely that's a good thing?"

"Maybe." She stood and brushed her hands on her white summer dress.

"Here, wash your hands, you'll get it dirty."

Frieda followed him to the riverbank and dipped her hands in the cool water. "It's an old dress anyway. I made it out of some material that Madame Rosie had left over." She flicked the excess drops off her hands then sat down. "Join me?" She patted the damp grass next to her.

"You'll get grass stains now."

"Doesn't bother me, a bit of dirt here and there. Werner would rather have me cooped up, all pretty and clean at home. But it's boring, isn't it, trying to be so perfect all the time?" She looked at Michel, her eyes unblinking and serious.

"I'm not sure I have ever been perfect."

"I'm sure your mother thought you were perfect."

"Maybe, when I was young."

"I'm sure she still thinks you are."

"She died, some years ago. I think if she was here now she'd cuff me behind the ear and tell me to get myself a proper job."

"I'm sorry you lost her." Frieda laid her hand on his.

Michel looked at her hand, then at her. She held his gaze, then took her hand away. They both turned to watch as a dragonfly hummed on the surface of the water.

"Anton says he found a radio channel that comes from England. He says the war is moving on, that things are getting worse." Frieda pulled at a blade of grass and wrapped it around her finger.

"Did you hear it? What they said?"

"No, Anton just tells me what he hears. Says there are warships in the Channel, bombs dropping."

"It feels unreal to me," Michel said.

"I know. We are sitting here whilst fish are leaving small bubbles on the water as they eat their breakfast, the birds are flying in the clear blue sky, the trees are swaying in the breeze—all of it seems so normal."

"I feel guilty. Like I should be doing something, but I'm not sure what."

"You are doing something, Michel; you are caring for the horses. It's a kindness and a help. What more could you do?"

"I—" Michel began.

"I have to go." Frieda suddenly jumped up and looked around as if someone had been watching. "I was only meant to be five minutes or so. Must get back, costumes to be fitted!" Her voice was high, but her expression was serious.

"Frieda..." Michel stood. "I'll walk you back."

"No! I'll go. You stay here and take care of this lot." She touched his hand again. "I'll see you later, though?"

Michel nodded and watched her lightly run back towards the camp, the smell of lemons lingering in the air.

*

Michel waited next to the riverbank until the heat had dipped enough to walk the horses back to camp.

Felix had set up a roped-off area for them to graze in as he continued banging and clamoring over the engine.

"Not gone then?" Jean sat outside Michel's tent, his legs stretched out in front of him, the chair underneath barely visible.

"Still here, for now."

"I've just been to see Madame Rosie. You met her yet?"

Michel sat on the grass next to Jean and took a cigarette from his shirt pocket. "I heard she's the circus fortune teller, yet she is a whisper, a ghost—always heard and never seen."

"Quite poetic of you, Michel. She lodged in town this week. Had a cough, or so she says, and needed a private room. Giordano says she only wanted that so she could earn more money—selling trinkets and things of hers."

"She's back now, though?"

"Back and brighter than ever. Her tent is up. I just popped in to see what she had to say about my fortune for the evening."

"And what did she tell you?"

"That she was tired and busy, and until I had money in my hand, my fortune wouldn't reveal itself."

"When's dinner?" Michel looked about but could not see the food tent.

"Ah, yes. No dinner tonight, but there are some local vendors selling food."

"Why not?"

"Seems the cook and his lot got a better offer. Or, if you listen to the rumors, they walked out after not being paid. Depends who you want to believe."

"Will we get a new cook?"

"Listen to you! *We*. I thought you were leaving. You're one of us, then?"

Michel looked up and saw Frieda talking to a workman outside the Big Top, her hands gesturing. Then she patted the man on his shoulder. "Perhaps I am." Michel smiled.

"Better get some rest then. Going to be a late one. I'm off to have a nap myself...although"—he stood—"it depends if Giordano is snoring or not!"

Michel took his advice, and ignoring the noise of voices, of hammering and yelling outside, he lay down on his bed and fell into a dreamless sleep.

The warmth from the torch flares and the day's heat made Michel's cheeks red and plump like a small child as he sat at the entrance to his tent. He leaned back in his chair and watched as the triplets, Eliška, Edita and Eliáš, walked past, their heads held high, their batons twirling in unison, the light blue sequins of their performance-day costumes catching the glow of the flames.

Michel was nervous. Beau needed to perform—though even just to behave would be an improvement.

He got up and walked over to Beau, who stood watching as the circus came to life. Michel talked to him and rubbed at his cheek until Beau's ears twitched forwards once more, his eyes wide and ready.

Michel turned to Claudette, who was dressed up for the evening's performance. She wore a bejeweled bridle, a baby-blue feather crown tied to her head to match the triplets' and Odélie's costumes, and her saddle was decorated with cheap azure gems, which when the light snatched hold of them, made them look as expensive and lustrous as diamonds.

"Madame," he said, stroking the mare's neck. "You are looking wonderful this evening. I'm sure you will have the audience cheering for you."

Claudette stamped her foot in reply then nuzzled into his neck.

"A story? You want a story?" Michel pulled a bale of hay closer to Claudette, and as he did, Bisou the pony and Beau walked towards him, as if they too wanted to hear the tale.

He pulled his book, *Le Lotus Bleu*, from his bag and smoothed his palm over the cover, feeling the worn blue leather and the gold embossing of the title.

"Well, let's see then—where is Tintin on his adventure?" Michel opened the book and began. But as he started to read, a voice nearby called out to him.

"Michel!" Jean-Jacques appeared, his costume the same as at rehearsals, his regal wig slightly askew. "Isn't it glorious?"

"I haven't seen it yet—I didn't want to get in the way."

"Leave them for a while, and come and play *mouche* with me. Then we'll seek out some food."

"You think Werner wouldn't mind?"

"Trust me: he's so busy flitting here and there, he won't notice."

Michel and Jean sat outside Michel's tent, each on a picnic chair with an upturned box serving as their card table.

Jean took a deck of cards from his pocket. "Now. Tonight I will win, and you will lose, and everything will be right with my world once more. Here, take this." He handed Michel a small silver flask. "Génépy—calms the nerves."

Michel took a swig; it was thick and hot at the back of his throat. He passed it back to Jean.

"Ah. Hugo has it wrong again. Not enough wormwood, too much vodka," Jean-Jacques commented.

"Where is Giordano?" Michel asked, coughing a little as the potent alcohol slid down.

Jean's enormous hands shuffled the deck. "Busy. He is worried about his hair. He says he's found a gray one and now will not perform until it's gone. So, he is seeing Madame Geneviève, who may be able to help. I assume she will use shoe polish—what else is there these days?"

"He could see the Great Vassily; perhaps he can make it disappear!"

Jean grinned. "Giordano can't help being vain—he's Italian and his looks are everything to him."

"How did you two meet?" Michel suddenly asked.

Jean-Jacques picked up a card and studied his hand. "Ah, now. A giant and a dwarf—how else do they meet but at a circus!"

"Werner's circus?"

"Maybe a little bit before."

"Did you come to Werner together for a job?"

Jean-Jacques looked up. "Something like that."

"And Werner made you an act?"

Jean shrugged. "Are you going to look at your deal? Do you need a card?"

Michel leaned back in his chair, studying his cards. "You think you can win?"

"I can only try."

"Try this." Michel played his hand.

"Are you sure you're here to look after the horses? I am starting to think that you should be a magician; I'm sure you're keeping cards in your sleeves."

Giordano, wearing his jester's costume, appeared. Jean took one look at his face and offered him his chair. The dwarf sat down, his legs dangling. Jean-Jacques offered his partner a drink, and Giordano took a swig.

"What's wrong?" Michel asked.

Giordano grumbled under his breath; something about the customers, the job, his hair.

"Did you fix your hair?" Jean-Jacques asked.

"She put shoe polish on it," Giordano said sullenly into his chest.

Michel laughed.

"I told you she would," Jean said.

"You would think a lady with a beard like she has would know something more about hair!" Giordano exclaimed, then reached up and took the jester's cap off his head, where they could see a thick black stripe down the middle, the rest of his hair a mahogany brown.

"I always thought I had black hair, and so she put black polish on it, and it shows I do not have black hair, I have brown! What kind of Italian man am I? No shiny black mane like Beau!"

Even though the man's tone was light, Michel could see that Giordano was near tears. He stopped laughing and handed him the flask.

"Well, the show goes on and I must perform," he said stoically. "I am a professional." He pulled the cap back onto his head.

"Can you smell that?" Michel asked suddenly.

Jean lifted his face upwards, his nose sniffing the air.

"Smells of butter," Giordano said.

Michel closed his eyes and breathed in deeply. Then, opening them with a start, he said, "Pancakes!"

"We shouldn't—people are arriving," Giordano said, but his eyes were fixed on the direction of the scent.

"We won't be long. Five minutes." Jean was already walking away, and Michel stood up to follow.

Within seconds the trio were out of the camp and amongst the growing crowds. Multicolored lights were threaded through the branches of trees and around posts, and blazing torches lit with petroleum led the way through the fair towards the Big Top. The small purple tent of the Mysterious Madame Rosie was lit with only small white lights and one torch, and visitors were assaulted by the thick scent of burning sage and lavender upon entry. Around the next bend was the tent of the Amazing and Strange. Later in the evening, Madame Geneviève would go there to groom her beard, the Great Vassily would astonish with his magic tricks, the strongman Maximillian would lift his daughter Adeline above his head, and Serge would delight by swallowing swords so long it astonished Michel that he was still in one piece.

A light breeze rippled the canvas of the tents, creating a flap-flap noise which reminded Michel of the pigeons fluttering in the eaves at the Gare d'Austerlitz. The breeze picked up the sweet smell of caramel, mingled with the peppery grease of the sausages cooking over large skillets of onions, and sailed out towards those who queued between two ropes at the ticket booth; small children standing on their tiptoes to try and see the magnificent curiosities awaiting them.

Michel stood aside to let a young family past, inadvertently leaning against the thick canvas of the Big Top, its red-and-white striped peak overlooking the many visitors. From inside the tent, he could hear the grumble of Aramis the lion.

It was remarkable to Michel how the circus had transformed itself. During the day it was empty and abandoned; far too quiet, the white canvas tents grubby and unloved, the Big Top fraying at the seams. Even the animals were duller, quieter and lethargic. The peeling paint on the stalls had not been restored, the lettering on the signs was beginning to fade, and the costumes had small tears, patched with any material they could find. But by night, the circus came alive. Its broken parts and worn paint were unseen, the animals woken from their stupors, and the performers became strange and magical creatures, glittering under the twinkling lights.

Michel walked past Kacper, who nodded a hello at him as he played his accordion, his small monkey Gino dancing, ready to be handed a banana for his troubles.

Jean-Jacques suddenly stopped the trio and pointed his long finger towards a stall awash with people. "Look!"

Michel followed the direction of the giant's finger and saw a man laughing with his customers as he poured thick batter into a pan, adding butter and cloying syrups. They patiently queued until Michel was finally handed a pancake for a coin; he groaned with pleasure as he took the first bite.

"It's the butter," the vendor said proudly. "My own. My cows made it."

Michel wiped the grease from his chin and walked after Jean and Giordano, who were making their way back towards Michel's tent.

Madame Geneviève stood outside her own tent, dressed in a tight red bodice dress, her large bosom spilling over the top, her thick beard oiled and perfectly groomed. She held a handkerchief to her face and dabbed at her cheeks now and again. When she saw Giordano, she bawled at him. "You said you had gray hair and now you do not have gray hair! I did what you asked! I am no magician! You made me cry just before the show!"

"Ah, come now, Madame, don't cry," Jean soothed, while Giordano shouted something back at her in Italian, his face as crimson as her dress.

The Great Vassily walked past at that exact moment, producing out of thin air a fresh bunch of tulips for Madame and a new blue hat for Giordano. "Come see me next time." He winked at Giordano.

"Michel!"

Michel turned at the sound of his name, and saw Werner stepping out of the train and heading towards him, followed by Frieda.

"Michel!" Werner waved at him. He was dressed, ready for the evening, his plump body decked out in striped trousers and a red jacket, finished off with a large black top hat, and his ridiculous mustache nicely waxed.

Michel made to move towards them but could not; his feet had planted themselves into the soil as soon as Frieda appeared. He could feel his heart beating faster and his mouth was dry. He watched every movement she made; the way she flicked her hair away from her face, her hand as it returned to her side, the way she gracefully turned, her whole body shimmering with sequins as she kissed Werner on both cheeks.

"Michel!" Werner shouted again. Finally, Michel had no choice but to respond. "Are you deaf? Could you not hear me? Is Beau ready?"

Frieda stood behind Werner and gave Michel the tiniest of smiles.

"Michel! Is he ready?" Werner's stern voice broke through Michel's thoughts.

"Yes..."

"Good."

"Frieda." Anton appeared next, dressed in a similar sequined costume. He bowed slightly and took Frieda by the elbow, guiding her away.

"Now. Let us get Beau, shall we? Did you change the saddle for my old one? I don't like that new leather; it irritates me." Werner smoothed his trousers over his ample behind as he spoke. "You like it here, don't you, Michel?" he continued unexpectedly.

"Most of the time I do..." Michel replied, his eyes still on Frieda as she was led away by Anton.

"Felix tells me you were asking him questions, on your first night with us."

Michel looked at Werner with surprise.

"Some of my workers don't like strangers asking them questions. In fact, none of us do."

"I'm not sure I know what you mean..."

"I mean that I gave you a week to prove yourself, and I am in doubt as to whether you have succeeded."

"I did as you asked. I have trained Beau. He's not perfect, not yet. But he has the potential."

"I also asked you to work and nothing else."

Michel thought of Frieda, of their swim, of their talks. Then he thought of Odélie.

"Your tongue fallen out of that thick head of yours? I wish it would."

"I haven't done anything wrong. I just tried to fit in," Michel said.

They reached the horses and Werner looked at Beau, then held his hand out to him. The stallion sniffed it then allowed his master to pet him. The tiniest of smiles appeared on Werner's face—so briefly Michel thought he might have imagined it.

"Don't try to fit in. No one can. Keep to yourself, Michel."

"I can stay?"

"We'll see."

Werner clambered aboard Beau and, heartened by his dignified stallion, trotted out into the crowd, laughing and joking with the customers.

Michel spent the evening sitting on a chair next to the horses' enclosure, ready to bring out each one when required. Around six, he heard the band start up with a trombone—*umpah pah, umpah pah*—as the crowds milled into the tent. Hugo, in his thick clown's makeup, stood on stilts, ruffling children's hair and honking his bright red nose as they passed.

Soon, it was quiet outside the candy-cane canvas. Still, Michel sat and waited. Suddenly the band slid into their next number, which meant only one thing. Werner's voice boomed around the tent and floated out towards Michel. The ringmaster welcomed the crowds, promised them an evening of amazement, and introduced the first act—the flying trapeze. The audience cheered and clapped, and Michel stood up, ready to deliver Claudette. His palms were so sweaty as he took the mare's reins that he dropped them twice. Claudette sensed Michel's lack of confidence and pulled away from him a little, stamping her hoof on the dusty floor, as if demanding an explanation for this change in behavior.

"I'm sorry, *ma chérie*." Michel kissed her nose, held the reins tighter and walked her out of the tent to the Big Top, where Eliáš waited. He accepted the reins from Michel, who took the opportunity to snatch a glimpse of the show happening on the other side of the curtain.

"You need to move out of the way," a stagehand said, pushing past Michel and grumbling at his uselessness.

But Michel did not hear him. He did not hear the crowd cheering, clapping, laughing—he did not even see them. All he saw was Frieda, tumbling down to earth. He gasped when she bounced into the net alongside Anton, but then they stood, held their hands high and took their bow. They turned and did the same for the audience behind them, and for a moment Michel caught her gaze; in that instant he felt incredibly powerful, and for that brief second, he knew he could not leave the circus—leave her, even though he could not have her.

"Take Beau," the stagehand prompted, handing Michel the stallion's reins. "The boss is done with him."

He did not move.

"Take Beau! He's finished for tonight."

"I'll wait for Claudette after the acrobats are done," Michel said, as Frieda and Anton climbed out of the landing net.

"No room. Get Beau out of here before the ringmaster sees you."

But Michel took his time gathering up the reins, turning Beau, waiting, hoping…

"I *said*, get him outta here!" The stagehand's face was puce with rage.

Beau pulled Michel on, and out into the night, the flap of the tent closing in their wake.

Eliáš brought Claudette back to Michel just after ten. People were streaming out of the tent like ants and scurrying towards the exit, the village beyond, leaving the grass strewn with papers, bottles and napkins in their wake.

"Here," Eliáš said, his French thick and unnatural on his tongue.

"Where are you from, Eliáš?" Michel asked.

"Why do you want to know?"

"I was just asking—your accent is different."

"Czechoslovakia," Eliáš said, and turned quickly away, striding to his own tent, his shoulders hunched.

A few hours later, Michel was deep in a sleep that had him dreaming of his apartment in Paris. Only this time, both Beau and Claudette filled the space, and on the chair near the window sat Frieda. As Michel moved towards her, others appeared—first Jean, then Giordano, Serge, Werner, and then Odélie…

"Odélie…" he said, half asleep.

"I'm here."

The voice was louder, closer.

"Odélie…" he said again.

"Michel, wake up." He felt a hand on his face, opened his eyes and saw the real-life Odélie standing over him.

"You were dreaming."

"Yes."

"Of me." She smiled.

He nodded and Odélie bent her head to his, kissing him, moving her body onto his.

"You dreamt of me," he heard her murmur once more, as she slipped her dress over her head and brought Michel close to her.

CHAPTER SEVEN

Le Vent du Changement

Michel awoke before dawn and once more Odélie was gone. He lay on his bed for a moment and let the trill of birdsong spread throughout the camp, building with each minute that the sun rose.

The clanging resumed behind him as Felix set to work on fixing the engine. Michel dressed and left the tent, rubbing his eyes and yawning as Anton passed him, his radio under his arm again, heading for a small gathering that had sprung up around Madame Rosie and Madame Geneviève, who were dispensing hot coffee and stale bread.

"Michel, is it not?" Madame Rosie greeted him as he took a tin cup of coffee from her. Her black hair was scraped back into a twist, a string of gold coins around her forehead, a small gold ring in her nose.

"It is."

"I have heard about you."

"Good things?"

She cocked her head to the side as if deciding. "Things."

"Move it." A workman from behind pushed against him. "Got to get the tent down by four."

Michel moved away from the queue and made his way to the horses, greeting them each with a pat on the nose, then fed them the last of the hay that Felix had dumped nearby.

Werner emerged from his carriage, dressed unusually in plain navy trousers and a pale green shirt. He said something to Felix, whose face was smeared with grease as usual, his dungarees almost falling off his wiry frame. Michel saw Felix nod, then return to the engine, and Werner made eye contact with Michel, hitched his waistband up over his belly—which immediately fell back below it—and walked up to him.

"That's the last of the hay," Michel told him.

Werner stroked Beau's nose.

"I can ask the farmer for some more?"

Still Werner did not speak.

"The show went well..." Michel ventured.

"Did it?" Werner turned to him.

"I think so."

"Did you see it?"

"No. I just worked."

A small smile appeared on Werner's face. Michel shifted uncomfortably and placed his hands in his trouser pockets.

"You worked. Is that what you did?"

"I did as you said to do. Worked and nothing else."

Werner nodded, then said, "Beau rides well. He didn't have a hint of fear about him, not even when the band struck up."

"I'm glad."

Werner scratched at his early morning stubble. "You can stay, Michel. Don't even ask me why I'm letting you. I know I'll regret it. You can thank that long-legged idiot friend of yours, Jean, for vouching for you. I told him that if you mess up, he goes too—and the little Italian."

"Thank you, Werner."

"Keep your head down, work hard, do as you are told, keep your nose out of everyone's business, and you'll get along fine. But I warn you"—Werner leaned into him so there was less than an inch between them—"keep away from *the performers*. Leave them alone. You are nothing but an animal yourself; *your friends* are the horses. Know your place and for God's sake, keep your mouth shut—no questions, no talking back. Understood?"

Michel nodded, his face growing warm.

Werner grinned. "Good." He walked back towards the train.

Michel's breathing came quickly, his fists bunched in his pockets. He wanted to run after the man, push his fat little body to the ground and watch him squeal. But he didn't. He stood and watched and waited until his breathing calmed, all the while keeping an eye on something, or rather someone, who had just appeared from the train, her cornflower-blue dress already stained with an oil smear from handing Felix his tools. She laughed at something Felix said and Michel felt his body relax.

He began to pack his things, then pulled down his canvas tent, storing it safely in the back of Beau's carriage along with the fold-out table, chairs and bed.

Around him, tent pegs were being pulled from the ground with the help of the four large carthorses that no one had bothered to name. With each peg, the tents deflated like sad balloons, until all of them lay on the ground, skeletons of the night before.

Shacks and stalls were dismantled with care and stored in the rear carriage ready for their next show.

Michel worked all morning, unpegging canopy after canopy from the summer-hardened ground, packing costumes, food and props into large wooden crates and sealing them with a few knocks of a hammer on nail.

"You need to work quicker, Michel." Felix was beside him, wrapping rope around his arm, the length of it quickly trailing towards him over the flattened grass.

"The train fixed, then?"

"No. I'm packing rope because it's still broken."

"Funny."

"My mother used to say, ask a stupid question, get a stupid answer. If you ask me an intelligent question, I shall oblige you with the same courtesy."

Michel stood and rubbed at his lower back. "Why are you so angry all the time? Surely that's a question that deserves an answer."

"You haven't noticed? There's hardly anyone here. Five workmen we've got now. That's nothing—not enough."

"Where'd they go?"

"You're back on the stupid questions again—how am I meant to know?"

"Fine. *Why* did they leave?"

"Money. None of it."

"What, after last night? The show was packed."

"Was it? What I saw were half-empty seats. You know, it all used to happen in that tent—none of this business of having little stalls here and there. It's more of a hassle now; takes longer to arrange. Want to get back to it, or are you going to stand rubbing your back like a pregnant woman all day?"

"You could give me a break, you know. I've been working since dawn."

"Haven't we all, Michel. No more questions now, not even intelligent ones—just work so we can get out of here."

They labored for another hour, dismantling the next tent, until Felix, wiping sweat from his brow, sat down on an upturned wooden crate and invited Michel to do the same.

"Smoke?" Felix offered.

Michel took a cigarette from him. They sat and smoked whilst others continued to pack the train wagons and Serge tried the engine, which rumbled and groaned.

"It won't last much longer. That engine's older than I am." Felix laughed.

"What will happen if the circus runs out of money?"

"We've only two choices: either leave and go our own way, or sell the train if we can and make it on foot, like the Roma do—caravans and such."

"I'm not sure where I would go. Before, I had this idea that I would go to my grand-mère's village . . . but now I'm not so sure."

"Michel, I'm not sure where you got the idea from that I want to hear the thoughts that run through that head of yours. Let me be perfectly clear—I don't care. I have to think about me. Me"—Felix pointed at his chest—"is the only thing that matters."

Michel stood, ground the cigarette out under his boot and walked away.

"Where are you going?" Felix shouted after him.

"The horses. Just me and the horses. That's who I'll think about."

"Good lad, Michel!" Felix laughed. "You're learning! Not so stupid after all."

By early afternoon the field was cleared, the only trace of what had been in strange outlines on the ground—brown, pressed grass in squares, circles and rectangles. Michel wished he could see the sight from high above; a map of something that had left, soon to be covered with fresh grass over the ghostly shapes.

The train whistle screeched in the balmy afternoon air, ringing out a call to everyone that it was time to leave. Michel stood outside Beau's carriage and watched everyone board. First Werner climbed on, strutting towards his own carriage, then Serge with Odélie on his arm, followed by the triplets, Geneviève, Hugo and the other performers.

Another whistle, then steam streaked from under the chassis and Michel swung himself up into Beau's carriage, closing the door almost all the way, leaving enough room so that he could sit, his legs dangling as the train pulled away.

"We not good enough company for you?" Jean dragged the inter-carriage door aside and stepped over the empty air in between with one stride.

Michel turned and smiled. "I just like the air. The scenery."

"Werner tell you to stay here?"

"Not in so many words. But I figured he didn't want me in the seating car."

Jean sat down next to Michel and offered him a cigarette. Michel blew the smoke away from him and watched as it was dragged back by the speed of the train.

"You shouldn't stay here—go and sit in a comfortable seat," Michel said.

"Are you bored of me?"

Michel shook his head. "Felix and the others are in the stock car; they don't sit with performers."

"So? They used to when we had more space—we had two seating carriages and bunks. In fact, the night you clambered aboard they were in the stock car to start with, where I found you, but Werner made us all squash into the seating car—said it wasn't safe for them in the stock car."

"He's a caring man," Michel said.

"Sarcasm, Michel? It does not suit you."

"I'm thinking that maybe I'll leave soon. Felix says the train won't last much longer."

"Ah, now you want to leave again. Well, that's true enough about the train. But I can bet all Hugo's génépy that Werner will die before he lets his circus fall apart. What's got into you? I thought you would be happy now—I spoke with Werner."

"He told me."

"So?"

"So, thank you for speaking up for me, but he's just so frustrating, so patronizing. I think if I stay much longer we will come to blows."

Jean slapped him on the back. "You're overreacting! He's tough on everyone at the beginning. He just wants to see how much you want it, that's all—you know, to prove yourself."

"If I'm going to do that, I can't talk to you anymore. Workers and performers don't mix—he said so this morning. And I can't mix with the workers either—Felix has made it clear that I am not welcome there. I'm on my own. I don't fit anywhere here."

Jean shook his head. "He doesn't mean it," he said quietly. "Felix, or Werner."

"He called you a long-legged idiot, you know. Yet you still defend him. What's he got on you anyway?" Michel looked at Jean, who would not meet his gaze.

"He's just joking," Jean replied with a weak smile.

Neither spoke after that, and Michel concentrated on the fields of green, then tilled brown soil, vines and thickets of trees rushing by. Jean shifted a little and coughed.

"I have only been on a train a handful of times before," Michel said eventually.

Jean looked at him, his face eager for the conversation. "Really?"

"When we visited Grand-mère. Other than that, I'm used to my legs."

"Giordano is unhappy about the train."

"Why?"

"He is convinced that if the train goes, he will go—his legs are too short to ride or walk for long. I told him it will be fine, but you know what he is like."

The train rounded a bend, the silvery new heads of corn visible amongst the green stalks.

"I fell in love once," Jean-Jacques continued, gazing out over the fields. "Just the once. With a girl with long legs. Just like those legs of corn. Long. Thin. Her head seemed to be sitting atop them."

"She'd have to have long legs with a man like you."

"Indeed! Yes. I suppose so. I never really thought of myself as tall until I met her, and she was tall—her head was at my shoulder. For a woman that is tall, I suppose."

"Where is she now?"

Jean shrugged. "She was beautiful, Michel. Blonde hair streaming down her back, blue eyes, and a smile that bowled me over. She was with us in the circus for a while. A snake charmer, if you can picture it! She was my goddess. We all have one, Michel. A goddess."

"Not me."

"Are you sure?" Jean stood and stretched his arms above his head, his hands reaching the roof of the wagon.

"My mother was tall," Michel said.

"She was?"

"Not as tall as you, or even your shoulder, but tall. She was thin and tall; she called herself a pencil."

Jean laughed.

"She was a good woman. Kind, thoughtful—cared for anyone she met."

"How long since...?" Jean asked.

"Five—no, six years now. I was a teenager. A shy, stupid boy with a stutter. Monsieur Bertrand, my old neighbor, helped me—found me a job, cared for me."

Jean sat down beside him once more, his legs dangling so far off the side that Michel was worried his feet would touch the moving earth and he would be swept away.

"My mother died before I knew her," Jean said softly.

"I'm sorry."

"Don't be. I had a father and he was a fine man. Tall too, though not as tall as me."

"He's still alive?"

"Somewhere, yes. Not in our town anymore. He moved. I'll find him again. We always find each other."

"What does she see in him?" Michel suddenly asked.

"Who?"

"Frieda and Werner."

Jean shrugged. "You know the girl I told you about—she was killed. Well, I think she was. She was taken by the Germans at the beginning of all this mess—they came into this German town we were traveling through to get back to France. We were stopped and we handed over our papers. It was fine at first—you know Werner has his German heritage, the right papers, the right bribes. We thought we were going to be let go, but then they decided to take a better look at us and found her papers—the wrong kind."

"A Jew?" Michel asked.

Jean nodded.

"And are you?"

"Am I what?"

"A Jew?"

"Perhaps once I was."

The train reached a bend and the wheels screamed as the brakes took hold and guided them onwards.

Once the quiet tack-tack of the train had resumed, so did Jean. "It does not matter who we are, Michel, we are all here and we work together. That's all that matters."

Michel glanced quickly at Jean, then changed the subject. "So, the next show will be different, you think? Smaller?"

"Smaller, definitely. You saw the workers go this morning? More will soon. You won't really go, will you, Michel?"

"I really don't know...I have no money to get me far anyway."

"Good. Stay awhile. Werner will calm down soon enough. He's just worried about the war, money. These are funny times, Michel, strange funny times. Who knows what will happen? Just live for today. We can worry about the rest later."

Michel nodded and swung his legs back inside the carriage, then leaned back against the inside of the wooden car. Jean followed suit, and soon the two friends had closed their eyes as the train rocked them to sleep.

The train was slowing, its wheels grinding as it pulled into a station, finally coming to a shuddering stop. Michel awoke and nudged Jean in the ribs.

"We've stopped," he said.

Jean yawned and raised his arms above his head in a stretch.

Michel jumped down onto the gravel of the tracks and waited for Jean to follow—but he did not.

Serge emerged first, then Werner and Felix. Steam billowed from under the train and Felix shook his head at it. He spoke with Werner, who shouted something then pointed at the engine. Felix shook his head again.

The tracks ahead were covered with weeds and broken-down carriages, and Michel watched as bulky Serge and stout Werner wandered further up the track, each looking left then right as if trying to understand where they were.

"What's happening?" Jean asked, his voice soft with sleep.

"Nothing."

Jean sat on the edge of the carriage whilst Michel walked backwards and forwards as he waited, now and again scuffing at the gravel with the tip of his boot.

Soon, Werner and Serge made their way back towards them, Serge climbing aboard and Werner approaching Michel.

"We're staying here tonight," he said.

"On the train?" Michel asked.

"Where else? You want to set up camp on disused tracks?" Werner pulled a slim silver flask from his pocket. He swigged then, uncharacteristically, offered it to Jean and then to Michel.

"Make sure the horses are fed, take them for a small walk, then come to the seating car, get food and whatnot, then sleep here."

"It was hard enough to sleep with all of us sitting up in the seating car last time—how about I stay in here with Michel?" Jean asked. "I've long legs, after all."

Michel tried not to smile at Jean's dig at Werner.

"I'll tell Giordano to join you too then, seeing as you'd rather stay here—I'm sure your partner wouldn't want to be left out. That way there should be room for all the performers to sleep."

"Giordano won't like that."

"He can suffer one night of discomfort." Werner turned and walked away.

Michel dragged the wooden ramps onto the gravel and secured them so Beau, Claudette and Bisou could disembark.

Lead ropes in hand, he took the horses to the edge of the tracks, down a small grassy verge and out into the fields.

He took off his shoes, the blades of grass a soft cushion for his bare feet. Only once he reached the middle of the field did he stop. He untied the ropes and set the horses free. They immediately galloped away, running in circles around him, their long tails high and swaying with joy, their ears pricked forward and nostrils flared. Only Bisou remained by his side, content to chomp on the fresh grass. Behind him, Jean led the four workhorses to the field and set them loose.

Michel sat and drew his knees upwards, resting his arms on them as he watched his charges play.

"They've no names, you know, the workhorses," Michel said to Jean, who was scanning the horizon.

"Then give them some. I think I can see a church spire down there."

Michel shielded his eyes against the lowering sun. "I can't see anything."

"You'd be able to if you were my height."

"What should we call them?" The larger black-and-white male carthorse stuck with his smaller female counterpart; the other two, younger tan geldings, plodded slowly around, investigating everything.

"Those two we should call Abigail and Jacques." Jean pointed at the couple.

"Was that her name, Abigail? The girl with the long legs."

Jean nodded, and watched them walk and eat in unison.

"And the other two?" Michel asked.

"They are the nosiest pair I've ever met. Always into boxes, investigating things. Once, one of them managed to open a box of costumes and ended up with Geneviève's petticoat stuck on his head!"

"Let's call one of them Bertrand—my friend from Paris—gentle but hardworking and inquisitive."

"And the other?"

"I don't know."

"What's your middle name, Michel?"

"Louis."

"Then let's call him Louis—a questioning sort of fellow."

Michel play-punched Jean in the arm and then they sat quietly, Jean with his eyes on Abigail and Jacques, and Michel watching his horse counterpart with his best friend Bertrand.

A crow cawed from a nearby tree, its yellow eye focused on Michel. He watched it as he took a cigarette from his shirt pocket and lit it. The bird followed the movement, then tilted his head to the side.

"Have you any paper, Jean?"

"Writing paper? I do."

"May I borrow some, and a pen?"

"Feeling reminiscent now, Michel?"

"A little." Michel stood, went to the newly named Louis and Bertrand, and patted their flanks as they walked around the field together.

*

That night, as the others ate and talked, Michel sat with the horses in their carriage and smoothed down the piece of paper with the palm of his hand. The fountain pen Jean had given him leaked as he wrote, staining his fingers a deep navy blue.

Dearest Bertrand,

I write to you now from a sloping hillside somewhere in the country—where, I do not know. The evening breeze is welcome as it has been another hot day, full of work, dust and little rest. I yearn now for a wash, but we are stuck here overnight, and I smell worse than the horses, who you may like to know are my bunkmates.

If you ever wondered what train you forced me to stow away on, it was a train carrying a circus troupe, and after some trials I have been welcomed into their family (well, by most!). I'm training their newest horse, Beau, a beautiful black stallion, and caring for the others. In fact, just this evening, I christened two of the workhorses Bertrand and Louis—an inquisitive pair who get themselves into mischief. It made me think of you, and an ache appeared that I had been trying to keep down since I left by working all the time—a homesickness for Paris, for your apartment, for our conversations and your guidance.

I wish I could ask for your guidance now. This job, whilst a joy in some ways, is not without its troubles. There is no money—at least none has been given to me—and the boss hates me so much that I wonder why he bothers to let me stay.

What should I do, Bertrand? Leave? Go to Saint-Émilion? Hope that I find a job and a place to stay somewhere else?

I just laughed to myself as I heard your voice instantly in my mind—"You have a job, Michel, a home, food; why are you risking this? You always were a hothead."

You are right, of course you are.

There is a woman, Bertrand. I am amazed by her. You once told me that you cherished your wife. I never knew what you meant by that before, but I think I do now. I cannot win her love—even talking to her is difficult for me. All my words get stuck and come out in a jumble, and I sound stupid. Even if I could speak to her, she would not be interested in me—I know this, and I have to remind myself of this fact—she is far superior to me.

And there is Odélie, an acrobat in the troupe. She likes me, and I her. But it feels fleeting, like those women I met at Odette's café—a night, a week, a month perhaps, but that is all. And yet I wish it weren't that way. Odélie is beautiful too—a little older than me, intelligent, quick-witted—why can I not cherish her instead? Why do I want what I can't have?

Enough now. Enough of me and my thoughts. How is Paris? Has it changed? How is Odette?

I have heard so little of the war since I left. A man here, Anton, a trapeze artist, has a radio. He tells the others now and again of the war. I have not listened to it all—I don't want to, not for now. I'd rather sit here and enjoy this summer evening, as the birds sing and circle before becoming silent, tucked in their nests, as the air becomes still and cool before the stars begin to appear. Here it is easy to pretend that all is well. I know, once more, you would chastise me for this; tell me how things are, what I should and should not do. You are right, of course. But what could I do if I knew more? I cannot stop the war; I cannot save anybody.

Our workman and train driver is called Felix. He's from Poland. He's a hard man and I'm sure he has seen much, yet he does not say so. He told me one needs to look after himself and no one else. I don't agree with him—but I am alone, so I suppose I can only look out for me right now…but to be honest it fills me with sadness. I feel like I have less worth. Does this make sense?

I'm tired, Bertrand, so I apologize now for my ramblings, but I had to write to you, I had to talk to my friend.

I have enclosed an address in Vodable. A friend from my travels called Lucien who showed me kindness lives there. I am sure he will not mind if you send letters to him. I shall write to him and forewarn him in any case. Perhaps we will return to that part of the country at some point, or perhaps I will leave here and go to him and stay. Please do write, Bertrand, I promise I will find your replies.

Stay well. Give my love to Odette.
Michel

That night Michel slept next to Jean; Giordano had found safety from a night with the horses and had begged a place in the main seating carriage with Geneviève, insisting that he had to be there to look after the women.

"Wake up, Michel." Jean shook him from a dream so deep that when he opened his eyes he did not know where he was.

"My apartment…" Michel said.

"If your apartment in Paris was like this, you were a poor man indeed!"

Michel sat and rubbed at his eyes, the milky early dawn seeping into the gloom.

"What's happening?"

"Werner has found us a spot to set up, a mile or so away."

"We are leaving the train here?"

"Even Werner must sleep in a tent from now on." Jean winked, a cheeky gleam in his eye.

A haphazard procession began to emerge just after the sun rose over the hills. Performers and workhands alike carried luggage, food rations and costumes, whilst the four carthorses pulled at a large worn wooden carriage piled high with the tents and stalls; so much so that the wheels screamed as the carriage moved, and Michel thought they would soon give way.

Michel gave lighter loads to Beau and Claudette; even Bisou was given the task of shouldering a woven bag containing a few lead ropes and bridles. Michel joined Hugo, who had decided that the ingredients for his génépy were the most important things to take with him, and asked Michel for Claudette to carry his bag with his clothes and personals.

"We have not talked much since our card game, you and I," Hugo said.

"No. Not much."

"Jean gave you some of the génépy though. He told me you liked it."

"I did."

"This batch will be my greatest—you'll see. I'll let you know when it is ready, and we will drink together and maybe we can talk then." Hugo ambled off to secure his perfect tent position—not too close to anyone, so that his stash of alcohol and ingredients would not mysteriously disappear.

Michel became distanced from the group. The horses insisted on stopping every now and then to chew at grass, stubbornly unmoving, an air of mischief about them since leaving the train behind.

He looked ahead and saw that most of the troupe had turned a dusty corner near an old oak and disappeared from view. He tried to reason with Beau that they should move more quickly, but the stallion was anchored in his desire to take his time and try each leaf or patch of new grass.

"You were waiting for me?" Odélie appeared at his side, her cheeks red with the growing heat, her breathing slightly quickened as if she had run to catch up with him.

He smiled at her. "Beau wants to sample every blade of grass, it seems. He has encouraged the others too."

"So, you were *not* waiting for me?" She pouted like a spoiled child, then laughed. "Come, Michel, let's catch up and perhaps place our little canvas homes near one another?"

Odélie took the lead rope of Claudette, who was unhappy to be dragged away, but as soon as she began moving, the other two sensed adventure and decided upon a quick walk to catch up.

Once Michel and Odélie turned the corner by the oak, there in front of them was a steep hill, and a sign marking that the village was now only one mile away.

On the right side of the track was a low farmhouse and two large hay barns off to the side, and on the left a field, mottled with coarse bushes, the grass already brown and patchy. In its middle, a storm of gritty powder was being churned up by those who were already making camp and smashing poles into the ground to erect their tents.

"Not great," Odélie muttered. "Dirt. Couldn't he have found a decent field? Perhaps by a stream or river?"

As they joined the others, Maximillian the strongman and his daughter Adeline, their bags over their shoulders, pressed past them and headed in the direction of the village.

"Where are they going?" Michel asked.

"Leaving." Odélie waved her hand dismissively.

"Leaving?"

"Probably. He was moaning the whole night about the war and the soldiers and all that. Said it was too dangerous for his beloved Adeline."

"And you aren't scared of the war?"

Odélie looked at him. "Why should I be? It will all blow over. You'll see. A fuss about nothing. Besides, I always get by—there's always someone who wants to take care of me."

"Michel, over here!" Werner shouted from in amongst the bustle.

Michel took Claudette from Odélie, who was suddenly eager to get to the triplets when she saw that they had found the best pitch, close to a thicket of blackberry bushes. They were already picking the ripe berries and eating them from their cupped hands, like squirrels.

Werner was distracted. "Michel—I want you over there, far corner, bordering that next field. See? Grass for Beau and the others. Rope off a section for them; we'll fashion an awning of sorts now. Felix will help you."

"And me?"

"And you what? You'll be in your tent next to them."

Michel led the horses to the far corner as instructed, and with the help of Felix set up his own area, away from the others, away from Odélie.

By six, the troupe had thinned: some had returned to sleep on the train for one more night and guard the rest of their equipment; others had dozed off in the warm evening air, and still others had ventured into the village to get supplies.

Michel threw down the hay he had procured from the farm for the horses, who ate slowly, tired from the day, the heat and the sudden changes.

"You look as tired as they do."

"Odélie." Michel turned to look at her, pretty in her pale yellow cotton dress, her feet bare, her lips painted red like her nails.

"We should sit together this evening; drink some wine, tell some tales." She smiled at him and took a step towards him suggestively.

"Michel!" Giordano appeared, dressed smartly in navy-blue trousers, a crisp white shirt and shined shoes. "Jean and I, we heard of a café—good wine, cheese, bread. You will come? Jean says you must. Cheese, during war! We need to eat as much as we can now."

Michel looked to Odélie, then back to Giordano. Then, he thought of Frieda.

"I'll be there in a minute. I'll just wash and change," he said.

Giordano walked away with a little skip in his step. Without a word, Odélie turned and strode away, her back straight, her shoulders squared.

Michel wiped his face with his kerchief and waited until she was out of sight before he went inside his tent to get ready.

The walk into the village took twenty minutes through long grassed fields, over styles and along a small stream. The church spire peeped at them as they walked, never out of sight, guiding their way.

"Do you even know where we are?" Michel asked Jean.

"We were heading south before the train died. Somewhere in the middle?"

"He was never good at geography," Giordano muttered.

"And you are? Tell us then, oh wise one, where are we?"

Giordano stopped and surveyed the landscape. "Mountains over there. See? We are on a hill. I'd say we are in the countryside."

Michel and Jean laughed.

"That is your expert opinion, Giordano?"

"Indeed, it is. When I see more clues, I will tell you exactly where we are."

The trio entered the small village. The houses, packed close together, ran up a cobbled street. Some shops were boarded up; the streets were eerily quiet with no children playing, no one coming home from work.

With nobody to water them, the flowers in the window boxes were brown and wilted; a lone dog trotted towards them, skinny and with wary eyes. It peed against a lamppost before hurrying on.

"Where's this café you say sells cheese?" Jean asked, his voice forcibly jolly.

They came to the market square, where only one café remained open.

"There, that one," Giordano said, and hurried towards it.

"Hardly a detective, is he?" Michel said.

They sat down at a small wobbly table, and the local woman who ran the café bustled over, clearly thrilled to see customers.

"Where are we, Mademoiselle?" Giordano asked her.

"You don't know where you are?" She raised her eyebrows suspiciously.

"We have been traveling far. Please forgive us."

Jean smirked at Michel and hid his smile behind a menu.

"You're not far from the city of Clermont-Ferrand—it's a few miles away."

"Ah, see! A volcanic town, is it not?"

"It is."

"My geography is intact. Jean, you owe me a drink."

"Did I agree to that?" Jean asked.

"Mademoiselle, my friend here will be buying the drinks."

"You flatter me," the woman said, patting her gray hairs into her bun. "I am a Madame."

"Oh! I did not realize. I do apologize."

"No apology necessary." She smiled at him.

They clubbed together what little money they had and ordered a bottle of wine. The food was brought without them asking—a thick cassoulet of beans and sausages that burst from their skins in the rich tomato sauce, fresh bread, a brie, and a whole camembert so ripe it was one day away from being inedible—the perfect age.

"No goose tonight," the Madame said by way of apology, as she placed the bubbling cassoulet in its terracotta pot in front of them. "Soon, no cheese, and then, no wine!" She fanned herself and looked as though she were going to cry. "They are coming, you know—everyone has left. We get no newspapers now; the telephones don't work. My sister lives in the village a few miles north of here; she says they came and took the church and the mayor's office for their own. My sister can't go out at night now—no one can. They must stay at home all day—all night. No cheese, no wine either, she says. They have to live on tinned vegetables."

"God forbid!" Giordano stood and wrapped his small arms around her ample waist, his hands not quite meeting. "No, no, Madame. It will not come to this! Do not fear."

The Madame was cheered by this and gave the trio another bottle of red on the house.

"I used to think that wine grew on vines," Jean-Jacques said. "Literally. Bottles hung on vines. That's what I thought when I was young." He shoved a piece of bread in his mouth, then with the silver cheese knife cut a wedge of melting camembert and filled what space was left.

Michel smiled. "When I was young, I used to think that there was only one country—France. Then, Monsieur Bertrand showed me a map and it was magic—utter magic—all those other countries."

"I used to think that I was the most handsome man in all of Italy!" Giordano said, his lips stained purple from the wine. "I still do, too!"

Jean and Michel laughed.

"Werner hasn't got rid of you yet, Michel Bonnet? Still here?" A voice and a scrape of chairs nearby interrupted their merriment.

Serge had sat down at the table next to them, Odélie on the chair opposite. She was dressed now in a flounced red dress, black heels on her feet, her hair pulled back into a tight bun at the nape of her neck. She looked older. Older and angry.

"Why shouldn't he be?" Giordano asked, pouring himself the last of the first bottle.

"I just thought he wasn't needed anymore. Beau is trained, so why is he still here?"

"I'm taking care of all the horses now," Michel said, draining his glass.

There was a pause as Serge and Odélie ordered. Serge waved his hand and shook his head when the Madame insisted that the whisky not be drunk on an empty stomach. Serge patted his well-built midriff, and the Madame smiled.

Odélie sniffed at the glass of white wine handed to her, a crease on her brow, then sipped at it. Serge glugged his whisky back in one go, eyeing Michel as he did so.

"You like it here, don't you, Michel?" Odélie asked, leaning across to their table. She lit a cigarette, the paper almost too white between her red nails.

"I do, yes, Mademoiselle."

Odélie laughed. "So formal, Michel! Did you hear that, Serge—Mademoiselle!"

Serge laughed loudly and Michel felt his face flame.

"So serious, so formal…" Odélie's laugh trailed away, and she turned from Michel and his friends to speak in hushed tones with Serge.

"I don't trust them," Giordano said, his voice slurred and a little too loud.

"Hush," Jean said, and passed him some bread.

"I don't!" he whispered. "Never have. They came here together, you know. Had a story. Werner believed them. I did not. Not. A. Word. Lies." His voice rose again.

"Hush!" Jean repeated. Serge looked over, then grinned.

"When will the next show be?" Michel asked.

"Tonight!" Giordano raised his glass in the air and they laughed. "I will open the show. The Great Giordano with his hair and his brain and his handsome face! They shall come from miles around to see me! We must tell everyone. Madame! Madame!" He waved to her. "I am the most handsome man you will ever meet. And, because you are so lovely and your food so great, you will be my guest at our next show!" He kissed her hand and her husband, who until that moment had busied himself reading a paper behind the bar, now raised his head, and leaned over the bar to listen to what was happening.

"Monsieur, of course you are," the Madame politely said, taking her hand away.

"Indeed. One more bottle. And some beer! Yes, beer. Michel? Jean? Beer? Yes, three of them and wine too."

The Madame nodded. "Perhaps some more bread? A little cheese?" She looked to Giordano, then Jean.

"Yes. Yes. Bread is good. My friend will appreciate that," Jean replied.

Michel started to relax again and soon forgot Serge and Odélie, listening instead to Giordano talk of hair, of women, and how he was sad that he had no girlfriend right now—why, he was used to two or three at a time!

"Maybe the next show will bring you some lovely admirers," Michel said.

"Indeed. Indeed. Yes, Michel. The next show. You are correct."

"Michel knows all about admirers, don't you?" Odélie had turned her attention once more to him.

"I'm not sure what you mean."

"No?" Odélie shrugged.

"It is a hot summer, is it not?" Serge asked the trio.

"*In-deed*," Giordano slurred.

"Quite. It will cool soon. Not to worry." Jean raised a glass to Serge, then the pair knocked their drinks back in unison.

"Hard to keep cool though."

"Indeed," Giordano said again.

"Michel, know any ways of keeping cool?"

Michel shook his head and Odélie smiled, then drained her glass.

"Shame there is no river here," Serge said.

"No river, but we do have a lake or two—not large ones, mind you." The Madame had appeared with a tray of drinks and more food. "A mile west. A greater lake which feeds into a smaller one. I took the children there to learn to swim when they were young. It'll be low by now, but you can get some respite."

"Aha! There you go, Michel, a lake. Michel is one for swimming," Serge said, then stood, took some coins from his pocket and flicked them onto the table, letting them clatter and roll.

"He does like swimming. Not always alone…" Odélie added and stood.

"Well, I take the horses. When they are hot."

"The horses? Just the horses?" Serge asked, and held his arm out for Odélie to take. "I'll check with Werner. Maybe he won't like you swimming with the horses."

As they walked away, Jean asked what it had all meant and Giordano began to sing a lover's song to the Madame, whose husband had decided there was no menace to be had with his guests and had once more retreated behind his newspaper.

"I don't know—who knows what anything means," Michel said, and looked at his shoes, where one of Serge's coins had come to rest after falling from the table. He did not pick it up. Instead he placed his foot over it, drank half of the warm beer, and allowed his mind to wander.

On the route home, Jean and Giordano began to sing a song Michel did not know the words to. As they walked and sang, Michel felt a warmth, not only from the summer evening air and the alcohol, but the warmth of friendship when Jean placed his arm around his shoulder and drew him near as they blasted out the chorus to their tune.

"You are scaring the wildlife!" Michel laughed as an owl overhead gave an irritable twit-twoo.

"Twit!" Jean cried.

"Twoooo!" Giordano finished.

The three of them began to laugh and sing again, almost forgetting their way home, and turned and retraced their steps three or four times before they decided upon the correct track across the field, towards their tents and their beds.

Michel awoke the following morning, his head full of cotton wool. He sat for some time on the edge of his bed, waiting until his eyes adjusted to the light and he remembered where he was.

He tested his legs and, although they felt heavy, he was able to move them. He stumbled outside, shielding his eyes from the glare of the morning light.

Things were already happening. People moved in and out of the field; the cart horses pulled in a large gypsy caravan, followed by three smaller versions. Newer carts were drawn in with the rest of the supplies from the train, and amongst it all stood Werner, smoking a pipe, directing people left and right.

Jean walked up to Michel, waving lazily, his gait much slower than normal. "It's gone," he said, then sat on the dirt, his head in his hands.

"What is?" Michel sat next to him.

"The train. Werner sold it last night. Used the money to some caravans. We have to go on foot."

"He works quickly."

"You don't say. He, Felix and a few others sorted it. Felix says he hasn't slept and doesn't expect to ever again."

"At least we can all stay together." Michel patted Jean on the arm.

"Oh, no! I am not upset by that." Jean raised his head. "My head! The light! The wine and the beer! I can't cope."

"Where is Giordano?"

"Making coffee with Vassily. Apparently, the magician has a cure. I told Giordano not to find us unless it works—he must try it on himself first."

"I heard Anton's radio this morning, I think—but then it could have been a dream."

"No, you heard it. He told everyone this morning that the government are seeking an armistice with the Germans and the Italians."

"What does that mean?"

"That we will surrender. It is just a matter of time."

"And then what?"

"And then they will come. In droves. They'll seek us out more quickly than we can imagine."

"What does Werner say?" Michel asked.

"Ah, now you trust him."

"Not quite. But he seems like he may know what to do."

"My head hurts, Michel. I cannot answer this now. We keep moving, never stopping, that's all I know."

Michel lit a cigarette whilst they waited for Giordano's miracle coffee. He looked for Serge, for Odélie, but they were nowhere to be seen. Then he looked for Werner and wondered what they had told him about his day in the river with Frieda. Whilst he waited and his eyes scanned the crowd of workers, the person he longed most to see walked across the grass towards Werner, as he revealed himself from a large gypsy caravan painted with red flowers, edged with gold trim and mounted on lacquered black wheels. He greeted her fondly, kissing her cheeks and escorting her inside. Michel shielded his eyes and squinted, trying to see her more closely as she walked up the few steps, then just as she turned to look in his direction, his view was obscured by the shadow of Giordano, who stood before him, a cup in each hand, grinning as if today were the perfect day.

"It works!"

The day was spent moving into the caravans: one for Jean and Giordano, one for Frieda and Werner, another for Madame Geneviève and Madame Rosie to share—the fortune teller had threatened to leave if she did not have one—and one more to be shared by Odélie and the triplets. The rest would camp—even Serge.

Michel helped fix tents, erect posts, and carry boxes of food to a small cooking tent manned by a tired Felix; always keeping an eye out for Frieda, but only seeing Odélie, who ignored him and flirted with Serge.

Before dark the following day, Michel was summoned to see Madame Rosie.

He pulled the purple curtain of her tent aside, revealing the fortune teller lit from above by soft light. She sat at a small round table, a glass ball in front of her.

"Madame?"

"Ah Michel, finally you have come to me," Madame Rosie said. Her accent was strange, but beautiful. Her w's and v's were switched around, her voice throaty and rich. Michel found it slightly hypnotic.

He sat down across from her, unsure of what to expect.

"I've been waiting for you to visit."

"Jean said you needed me for something?"

"Give me your hand," she said.

"He said you needed help with the tent?"

"Give me your hand," she repeated, her green eyes, almost yellow in this light, boring into his.

Michel placed his hand into hers; they were soft like a baby's.

"You will live a long life, Michel."

"I am sure you say that to everyone."

The Madame smiled at him, revealing a gold-capped incisor. "Perhaps. For those who pay."

"I have little money."

"I have not asked you to pay."

"I don't have anything I want to know."

"I think you do—that's why I asked Jean to send you to me."

"I'm just here to work, Madame." Michel stood and pulled his hand away.

"But what of the woman you wish to cherish?"

Michel stopped. "Cherish?"

"That is what you feel, is it not?"

Michel sat down heavily in the chair. "How do you know?"

"I know many things, Michel. Some of it I see, plain as day, when no one is looking."

"You saw us?"

"I have seen the way you look at her."

"I just think she is pretty," he said stupidly.

"Just pretty? No. Michel. There is more. What do you want to know?"

Michel gave her his hand again; she grabbed it strongly between her fingers.

"Is Bertrand, my friend, all right? Is he well?"

"Your friend is well." She studied his palm. "But that is not the question you wish to ask."

"Will the war end?"

"Yes."

"Will I be safe?"

"Yes. But again, Michel, you are not asking the right question."

He took a deep breath in. "Will I be alone in my life?"

"Sometimes, yes. But you will think it is the end when it is not. Remember this. Do not be disheartened."

"Can I ask you something else?"

"Yes. Anything."

"And you will tell me the truth?"

"If I can see it, then I shall tell you the truth."

"Will Frieda leave Werner? Will her heart be mine?"

Madame Rosie dropped Michel's hand. She leaned back in her chair for a moment, then from a pocket in her scarlet dress she took out a stick of incense. She lit it, and from it a strange scent and smoke filled the tent.

"She loves many," her voice said through the cloud.

As the smoke dissipated, Michel saw Madame Rosie through the gloom, her eyes too bright, her gold tooth shining. He felt his head swim and dip.

"Frieda is a mystery to me. She does not want to reveal her truth."

"But you said you could see the future?" Michel's tongue felt fat, his speech slurred.

"There are mysteries everywhere, all around us. But we are lucky and have signs to follow—a painting, a photograph, a letter; mysteries, yes, but at the same time we will have our answer if we truly want it and look for it."

"I don't understand," Michel said.

"It is because you are not sure you want these answers. You need to look at what is everywhere—what is right in front of you."

"I do not understand," Michel said once more.

"You will. You will. You must look, Michel."

From outside came laughter, then Kacper's accordion struck up a tune.

"They are celebrating our new home. Hugo will have made génépy. Come, Michel. Let us join them."

Michel followed the Madame, his head still clouded. Once outside he took a deep breath of clean summer air and allowed Madame Rosie to lead him towards the others, who had set up tables and chairs, some food and drink. At the head of the troupe sat Werner, his smile radiant, his foot tapping in time with the music, his eyes on Michel.

It was after midnight when Michel fell into his small bed, his eyes closing immediately, his feet still encased in their heavy boots. He felt as though he was slipping into some deep sleep of the dead when he heard something. His eyes opened only a fraction—the lids heavy—and in front of him was a cloaked shadow. The figure moved towards him, and Michel could not sit up. The shadow then bent down and kissed Michel lightly on the cheek, stroking his hair and whispering sweet dreams to him.

"Frieda?" he asked. But already the figure was gone, and he was alone in the night.

His eyes closed, cementing themselves shut, and his brain danced about, dreaming of Frieda tumbling through the air, swimming in deep waters, and then appearing to him, cloaked in black, her voice soft, her kiss on his cheek.

PART TWO: AUTUMN

On russet floors, by waters idle,
The pine lets fall its cone;
The cuckoo shouts all day at nothing
In leafy dells alone;
And traveller's joy beguiles in autumn
Hearts that have lost their own.

"Tell Me Not Here, It Needs Not Saying," A. E. Housman

CHAPTER EIGHT

L'Amour

The light had changed. No longer did it rage down upon them from dawn until dusk; now, its subtle early September glow, which filtered through drooping leaves and dappled the ground with specks of warmth, signaled that autumn had arrived.

A fresh wind blew through the tent one morning, bringing the smell of crackly leaves, bonfires and crisp air. Michel climbed out of bed and sat on his chair outside, enjoying the cooler air. The change calmed him and allowed him to sit back and relax, enjoying the slower pace and the laziness that the season inspired.

Anton walked past, a beard now thick on his face, his eyes rimmed red, his radio tucked under his arm. Michel shook his head—he was tired of that radio. All summer it had been a constant noise of news and static, informing and yet irritating the troupe from sunrise till sundown. Bombing raids on England, retaliation with a bombing of Berlin, food shortages, death, war at sea; the news did not cease with the barrage. When Anton could not get a signal, he wandered frustrated around the camp, the radio always with him, humming with white noise until a voice could be heard.

The summer had dragged on. Each week they moved, pitched up on the outskirts of a new town, and as the summer reached its peak in August, the troupe settled for three long weeks in a field beside a farmhouse—a friend of Werner's. Michel counted the months—now three—since he had been with them; he had not spoken to Frieda since the day on the riverbank when she fled.

He looked for her now, and within minutes she was in his eyeline, talking to Madame Rosie with a crimson costume in her hands. Rosie took it from her, and the two women hugged. She did not look in his direction.

He pulled out the paper Jean had given him months before, and once again wrote to Bertrand.

Dearest Bertrand,

I wrote you a letter in the summer telling you I was fine, telling you about my new job. I imagine you still, sitting at your desk and carefully asking me questions, telling me about your day, about Odette, about Paris.

I yearn for home still. No matter how much an adventure, no matter how much my heart must be here for now, it still beats for Paris, for home. You said once that home is where your family are, and my family is you.

We have traveled far since I last wrote, first further south and now towards the west. I imagine we will near the coast soon. I would like to see the sea—I do not like it when we are landlocked. Water makes me feel a little at home and whenever I see it, I imagine I am standing on the Pont Neuf, watching the Seine wind its way through the city.

Thankfully, just this morning autumn has arrived on a cool breeze that flaps against the canvas tents. I have not left, just as your voice told me not to do. With the advancement of the war, I truly have nowhere to go.

I still have not received pay—I know you will say he is a gypsy, but we all are now. Traveling in caravans, pitching up and playing tricks in town squares to earn enough to eat.

Tonight, we have a show prepared. Our first since July. It will be a small affair, yet it heartens me to see the red-and-white striped tent once more reaching for the sky.

It has been hard these past months, I cannot lie. More and more people have left so that we are stripped back to the bare bones.

We reached a town in the east and foolishly set up camp, not realizing that it was full of German soldiers on leave. Felix went into town that night with two others. He did not return.

The boss told us Felix was arrested for fighting, but his face was pale and his hands trembled. Then he barked orders for us to leave. He never once mentioned Felix's name and has not since.

I miss Felix, Bertrand. His gruffness had become a sort of kindness. That sounds strange, I know. But I understood him, I think. I knew that he meant well, he meant for me to be safe.

I told you in my last letter about a woman I cherish. I want to tell you now that I believe I may love her. Even though I have not spoken to her in months (!) it does not seem to matter—it is as though every day is a good day as long as I see her. On those days I do not, I am like a teenager again—sullen and unresponsive. I wonder sometimes if I am going mad—one day so happy, and the next I can wish for never-ending sleep.

Sometimes she watches me when I train Beau, just far enough away that my voice does not carry, but she will wave at me and I will wave back and I imagine that she is smiling at me.

Other days I ride Claudette the horse past her caravan and I see the curtain twitch and wait for a quick glimpse of her face, her smile.

There are times when we walk past each other, and once or twice I imagined that our arms had touched. I think they did—I hope they did.

These moments are what I seem to live for. I know her routine—how she visits the horses at dinner-time—and I have delayed myself so many times and missed a meal just so that I could nod hello, then watch her as she speaks to the horses, patting and fussing over them.

The boss still does not talk to me unless it is something to do with the horses. I have friends though: Jean and Giordano, Madame Rosie and Geneviève, Hugo and Vassily. These friends are dear to me now; they are almost like family. We share what little we have and cheer each other on the days when things do not go so well.

I told you of another woman in my last letter, Odélie. A woman who liked me. I think I failed her in a terrible way. She liked me more than I liked her, I see that now. And my rejection, or rather my ignorance, has caused some tension. She has an ally, her friend Serge, and between the two of them they enjoy teasing me, hiding things, talking about me to the others. Yet they do not realize that my childhood was full of these things—my stutter set me apart, alone, and I endured. So, I will endure this.

As sparse as the circus has become, people still flock to us, eager to see some color, some fun, just something different. Kacper plays his accordion, and Gino the monkey dances and brightens children's faces; Frieda tumbles and turns, bedecked in sequins, and high up she looks just like a star about to fall to earth; Serge swallows swords, bare-chested and muscles bulging; Hugo the clown delights everyone by balancing on a child's tricycle and throwing cheap bonbons to the crowd; and Jean and Giordano do their new act, where they sing and dance and act like fools. The finale is always the ringmaster himself, fending off Aramis our elderly lion. Then he rides Beau, who dances, whilst Odélie and the triplets twist, turn and flip, all the while with Frieda still overhead grasping the trapeze, spinning in the air— then with the crash of cymbals she lets go and allows Anton to catch her. It carries on, night after night, like a recurring dream, and one which always ends the same way—with Frieda spirited away from me, leaving me with only the scent of her lemony perfume lingering in the air, and the memory of her.

If I were sitting across from you now, you would tell me I had become a romantic, which has made me foolish. You are right, of course you are. I am a fool.

I must go now, my friend. I hope this letter finds you well. I hope you write me back. Tell Odette I said hello. Tell Paris I will see her again.

Michel

Michel folded the letter and wrote the address on the envelope. He sealed it with a stamp given to him by Madame Rosie and placed it into his bag to be posted.

The crimson feathers stroked Michel's palm as he dragged them across it, ready to put into Claudette's new headdress. He felt the softness of each feather, and the hardness of the quill, almost bone-like, that held them all together. That night they were performing in a small town outside Médis. There were no food stalls this evening, simply the Big Top and a few scattered tents holding Madame Rosie, Serge and Madame Geneviève—a sorry rag-tag bunch of players, who all clung together because they had no other option.

Michel left his tent and meandered about, admiring how, despite the lack of money, the company had managed to transform this small town's field into an evening of magic and mystery. Lights were strung in trees and along posts, though every few bulbs were dark and needed replacing.

The Big Top still stood proud, red-and-white striped, a small flag on top with a picture of a horse and rider; Werner sitting atop Beau. There were no tiered seats anymore, just a roped-off section so the few who managed to visit could stand and watch.

Michel turned towards Rosie's tent, from which the comforting scent of lavender wafted towards him on the cool air. He was busy admiring her newly painted sign—her name peeking out from amongst twists and turns of green ivy and small rosebuds—when he walked into something. Something warm and large.

"Serge." Michel took a step backwards.

"Where are you going?"

"I thought I'd talk to Odélie about tonight," he lied.

"She's busy."

"I'm sure she is. I just wanted to check on Claudette's headdress, that it was right, but if you don't think that Werner wants it to be perfect..." Michel shrugged.

Serge stood aside and as Michel walked past, their shoulders brushed against each other. Michel turned to look at Serge, but Serge did not turn around.

Michel bypassed Odélie and the triplets' caravan and made his way instead to Jean and Giordano's. From outside, he could hear Giordano practicing his newest song, and when he opened the door he saw Jean-Jacques copying Giordano's movements as if they were a mirrored reflection of each other—yet one tall and one small. He stood and listened to the tune; it began with a story about a boy, a boy who longed to have a friend, and the friend he found was in his long shadow that followed him everywhere. The boy and his shadow grew together and eventually became one; at which point in their routine, Jean would appear and carry Giordano on his shoulders, a giant cloak covering them both—a nine-foot-tall boy who was now at one with his shadow.

Michel waited until Giordano had reached the point of his narrative when his shadow would take him and make them one, then entered.

"No, no!" Giordano shouted. "You ruined it! Almost there, almost at the end! Michel, what were you thinking?"

"You performed it last week and the week before in the town squares; you're fine."

"It's still new, not perfect!" Giordano threw his hat on the ground then slumped into a chair, his chin on his chest as he pouted.

"Ignore him, Michel—sit, sit." Jean directed him to the other chair, then sat on the end of his bed.

"Your feet must hang off the edge when you sleep." Michel nodded towards the short single bed.

"They do. I don't think I've ever had a bed that my feet stay in all my life."

"Not even when you were young?"

"*My* feet have always stayed in my bed," Giordano interrupted, keen to be included in any conversation. "They know where to stay. Give me a drink. I'm nervous. I must calm my nerves now."

Jean stood and poured each of them a shot of Hugo's génépy, which was stronger than ever. Michel placed his own glass on the ground, still mostly full.

"Too bitter, he can't get the right ingredients anymore," Jean said and followed suit, placing his full glass on the floor.

"Tastes good to me." Giordano knocked back the rest of his génépy.

"You would say that. You said that the first time I met you!"

"In that bar?! In Montmartre? Yes. I probably did say that. I was in Paris three days before anyone spoke to me. 'The small Italian,' they called me behind my back. *Le petit étalon italien.*"

"They were calling you the small Italian stallion, my friend." Jean laughed, and Michel joined in.

"Who cares what they called me? They were jealous. Jealous of the Italian who robbed the French of their women! Pour me one more, Michel, to numb the nerves."

"I was glad I met you that day," Jean said, a look of melancholy on his face. "Who knew we were to be friends? The giant and the stallion?" He laughed again.

"You needed me," Giordano said, between sips. He turned to Michel. "He had lost his job in another circus."

"So had you!" Jean shot back.

"I did not lose my job. I simply decided it was not for me."

"Let's just say, we found each other, and we needed each other." Jean poured some more génépy into his own glass.

"How did you come to be here?" Michel asked.

Jean shrugged.

"It was those people," Giordano blurted, "those ones, you know? The ones who said we were not right?"

Jean placed his glass on the ground and looked at Giordano.

"You remember, Jean-Jacques? We were in that small apartment near the graveyard, and we would juggle and sing, and play hide the queen under the cups. The police, they told us to move; the people, our neighbors, they told us we were wrong and then that day, that day in the cemetery when we took our lunch against the falling grave, Werner appeared."

"Hush now, you're drunk." Jean made to laugh but it rang false.

"Tonight will be a good performance, I'm sure of it. Beau has mastered some more tricks," Michel said, seeing Jean's discomfort and trying to change the subject.

But Giordano continued: "He was there. We were sitting, our backs against that grave. You remember? Pour me more, Jean. One more for the nerves. Pour me one more, I said! I'm small but not weak! Thank you, Jean, thank you. Where was I? Yes, the grave. We had our backs to it, and we ate bread and cheese. Then Werner came and said, 'I hear you play tricks?'

"We told him we did, and he asked us if we wanted a job. See, Jean? See? I told the story as it was. No more, no less. We got a job; it got us away from that moldy apartment, got us back in the circus."

Before Michel could ask more, voices outside, deep and authoritative, shouted in muddled French with thick clipped accents. Madame Geneviève screamed out that her jewels were being taken.

Michel ran from the tent to be greeted by the sight of armed, uniformed soldiers, black swastikas on their sleeves like menacing spider legs, their shining boots too clean and too bright in the autumnal dusk.

The soldiers threw belongings from Madame Geneviève's caravan, then moved on swiftly; they pulled Anton out of his tent and kept searching.

Dissatisfied, one soldier kicked Anton in the stomach, then laughed as he howled and curled up on the ground.

Michel made to move towards the man, but felt Jean place a hand on his arm. "Don't move," Jean whispered.

One by one, the performers were dragged from their caravans and tents, and made to stand outside as their belongings were thrown to the ground. Michel saw shadows in his own tent; then his beloved book was tossed onto the grass, the pages open and fluttering in the wind.

A man in a long gray overcoat smoked a cigarette nearby, his thin mustache twitching as he smiled at his soldiers' handiwork.

"What is the meaning of this?" Werner appeared, his top hat askew, his bow-tie half fastened.

"Papers, Monsieur," the man with the twitching mustache replied. "Papers. Do you have a permit for this..." The man gesticulated to the few tents, a stall or two. "This thing?"

"It's a circus," Werner replied, drawing himself up to his full height, and righting his top hat to give him those few extra inches.

"Quite. Well. Perhaps it once was..."

"I have a permit. I obtained it today from the mayor. He said one night only."

The mustached man took the papers from Werner and scrutinized them.

"The mayor? Unfortunately, he is no longer mayor now. I am. I am mayor, policeman, judge and jury. Have you asked my permission?"

Werner shook his head with confusion.

Before the mustached man could speak again, Frieda appeared from behind Werner with a smile on her face that Michel had never seen before. He held his breath.

"Herr Captain," Frieda said. "Welcome. I'm sorry—I do not know your name?" She stepped forward and curtsied.

The German's wide eyes followed her every move.

"Madame," he said, and took her hand in his, gently kissing the soft skin just above her wrist. Michel felt a ball of anger rise in the pit of his stomach; he clenched his fists and saw that both Werner and Serge had done the same.

"You must join us this evening, as our honored guests."

"I am no captain," the mustached man said, his voice softer now, a slight pink glow on his cheeks. "I am merely an *oberleutnant*. And my name... Yes. You can call me Herr Köhler."

"And you may call me Frieda."

He nodded and did not let go. She gently stepped back so that her hand finally fell away from his grasp.

Herr Köhler waited until his soldiers had finished their task, but they found only a bottle of Hugo's génépy as a prize. "This is illegal, you know," he said, and smiled.

"It is medicinal," Frieda said, her voice purring. "Just to help with the nerves when I perform. It is scary to perform in front of so many—especially when they are handsome."

Herr Köhler's eyes strayed from Frieda's face as he examined her from head to foot. "You have one evening," he finally said.

"Thank you."

"You will bring everyone's papers to me tomorrow morning before you leave. It will give me the chance to note down our visitors—names, origin. I'm sure you understand." He clipped his heels together, alerting the other soldiers that the search, for whatever it was, was over.

Michel looked over at Frieda, whose smile had disappeared. Werner took her by the elbow and steered her towards their caravan. Serge escorted Oberleutnant Köhler and his soldiers towards the stall selling Hugo's génépy.

"You OK?" Michel felt Jean's large hand on his shoulder.

"I am. You?"

Jean's face was pale, Giordano's even more so. "What were they looking for?"

Jean's Adam's apple bobbed in his throat as he swallowed, his voice dry. "Nothing. They just like to cause trouble." He turned to look at Giordano.

"Jean, tell me," Michel whispered urgently. "What's happening? What were they looking for?"

"Nothing," Jean repeated, looking Michel dead in the eye. "They're just seeing if they can stir things up. That's what it's like now—ask Anton, he hears it all."

Jean and Giordano returned to their tent and Michel left them. "Madame," he said to Geneviève, "let me help."

He bent down to pick up her clothes, the shoes, a book, which had been thrown out into the night. She did not speak, but now and again gave a muffled sob as she dusted off her belongings.

"Thank you, Michel," she said finally, carrying the last of her things inside. "I would invite you in, but as you can see, I am in a bit of a mess at the moment." She gave him a watery smile.

"Madame, no matter." He took her hand, kissed it, and gave a little bow. "If you need anything?"

"*Merci*, you are a true gentleman."

Michel made his way back to the horses, aware of the clump of soldiers who still stood nearby, laughing with Serge.

"You are quite the charmer still." Odélie appeared at his side.

"Madame Geneviève? She was upset." Michel frowned.

"No, no! I'm sorry. I did not mean it like that. It was a joke, nothing more." She touched his arm. "It is emotional, all of this, for all of us."

"It is." He scratched at the stubble on his cheek; when had he shaved last?

"You look tired, Michel."

"I am."

"Then go and rest for a while."

He smiled at her, and she smiled back.

"Will you help me if I need anything?" She tilted her head to the side; her eyes narrowed a little and the smile seemed less sincere.

"Of course," Michel said. "Just as I would do for Serge, or Jean-Jacques, or anyone here."

Odélie's smile dropped. "I need Claudette with blue feathers, not crimson."

"You said crimson before."

"I've changed my mind," Odélie snapped. "A woman is entitled to change it whenever and however much she likes! Blue."

Michel watched as she stalked away. He sighed.

He was exhausted but did not rest as such. Instead, he sat outside his tent watching and waiting to see if Frieda would reappear.

The crackle from Anton's radio made him look to the left. Anton was in his tent; no light, just the radio. Michel listened hard and heard voices—German, not French—and then Anton's voice as if he were having a conversation.

Moments later, Werner hurried past, striding towards Anton's tent. As he entered, the voices disappeared and Michel caught Werner's voice—low and threatening, but the words were mumbled.

Michel waited until he saw Werner leave, followed by Anton, his eyes downcast, his limbs slow and heavy.

He hesitated until they were gone, then quickly ran to Anton's tent. Inside was not just one radio but three, plus wires, headphones and a microphone.

He closed the tent flap and walked back to his own. The wind blew, but this time it was cold and made him shiver; Bertrand would have called it the wind of change, and Michel believed it.

That evening, Michel was at the rear of the Big Top, watching the show from his seat on an upturned bucket. The dancers danced, the clown clowned, the acrobats contorted and flipped and spun. Frieda flew in the heavens above them and Werner rallied the crowd, as the pared-back band comprising Kacper and his accordion, accompanied by a workhand on the trumpet and Serge thumping a drum, tried to fill the tent with mellifluous notes. The audience clapped with delight under the twinkling lights, only seeing what they were meant to—the performers, the colors, the act.

Michel knew different, though. The troupe's faces, although made up as usual, were more mask-like than ever. Hugo was paler, his eyes larger and sadder; Werner's smile was frozen in place; the triplets and Odélie were almost ghost-like in their pallid blues and whites, as though hoping to simply disappear in front of their audience.

Sitting front and center were Herr Köhler and his men. Hugo's génépy had worked a treat, and they laughed and slapped their thighs as Hugo honked horns and pretended to fall over his own foot. By the end they were half asleep, and Herr Köhler had to be carried back to the village.

Michel waited until the very end, when Frieda tumbled into the safe hands of the net, her long stockinged legs strong and supple, her curves enhanced by the sequined bodysuit.

He imagined that instead of the net it was his arms that held her, pulled her to him so she was safe. Then, he imagined her standing in a parlor filled with light and birdsong from the trees outside. In his daydream, he took her in his arms, and they moved together as if they were one and the same.

He snapped back to reality. If, just if, she ever spoke to him again, what could he do? Woo her? With what—the few francs he had kept from Lucien or won at *mouche*? And what of Werner? He would not let her go without a fight—one which Michel knew he would lose. He felt his hope slipping away. She was not his she never would be.

He stood and took Beau's reins, then Claudette's. He waited, counted to ten, then twenty. Finally, she walked past him, the scent of her sweat and lemon perfume sweet yet fresh at the same time. She turned to look at him and smiled: not a smile she gave to Herr Köhler, nor a smile she gave to Serge or Odélie, but a shy smile Michel knew well—one that Estelle in Paris had given him, one which told him he was right to stay, to wait. *Patience, Michel.* That's what Estelle had said. *Patience.*

As the troupe quieted, lights were switched off and torches doused, Michel sat out with the horses, stoking a fire in a steel drum, and wrapping them in his own blankets. They soon settled onto the bed of straw, each using the other for warmth. Michel watched them sleep, their breath steaming in the cold air. He would speak with Werner tomorrow. This could not go on. They needed stables; the weather would soon be worse.

Beau would not settle completely, and whinnied and kicked for no reason. Michel sat close to him, stroked his nose, and began to tell him a story.

"When I read to you before, it was always the story of Tintin and his adventures. Well, this story, now, is not from the book. It is my story. Once upon a time, I was born in Paris to my mother, Marie. My father had died in the war, so she was alone, with me, in Paris and no money."

Beau quieted, but there was a noise, a rustle behind them—something was there that should not be.

Michel stood.

"Keep going," a voice said.

"Who is it?" he asked, even though he knew the answer; he just wanted her to speak again.

"Frieda." She moved close to the fire, the orange glow lighting up her face under the cloak she wore.

"You should be inside; it's cold."

"So should you. Leave them, just for a moment. Come and warm yourself inside. I have some wine that can warm you too." That smile again. The one that was just for him.

"What about Werner?"

"He's gone into town to celebrate with Serge. He won't be back for some time. Trust me."

Michel hesitated, unsure of himself, aware that words had failed him once more.

"Come. Please." She held out her hand.

Michel took it and allowed her to lead him towards her and Werner's home, feeling as though this were all simply a dream.

Inside the caravan the ceiling was painted with pink-cheeked cherubs that floated on clouds against the purest of blue skies; bunches of rich purple grapes decorated each corner, so realistic that Michel felt the urge to raise his hand and pluck a plump fruit from the vine.

A bed covered in a rich red-and-gold blanket dominated the space. Beside it were a chair, some clothes, a small warming stove and a brass stand holding some potted herbs, a few cups and a jug of wine the color of the painted grapes. A door led to another room, but it was closed.

"Here, sit," she commanded, pointing to the chair near the stove.

Michel sat.

"Take this." She handed him a glass filled with the thick, red wine. "Drink."

He drank.

"It will warm you; keep drinking."

The wine was not like anything Michel had tasted before. A spice had been added—perhaps cinnamon; no, cardamom— something that made him relax back into the seat.

"I like the way you talk to the horses. You calm them. Even if it means you catch your death of cold. Tell me, why do you read to them so? It's odd. Who are you, Michel?"

"I'm not sure I'm anyone."

She smiled and her eyes narrowed. She sat across from him on a footstool covered in a dark green velvet threaded with gold—as if sunlight were trying to escape through a canopy of leaves.

She poured herself some of the spiced wine, the slop as it hit the glass like heavy rain on a windowpane. She sipped at it, then, licking her lips, she said, "Tell me your secrets. Tell me who you are. And then I will tell you who I am."

"I have no secrets," he answered. He placed the glass onto the brass table and felt his head swim.

"As you wish." She placed her hand on his knee. "Sit back. It is the warmth; it is making you sleepy."

Michel did as he was told and enjoyed the feeling of heat that came from her hand.

"If you will not tell me your secrets, tell me a story instead. I hear no stories; I know so little of who you are."

"What story would you like?" Michel looked into her emerald eyes and held her gaze.

"Tell me the story of the man who can talk to horses."

"And what will I get in return?"

"A story of a girl who is always hiding, but what she wants more than anything is to ride away on a jet-black stallion to a home of her own."

"You?"

Frieda took her hand from his lap. "First, your story."

Michel sat up slightly, and Frieda poured more wine into his glass. "There is not much to tell."

"You were born in Paris, your father had died. Continue…"

"My mother and I lived in an apartment in the 14th arrondissement. She liked to paint and filled it with color. We had little, but she made everything bigger, more wonderful. Monsieur Bertrand and his wife Amélie were our neighbors. They would watch me when Maman had to work. Monsieur Bertrand taught me to read. He bought me the book you hear me read to the horses. I was not good at school; I had a stutter, and I could not find the words when the teacher asked me questions. They made fun of me, until I grew a head taller than them. Then they stopped. Monsieur Bertrand taught me to read aloud, to master my stutter. Then he found me a job when Maman died and I had no money. I was a stable-boy and I read to the horses, to calm myself, and then to calm them. I learned to train them, to ride them. And now I am here."

Whilst he had spoken, she had closed her eyes and Michel wondered if she had fallen asleep.

"You think it is a small story, don't you?" She opened her eyes.

"It is what it is."

"I like it."

"You do?"

"I like it, but you could make it more like it was, Michel. It could be full of color, laughter, what your mother said to you, what she smelled like, what Paris was like in the rain!" Her voice was higher now, her words rushing out. "The smell of baked bread from the boulangerie, or how the sun rose above the city's rooftops, or how the gardens looked in the summer, or how the people sat at cafés and sipped coffee and ate cake!"

"I could. But I am not really a storyteller. I am a horse trainer."

"Do you miss Paris?"

"I do."

"But you will not return?"

Michel shook his head. "I want to. But with the war, I am not sure what is there for me anymore."

"But there are things for you here?"

He nodded then drank the rest of his wine.

"Michel, there are those who long for home, who cannot find themselves comfortable anywhere but with that which they already know. But there are those who welcome a change of sound, of sight and of smell. They long for the unknown just as others long for the known."

"And you are one who welcomes change?" Michel said.

"No. I am the one who longs for home."

Suddenly a knock on the door made Frieda jump up from her seat. Her smile was gone, her face suddenly pale. Before she could answer the door, it was flung open by a red-faced Werner.

"You! Out! Now!" he yelled at Michel, who stood obediently and climbed down the steps.

Frieda rushed to the door.

"Close it. Stay inside." Werner's voice was low; Frieda's bottom lip trembled. He turned to Michel and gazed down at him from the wagon.

One by one, Werner clomped down the steps after him, the sound echoing in the still air.

"We just talked, nothing more."

"With her! You talked with her, where we sleep! Who do you think you are, *Michel Bonnet*? Eh? You already charmed Odélie— yes, I know of this. If you think I don't know what is going on then you are stupider than I thought."

"We just talked."

"You *just talked*." Werner mimicked his voice and Michel felt his jaw clench. The ringmaster shoved him a little, so that he was forced to step backwards.

"There's no law against talking, is there?"

"My law says there's no fraternizing between worker and performer."

"I am friends with Jean. Giordano and the others. Why not Frieda?" Michel said, emboldened by the alcohol.

"Not this performer." Werner stepped down and pushed Michel again. "You think you know it all, don't you, Michel? Making friends. Being part of this. I let you, you know. By my grace I ignored it. But you have stepped too close. Too close. And you stand here and tell me you were *just talking*?"

"We were." Frieda opened the door, the light behind her illuminating them all. "We just talked. That's all. About the horses, about what Beau could be trained to do next." She nodded slightly at Michel.

"She's right. I was saying that maybe I could teach Beau to dance like the Spanish horses. She thought it would be a nice surprise for you."

"Come. Come inside now." Frieda moved between the two men, placing her hands on Werner's shoulders. "Please. I asked him to come and talk to me about Beau. That's all."

Werner's eyes bulged in the darkness. He opened his mouth to speak, but nothing came out. He raised his arms, but then dropped them heavily to his sides as if all the fight had been knocked out of him already.

"We leave at dawn—make sure the horses are ready."

Michel stood in the pitch darkness, watching his breath curl in the icy air. He watched Werner walk up the steps to Frieda, and only then did he return to the horses.

The next morning, the troupe left before the cockerel crowed and took a rough track away from the town—away from Herr Köhler and his office, where he would be sitting waiting for their papers, waiting to know who they really were.

They moved the horses on quickly, stirring up dust in the wake of their caravans. Michel rode Beau, Claudette on a lead rope next to him. Bisou—too small to keep up—was in Jean and Giordano's caravan, annoying Giordano by knocking things over and leaving smelly deposits on the floor. No one spoke, no one asked where they were going next, and Michel was too tired, too unnerved by the evening before to think about it—all he knew was that Frieda was in danger with Werner and he had to save her from him.

They rested mid-afternoon outside a settlement of a few houses nestled into the rocky western coastline. Michel had not seen the sea in a long while and he stood on a cliff edge, taking in large lungfuls of fresh salty air whilst the horses rested and ate the lush grass.

"No show tonight." Werner appeared. "The Boche will be here soon enough. Tonight we rest, and move tomorrow. There is a field, a mile or so down the track, for us to camp on. Make your way there. Serge will lead you."

The troupe sluggishly climbed back aboard the wagons, following Serge and Odélie, who led the procession.

Michel waited for Claudette and Beau to finish grazing, reluctant to leave the view of the sea. When he turned back, he realized Werner had not returned to his caravan and sat on the grass, smoking a cigar.

"This is my last one," he said.

Michel nodded.

"You are angry at me for last night? The way I treated you?"

Michel did not answer and patted Claudette's neck.

"She explained that it was a surprise. A gift."

"Beau needs to be re-shod," Michel said.

Werner looked out into the ocean as if he could find words in the salty surf.

"Tell me, Michel, why do you stay? What have we got here now that entices you so?"

"It is a job."

"One I have never paid you for."

"I couldn't stay in Paris. I have nowhere else to go."

"Don't speak to her again," Werner said, but there was little threat in his voice, only fear.

Michel took the reins in his hands and walked the horses on to the camp. He looked back once at Werner, who still sat gazing out to sea, looking as lost as Michel felt.

The troupe had made camp quickly and returned to their caravans and tents, so Michel was alone in putting the horses away for the night.

Jean, perhaps, had erected his tent, and Michel sat inside, his stomach empty, his nerves frayed, and wrote his thoughts to the only person he really trusted.

Dearest Bertrand,

It is night. The owls are quiet, and the wind is blowing through the trees with the promise of a gale.

I am in my tent, alone as always. Yet I feel a little joy at the fact that I visited her yesterday. We talked. And it was enough for me—just to hear her voice again. I cherished her, every moment. It was enough.

I do not think I will be here much longer; my desire for her was seen by the wrong man—by the boss. She is not mine, and despite the fact that I know she cannot be, I hold out hope—fruitless foolish hope.

What should I do, Bertrand? Tell me.

I try to hear your voice, to hear your counsel, yet there is nothing tonight. The wind has picked up even more. Rain is not far away.

The horses are cold. I have used my own blankets to warm them, but they look at me with sad eyes—they are tired of moving, of running. I think I am too.

Bertrand, I wish you could tell me a story—those stories you told me when I was a child and, when I think of it, even as an adult, they made the world seem a magical place, full of adventure. The reality of this adventure is too much for me. The war is raging around us and it will not be long until it finds me and drags me to it. I wonder if I should have stayed in Paris—looking back, there seems little reason for me to have left. There is nowhere safe to run to.

I worry for you, Bertrand. I heard from Anton that bombs were dropped near Paris, that the city is infested with Germans, their language, their rules. Are you well? I hope that you are. I pray that you are.

I must go now, my friend. Let this letter find you in good spirits.

Your friend,
Michel

The wind that evening continued to grow, bringing with it a spattering of rain. Michel wrapped his coat around him to scare away the cold. One by one, the troupe blew out their candles until it became completely dark. He listened to the wind groan as it bent the tents easily to its will. He wondered whether it would grow strong enough to lift the tents clear off the ground, sending them sailing over the ocean like balloons a child had let go. He turned onto his side and pulled his coat up further, shivering and worried for the horses who must now be damp with only his blankets for cover.

At first, he thought the wind had destroyed a tent. The shouts from outside were frantic; then lights came, first torches, then other lights that shone into Michel's tent and almost blinded him.

"Where is he?" the voice behind the light said.

"Who?" Michel sat up, shielding his eyes.

"Darbonne."

"I don't know anyone by that name."

A shout made the man leave Michel, who ran quickly out of the tent to find Anton facedown on the ground, a soldier cuffing him as a black car waited, its flag of red with the black insignia flapping in the wind.

"What's happening?" Michel asked Jean, who stood watching from his caravan steps.

"They've come for Anton."

Michel saw Frieda watching, her hand covering her mouth, as if stopping herself from screaming out to her trapeze partner—the man who had caught her mid-flight and never once let her fall. Michel wanted to go to her, to wrap his arms around her, but he could not move. He was rooted to the spot as the wind blew and the rain pelted down, and Anton was heaved upwards.

For a moment, Michel met Anton's gaze—the man's eyes were wide, his mouth agape. It reminded Michel of when he had fallen as a child—that look of shock and panic.

"What has he done?" Michel croaked, his throat tight.

"I don't know," Jean said.

"Can't we—" Michel made to move towards Anton, but Jean pulled him back.

"Come inside; there's nothing to be done."

"But...what has he done?"

"I told you, I don't know," Jean said, and turned away from Michel, who followed him inside.

"Don't lie, Jean! What is going on?"

Jean sighed and rubbed his eyes. "They say...they say he was distributing anti-German leaflets in town. They say he is with the resistance—they are arresting him for being a spy."

Michel thought of the radio that never left his side, the wires in his tent and Werner threatening him.

"It's happened before," Michel said.

"Once, just before you joined. He was with some sort of resistance group—sending messages over the radio. He said it was the only way he could help."

"And Werner stopped him."

"He thought he had. But then, obviously Anton didn't."

Michel stood at the door and watched as Anton was pushed into the back of the car. A soldier approached Werner and Michel saw the ringmaster pass the soldier some money. It was a quiet, fleeting exchange. Then Werner went inside his caravan and did not look back as Anton was driven away, the car's rear lights red in the gloom of the night.

CHAPTER NINE

Ringmaster Werner

That morning, before the sun had a chance to rise, the troupe quickly packed up. Michel rode Beau over to Jean, who was steering his caravan, Louis straining against the reins.

"He's tired," Jean said, and rubbed at his own eyes with one hand.

"We all are."

"I saw something last night, just before they left with Anton. Werner gave some money to one of the soldiers."

Jean did not take his gaze away from the road ahead.

"I saw it with my own eyes," Michel told him.

"So, what are you trying to say?"

"That Werner tipped them off about Anton. He saw the wires and things in Anton's tent and got mad."

"Must have been a trick of the light. Werner would never have tipped them off about Anton."

"Why do you keep trusting him, Jean? Why? He doesn't pay any of us. He treats Frieda as though she is his property, and he clearly paid the Germans to take Anton away."

Jean did not answer. He flicked at the reins and stared ahead.

"Jean. Answer me, please. I thought we were friends?"

"We are, Michel. We are friends. But I don't know the answer. I don't know what happened."

"Then who does?"

"Werner. You want to ask him?"

"If I do, what will happen?"

"You already know the answer to that."

"So, I do nothing?"

"For now, at least."

They rode until midday and rested for a few hours, until Serge told them to continue on.

"The horses are tired, Serge," Michel told him. "They need to rest, to eat."

"So do I, so I suggest you shut up and we carry on until we can find somewhere decent for the night."

Michel swapped the horses around, so that Jacques and Abigail could rest from pulling Werner's large caravan and take on the smaller ones. Michel rode Claudette, who restlessly flicked her head, now and then stopping to stare at the ground.

He talked softly to her all throughout the afternoon, until they reached a hamlet of five or so houses clumped together in a small valley, the smoke from their chimneys hanging heavy in the damp air.

Werner took control and spoke to the occupant of the first house, who directed him to the largest property, one with stables and a barn. Werner returned within minutes, a smug smile on his face. "Lodgings have been procured. The horses need rest, stables, feed. And Michel sleeps in the barn."

"As if I wasn't aware they're tired," Michel muttered to Jean.

"At least you'll be warm and dry in the barn?"

"Serge, Vassily, Hugo—you're in the barn with Michel too," Werner shouted before he led them on.

That night, the troupe was quiet. For a few francs, the lady of the house had prepared soup and potatoes, yet they ate without gusto—each thinking of Anton, yet not one mentioning his name.

Michel retired early to the barn and soon, Hugo, Vassily and Serge joined him, carrying their bags and a gas lantern.

"Here, I still have a few bottles." Hugo pulled his famous liqueur from his bag. "We can toast Anton."

Michel looked to Serge, waiting for him to decline. Instead, he took the bottle from Hugo and drank deeply, wiping his mouth with his sleeve. He passed the bottle to Michel, who also drank, enjoying the warmth.

"If I could have, I would have spirited Anton away…but alas, I am only a master of parlor tricks," Vassily said, his thin fingers rolling a cigarette.

"So, you're not really magic then?" Hugo laughed, his face already growing red from the alcohol.

"Where's Kacper sleeping?" Michel suddenly realized he had not seen him all day.

"He's got a cold so he's sleeping in with Jean and Giordano. The monkey is driving Giordano crazy!" Hugo said.

"I wish I could have had my own caravan." Vassily lit his cigarette. "I would have liked that very much."

"Why didn't you get one?" Michel asked.

"Giordano had some money ferreted away. Gave it to Werner. It was only supposed to be the women and Werner who got a house on wheels. Giordano is a precious soul—cannot and will not camp lest he ruin his clothes!"

Serge laughed. "I do like his clothes though. He annoys me, but the clothes—I always wanted to have nice clothes like that."

Michel watched Serge as he spoke of clothes, shoes, a house with nice furniture. The alcohol had relaxed his features, so his jaw did not seem tense and the permanent crease between his eyebrows had disappeared.

"I think one day, I will have all those things," Serge finished, and drank back some more génépy.

"I had those things once." Hugo swayed a little. "But then I became poor—lost my job, my home, my wife…" He burped.

"But now you have us." Vassily patted his arm. "And all this!" He opened his arms as if he had just conjured the barn from thin air.

"Then I am a lucky man!"

"Come now. Bed, no more of this talk." Serge stood, and Michel saw that the crease between his eyes was back, his jaw set once more.

"Always the first to leave the party. Always the one to ruin the fun." Nonetheless, Hugo allowed Serge to help him up and lay him down on a blanket. He covered him like a baby then lay down, turning off the lamp so that Michel had to find a place to sleep in the gloom.

The troupe traveled inland for two more rain-filled days with no indication from Werner as to where they were heading.

"I saw a sign not long ago that said Paris was three hundred miles away," Jean told Michel, as he rode next to the caravan.

"You don't think we are heading to Paris?"

"Who knows? Can't carry on like this much longer. I think Giordano will kill Gino if he has to sleep with him in there another night."

"How is Kacper?"

"Better. He gets a cough easily—especially with this weather. Bisou is driving Giordano crazy too. We have him settled at the rear, but he thinks he is a dog and wants to sit on the bed."

"He wouldn't be able to manage the distance if we walked him." Michel thought of Bisou's stumpy legs.

"I know. I don't mind him. It's just Giordano. Says his clothes are full of horse and monkey hair."

Michel chuckled.

"It's not funny. It was at first, but now it's tiresome. Giordano's right—it's like living in a zoo."

"I feel for Aramis." Michel looked to the small crate being pulled behind Werner's caravan. "He's not been let out of that thing for days."

"He's sick, Michel. I doubt he would go out even if we let him."

"Sick?"

"Has been for a while. Werner has tried his best—got him medicine when he could afford it. But he's old and tired. It won't be long now. The last of the wild animals gone."

"Apart from Gino."

"That's if he survives Giordano." Jean smiled weakly.

Michel was surprised to see that he remembered the road on which they now traveled. The row of trees, the dip in the land from the rocky outcrop that jutted out over the small village like a welcoming sign. They were back in Vodable. And Michel's heart soared as he thought of Lucien, of the dog Coquette. He almost felt as though he had come home.

Michel rode Beau ahead and slowed alongside Werner's caravan, the ringmaster at the reins for a change and Serge nowhere to be seen.

"I know where we can stay," he told Werner.

"And where is that?"

"A friend, he has a farm. I will show you."

Before Werner could disagree, Michel rode out in front, leading them towards Lucien and Isabelle.

Lucien did not seem surprised to see Michel, and as he rode up the drive to the farm, Lucien simply turned from digging in the garden and waved his arm in the air.

"You came back!" The old man took Michel into an embrace as he dismounted. "I got your letter. Your friend sent some too—come, I'll show you."

"I've got a favor to ask, Lucien. You remember the circus I told you about in my letter—the troupe from the train? Well, there's no train anymore, just a bunch of us in caravans and tents, and we need somewhere to stay. Can you help?"

"Of course, of course. You can camp where you like! It's so good to see you, Michel, so good! We needed something to cheer us. The Germans came, you know, just after you left."

"They are everywhere."

Lucien nodded. "Like rats. Thankfully, our resident rat is a fat, slovenly man—Oberfeldwebel Gehring. They took over a few buildings to use as lodgings for soldiers on leave, but we have found that as long as Gehring is well fed and his pockets are full, he leaves us be."

"You think he would leave *us* be?" Michel indicated the caravans and wagons that rattled down the track.

Lucien shrugged. "We can only try."

Isabelle was not convinced that allowing a circus troupe to camp on their land would be as acceptable as Lucien believed. "You are a madman!" she yelled at him as Michel, pretending to be invisible, bent down to pat Coquette in their warm kitchen. "You think that everything will be all right—you have no brain in your head, Lucien! Your mother always told me you had no brain—well, I wish she were alive now to see this!"

"What's so wrong with a few friends to stay for a while?" Lucien placated. "It is our land—we can still do as we please with it."

"And what will happen when the Boche see who our visitors are? They'll come asking for papers."

"I'm sure they have them—all good French folk." Lucien nodded at Michel, who smiled at Isabelle.

She slammed a milk jug onto the wooden table, the cream slopping over the edge and dripping down the sides. Suddenly the twin cats appeared, and with a quick glance at Michel and the dog, began to lap up the drops before Isabelle swatted them away with the back of her hand.

"It'll just be for one night." Lucien took her hands in his and kissed them. "One night. And if Gehring is amenable, maybe one more night."

"I just don't know, Lucien. I just don't know. Maybe they will think they are gypsies? I heard from Madame Foucault that they took that Roma family away from Saint-Vincent. They were told they could not travel anymore—forbidden, she says. They were sent to a camp to stay. What if they do the same to Michel—to his friends?"

"They're a circus!" Lucien cried. "Not Roma."

Isabelle looked out of the window at the caravans—Jean and Giordano were trying to coax Bisou outside. "Doesn't look like much of a circus to me—looks like gypsies. And I dare say Gehring will see the same thing."

"He sees what we make him see. You know that. Why else do we still have our food, our farm? We will make it OK with him, I promise you. Hand on heart, see?" Lucien pressed his right hand against his heart.

"And how will you make him amenable, Lucien? You are already plying him with some of our best wine, duck and pork. What next? Me?"

"My dear, I could never, would never, turn you over to him!" Lucien kneeled down on the flagstone floor as if seeking penance.

"Get up, you old fool." Isabelle looked at Michel, who fidgeted with his hands in his pockets like a small child. "Fine, *one* night. If there are any problems, you, my friend, are gone, and you say we had nothing to do with it. Understood?" She raised her eyebrows.

"Madame, absolutely."

"*Absolument!*" Lucien stood and hugged her. "But think, if it is OK, and they stay, then we can see a circus, my love! A real-life circus! Think, a night of food and wine and dancing and tricks! It is what we need. It is what the whole town needs."

Michel saw Isabelle smile despite herself, and her eyes widened like they had months before when Michel had told her of the sights of Paris.

"*Merci*, Lucien, Isabelle." Michel kissed her on both cheeks and went out to tell the others they had a home for the night, at least.

Late that afternoon, as tents were pitched, fires lit, food sought, Michel left the troupe and walked towards the river he had left months before. In his pocket he took with him Bertrand's replies to his letters. He wanted peace and quiet to read them.

He found a dry enough log under a canopy of leaves and watched the swollen river, now a dirty brown from the mud that had been churned up by the recent rains.

He pulled the cream envelopes from his pocket and smiled to himself at Bertrand's familiar scrawl. He held one to his nose and believed he could smell home.

He opened the letter dated July, and read:

> Michel, my friend,
>
> I received your letter today, and I was so heartened by it—to hear that you are well, alive, and in a circus no less?
>
> I am glad, in a way, that you found a home for yourself amongst the players and the artists; when Amélie was alive, she loved the circus—the music, the costumes, the acts. She always told me I would have made a fine clown. I think she was probably right.

You talked of cherishing a young lady. My dear Michel, how wonderful for you to have found that feeling, but alas, as you say, it is complicated. Love is complicated, even when it seems not to be. All I can advise you is to be her friend. You say you cannot have her, cannot be with her. Why is this? Is she married?

The best you can be, to anyone, is a friend. And I can say from my personal experience that you are one of the best friends a person could have. In this way, you can still cherish her.

You see, I have surprised you with my response, have I not? I have not told you to ignore your feelings. But then, I am an old romantic at heart and believe love can and will conquer all.

I have a confession to make. I now regret not leaving with you. Things have changed so quickly. Monsieur Freidman had his shoe shop taken from him. He is still here, living in his apartment above me as always, yet he is now under surveillance because his son—you remember him—is, or rather was, a lawyer, and he has been fired, along with all Jews in official roles.

Monsieur Lippmann, the journalist, was arrested. No one knows quite what he did. Although it does not really matter now, does it?

The rationing has begun in earnest and crowds flock out of doors. I am glad I kept so much cognac—I hope it will see me through to the end of the war, or my death, whichever comes first.

You must forgive me for being so maudlin. It is just that life—the color, the hope—is gone now, and I fear it will become worse.

We have curfews now—lights out, drawn curtains, no going out after 9 p.m.

Madame Odette is faring well—she is a wily old bag, always was. She has made the acquaintance of a lieutenant who enjoys her company, the café and a drink, so she seems to be doing quite a bit of trade these evenings. I, of course, do not and cannot go there at night. But I do go and see her in the day, for a coffee, a chat with whoever is left.

I think I must stop now, Michel. I feel myself spiraling further down into a pit of despair.

I pray you are well; I pray you still see some color in your life.

Your friend,
Bertrand

Michel folded the letter and placed it back into its envelope. He felt a tightening in his throat at the thought of Bertrand alone; at the fear that was clear in his letter.

He lit a cigarette and waited until it had burned itself out before he opened the next letter, his hands cold, the lump in his throat still there.

My Dear Michel,

Another letter has arrived! You cannot know the absolute joy I felt when I received it. I did not open it straight away, but saved it all day in my pocket, ready to savor this evening when the curtains are drawn, and I am a prisoner in my own home.

You are indeed correct that I write this now from my desk. My latest reply to you.

There is not much to tell you about this life; the only thing I can say is that because the Boche enjoy our fair city so much, they have not destroyed it. The only bombs we had were in June, and since then it has been relatively quiet. I say quiet, but what I mean is I have not heard that dreaded thud and smash as the bombs fall. We have those damned sirens that whine almost every night, and some of us have stopped bothering to go to the air raid shelter. There seems little point to me—let them bomb me in my sleep!

Food is the biggest problem we face now—the shortages are fraying everyone's nerves. I manage with what I can get my hands on and Odette seems to get her hands on much—and will sell it to us for a price! I think I may have to pawn my father's pocket watch—it will give me a few more francs to manage on. I was sad when I first thought of it, but then, if he was here, he would tell me to stop being so stupid and sell it to buy food.

I am sorry to hear of your friend Felix. It seems as though anyone can disappear these days. Odette's cousin's husband was arrested for fighting with a soldier in the street. When she went to the prison to visit him, they said he was not there. I do not think we will hear of him again.

Now, enough of my miserable life here. Let me talk of important matters—those of the heart.

First, your lady friend, Odélie—or rather your previous lady friend. I am sure that her heart has healed and that you did not treat her as badly as you thought. If it still weighs on you, Michel, then perhaps apologize to her, explain to her that your feelings are not strong enough for her and she deserves to be loved in the best way possible. That, I am sure, will bring you peace of mind and it will mean much to her.

Your love for Frieda sounds wonderful, and I congratulate you on feeling this way! Those moments you describe remind me of my early days courting my dear Amélie—treasure these days, these moments, as much as you feel frustrated. Women are strange creatures, Michel, and it sounds as though she may feel something for you too—but you say she cannot be yours, for a reason you have not expanded upon. I do wonder whether that is because you still have hope that maybe you are wrong?

I must close soon; I am due at Odette's, who has procured me a pound of butter and some fresh meat with her wily ways! But before I depart, I am going to sit here and look out at the street, letting my mind wander as I think of the colors and sounds of the circus show, of where you may be now, and what you may be doing. This daydream I am sure will keep me going for some time, until I receive your next letter—which, Michel, I dearly pray that I do.

Take the best care, Michel.
Bertrand

Michel folded the letter and placed it on top of the other. He thought of Bertrand's words. In his last letter he had explained the situation with Frieda and Werner—did that mean he had given up hope? To write it on paper made it too real—a defeat—yet Michel realized that he was not yet ready to be defeated.

He stood and put the letters in his pocket, leaving the river behind and heading into town, wanting to be alone for a little while longer.

Very little had changed in Vodable. The Madame's café was still open, though now it served a few uniformed soldiers who sat and laughed with the locals. Michel spied a man, his legs long and thin, his arms the same, but with an enormous potbelly as if he were pregnant, perched on a bar stool close to the door, his feet dangling, his face round, flushed and joyful. He wore a uniform too, but his was unbuttoned and messy, as if he wore it only because he had to. Oberfeldwebel Gehring.

Michel did not go in, but turned instead to the patisserie and bought himself a slice of rich chocolate cake layered with cream. He found a bench by the side of the church overlooking the cemetery and ate his cake slowly, luxuriating in the sweetness. It had cost him more than he could afford, but it was worth it, just this once.

He waited in the quiet until the sun began its descent, and then stood to walk back to the farm before dark set in.

Then, he saw her. Frieda.

She sat down on the bench and he did the same.

"I wondered where you were. Jean was sent to get some extra bread before the baker closed and I said I would go with him. Have you been here this whole time?"

"A little while. I just wanted to walk and clear my head."

"Is there much on your mind?"

"Just one thing," he said.

"Werner is thankful you have found us a nice spot to stay for the evening. Lucien has been keeping him company—talking of wine and women and animals. They are making their way through their second bottle."

"Lucien is a wine connoisseur. He is good company."

"As are you, Michel." She leaned against him, her head on his shoulder.

"Frieda, you shouldn't be here. I'm not allowed to speak to you—remember?"

Frieda lifted her head from his shoulder. "I know, but I miss your voice."

Michel turned to look at her, their eyes locked.

"There you are!"

"Jean!" Michel stood quickly.

"Bread—here, take a loaf. I could only get two. Hopefully it will be enough."

"I'm sure it will be plenty. It's time to go home."

The trio walked back, Jean out in front, whistling a tune. Michel felt his hand brush against Frieda's, and in a moment of spontaneity he took her hand in his. She did not pull away and her thumb stroked his, just once. It made him feel breathless with the want of her.

He knew in that moment that he would fight to be with her. She was Werner's, but she had shown him that perhaps she would someday be his.

They walked silently back to the farm, Michel enjoying her warmth, her scent, even her silence.

Just before the turn in the bend that would lead them down the track, she pulled her hand away.

The following morning broke with a frost on the ground, blue skies and a light breeze that stirred up the crunchy golden and bronze fallen leaves. Michel woke in an uncomfortable position, balled up on Lucien's couch as Kacper had taken the spare room. He stretched and realized he would have to erect his tent, as cold as it was—he couldn't sleep on this again.

Michel breakfasted late with Lucien and Isabelle after they had finished feeding the troupe.

"I gave them the shed," Lucien told Isabelle.

"Good. And some blankets?"

"Blankets too. They asked for a candle. I gave them one."

"What for?" Michel asked.

"That lion is dying. Werner was up all night with him. We moved him to the shed at daybreak."

"Why did no one wake me?" Michel stood.

"Sit down. Werner says he wants just him and Frieda."

"I should at least take a look, see if there is any way I can help?"

"Fine, a quick look, but there's nothing you can do, I'm afraid. It's the end."

Michel went to the rear of the barn, where Lucien's shed had been emptied of its tools and detritus to give room to the elderly lion.

Michel had seen Aramis only once, at a performance. His gait had been slow, his eyes glazed as if blind. He knocked lightly on the wooden door and waited.

"Michel." Frieda opened the door, her eyes filled with tears.

Without thinking he took her hands in his. "I'm so sorry."

She moved aside so he could see past her. There lay Aramis, his breathing slow and raspy, his tongue hanging out of the side of his mouth. Werner lay on the floor next to him, his little hand stroking his mane and whispering gentle words as the lion pulled each breath in.

"He won't leave his side," she said quietly.

"Is there nothing that can be done?"

She shook her head.

"I should go in."

"Michel?" Werner turned towards the door. His eyes were red, the skin underneath puffy.

"Werner, I'm so sorry."

Werner stood and coughed, wiping tears from his face. "We can't leave today"—he gestured at Aramis—"but Lucien's wife is worried about our presence here. I told Lucien one of us would go with him to see this Gehring, to try and get approval to stay awhile."

"I can go," Michel said.

"No. I was thinking Serge—can you summon him?"

"I think Michel would be better," Frieda said. "You know how Serge can be, and his very bulk may cause offence."

Werner looked Michel up and down. "I suppose Michel looks harmless enough—and he has the face of a simpleton. It may beg some sympathy."

Despite the slur, Michel smiled a little—it was almost good to see that Werner had not yet lost all of his gruffness.

"I'll go right away." Michel nodded at him. "And I'm sorry again."

Werner turned from him, then lay down on the floor once more, to talk to his friend for one last time.

Isabelle had two bottles of wine ready for Michel to take, as well as fresh bread, bacon, and some money Lucien had loaned the troupe.

"I'll get it back from Werner when he's better," Lucien said.

"You're ready to go?" Michel pulled on his coat.

"I'm sorry but I can't—you'll have to go it alone."

"He's got work to do," Isabelle explained, her voice flat, as if there had been an argument before Michel had entered.

"You think he will listen to me?" Michel asked.

"He'll listen to anyone as long as they've something in their hand," Lucien said. "Don't worry."

As Michel followed the track to the town square, he heard the tip-tap of light feet behind him, followed by an even lighter footstep. He turned to look, and saw Frieda running towards him, Coquette—her tongue hanging out—at her heel.

"You did not hear me shout at you?" she said breathlessly as she reached Michel.

"Did Coquette follow you or did you follow her?"

"She followed me. Lucien said to let her come, as she pines when animals die. She's sensitive."

"Werner allowed you?"

"He wanted to be alone with Aramis..."

"You shouldn't be here. What if he finds out?"

"I can help you. I have learned how Werner charms people to get what he wants. Besides, a woman's charms will surely be useful now."

"If you're sure...?"

"I can't stay there—I can't watch Aramis die, and I can't sit in a caravan or listen to the others talk of all those animals they have loved and are now dead. That's all they are doing—Giordano is lamenting his dead cat from his childhood. I can't bear it. Please. I promise if Werner says anything, I will tell him I insisted."

Michel started to walk again, and every few steps bent down to ruffle Coquette's ears.

"You love them, don't you?" Frieda whispered.

"Who?"

"Animals. All of them."

"Sometimes they are easier than humans. Kinder. More patient. More loving."

"You didn't even know Aramis, yet you feel pain for him passing."

"I do," Michel said, then patted Coquette again.

Frieda threaded her arm through his and rested her head on his shoulder. With the touch of her, he felt his stomach do a somersault and told himself to remember this moment.

They continued quietly to the town square, where a group of four girls had drawn a hopscotch grid in chalk and were singing as they jumped.

Oberfeldwebel Gehring, followed by two of his soldiers, walked towards the café. The girls did not stop their hopping, but they became quieter; an old woman who was making her way down the church steps now turned and walked back inside.

"Stay here," Michel told Frieda. "It's probably better if I try on my own first—just in case it does not go well."

"You must be joking." She walked towards the café that Gehring had just entered, and Michel quickened his step to catch up with her.

Inside, Gehring stood holding court at the bar—about how things could be, and how things were with him.

"I am a humble man. A servant to the Reich. But I am aware of where I am. Here, I am in a town—a village, no less—where there is little. Some farms. Some wine. This does not interest the Führer. You have nothing here he could want. So, we live in peace, you and me. I want no trouble. Just peace."

Michel paused at the bar to order a coffee, then took a seat nearby, Frieda next to him and Coquette under the table, her eyes watching the feet of those at the bar.

"As you know, I am a man of peace. You have seen this. I just ask that you remember that. Understand how none of us, least of all me, want a life disturbed by friction."

Michel saw Gehring briefly glance in his direction, then settle onto a bar stool and call for his morning coffee, sending the soldiers to the bakery for warm croissants.

"Are you going to talk to him?" Frieda asked.

"Not yet. Patience." Michel sipped at his coffee.

Minutes ticked by on the clock that hung above the bar, smoke from cigarettes curled like gray cats' tails to the ceiling, and the radio crackled with German voices scuttering across the air towards French ears from an approved station.

Finally, Gehring could bear it no longer and turned to them. "You are new."

"We are," Michel said.

"I wasn't asking you," Gehring said, and lit a cigarette, squinting as the first plume of smoke left his mouth and stung his eyes.

"We are staying at the farm of Lucien Demotte," Frieda added with a smile.

"Demotte? Good wine. Good man. And why are you there?"

Michel coughed and stood. "May I?" he asked, indicating the bar stool next to Gehring.

"If your lady friend will join us too." Gehring grinned at Frieda with his cigarette between his teeth.

They both sat, having dragged the stools across the floor. The Madame raised her eyebrow in annoyance at the sound as she polished glasses with a crisp white cloth.

"May I buy you another coffee?" Michel asked.

"You may."

Whilst the Madame poured fresh coffee into their cups, Gehring's officers reappeared, brown bags in their hands, the buttery grease from the warm croissants already staining the paper a darker brown.

"Leave them here," Gehring told them, slapping his hand on the bar. Then, in German, he spoke quickly, and so ferociously Michel shivered and goosebumps appeared on his arm. The soldiers left and Gehring opened a bag, tearing into one of the croissants as if it were a turkey leg.

"You enjoy our pastries," Frieda noted, then nudged Michel in the ribs and gave a slight nod towards the bag of food and drink that Lucien and Isabelle had given him.

"I do. I do," Gehring said, spraying crumbs.

"Perhaps you would like some fresh bacon and bread to take home with you for this evening?" Michel picked up the bag.

Gehring stopped eating and looked at it, then at Michel, flakes of pastry stuck to his lips. His tongue nipped out of his mouth and cleared the crumbs away. He placed the remaining pastry on the countertop, picked his smoldering cigarette out of the ashtray, and flicked off the large graying tip of ash.

"Who are you?" he asked. "Why are you here?"

"I am Michel. From Paris. I am working for Werner Neumann, the ringmaster of Neumann's circus. Perhaps you know of him?"

Gehring shook his head.

"We are just passing through, a few of us. We thought perhaps to stay a few days, perform a few tricks?"

Gehring smoked, then gulped his coffee down and nodded at the Madame to refill it.

Michel could feel himself grow hot, and sweat trickled down the back of his neck. He had made a mistake. Lucien was wrong. Gehring was not going to agree.

"Neumann..." he finally said.

"He came from Austria originally—just like the Führer," Frieda said. "*Ein Volk, ein Reich, ein Führer.*"

Gehring smiled. "It is better when it is said loudly. At the rallies, where there are thousands shouting this. *Ihr Deutsch ist gut.*"

Michel looked confusedly at Frieda—her German sounded perfect, strong, confident. He saw her smile and blush at the compliment.

"A few days... OK. You have something in the bag, you say? A gift for me?"

Michel passed him the bag and the bottles of wine. He placed the money flat on the bar, and Gehring's hand snatched it away so fast that it was as though it had never been there.

"We should be going." Michel scattered a few coins on the bar for his coffee.

"Tomorrow night," Gehring said, his mouth full of pastry once more.

"I'm sorry?"

"Tomorrow night. In the square. Entertainment. I like magic shows especially."

"Of course." Michel nodded. "Tomorrow."

As they left, the gummy man, Armand, from Michel's first visit to the town was pulling out a chair and settling himself down.

"Back again? And you brought another?" Armand said.

"Monsieur." Michel smiled.

"Don't you Monsieur me! Tell Lucien I know what he is up to! Gehring! Gehring! What do you make of this nonsense, then? All these *performers* . . . ?" He spat the words onto the floor.

Gehring shouted from inside, "Monsieur Armand, I have it all in hand. Don't worry."

"Ha! See! He will sort you out!"

"I am sure he will, Monsieur Armand."

"Tell Lucien I am here, and I am waiting. I do not like him, not one bit. But he plays backgammon well. Tell him! Can you do that?"

"We will," Frieda sang, and took Michel's arm as they walked through the square, Coquette once more trailing behind them.

"You seem angry at me," Frieda said after a while.

"I'm not."

"Don't lie."

Michel glanced at her, then turned to look at his feet as they walked. "Why do you stay with Werner?" He kicked at a stone.

"I have no choice."

He stopped and, sensing his chance, he took it. "You do. We could leave together."

"And go where?"

"I don't understand what you want from me, Frieda!" he suddenly said, his voice edged with desperation. "You are with him, but I know you want something more with me. You held my hand; you rest your head on my shoulder like you want to be with me—"

"Hush," Frieda soothed. "Yes. You know how I feel. I know how you feel. Can't that be enough for now? Please, Michel, walk with me, enjoy this moment. Who knows what will happen or what *can* happen? Things are changing so much around us—soon it could change for us too. Please. Trust me."

She looked into her eyes and knew he would do anything she asked of him. He stepped up to her and kissed her, his arms pulling her to him, her body relaxing for a moment into his.

Gently, she pulled away and took his arm once more, ready to resume their walk. "I like Monsieur Armand," she said.

"The toothless man?"

"Yes. He's funny."

"He's angry and bitter."

"It can be overcome. I just like the way he talks—*Don't you Monsieur me!*" she imitated Armand.

Michel laughed. "Very good! Who else can you imitate?"

"*But Giordano, please, please give me my necklace back.*" Her voice was high-pitched and whiny.

"Madame Geneviève!" Michel guessed.

"*I have de most beautiful hair in all the world!*" Her Italian accent was flawless but exaggerated, and she ran ahead of Michel and twirled around. "*Can you not see how my hair, it glows, my feet, they dance? Why, I am so clever, so talented!*"

"Giordano!" Michel laughed.

"Do not tell him I did this! I love him, really. I do." She took his arm once more. "They are my family. All of them."

"And what am I?"

Frieda stopped walking and Michel faced her. As she opened her mouth to answer, Coquette barked and ran off towards Lucien's farm.

"Where have you been? Werner is beside himself!" Jean-Jacques was running towards them across the field. "Aramis has died. Werner is drinking with Lucien and crying. He thought the German lieutenant had taken you both away! Come. Come quickly."

Michel and Frieda hurried with Jean back to the farm.

"Come, show him you are both fine. I have never seen him like this before. Never. Tears streaming down his face, talking of wanting to go home, of his mother! I did not know he even had a mother!"

"Don't be silly. Everyone has a mother," Michel said.

"I thought Werner just, you know—appeared. Who knew?" Jean raised his arms in the air as if waiting to see what else would fall from the heavens.

As promised, Werner was distraught, hunched inside his caravan, Lucien topping up his glass with a rich red every time Werner emptied it.

"You're alive!" Werner shouted upon seeing Frieda. He grasped her in a wobbly embrace.

"Shhh, don't worry." She turned to Lucien and Michel. "You can go now. I'll take care of him."

"No! No one leave! We are burying Aramis, is that not so, Lucien?" Werner asked.

"Yes, of course. There's a spot under an oak at the bottom of the field. Bluebells grow underneath in spring, and in summer the field is full of wildflowers."

"Get Serge. Get him to dig a hole, and when it's ready we'll all go and say goodbye..." Werner's words trailed off, his lip wobbling.

Michel stepped out of the caravan, found Serge, and together with Jean they dug a hole at the base of the old oak.

No one spoke but Giordano, who sat on a blanket and barked orders. "Needs to be deeper! He'll come up otherwise, when it rains."

"If it matters that much to you, you could help." Jean wiped the sweat off his brow.

"Only one boss needed—me. Too many cooks otherwise. Come on now, Michel, dig quicker. It'll be dark if you carry on like this!"

*

By late afternoon, the grave was dug, and Aramis's body had been brought to its resting place by the strong arms of Serge, Michel, Jean and Vassily.

The troupe walked in pairs across the field, Werner at the helm, Frieda by his side. He held a crimson blanket, and when he reached the grave, he laid it on Aramis. "Goodnight, my friend. Goodnight."

Michel stood next to the hole, a spade still in his hand, ready to fill it in. He felt the sadness they all felt, even though he had barely known Aramis. But it was a sadness beyond the death of the lion. It was everything—the death of the entire circus, of what it once was, of what it could never be again.

Kacper played a soft, mournful tune on his accordion whilst each member of the troupe threw a handful of soil into the grave.

Madame Geneviève and Rosie held on to each other and wept at the sight of Aramis. Vassily threw in a flower and Hugo poured a little of his génépy onto the lion's body. "See you on your way, my lad," he said.

"Fill it now," Werner said. "Fill it and then tonight we drink to Aramis, our loyal friend, our beautiful..." He trailed off and began to sob. Frieda placed her arm around his shoulders and led him back to the farmhouse.

No one offered to help Michel, and he did not ask for any. He shoveled the dirt onto Aramis and thought of his mother and the day of her funeral. He sent a prayer to her and wiped away a tear, realizing he had been crying as he covered the grave.

"I didn't realize that you were so fond of him, Michel."

He looked up to see Odélie standing in front of him, wrapped in a shawl against the chill in the air.

"It's sad," he said simply.

"It is. You know, I loved Aramis—I did. I fed him at night, and I think he liked me the best. When his teeth fell out and he couldn't chew the meat, I chopped it up small for him, just so he would still eat. I think he knew that I loved him—do you think animals know that?"

He looked at her, her eyes spilling over with tears. He dropped the spade and took her in an embrace. "I'm sure they do, Odélie."

She moved her face from where it was buried in his shoulder and tried to kiss him. He pushed her away gently. "I can't—I'm sorry, Odélie, I can't."

"What is it with you, Michel?" she spat. "One minute you want me, then suddenly you ignore me as if I did something wrong."

"I know. And I'm sorry. My behavior towards you was not right, Odélie. But it was because I knew you deserved better than me...someone who could give you everything you want—"

"Spare me the apology, Michel. I know I deserve better than you. You were just something to pass the time with, a toy."

She turned and stalked away, but despite her harsh words, Michel was pleased to see a small smile on her lips. Her place was righted—*No one rejects Odélie; she rejects them.*

As afternoon made its way into evening, the troupe sat with Lucien and Isabelle around a makeshift campfire and drank some of Lucien's most precious bottles of red.

"I can't believe you gave up your finest," Michel said.

"It's just wine, Michel. Just wine." Lucien raised a glass.

"He's drunk—he must be, because he wouldn't say that unless he was!" Isabelle grinned. "Come on, you old fool, inside with you."

Kacper stood and followed the pair inside the house, as did Vassily, who would share the spare bedroom with Kacper.

"You can sleep on the couch again, Michel." Isabelle turned to him. "Or there's the barn?"

"I might take the barn tonight." Michel smiled. "The sofa was a little short for my legs."

"If you won't take the sofa then I will," Serge said, hurrying after them. "I don't care if my legs fall on the floor, I'm sick of that tent."

Madame Rosie helped Geneviève to their caravan and Odélie herded the triplets to their beds—the three of them paler and skinnier than ever.

"They're not doing so well since we lost the train," Jean said. "Odélie says they hardly ever leave the caravan and won't even talk to her anymore—just when she thought they were coming out of their shell."

"They've been through much," Werner said, his voice thick with drink, his eyes set on the flames as they danced.

"Come now, we should go to bed." Frieda took hold of his arm.

"You go. You go. I want to sit. Jean, Giordano, you'll stay with me, won't you? And you, Michel? Thank you for digging the grave. I don't say it often, so you need to take the thanks now."

"That's all right, Werner."

"We'll stay with him. You go and get some rest," Jean assured her.

Frieda smiled then yawned. "It's been a lot, today and last night with Aramis. Goodnight, all."

"Goodnight, my dear. Sleep well. I shall be there soon enough." Werner waved in her general direction. "Do you know, Michel, I loved that lion, I really did. I tried my best to keep him safe. I rescued him, did you know that? He was being treated badly, so badly—beaten, starved. I took him, cared for him. I never made him perform much—not much at all—and the way I got him to perform was to have meat in my pocket, just like a dog...he could be trained with kindness."

"You did all you could for him," Jean said.

"I felt terrible when he was stuck in that crate, when we could find nowhere to stay. But we did find somewhere, a resting place for him." Werner began to cry once more.

"I should head to bed myself." Michel stood.

"And you, Michel, you found *us* somewhere to stay, didn't you?" Werner was slurring now, his eyes tight. "The wonderful Michel." He stood and twirled, his drink spilling on the ground, drops hitting the fire and making it hiss and spit. "The wonderful, marvellous Michel!"

"Come now, Werner." Jean stood too. "Let's get you to bed."

"I'm the boss!" Werner looked at Jean and pointed at his own chest. "Me. I'm the boss. Sit down. You too, Michel. Sit."

Michel, seeing how drunk Werner was, and how he too had a muggy head, knew no good would come of staying. "I'll just go to bed..." he said again.

"Sit down!" Werner boomed. "I'm the boss, you idiot, orphaned pretty-boy. Telling me what I should do—I tell you what to do."

"I didn't tell you what to do," Michel said.

Werner marched towards him and pushed against his chest, sending Michel back a few paces. "Smart little mouth you've got!"

Michel, whether from tiredness, the wine, or the distaste he had for Werner, pushed back against him, knocking his body to the floor. He stepped forward and Jean moved between him and Werner. "Don't do anything you'll regret," Jean warned.

"Let him! Let him hit me and then he can go!" Werner shouted from the dusty ground.

"Michel, don't." Jean held him back.

"Go!" Werner was now crying, fat heavy sobs. "Go. You know nothing about us!"

Michel relaxed his arms, and Jean turned to help Werner sit up by the fire, filling his now empty glass. "Drink this, calm yourself and then to bed," he soothed.

"And then to bed," Giordano repeated, his eyes wide.

Werner calmed, his sobs slowing. He wiped his eyes then blew his nose. He looked at Michel. "Don't go," he said quietly. "I've had a little too much to drink. And with Aramis..."

Michel dragged a palm over his face and rubbed at his eyes. "I'm going to bed."

"No, wait. Please, Michel. Sit. Please," Werner asked.

Jean nodded at Michel. "Please, Michel?"

Michel sat, his knees drawn up to his chest, all four silent and watching the flames.

"We've been here before, haven't we?" Werner suddenly said.

"I don't think you tried to punch me though." Jean laughed.

"Me neither," Giordano chimed in, now the tension had gone. "You just sat us down quietly after you had shouted at us in a rehearsal, told us we were useful. We thought we were going to be fired!"

"You had only been with us a few days then," Werner said. "But you could see who we were."

"Because we were like you too," Jean offered.

"Quite right. You are." Werner turned to Michel. "You're wondering what we are talking about, aren't you?"

Michel nodded.

"Lucien said you sorted things in town today. And then you dug the grave for Aramis. Filled it in yourself. I have to admit, I was too hard on you, Michel. But I had to be. We have so much to lose."

"I won't leave," Michel said.

"That's not why I am saying this—leave or stay, that's not the point! I'm saying it because..." Werner looked around wildly. "Because I trust you. Because I'm drunk. Because it's all changing."

Michel instantly felt his face flame and his stomach turn. Werner trusted him. *Trust. Frieda.*

"Some more wine for Michel, Jean, pour him some more wine."

Jean did as he was instructed and Michel raised a toast to Werner, all the while feeling the guilt creep across his chest.

"Now, Michel. If you'll permit me, I'll tell you a story. It will help you to understand why I was so hard on you. The others know—I told them at a given time, when I knew they were one of us. Now, it's time for you to know."

Despite the wine, the tiredness, the guilt, Michel sat forward, intrigued to find out the secrets of the circus.

"I met her on the longest day of the year. The summer solstice. I was in Hungary with my troupe—a different one to this bunch, and I wasn't ringmaster yet. Just a wide-eyed novice—like you, Michel. I worked with the horses, I sewed costumes, I helped choreograph the evening. I did everything and anything to learn it all. I was obsessed, you see. Obsessed with becoming a ringmaster.

"I had been to a show as a child and wanted to be that man who commanded an entire circus. Like a conductor with his baton, he was in charge of his musicians and the music they would make. So that was my dream—a simple one, as I had no schooling, no parents; only a grandmother, who I am sure was glad to see me leave and join the circus that came through town when I was fourteen.

"Anyway, where was I? Yes, right. The summer solstice. We were in Budapest, in a park next to the Széchenyi Baths—the hot springs—and you could see the steam from them rising in the violet sky. It was a strange night. The sun was behind a cloud and yet glowed brighter, as if trying to make itself known. The orange glow, the purple of a midsummer sky, and those ancient waters and their steam...it felt as though we were on a different planet and something magical was about to happen—something that would change me forever. I sound romantic and foolish, don't I? I thought this of myself too, as soon as the thoughts had appeared in my mind, so I turned away from the steam and the sky, and went about my business—for there was a lot to do.

"We were the guests of a count and his elderly, sick wife who had a love for tricks and magic. We had brought in more acts: travelers who could tell fortunes; exotics that could bend their bodies, breathe fire and dance like otherworldly creatures.

"I walked towards the main tent, ready to greet the important guests before the show, when I saw her.

"She walked in front of me, a long mane of blue-black hair tumbling down her back. She wore a costume of silver sequins with a matching headband, and her long legs flashed out from the hem of the little skirt as she strode towards the tent, and the trapeze.

"I was shorter than her by some inches and my legs had to work twice as hard to catch up. But I did. And when I did, I tapped her on the shoulder so she had to turn to look at me, and then, just like that, I could not speak. She was beautiful. Her green eyes were ablaze with light from the torches, her cheeks flushed, and her lips painted a deep red.

" 'Yes?' she said.

"I said nothing.

" 'Yes?' Her accent was thick.

" 'I am French,' I said stupidly.

"She cocked her head to the side like an inquisitive bird. 'So you are,' she replied, now in French, perfectly accented, as if she were magic and could speak any language she wished.

" 'I am Werner.'

" 'Werner the Frenchman. Your name is not so French.'

" 'My father was German. My mother, French. I am French.'

" 'All right, French Werner. I'm just here for the night but I thought I'd talk to the others—gets a bit lonely when you are on your own—' "

"I know that feeling!" Jean interjected. "My first circus, I was alone."

"Then you met me." Giordano smiled.

"I did. But now Michel is alone. We must find him a Giordano!" Jean raised his glass, as did Werner.

Michel smiled weakly. He wasn't alone. He had thought he had Frieda. But now, hearing how Werner had met her, how he had cherished her from first sight, he felt sick with the knowledge that he had already lost the fight—he had never really been in with a chance.

"Drink, Michel!" Werner said. "Drink."

Michel drank, wishing that the story would end quickly so he could go away, be alone and decide what he was going to do.

"Now, where was I? Oh yes, she said she was there for one night—just one. So I said to her, my voice all stupid and high, 'I am here all the time.'

"She laughed loudly. I couldn't blame her; I sounded simple. I wanted so badly to impress her, but I knew that I could not—she was the otherworldly creature that fell from the heavens. She would not be interested in me.

"As I opened my mouth to apologize to her, she turned and walked away. Again, I did not blame her.

"I did not watch her perform that evening; I could not bear it. The embarrassment of my failings haunted the show and I did not enjoy it or relax for the entire night. In a way, I was glad she was only there to make up the numbers and would be gone by dawn; I could then return to my life and concentrate on my career as ringmaster.

"The following morning, I had little time to think of her as we busied ourselves packing and sorting. We had no train—that was something I wished for dearly and would make true in a year's time—but back then we traveled as we do now, on foot, our horses pulling the weight of our lives and our costumes.

"I climbed aboard the front of a caravan I had been gifted by the ringmaster—an elderly man who was looking for someone to take over, someone he believed could be me. My caravan was painted red, the name of the circus in gold swirling letters on the side. Inside I had little—a bed, a stove, a few belongings—but I was mightily proud of it. It was mine and mine alone.

"As we began our journey, I talked gently to my mare Sophia, named after my grandmother, and told her of where we were headed next.

"Suddenly, a loud bang came from inside my caravan. At first, I thought perhaps I had not secured a book or some such—but I realized it was far too loud a noise for any possession I owned to make.

"The small hatch flung open and a face appeared.

"'Coffee?' she asked.

"I stared at her face for too long and she shouted at me, 'Look where you are going!'

"I spun around and concentrated on the road once more, pulling my mare Sophia away from oncoming traffic.

"'So,' she said. 'Coffee for the French-not-German Werner?'

"'Coffee? Yes. I'd like that.'

"I heard her whistle a tune as she made me coffee, and I thought I was in a dream.

"I loved her—loved her so much I asked her to marry me. She said she would, and while we saved to buy the train we plotted our lives together. We would travel the world, see it all...and then things changed."

Werner stopped and tears appeared in his eyes again. Jean passed him a handkerchief and let him take a moment to blow his nose.

"If it is too hard, you do not need to say any more," Giordano said.

"I have to. It is right. It is right to talk of her. To talk of the daughter she lost."

Michel looked to him. *A daughter? Frieda had a baby?* It all made more sense now—her reluctance to leave, the way she had been kept almost wrapped in cotton wool, forbidden from doing anything that could harm her. Michel saw Werner with new eyes. He was simply a man trying to protect his love—protect her from the world because she had already lost so much.

"She fell pregnant before we could marry," Werner said sadly. "I told her we would marry as soon as we could afford it, but she said she did not care. She felt loved and was so happy to be having our child.

"We were back in Hungary when she delivered the baby. The troupe had traveled to her home country—I did it to make her happy.

"When I held our daughter in my arms, I was so happy and full of love—it welled up in me so much that I was sure I could not contain it. My little girl wrapped her pink fist around my finger—there she was, the ringmaster's daughter. All of this was now hers.

"I gave the baby back to her mother and told her we would remain in Hungary, that her parents were due to arrive. She held our new daughter in her arms and screamed at me for being so stupid.

"I didn't understand. I thought she would have wanted to see her parents, her sisters. I'd telegrammed them, and they knew where we were.

" 'We need to leave, now.' She leapt out of bed and almost fell. I took our daughter from her.

" 'But you must rest. See a doctor.'

" 'I don't want a doctor. I don't want my family either. Please, Werner, please, let us go.'

"I agreed, of course I did—I could not deny her anything. But before I could tell the troupe, there was a knock on our carriage door—a policeman, and with him, her parents.

"They did not speak to me. The father pushed past me to her and grabbed his daughter's arm, shouting in Hungarian—harsh, quick words. I was still holding the baby, but then the mother snatched her from me. I stepped in front of the brute of a man… but as you can see, I am short and I could not push him away.

" 'What's happening? What's going on?' I cried.

"She screamed for our baby, who was now wailing. Her mother turned to leave.

" 'The baby!' she cried. 'Get my baby!'

"I did not know how I was going to achieve it. I ran to the woman, but her husband was quicker. He punched me three, four or maybe five times. He knocked me unconscious.

"When I woke, the carriage was quiet."

"The baby was gone, and Frieda?" Michel asked.

"Yes ... the baby was." Werner looked at him, confused. "But my darling girl sat on the bed in tears, rocking and crying for her child. I held her to me, kissed her, promised her we would call the police, get our child back.

" 'But he is the police,' she explained. 'He is. I ran away, Werner, because they wanted me to marry someone I hated. So I ran and ran, and I found you—we found each other.'

"Her mother was devoutly Jewish, her father goodness-knows-what, other than a hard, mean man who had viciously beaten her and her mother.

" 'We've lost her,' she cried. 'She's lost to me.'

"She lay back on the bed and stayed that way for weeks. We were forced to move to another town as the police had been sent out to us—her father's handiwork—"

"Did you get her back?" Michel interrupted.

"Frieda—well, yes, yes I did." Werner raised his eyebrows at Jean and Giordano.

"No, I mean the baby?"

"Yes, the baby came back," Jean said. "Are you feeling all right, Michel?"

"Wait, so the baby came back?"

"Yes." Werner nodded.

"OK, so what happened to Frieda?" Michel said slowly.

"She. Came. Back," Werner said slowly.

"From where?" Michel asked.

"From her grandparents."

"So, after the mother took the baby, Frieda went to them?" Michel asked.

"Oh my goodness! What are you not understanding, Michel? The baby *was* Frieda!" Giordano stood, waving his little arms in the air.

"Wait...you thought...Frieda and I? That Frieda gave birth?" Werner was laughing now. "You fool! You fool!" He held his belly as Jean and Giordano joined in.

Michel could not speak. His face was slack, eyes wide.

"But, but..." was all he could manage.

Werner's laugh slowed. "All this time you thought Frieda was my wife?"

"You said I couldn't go near her. Everyone protected her, said she was yours. Even Jean warned me away."

"Of course I did! Go after the boss's daughter? Not a great idea!" Jean exclaimed.

"I needed to protect her, Michel. That's what a father does. It took me years to get her back—years. And when I did, I swore not to let her go again."

"And her mother?" Michel asked quietly.

"Éva? She left me. She had a choice to make and she chose Frieda—better to have one parent than none at all."

"Could she not have come back to you with the baby?"

"I told her not to even try. I wanted them to be safe, so she arranged with her parents that she would go to live with her sister, who would take care of them, and she would be away from the hands of her father."

"He never saw her grow—never saw his daughter's first steps," Giordano lamented.

"My friend, you are drunk. You always cry when you get this drunk." Jean wrapped his arm around Giordano's shoulders.

"I am not! I am not! I am sad."

"Hush, Giordano. I got her back, didn't I?" Werner said.

"How?" Michel asked.

"Well now, that's the next part of my story. You know, Michel, I may seem mean to you, but I am not—not deep down anyway.

I work hard, and I work hard to protect others too. Frieda came to me when she was just ten years old. A vision of her mother. I knew what she would say before she said it.

"I was in Paris back then, a place I have always called home. It was raining and cold, and the water clogged up the gutters, and the drains gurgled with the vast quantities of water trying to push through them. I sat in my apartment—my mother's childhood home—and listened to the rain on the window, the sound of quick footsteps on the pavement as people hurried home.

"'There was a knock at the door. I thought it was Serge. He was due to come around and give word on the train, how much it was going to cost to fix it and get us back on track by spring. I opened it and there she was. 'Papa,' she said. Just like that. 'Papa.'

"I hugged her to me, and she cried into my chest. She cried because her mother was dead from a disease that had wracked her in the past few years. She cried because her mother's family had not helped her. She cried for me, for me and her mother and the love we had.

"When she had calmed down, I sat her in a chair and wrapped a blanket around her shoulders.

" 'It is dangerous for us in Hungary,' she said. 'I had to come to you—she told me to come to you. She told me to get a train and give a note to the conductor which asked for him to help me. He did. He helped me all the way to Paris and then put me in a taxi and it brought me here.'

"I was astounded at her—so brave for one so young. I had written often to Éva, but I had never received a reply. I assumed that the letters had been put straight into the fire. Only a month before, I had written to tell her of the train breaking down, of having to stay in Paris for a few months.

" 'You found me,' I said.

" 'Mother said you liked to come here for the winter. She knew you would be here—she showed me your letters.'

" 'But she never wrote back,' I said.

" 'She wrote you this.' Frieda handed me a letter.

"I could not wait; I opened it right there and then. I cannot tell you word for word, nor do I wish to tell you everything she wrote to me. But she told me of her illness, that she had little time left. My letter had come at an opportune moment: she acted fast and sent Frieda to me when she knew exactly where I would be. She told me she loved me. She told me to take care of our daughter.

"When I had finished reading, I took my daughter's hand in mine. 'You are here. You are mine. You are safe.'

"I gave her my surname and Serge found a man to make her some papers. She did not want to hide—she was proud to be Jewish, proud of her heritage, her mother. But I explained to her that things would be easier this way. All she had to do was go along with pretending to be someone else for a while, and she would stay safe.

"She listened to me. How could she not? She had nowhere to go. The war, although still ten years away, was already beginning back then, Michel. I had seen on my travels the way Jews were being targeted; I had heard of Hitler, of his plans, and seen how many listened to him. She had to be Frieda Neumann, as much as I now despise the origin of that name. I taught her German history, not that I knew much of it myself. I taught her to disguise her accent and speak French fluently. Then we started on German. She was a good student and taught herself in half a year.

"Serge, an outcast from his own family, was the one who suggested she learn the trapeze. Her mother had been a natural— perhaps she would be too? I did not want her to be part of our act. I wanted to keep her safe, but she was bored and determined, and once she saw photographs of her mother performing, there was little I could do to stop her."

Werner stopped talking and rubbed at the tiredness in his eyes.

"More?" Giordano held the bottle of wine over Werner's glass.

Werner nodded, then took three deep gulps.

"You can stop," Michel said, not meaning it, but he could see the effect it had had on Werner. This story had reduced him to a smaller man still; his chest was deflated, his eyes sunken.

"I have started so I will finish," he said.

"Frieda was a force. As things progressed, she picked up waifs and strays wherever we went. Mostly those on the fringes of society—those of different faiths, the disabled, the different. She saw talent in everyone she met. As I said, this was before war broke out, but there are many who have always been persecuted—gypsies, orphans, thrown in homes and hospitals, locked away as if they are mad." Werner looked to Jean and Giordano, who nodded in agreement. "Anyone who did not fit. Anyone who needed sanctuary. I was thinking of her when I hired Jean and Giordano, knowing what they were facing in Paris—no work, the looks they got...I thought I could offer them more.

"As time wore on, the face of our troupe changed, and soon the only original members were Serge and Odélie. Serge realized sooner than I did that we now had a large group of people who were not only performers, but who relied on us to keep them alive. I made myself more German when war was talked of. I spoke German, I shook Nazi hands, I bribed. I got myself so deep in lies that by the time war did break out we had to see this through. And then, one day, a stranger climbed aboard our train, and we gave him a job. A stranger who could be anyone. A stranger who could find out the truth and give us all away."

"I would never—" Michel began. Werner held up his palm to silence him.

"You cannot trust everyone, Michel. I just hope that I have not made a mistake in trusting you with this."

Michel sat for a moment, digesting everything. *Frieda is not Werner's wife or girlfriend. Werner is not the man I thought he was. The troupe is in more danger than I realized.*

"It is a lot," Jean said. "I'd understand if you ran away, to be honest. We are in a very shaky predicament now, Michel. Most of us are Jewish, and if not Jewish, we have our own secrets that would land us in prison, or worse."

"I have one question," Michel said.

Werner smiled. "I suppose you have the right to ask questions now, after I forbade you for so long."

"Anton. I saw you pay off that German soldier. I saw it with my own eyes, so don't deny it."

"I won't. I did pay him."

"Why? Why would you want to get rid of Anton?"

"I didn't pay them to take him away. I paid them so they would let us leave. Anton was once a politician, you know. He left politics and joined a group—now we call them the resistance, but back then it was just a bunch of politicians and academics who understood what was happening and wanted to stop it from getting this far. He wrote articles in newspapers, pamphlets—all sorts of things. I met him when he lived in Marseille. He was in trouble then, even before my German cousins arrived. He had written something for a newspaper, an investigative piece of sorts, highlighting the corruption and fascism of a few politicians, judges and high-ranking officers. Let us say that they did not take kindly to his accusations and he needed to disappear, quickly.

"I met him at a friend's house, just after this friend had married for the third time. My friend was helping him then—another one of us who could not stop talking, fighting and wanting to help. He asked me to take Anton with me. I did. What else could I do? He proved adept at the trapeze—strong, supple. He promised he would not cause trouble...but this war, Michel, it has sent people mad. He could not resist getting involved, and started up again with his damned radio and his leaflets. Remember when we were in Toulouse, the three-day event we held? He spent a lot of his time helping send messages over the wireless radio in one of his contacts' houses. I didn't know then, but after the raid, after Herr Köhler asked for our papers and began a search, I knew something was wrong—that they suspected us. Anton came clean. He offered to give himself up. I told him not to, that we would leave at dawn and get out before they asked any more questions. It turns out that we were just not quick enough. It's hard to hide a circus when you look like us. I couldn't get him to safety, and for the rest of my days I will regret not being able to save him."

Werner stood and sighed. "I think it is time for me to go to bed now."

Jean and Giordano stood too, the trio wobbling towards their caravans. As they did, Michel noticed a shadow melt back into the night. Then he shook his head. It was a trick of the light, nothing more. The evening had been so full of ghost stories he could not help feeling haunted.

He retreated to the barn and lay down on the straw, his coat covering him, and listened to the creak of the wood as it settled to sleep, the rest of the troupe already in their beds, only one light still burning from inside Werner's caravan, his memories keeping him company until dawn.

CHAPTER TEN

Henri Le Comte

Michel awoke to the crow of a cockerel and the snuffle of Coquette's wet nose on his cheek. He turned over and ruffled her head; she gave him a lick in reply.

He heard the morning break around him—Jean and Giordano arguing over the first batch of coffee by the fire, Madame Geneviève warming up her voice along with the song of the waking birds, Serge grunting and coughing up thick black spit from the pipes he smoked in the evening, and then a voice he had not heard for a while: Frieda talking to Isabelle, her laugh floating over to him.

He did not move, wanting to take a moment to register everything he had been told the night before. Part of him felt afraid—afraid that the secrets of the troupe were too much for him to carry—what if they were found? Would he be taken with them?

Claudette whinnied next to him, and he stood and patted her nose. "I'm a little worse for wear today," he told her.

She nuzzled into him and he heard Frieda laugh once more. As soon as he did, his fear was tucked away, replaced with happiness, with hope.

The troupe spent the day deciding on who would perform that evening, and what they would wear. Michel was desperate to see

Frieda, but she flitted about, her spirits high, her laughter infecting everyone, and he contented himself by listening to her, watching her and preparing the horses for their upcoming performance.

"We all ready?" Werner's voice boomed.

The troupe lined up in pairs, ready to walk their colorful selves into town. Michel held back and saw Werner assist Frieda down the caravan steps. She was wearing her short gold sequined dress, her long legs stockinged. She allowed Werner to take her arm and lead her towards Claudette.

"May I?" she asked Michel.

He did not answer but helped her sit side-saddle on Claudette, ready to walk into town. Odélie appeared around the side of her wagon and stared at Frieda, then at Michel. Her costume complemented the dancing red sequins of Claudette's bridle and saddle.

"She doesn't even match her." Odélie pouted.

"Doesn't matter," Werner retorted. He mounted Beau and trotted out in front, soon followed by Frieda, then Giordano on Bisou.

The others followed on foot; Kacper playing his accordion, Hugo on the horn and Jean banging on a drum.

Michel took up the rear and found Odélie at his side. "You gave her my horse," she said, her expression wounded, then ran lightly away to join the triplets. She did not look back at him.

"Isn't this fun?" Lucien appeared with Isabelle. "She could not be happier, could you, *ma chérie*?" Before she could answer, Lucien continued: "The colors, the music! You are lucky, Michel. So lucky."

Michel looked at the old man, whose cheeks were rosy as a child's and his eyes just as wide.

By the time they reached the square, Werner was already chatting to the thirty or so villagers who had gathered outside the café to watch. Gehring sat in prime position, a glass of beer in one hand and a cigar in the other, his expression already entranced by the colorful spectacle. He was the only one, though. The other spectators had their hands jammed into their pockets, their faces blank, their eyes watching the strangers' movements. Michel felt more nervous about the unfriendly crowd than he did about the five or so German soldiers who lounged behind Gehring at the café.

Children sat on the ground by their parents' feet, chins in their cupped hands, waiting, ready for the show to begin. They too seemed bored and restless, as if they had been forced to come and see this menagerie of outsiders against their will.

Hugo, his face painted as an Auguste—his nose red, his wig a mass of ginger curls, with blue-and-white striped trousers—climbed onto stilts and waved to the children who littered the ground. Suddenly, they became more animated. To them, the troupe had become something else—magical creatures, not the downtrodden outsiders of before.

Their squeals of delight echoed around the square, and in an instant it seemed to Michel that the town relaxed. Mothers took their hands out of their aprons and began to talk gregariously to their neighbors; men lit cigarettes and went into the café, returning with mugs of beer and short glasses of wine.

As the sky darkened, lights came on around the square, casting shadows on the performers' costumes that made them appear brighter and more exotic.

Kacper played tunes on his accordion as the troupe performed all at once, so that the spectators were captivated wherever they chose to look.

Near the church, Gino the monkey danced and accepted coins from children in his small blue cravat. Outside the café, the triplets backflipped and somersaulted, whilst Odélie became Serge's assistant, handing him knives to swallow, each one longer, sharper and shinier than the last. In the center of the square, Frieda rode Claudette, standing up on tiptoes as the mare trotted, then jumping to the ground before springing back into the saddle with one deft leap. Jean and Giordano acted out their story of the boy and his shadow, the mothers dabbing at their eyes when Giordano sang of his lament at having no friends. Vassily went from child to child, magically pulling coins, scarves and bonbons from their ears, whilst Madame Rosie told fortunes and sold charms at the café.

Michel realized that Lucien and Isabelle had left him alone, and so he perched himself on a low brick wall, just far away enough to see the whole spectacle as it unfolded. He lit a cigarette and watched Frieda, who never tired, never lost her footing or her smile.

Soon a fiddler appeared, one of the townsfolk, then a villager with a French horn and one with a hand-drum. Each set up next to Kacper, and somehow they found common tunes they knew, and the air became filled with notes, high then low, fast then slow, which encouraged feet to tap against the cobbles, heads to bob in time with the music, until Gehring himself could not sit still any longer and grabbed the hand of the Madame from the café, and began to dance. More people joined in, and whilst the children watched Vassily, Giordano and Jean, the adults danced and laughed.

Michel saw Frieda tie Claudette's reins to a railing and she too began to dance, her hair flowing behind her. Now and again her whole head tilted back, free and enraptured by the music.

Michel wanted to join her, but he did not want to disturb the vision of her wild, liberated and happy, laughing at her father Werner as he performed a complex tap dance, his little legs moving quickly. The triplets had for the first time separated from each other, and held the children's hands to sway from side to side with them. Even Serge was taken by the merriment, and smiled when a young woman in a red coat asked him to dance with her.

Madame Geneviève had not wanted to take part in the performance, but Michel saw her rise from her chair at the café and proffer her hand to Monsieur Armand. At first he shook his head and waved his hands. But then, strangely, something came over him as the jolly tune slowed to an old folk waltz and each person paired off.

With his knobbly hand, he allowed Geneviève to gently pull him to his feet, and he danced slowly, rocking left to right, his head on her shoulder and tears in his eyes.

"Will you dance with me?" Odélie appeared at Michel's side, a gentle curve on her lips.

He took her hand and allowed himself to be guided into the square.

"Thank you for your apology, Michel," she said quietly as he spun her slowly. "I know I say the wrong things sometimes. It's habit."

"I'm just sorry I did not say it sooner." His eyes strayed to Frieda, only for a moment.

"She's beautiful, isn't she?"

"She is," Michel agreed.

When the tune changed, he felt a tap on his shoulder. Frieda.

"May I?" she asked.

Michel turned to her as Odélie moved away. He took Frieda's hand and wrapped the other around her waist.

"You look happy," she said.

"I am."

As Michel led Frieda around the square, as she laughed and then rested her head on his shoulder so her hair tickled his cheek, Michel spotted Odélie. She was talking to one of the young German soldiers, her body close to his, her hand resting on his forearm, but her eyes never left Michel and her smile had faltered—it was clear that his apology had not yet erased the hurt he had caused and he felt a pang of guilt.

Kacper changed his tune and Michel knew it well—a song he had heard in Paris, at Odette's café—"La Java Bleue." As he danced with Frieda, he began to sing the words—words full of love for the person you danced with, of not wanting to let them go, but hold them close and try to keep the promise of love.

"I did not know you could sing." Frieda looked up at him and he stopped.

"I can't! Well, I can, but not well."

"I like it," she said. "Carry on."

He held her tight and sang the words—a song for dancing the Java with your love, the one you could not imagine life without.

By midnight the crowd had dispersed, one by one sluggishly walking home to their beds, children carried asleep on their fathers' shoulders, women giggling, giddy from too much wine and fun.

The troupe were also tired as they trudged back to the farm, Lucien leading the way with Coquette, who danced around her master's heels, not yet worn out from the evening.

Michel had to stay behind—the horses had, as horses do, left hefty, steaming deposits around the square, and he had been tasked by Werner to clear it before he could rest his head.

He finished shoveling the square within an hour, stuffing the dung into a wheelbarrow given to him by the priest, who had visited the festivities for a cursory glance and a glass of Lucien's wine.

As Michel wheeled the squeaking barrow down the lane towards the farm, he whistled "La Java Bleue" and thought of Odette in her café in Paris. He remembered the words, tested them, then sang them out into the night.

As he finished the final line, he heard footsteps behind him. He stopped the wheelbarrow and listened. Then he looked behind him, but the dark was absolute. Nothing. He started walking again, the squeaking of the wheel too loud in the night.

Still, he walked slowly, counting his steps, realizing that an echo was indeed behind him. He stopped once more. Before he could turn, a heavy force hit the back of his head with a thump. The last thing Michel heard was the twit-twoo of an owl as he fell unconscious onto the dirt track.

*

Michel awoke to a bright light above him.

"You're awake!" Frieda's voice, disembodied, floated around him. He closed his eyes against the glare.

"Where am I?" Michel's voice was scratchy.

"In Lucien's house."

"Frieda?"

"Yes?"

"What happened?"

"Someone attacked you."

"My head hurts."

"It will. You were hit."

"On my head?"

"Yes. You were hit on your head."

"Ask him his name." *A voice, worried—Giordano.*

"He knows his name, don't you, Michel?" *A question. A new voice. Jean.*

"Well, he does now, you foolish man! You are telling him his name!"

"Hush! Both of you. Let him rest. See? He is falling asleep."

Michel opened his eyes. He remembered the light; now there was none. He was rocking slightly in his bed, side to side, side to side.

"Frieda?"

"It's me." Giordano's small, round face appeared over him. "Do you want to sit up?"

"Who is rocking me?"

"No one. You are in our caravan."

"We are moving?"

"Yes. Do you want to sit up? I have water, some bread maybe?"

Michel allowed Giordano to place his hands underneath him and help him to a sitting position. Then he tucked pillows behind his back and handed Michel a glass of water. He turned up the lamp to brighten the space, and colors suddenly jumped about in front of Michel's eyes so that he had to blink a few times before they settled down into shapes he could recognize.

"What happened to me?"

"You were attacked."

"By whom?"

"Werner has a suspicion that maybe it was someone from the town, someone who didn't like us being there and thought this would make us leave."

"How long have I been asleep?"

"A day or so.

"Why are we moving?"

"We are heading for a town near Paris. Werner has friends there— he wired them—and we can stay with them and be safe for a while."

"Paris..." Michel said.

"Werner says we are safer when we know exactly where the enemy is, where we will hear what is happening and when. He thinks we are no longer safe in small villages."

Michel shook his head and winced in pain. He raised his hand and his fingers found his bandaged skull, the back of his head swollen and hot to the touch.

"Careful now, Michel. Careful."

"I left Paris because it was not safe."

"We are not going *to* Paris," Giordano said earnestly. "*Near.* Werner says we can get papers and perhaps leave France. He is trying. He has kept us safe so far; we must trust him. You must."

Michel drank down the water and Giordano refilled his glass.

"Madame Geneviève did not come with us. Neither did Vassily," Giordano said. "They have gone further south. Geneviève shaved her beard. She said her face had never felt so cold."

Despite himself, and the pain and sadness he felt at more people leaving the troupe, Michel laughed. It began as a chuckle, then as Giordano joined in, the laughter became loud and breathless, tears streaming down their faces.

"Her face was cold!" Michel laughed. "It was cold!"

"You know"—Giordano wiped the tears from his face—"she looked so beautiful without the beard. I was sorry I had not taken her for dinner or danced with her. I shall miss her." His smile disappeared.

"And Vassily."

"And him."

"Thank God we still have Hugo. I could not go on without génépy." Giordano shook his head sadly.

"Where is Frieda?"

"In Madame Rosie's caravan. She is keeping her company. She was sad to see Geneviève go."

"My head hurts." Suddenly, Michel felt nauseous.

"Lie down, lie down. That is enough for now. Close your eyes and rest. I will tell Jean to slow down a little, make it less bumpy back here."

Michel lay back and closed his eyes, listening to Giordano speak to Jean at the front of the wagon. He was not sure if Jean slowed or not, but soon the rocking soothed his head and he fell into a dreamless sleep.

The next time he awoke, Bisou's face was above his.

"Get out of the way!" Giordano was there again, pushing the small pony back. "He was in Werner's caravan so you could rest, but he ate a silk-covered pillow and Werner went mad. So, he's here with us again."

"I need to sit up," Michel said, but as soon as he did, the swimming in his head made him sick.

"Stay there. Stay still. We'll stop soon. Just rest, Michel. Just rest."

*

Three days followed of Michel being cared for by either Giordano or Frieda. He stayed awake a little longer each time, but soon his head would swim and throb with pain and he had to sleep once more. Madame Rosie brewed him a tea that took the edge off the headache, and applied a poultice to the wound.

That evening, Frieda appeared and woke him as her quick fingers took the poultice away. She wiped his face with a cloth, then held a glass of water to his lips.

"You are looking better." She sat beside him and stroked some hair from his face.

"I feel a little better now." He smiled at her.

"You have a letter," she said, and placed an envelope on his chest. "It came the morning we left Lucien's."

Michel sat up slowly, then saw the familiar writing of Bertrand. He opened the letter and tried to read, but the words jumbled and ran into one another.

"Can I read it for you?" she asked.

"Please."

Dearest Michel,

Once more your letter has cheered me completely. There is no news here apart from bad. The Germans seem able to defeat anyone in their path. I heard in Odette's that Jewish refugees are sent to camps in the south—have you seen such a thing on your travels?

It all seems so hopeless, but when I saw your letter my heart leapt with a little joy.

Alas, you tell me of your own experiences, and have explained why the woman you cherish so much cannot be yours. It makes sense to me now. I am sorry, Michel. But take solace that you have known how it feels to fall in love.

Your letter was short; you talked of cold, of weather. I can tell from your tone how bleak things have become. You wouldn't ever let me know how bad it is, so I can only guess.

I enclose in this letter a few francs—not much. I hope it finds you. There are many letters that go missing now, and this may well disappear into the void, especially with money inside. But it is worth the risk to know I have tried to help you as much as I can.

I did sell my father's watch—it bought me a little to get me by. I worry that this winter will be cold—too cold for these old bones—and with the higher cost of food now, I do fear that my savings will not last me long at all.

Pah! Listen to me, an old man indeed—talking of money and heating and the cost of food. When did I become an old man, Michel? It seems to me that it was just a year ago that Amélie and I met—I was young and full of love, full of hope for my life. I wonder what joy will be left in my life now. I look in the mirror and see my gray head, my wrinkled face, and sometimes I ask my reflection, "Who are you?" An impostor in my mirror!

Please write to me again, Michel. Do not fear telling me things—tell me everything. I wait in earnest for your next letter.

Be safe, my friend.

Yours,
Bertrand

Frieda stopped talking and Michel took her hand in his.
"I would love to meet him one day," she said.
"And I hope you will."
"You must write to him when you feel better."

"I will. Frieda, the letter talks of you and Werner. I shouldn't have said anything to Bertrand...it's just, I thought you were his. Werner's."

"Hush. No need to explain. Werner filled me in. I must admit I found the confusion a little funny."

"And what did you think of what I told Bertrand?"

"Cherish. I love that word." She kissed him lightly on the cheek, then helped him to lie back down. "I am glad you cherish me, Michel. Know that I cherish you."

On the fourth day, Michel woke to the sound of bells tolling the hour. He sat up and found he was alone. He dressed and opened the door. He was in a field behind a graveyard, the horses grazing nearby. The church bell stopped—four o'clock.

He sat on the caravan's wooden steps and lit a cigarette. He heard an accordion play a familiar tune in the distance and knew they were performing—small tricks, dances, anything to earn money before they moved on once more towards Werner's friend and the safety that he promised. It was strange to think of the Big Top lying crumpled in a box. Although tattered and aged, it was still the jewel that attracted people to the circus.

In the distance, Michel saw the sky darkening to its autumnal deep navy. Within weeks, it would change to the pitchest of blacks with only the stars to light the night.

He thought of Paris, and how the lights burned brightly so that the winter sky was never quite completely dark like here in the countryside. Was it still like that?

He shivered and retreated inside. He lit a small fire in the stove and made coffee. Wrapping his coat around his shoulders, he sat next to the fire and dozed, awaiting his friends, his family, his love—Frieda—to return.

*

"Michel!" her voice sounded faraway, worried. He tried to reach out to her.

"Michel!" His dream dissolved and she was in front of him, tears streaming down her face, her cheeks flushed, her breathing rapid. "Quick, please come! Please!"

Michel followed her out into the night, weaving through the gravestones. His head pounded and he felt dizzy, but he did not stop.

As they rounded the corner of the church, Serge appeared, covered in blood, supporting Werner, who was battered and beaten.

Michel helped Serge to carry Werner to his caravan. No one spoke. Only the grunting and breathing of Serge and Michel could be heard, punctuated with a gurgle of blood from Werner's nose as he tried to breathe.

Inside the caravan, Michel could see the state of Werner; his nose was broken and bent to the side, both eyes were swollen shut, and, as Serge undressed him, they glimpsed a deep gash in his side that oozed crimson.

"Frieda, get Madame Rosie now! Go!" Michel ordered. "Serge, fetch Giordano or Hugo and ask them for the génépy. Ask Jean to bring a needle and some thread. Quickly."

Michel was no doctor, but he treated Werner as he had once treated a tearaway stallion in Paris that had caught himself on a barbed fence. Michel had calmed him as he cried in pain and tended to the wounds with swift hands.

"Michel…" Werner tried to speak, his voice muffled by his swollen lip.

"Hush now. Hush. It will be fine."

Madame Rosie brought with her a potent liquid, a deep green that reminded Michel of the stagnant water of the Seine in the summer months. She poured it down Werner's throat, and within seconds his breathing calmed.

"It won't last long. You must be quick," she said. "I will help. You close the wound; I will sort his nose."

Michel held the wound closed as best he could, and Rosie, with a quick movement, snapped Werner's nose back into place. She then cleaned his mouth, his lip and his nostrils, so that he could breathe easier.

Michel saw he was missing two teeth as Rosie plugged the bloody holes with cotton wool.

"What happened?" Giordano burst in, the génépy in his hand, Jean behind, carrying the thick sewing needle he used to mend his costumes.

Michel grabbed the alcohol and poured it over the wound, then sewed it shut, the stitches pronounced and haphazard.

When he'd finished, Madame Rosie asked everyone to leave so she could clean and dress the ringmaster. "I'll watch him for a while," she said. "Go and get some rest. If he wakes, I can give him some more of my remedy."

No one argued. As if they all knew where to go, they followed Frieda and poured into Jean's caravan, Serge still wearing his shirt splattered with red.

"I should change," he said to nobody in particular, as Frieda handed around tumblers of whisky.

"What happened?" Michel asked.

"He would not stop. He wanted to drink after we had performed in the town square. Just me and him. We drank. No, wait—Odélie was there too. She was talking to some soldiers who were drinking and laughing. I told Werner that we should leave, but he insisted we stay. The others were at the restaurant, having a small meal provided by the chef for free—he liked Frieda, I think. I don't know . . ." Serge stopped, and Michel saw tears in his eyes.

"I told him—I said, 'You are drunk, we should go to the others, have something to eat,' but he did not want to listen. Finally I convinced him and we stood outside, getting some air, and then there he was—this soldier from the bar. He asked us for papers and Werner said he had forgotten them. The soldier, he wanted money, he wouldn't leave us alone. We started to walk away, and then suddenly Werner was on the ground, blood coming from his side. Then I fought the man, I punched him, but he was strong and I fell and he hit Werner, he hit him and hit him and I tried to stop him, I tried to stop..."

Serge held his head in his hands, his large shoulders suddenly smaller as they heaved up and down with each sob.

"Clean yourself up, Serge." Frieda placed her hand on his shoulder. "We need to leave, now. Jean, Giordano, get the triplets to help you pack up. Michel, ride with Serge and take our caravan. I will stay with Werner."

Michel watched her as she continued giving instructions to the others. Her makeup was smeared from her tears, but her face was set as she took charge—she was the new ringmaster.

Maybe it came from the incident, maybe it came from the quiet creak of wheels on the rutted road and the horses' hooves clopping, or maybe it came from weariness, the knowledge that everything was now different and could not be undone. Whatever it was, Serge softened towards Michel that evening.

"How is your head now?" he asked as he navigated Claudette and Beau, who diligently pulled their master as he slept.

"I feel dizzy sometimes. The air helps."

"You will be fine. I have been hit so many times on the head I am surprised it is still attached!" He chuckled then stopped, as if realizing the impropriety of it, and turned quickly to look at the caravan behind him as if Werner had heard.

"Do you think this is a good idea? I feel foolish to have escaped south just to return north again."

"I don't know. You can see, can't you, that we are not safe anywhere? It does not matter where we stop—it can never be for long. We will always stand out—we did before the war, we do more so now, and it is certain that if we live, if the war ends, we will be at odds with the world once again."

"Where is this friend of Werner's? Giordano said somewhere near Paris?"

"Just outside the city. He's an old friend, a good man. He has money and land."

"And we'll be safe there?"

"Safer than we have been."

A cold wind suddenly swept over them, and Michel shivered and wrapped his coat tighter around him.

"Winter's coming," Serge said.

"I used to like winter. The fires my neighbor would build, the wine we drank, the books we read as the snow softly tapped on the windowpanes..."

"I hate it."

Michel wanted to ask why, but instead lit a cigarette. He offered one to Serge, who accepted.

"I have never seen you smoke anything apart from your pipe," Michel said.

"I don't often smoke cigarettes—they clog the throat more than the pipe, I find. I need my throat to be open and well. Swallowing a sword is not as easy as you think."

"I never thought it was."

"I saw my first sword swallower in Paris, you know?"

"Yes, there are many circuses there."

"We are not a real circus though, Michel. We are a traveling group of misfits. Not like Cirque Medrano! Do you know it?"

"At the edge of Montmartre? I know it."

"I wanted to work there, but I could not. I was not talented enough. Werner, he worked for Medrano a little in his youth. He wanted his own show to travel, though. He said everyone should have the chance to see his performers."

"You are from Paris then?"

Serge shook his head. "Poland."

They lapsed into silence once more, until Serge broke it with a cough and flicked his cigarette to the ground, the sparks flying.

"You should not smoke so much, Michel. My father smoked. Every day. I cannot remember ever seeing him without a cigarette in his mouth."

"He's in Poland now?"

"No. He is dead. What family I have left are in Paris. Do you think Werner will live?"

Michel turned to Serge. "Yes, I do. He's strong."

Serge nodded.

"Where I come from is a small town in Poland, near the border," Serge began. "Have you ever been? I don't suppose you have—not somewhere to visit just now, regardless. Should I tell you more?"

Michel nodded and Serge continued, not pausing or really seeming to care whether Michel wanted to hear or not.

"It once was Germany, but after the first war, Poland took it back. My father was Polish, my mother German. But it did not matter so much back then what country you were from. Serge isn't what my parents called me; I was born with the first name Zygmunt. I was my father's apprentice—an ironmonger. I was no one and I was happy with that. But early on, before this war began, things changed for us. Our town grew hostile—Germans against Poles, against Jews, against everyone. My father could see where things were heading so we moved to France, to my uncle's home, and there, I grew up, from the age of twelve.

"My father worked with my uncle, both ironmongers, and I was still their apprentice. In my uncle's workshop hung two swords—swords he said were made by my great-grandfather for a battle. He had made hundreds of them, my uncle said, and these two he had kept for himself; to remember the war, those killed, and of course his skill.

"The handles of the swords were gilded, and he had added gems, red and blue, that glinted every time the light caught them. I loved to look at them—just look. My uncle said I could not touch them.

"I was perhaps fifteen years old when I went to see the circus with my family. When I say 'circus,' it was little more than a bunch of travelers playing tricks and telling fortunes. There was one performer, though, who claimed to be the strongest man and who could swallow swords whole.

"I wanted to watch him do this—I wanted to see a man who could defeat a mighty sword and walk away alive.

"My uncle and father told me I was silly and childish. I was almost a man myself—I was to do away with children's magic and illusion. Whilst they drank beer at a bar, I snuck away with my cousin, who you know."

"I do?"

"Odélie—my cousin. She flirts a lot, makes people think we were, or are something, but it's not like that. She just enjoys making men look at her, and back then she was the same. She wanted to see the performer too—not because he swallowed swords, but because he had winked at her earlier and she wanted to find out exactly what that wink meant.

"We found the man in amongst a crowd three or four deep, and pushed to the front. Odélie stood ahead of me, smiling at the man who simply and expertly swallowed swords of different sizes, as if he were a frog who could stick out his tongue for an insect. It sounds disgusting—and it would horrify most—but to me it was so extraordinary that it had me riveted.

"When he finished his act, Odélie made her way over to him and they spoke. I watched him afar. He placed his hand on her arm, and I knew they would soon depart together.

"'Monsieur,' he said to me. 'I wish to take you and your cousin for a nightcap. Will you join us?'

"I looked at Odélie—her smile said it all, and I could not begrudge her what she wanted. I agreed.

"He was a kind man who was flattered by my interest in his craft, and he taught me what he knew over the weeks and months that he and Odélie were together. It was a secret for her and me; my father would be angry that I was even thinking about joining the circus, and my uncle would disown Odélie if he suspected she was not a virgin.

"When the man left to join another circus in the south, Odélie convinced me to try out at the Cirque Medrano. Like I told you, I was not good enough. I went to a local bar that evening to drown my sorrows. Odélie came too and tried to cheer me up, telling me stories of the things she had done as a child—you know, like stealing a tart meant for dinner, or how she would hide under the bed to scare her father. While I drank an entire bottle of red until I could no longer think, Odélie had chatted up a small man, a man who called himself Werner Neumann. 'I have a circus,' he said. 'A traveling circus. Your beautiful cousin tells me you are a talented sword swallower?'

"I nodded. The wine had deadened my tongue.

"'Tomorrow, come and see me,' he said. He gave me his Paris address on a scrap of paper.

"I went. Of course I did. So did Odélie. I got a job. I argued with my father. I left. And Odélie followed. Although she had no talent as such, she learned how to ride, how to do acrobatic tricks. She learned how to get men to like her, to rely on her. And now, here we are."

An owl flew close and startled the horses, who stomped and chaffed at the bit. Michel soothed them until they walked on, their ears twitching for any new sound.

"Do you think Werner will be OK?" Serge asked once more.

"I do."

"I hope you are right. I am not sure what we would do without him."

"I don't think we have to worry about that for now."

Serge nodded and flicked at the reins, spurring the horses on. "Can I have another cigarette?"

"You can."

CHAPTER ELEVEN

Le Cirque des Amis

En route to their new home, in the region of Senlis outside Paris, the trees had shed their rust-colored clothes, leaving naked limbs whose skeletons felt no cold; in fact, they welcomed it, allowing the early morning frost to cling to them.

Michel, instead of shedding his own clothes, gained a few more. First was a patchwork-knitted jacket that Geneviève had left for him, then on top of that a long black woolen coat which Odélie said was left behind by some customers long ago, yet smelled strongly of cigarettes and a tangy aftershave Michel could have sworn he knew. He thought once or twice to ask her about the coat's true origin, yet the bare branches of the trees swaying in the cold morning made him think again.

"We are not far," Serge said. It was a Friday evening, and the sun had just begun its descent over the horizon.

As Serge navigated the road in the twilight, Michel soon became aware of a hazy shadow in the distance.

"This is it?"

"This is it," Serge answered, as a clump of brick buildings came into view.

The main house was set in an L-shape, the downstairs windows burning with lights from inside. A small gravel drive led to stables and a barn. But Serge did not stop; he continued to maneuver the horses past the stables, out into a field at the back of the house where the wheels sludged in the wet grass.

"We'll get bogged down," Michel said.

Serge ignored him and encouraged the horses on, both with their ears set back, foam at their mouths from the strain.

One by one, the others pulled into the field. Michel climbed down once Serge stopped and looked about him—on the left was the shadow of a cathedral's tower, and the rooftops of houses disappearing into the dark.

"This is it?" Odélie lit a cigarette.

"What were you expecting?" Madame Rosie asked.

"You said Paris, Jean. This is not Paris."

"He said *near* Paris," Giordano corrected. "This is near, is it not?"

"I can't see it." Odélie looked towards the horizon, as if the Eiffel Tower would appear before her eyes.

"It's dark; wait awhile," Jean joked.

"I suggest we all get some sleep," Serge snapped, dark, puffy circles under his eyes.

"Fine." Odélie climbed back inside her caravan, her voice loud as she complained to the triplets about their lackluster camp.

"Michel, you and I will stay with Werner. Hugo, Kacper—don't bother to camp. Find a space with Jean and Giordano. Get some rest. It will be fine. Frieda, it may be better for you to sleep with Madame Rosie tonight. I snore, and Michel can tend to your father."

She squeezed his arm. "He's asleep for now but he has a slight fever. Keep mopping his brow and please wake me if you need anything."

Serge nodded, and Michel took her hand—lightly, briefly—before she followed Rosie.

Michel unhitched the horses and let them graze. "We need something more for them."

"We'll sort it at daylight."

"Look, I know it's dark, but they need a stable," Michel insisted.

"And I *said* we'll sort it come daylight."

Reluctantly, Michel left the horses outside and sat in Werner's caravan, watching as Serge gave Werner water to drink and placed a cool cloth on his forehead.

"He's still sleepy," Michel said stupidly.

"It's a fever. And infection. We will need to get a doctor first thing."

"I thought you said Werner had friends here?"

Serge nodded and stretched out on the sofa. "They'll come. They'll find us. They know we have arrived."

Before Michel could ask more, Serge closed his eyes and it seemed to Michel he was instantly asleep. Michel stoked the log burner, feeding it and listening to it crackle as Serge snored, and Werner muttered strange words in his sleep.

Michel, though weary from the journey, took out some paper and a pen, and wrote back to Bertrand.

Dearest friend,

I received your letters—Lucien kept them safe for me and gave them to me when I returned to Vodable.

It was a joy to hear your voice, so distinct through your writing, and yet it brought me sadness and fear to hear of the way your spirit has dimmed since I left.

I understand, of course. I think we are all changed in such a small amount of time, and I wonder if we will ever go back to being who we once were.

You are right that the Germans are everywhere now. I have seen them many times with my own eyes. They fill the roads with their jeeps and black cars, which frighten me. There are more people on the roads too. On our journey here (we are now in Senlis, not far from you!) we saw many people carrying their belongings, their children. It reminded me of the day I left Paris—that same feeling of panic, of having the urge to leave and yet the fear of not knowing where you will end up.

These people on the roads were from other countries too; there were some who had traveled from Belgium and were picking their way further south. We passed them on our way up north.

You are wondering now why we are here? I am too. There is a part of me that feels we should have stayed south, but we had no money, and rationing was making things hard. It has got so bad, Bertrand, that Werner thinks we are safer with his mysterious friend—who I am yet to meet. He has talked of getting papers for us to leave France. I need to be honest; I don't think it will be possible. I think he is running scared like everyone else, just trying to find something, anything, to cling on to.

He is unwell. He was attacked by some soldiers in a bar. The truth is, I have come to like him. In my last letter to you, I told you of his wife. I have to tell you I was wrong. Frieda is not his wife, but his daughter. I wish I could tell you more, but as things are, I cannot.

As I sit here and write, I can hear the drone of planes overhead. Whose planes, I do not know. I like to think it is the British, perhaps here to end it all?

I have not eaten much for a while now. None of us have. Bread, coffee, cigarettes, and soup when we find something to put in it. I imagine if we carry on like this, we will soon disappear. I cannot help but remember how lucky I was to be able to buy mutton before, eat pastries and cakes. My stomach rumbles at the memory.

Are you eating, Bertrand? I hope you are keeping well. I thank you for the francs you sent; they helped indeed. Please do not send more. They would not reach me anyway, as I am not sure when or if I will see Lucien again. Keep the money for yourself; keep warm and fed.

I wish I could help you. The city is not far from here and I wonder if it is safe for me to visit you? I think it would be fine, but it is the getting there which may cause problems—I cannot very well ride into the city on a circus horse or with a caravan in tow!

I will write again soon.

Yours,
Michel

A knock on the door woke Michel. He had fallen asleep on a chair next to the fire that now burned low.

Before he could answer, the door was opened to reveal a tall thin man, dressed head to toe in a black suit, his beard neatly trimmed to a point and his eyes the brightest of blues.

"You made it!" The man said. "Do you know that your horses are in the next field?"

"They don't have a stable," Michel said.

"Indeed, they do. Indeed, they do!" The man's voice was melodious, his accent mixed, from countries Michel could not place.

"May I?" the man asked and stepped inside. "Ah, Serge, sleeping like the baby he is. And Werner. Oh God! Werner. What happened?"

"He was attacked."

"Good God. I'll go home right now, get my doctor. Wait here. Ah, you are already here...but don't go anywhere!"

The thin man practically leapt out of the caravan, and Michel watched his long legs sprint through the dewy grass towards the shadow of the large house.

Serge grunted then woke. "It's freezing, Michel, close the door!"

"There was a man here."

Serge sat. "What kind?"

"Tall, thin. He went to get his doctor."

"Henri," Serge said. "I told you he knew we were here. Michel, get that fire going. I am going for a piss."

Serge left and a bemused Michel added more fuel, then checked on Werner, waking him gently so that he could drink some water before collapsing back into a fitful sleep.

Serge returned with Frieda in tow.

"You scared Madame Rosie," she scolded Serge. "She opened the curtain, and there you were!"

Serge shrugged.

Frieda went straight to her father and stroked back his damp hair from his forehead. "Papa?"

Werner's eyes moved under the lids, but he did not wake.

"He's coming!" The door was flung open once more and the tall thin man called Henri was back, his cheeks flushed with exertion.

"Henri!" Frieda walked towards him, and he kissed her on both cheeks. "It is good to see you."

"And you, my dear, and you. And of course, dear Serge."

"This is Michel," Frieda introduced him.

"Michel, of course. How do you do?" The man doffed his hat flamboyantly, then laughed at Michel's confused expression. "I am a little over the top—it is my lineage, you see."

"Henri is a count," Frieda proudly said.

"Or so he would have people believe," Serge grunted.

"I am a count. A sir. A prince amongst paupers. And, I am at your service, Serge, as always."

"He lives in the house we passed; this is his land," Serge said. "Not that it always was his."

"It is mine. In name, on the title and in my heart. A gracious widow, God bless her soul, left everything to me. Can you imagine, Michel—a whole house and this land, just for the likes of me?"

Michel felt himself instantly warm to Henri: a natural entertainer, a comic and clown yet no one's fool, all rolled into one.

"Now, we must get Werner back to my house. There he can rest." Henri sat down by the fire. "Serge, coffee, perhaps? Even these days it is still proper to offer a guest a drink," he twinkled.

Michel watched as the burly bulk of Serge moved awkwardly around the small caravan, finding the kettle to put over the stove, cups, coffee. Henri, it seemed, was a magician as well, to be able to tame the wild sword swallower.

"Where are the others? I see only four caravans."

"They left, one by one. Money was tight," Serge said.

"Money? No, I think more likely they were scared by our German friends, no? When Werner wired me that the train had to be sold, I wept, my dears, I did! I knew what would happen. It is good you have come to me. You will be safe here."

"For how long?" Serge passed Henri his coffee.

"For as long as I can keep you safe." He threw up his hands. "You know, Serge, you do doubt me. When have I ever let you down before?"

As he spoke another knock at the door disturbed them; this time two of Henri's servants with a car they had managed to drive over the wet grass.

"Ah, yes. Let's get Werner into more comfortable surroundings, then bring in the troupe for breakfast. By then the doctor will have been and we will know where we are."

Henri instructed the servants to carry the deadweight of Werner to the car, and they set off towards the house, leaving Michel and Frieda standing in the cold damp field watching the smoke of the exhaust cloud the wintry air.

*

An hour later, the troupe had woken and walked the half-mile to Henri's home.

In the daylight, the farmhouse was more than that. It had been refurbished, the roof re-tiled in red slate, the stone cleaned. To Michel, the house spread far and wide, corridors leading off to rooms filled with secrets. Box hedges lined the drive and a car sat waiting at the front door.

They were ushered in by a servant who did not introduce himself. "He asked you to wait here." He directed them to the left, into an opulent living room, a fire burning in the grate, a chandelier winking overhead.

"I cannot believe we are in the home of a count." Giordano grinned and plonked himself onto one of the sofas, the thick cushions enveloping him.

"He is many things and nothing," Serge said. "He is an artist, that I know. He is famous for his paintings all over Europe. They say that even the Führer has one."

"If by 'they say' you mean 'Henri says,'" Frieda reminded him.

They all found seats, Michel balancing himself awkwardly on a spindly chair that he was sure had once belonged in a palace—its legs were gilded, the cushions a rich plum. Every available wall space was filled with paintings: women in profile, scenes of Paris and London. One portrait stood out more than the others—a young man staring at the painter, a sad smile on his lips, his heavy chocolate eyes following the viewer around the room.

"That one's Henri's," Frieda said.

The painting was titled *Pedro*, a bronze plaque affixed to the frame so that no one would ever need to ask.

"He is like the Count of Monte Cristo," Jean said. "A count yet at the same time not a count. But perhaps not out for revenge like our fictional friend."

"Perhaps he is?" Madame Rosie said.

"So what if he is not a count?" Michel was tired, confused, his hands still cold from the night-time journey. Jean lit a cigarette and passed it to him. Michel was thankful for the small warmth it afforded.

"He is Papa's oldest friend," Frieda began. "They met years ago, the same night he met my mother."

Michel smiled. It was the first time she had called Werner "Papa" in front of everyone, almost as though Henri had reminded her of her past—that she was Werner's little girl. "The summer solstice, in Hungary," Michel remembered. "He was the guest of a count."

Frieda nodded. "Henri—one and the same. He says he is a count of some noble family. A noble family that has bloodlines in all the major countries. He once showed me a family tree—it looked old, crinkled. When I was younger, I always thought that perhaps he was actually Count Dracula. It makes sense: he does not age and leaps about from city to city! Anyway, where was I?"

"Hungary," Giordano said. "And I am. Hungry."

Jean barked a laugh and Frieda shook her head wearily at him.

"Henri so admired the acts at the show that he made sure Papa was able to keep the tradition going. He gave him money, helped with permits, and when things were sometimes difficult, perhaps with the police, he made sure we were fine. He traveled with us and would return to Paris, or Milan, when he needed a break. One night, perhaps just after I first met him, he himself got into trouble. Papa did not tell me what had happened, only that the police, this time, needed to speak with Henri. Papa hid him in our spare room and told me I was not to go in there.

"Of course, I disobeyed. I was fifteen; I could not help myself. When Papa and Serge left the apartment, I knocked gently on the door and Henri told me to enter. His face was battered, much like Papa's is now, and he was crying.

"I held him in my arms as he wept and he told me, 'You should be careful who you love. Who you trust.' I did not know what he meant."

"But Werner got him out of whatever trouble he was in?" Michel asked.

"He did," Serge said.

"What was it, the trouble?" Giordano was ever alert to gossip.

"I was in love, that is all. Unfortunately, it was with the wrong person." Henri's voice broke in from the open door.

"Monsieur Count, I do apologize—" Giordano began.

"No need." He waved the apology away. "Come, breakfast is ready. Let us dine together as friends."

Henri had had his servant lay the table with fresh bread, jams, fruit, steaming pots of coffee and cream, pastries, and even bowls of hot chocolate that the triplets eagerly helped themselves to. Odélie appeared as everyone sat down, still yawning.

"Still too early for you, my dear?" Henri asked.

"I need coffee."

"Too early for me too," Hugo said. "But I made the effort."

"It's because there is food," Odélie said.

"Free, too." Giordano grinned at her.

Kacper sat feeding Gino small scraps of bread, his eyes watchful. Michel suddenly realized that he had never heard Kacper speak.

"The doctor says Werner is fine for now. The fever has lessened, and he shall keep an eye on him," Henri said, smoking a cigarette as his guests ate.

"Thank you," Frieda said. "You cannot know how much we appreciate it."

"How far are we from Paris?" Odélie eyed Henri.

"Ah, Odélie! How rude of me. How are you—you look tired?" he joked.

Odélie's face went puce. "How far are we from Paris?" she said again.

"Never one to take a comment on your looks, were you? We can all be tired from time to time," Henri teased. "You are still a beauty."

"Do not make me ask again."

"How far? How far? Let me think. A few miles—maybe fifteen, twenty, thirty? Who knows? Not far, my dear. Have you somewhere to be in Paris?"

They all looked to Odélie.

"No. I only wondered."

"Good. Good. You have a nice place to stay for now."

"This is nicer." She looked around the room.

"Ah, my dear, if I could have you as my house guest, I would. But, as you know, it would raise too many questions, too many. Better you stay where you are."

"How is it better? We are in plain sight."

"Right you are. Plain sight is better than hiding, as no one will think you have anything to hide. Anyway, I am working on things. In fact, Serge—we must go to Paris this evening. I have some friends, or rather some people, who may owe me a favor or two to sort out your situation."

"I am coming too," Odélie said.

The triplets looked to their faux maman, their expressions anxious.

"Madame Rosie will mind you." Odélie's voice was harsh, annoyed by their neediness.

The triplets looked over at Madame Rosie, who smiled gently at them. Then, adopting her as ducklings adopt a mother duck, they were satisfied.

"And my dear, what shall you do in Paris?"

"See my family," Odélie said, but she did not look at Henri as she spoke.

*

Later that day, as everyone settled in, lit fires and cooked what little food they had, Michel took the horses to Henri's stables where he fed and watered them, noticing how happy they were now they were warm and dry. He gave the letter for Bertrand to Henri, who promised to post it once in the city.

He sat and smoked in the barn whilst the others ate, strangely reluctant to go back to them.

He had just ground the cigarette butt under his boot when he heard footsteps approaching.

It was Kacper, Gino on his shoulder. He smiled at Michel.

"You know, Kacper, I was thinking at breakfast that I have never spoken with you, not once. I realize how rude you must think me."

Kacper shrugged. He patted Beau, then Bisou.

"It's all been a bit crazy, hasn't it?"

Kacper sat down on an upturned bucket and nodded.

"I am tired. You must be too. It's all a mess."

Kacper held his palms upwards as if to say, *What can you do?*

"I agree. Kacper, tell me about yourself."

Kacper raised his eyebrows, then pulled out a harmonica from his pocket. He began to play, and Michel sat forward.

"I know this one!" he said. "My mother—my mother loved this song." And Michel began to sing along—a song of talking about love, of wanting to hear it as much as possible.

"I told you that you were a beautiful singer." Frieda stood in the doorway watching.

Kacper did not stop playing so Michel turned to Frieda, and sang to her that he loved her, that he would tell her he loved her every day and never stop.

"Are you awake?" Michel's head swam in a dream and he thought he could hear Bertrand.

"Are you awake?" the voice said again.

Michel tried to open his eyes, the lids heavy and unmoving. "What time is it?" he muttered.

"Five in the evening, I think. It is getting dark."

His left eye opened and he saw Hugo sitting on the sofa opposite Werner's bed, on which he now slept.

"I had to sleep last night with his feet in my face. Can you imagine? Kacper's. And Giordano had the cheek to say I snore. Do I snore, Michel?"

Michel groaned and pulled the blanket up to his chin. His nose was cold, and he wanted to bury his face in the pillow.

"Why are you sleeping in the afternoon? I suppose you did not sleep much for the past few nights—days, in fact."

"Hugo, why are you still talking to me?" Michel opened both eyes and sat up, rubbing away the sleep.

"Do you think we are safe at last?"

Michel saw now that Hugo's left leg danced as he spoke, and his nails were bitten and raw. "We are."

"I don't know, I really don't. Madame Rosie says she saw something in her cards, something awful, like...a beast."

"A beast?"

"Well, something like that. Or death. Maybe she said death? Or maybe she said a beast would kill us. I cannot remember. It was late, I was tired. But I have been thinking of beasts all day and then Giordano says I snore! It's not good, Michel, it really is not." Hugo extinguished his cigarette, then lit another.

"You need to calm down." Michel climbed out of bed and quickly into his trousers, pulling a thin brown woolen sweater over his head.

"That's easy for you to say! You are not Jewish, are you? Or, are you? Well, you don't look it, not to me anyway. I am. Kacper is. Jean is. Giordano—well—he isn't but I hear they don't like freaks. Is that true? Don't look at me like that, Michel. I love Giordano,

I do. I am just saying. Frieda is Jewish too. And Madame Rosie. The triplets also. You know their father was killed for printing a pamphlet against the Reich? Frieda rescued them. She rescued all of us. But you are not Jewish, are you, Michel?"

Michel had dressed, tied his laces and lit his own cigarette by the time Hugo had finished. "No. I am not."

"There, see? I told you." Hugo was pleased that he had figured something out, even if it was of little importance. "But you won't tell, will you? You won't tell anyone?"

"I won't, Hugo. I promise you."

"You're a good man. Frieda says you are a good man, that she trusts you. If she says that then I do too."

"Thank you, Hugo."

"Felix too—he was Jewish. They took him. Werner said that he was taken because he was fighting, but I know he was lying—I know it!"

Michel looked at the frightened clown, his mind going over Felix's disappearance. He knew it would not have been fighting—he knew that Werner had been afraid at the time. *Why didn't I realize the truth?*

"I'm sure it was nothing," Michel lied to Hugo. "If Werner said it was for fighting then I'm sure it was true."

"So, he wasn't taken because he was a Jew?" Hugo asked hopefully.

"Génépy, you need génépy," Michel said and opened the door, leading them to Jean and Giordano's caravan.

Giordano reluctantly brought out his last bottle. Hugo said that in theory he could make more, but he didn't have the ingredients and maybe the Germans would find them because he was making it, so it might be better if he didn't?

"Hush!" Giordano snapped. "Drink and calm down."

Michel sat on a wooden chair close to the fire burning in the iron stove. His nose was still cold; his whole body ached.

"Where are the others?" Hugo stood near the window, smoking distractedly and drinking his alcohol in quick sips.

"Madame Rosie has gone to sit with Werner. Serge, Odélie and Henri left in a black car earlier. Kacper has gone for a walk around the grounds with Gino."

Michel smiled at the thought of Gino appreciating the architecture of Henri's grand house, and the town with its cathedral spire that pricked the clouds.

"What are we to do?" Hugo asked. "Just sit?"

"Read a book. Here." Jean handed him a volume bound in red leather with gold lettering.

"*The Count of Monte Cristo*," he read.

"Like Henri. Read it. You will enjoy it. He brought it for me as a joke after what I said, but I think you are in need of a riveting tale more than I am."

Despite himself, Hugo took it and sat down, the book on his lap.

There was a quiet knock at the door and Frieda entered. "Michel, can I borrow you for a minute?"

Michel left the others to their drinks and followed Frieda into her and Werner's caravan. "What can I do for you, my love?"

She drew him to her and kissed him deeply.

"That's all I wanted," she said when she pulled away. "I just wanted us to be alone for a while."

She opened the internal door Michel had noticed the first time he had come into the caravan, and inside was a double bed with a thick yellow duvet and plumped pillows.

"My bedroom," she said.

Michel looked at her. "It feels wrong to go in there," he said.

"Why is it wrong?"

"It's your room."

"I did not realize you were such a gentleman." She did not smile.

"I just don't want to hurt you, Frieda. I have hurt women in the past…"

"How many?"

"What?"

"How many women?"

"Not many, no, not many at all. It's just that the way I feel about you, Frieda, I want to make you happy."

She took his hand in hers. "It would make me happy if you would lie next to me, stroke my hair and tell me how much you love me."

He smiled at her and allowed her to take him into the bedroom. They lay down next to each other, just a few centimeters between their faces.

"You think we will be all right?" she asked.

"I do."

"I want to leave."

"And where would you go?"

She rolled away from him and let out a sigh. "The world—the whole world!" She lifted her arms up as if the space between her hands was the circumference of the earth.

Michel propped his head on his hands.

"The whole world is pretty big; can you think of one place?"

"One place… One place… How about California? It's warm there. Werner got a postcard once, from someone who had left to join a circus there as a trapeze act."

"Like you."

"Like me."

"Certainly, my love, we will go there."

She stroked his face.

"Do you mean it?"

"All I can promise you is that we will go away together. Start a life together. Be safe somewhere."

"Will we have children?"

"Yes."

"How many?"

"Three—no, four. Maybe five."

"Five? You are crazy, Michel."

"We will need them to have our own troupe."

"Our own troupe…" she repeated.

"It will be the Cirque de Bonnet—"

"And you will be the ringmaster."

"I will be the ringmaster. And you will be the star act. Our children will do whatever they like—perhaps they will be clowns, or tumblers, or fire eaters."

"And we can send for Jean and Giordano. And Madame Rosie, and Kacper and Gino."

"Of course. And Hugo."

"Perhaps not Hugo," she said. "He would not travel that far, I am sure; he would worry too much."

"And Madame Geneviève, and Vassily—"

"She would have to grow her beard back again," Frieda said, laughing.

Michel laughed with her, then kissed her. "We will have our friends and our family with us."

"A Cirque des Amis—a circus of friends," she whispered.

"A Cirque des Amis," he agreed.

She sat up and lit a cigarette for them both. "I'm sure Odélie is not coming back from Paris tonight."

"Oh?"

"Serge told me she wanted to leave. She has found her chance now."

"The triplets will miss her."

"They will. Will you?"

"No."

"Are you sure?"

"Why would I?"

"I saw the way she was with you in the beginning. You were hers. She told me so."

"I was never hers," Michel said. "She may have thought that, but I wasn't."

"You made love to her though."

"She practically ambushed me!"

"But you didn't say no."

Michel shook his head. "No. I didn't say no."

Frieda licked her lips then took another drag of the cigarette.

"It wasn't making love. It was a mistake. I thought you were married. I thought I could never stand a chance with a woman like you."

"You don't have to apologize, Michel. That was the past. I just wanted to make sure it wasn't going to affect our future."

Michel took the cigarette from her, then kissed her gently on the lips. "Nothing will affect our future. It is you and me."

"And our Cirque des Amis."

As they kissed, her hands roamed his face, his neck and then down his chest towards his belt. She stopped when he gasped, pulled away from him and smiled. She unbuttoned her black shirt, her breasts falling free like ripened fruit. He ached to touch her, but she was not yet finished. She undid her trousers and let them fall to her ankles, revealing the long legs he had watched for months.

She unpinned her hair so it cascaded down her back. He moaned with pleasure—the sight of her was enough.

"Do you really love me?" she asked, her voice testing, joking.

"I do love you."

"Do you want me?"

He had no words. His mouth was dry. He could only nod.

She looked at his trousers. "I can tell," she said and giggled.

He grinned at her and she climbed on top of him, undressing him with frantic fingers, until at last they joined together, both sighing with relief.

CHAPTER TWELVE

Monsieur Bertrand

"I read the cards," Madame Rosie said. "I read them, and I saw it again."

"What did you see?" Michel sat with Frieda, eating dinner in her caravan the following night.

"I saw the Tower, Death, the Lovers."

"They can mean different things," Frieda said, clearing the soup bowls, the bread and crumbs.

"I know. Don't you think I know that? But where are Serge and Odélie? They have been gone more than a day."

"They will be back soon."

"I don't know. There is danger. I can feel it."

"Sit, Rosie. Please. Take this." Frieda handed her a small glass of wine. "We borrowed it from Henri's basement. He'll never know."

Madame Rosie drank. "What if they are not back tomorrow? What then? Do we sit here and just wait?"

"If they are not back tomorrow, then I will go to Paris myself and find them." Michel placed his hand on top of hers.

Madame Rosie visibly relaxed. "I'll tell Hugo and Kacper; they will be so relieved."

When she left, Frieda sat back down at the tiny fold-away table. Her hair was loose, and she wore a red sweater and black skirt. "You look beautiful," Michel said.

"More beautiful than when I am wearing sequins? This sweater is so old." She plucked at the wool to make her point.

"More beautiful than sequins," he said, and leaned over to kiss the tip of her nose.

"You didn't mean it, did you? That you would go to Paris?"

Michel shrugged. "They'll be back. I won't need to go."

"We should go and check on Papa, see how he is."

"You stay. You were with him most of the day. I will go and sit with him for a while."

Michel kissed her goodbye and made his way to the house, up the carpeted staircase to Werner's bedroom.

He opened the door slowly. Werner was tucked under crisp white sheets and a green bedspread, his face as pale as the pillows.

"Werner?" Michel whispered, as he sat on a chair next to the bed.

His eyelids fluttered, then opened just enough to see who had spoken. "Michel," his voice crackled.

"Do you need anything?"

"Water."

Michel gently held a glass to his lips and allowed him to sip, then wiped his mouth with a cloth.

"I hear one of Henri's servants is looking after you? Frieda says he is driving you mad."

Werner managed a weak smile.

"Frieda also said the doctor had been again—that your temperature has dropped. That's a good sign?"

Werner closed his eyes.

"I'll let you sleep." Michel made to stand, but Werner's hand grabbed his.

Werner did not speak, but he did not let go of Michel's hand, so he sat down once more and held his hand until his breathing was quiet and even, his grip relaxed.

*

By four o'clock the following afternoon, nerves were frayed, and the troupe met in Henri's living room, much to the annoyance of his servant.

"You should go to Paris, Michel, you said you would," Madame Rosie said.

Michel looked to Frieda, whose eyes were wide and frightened like a rabbit's.

"I'll go with you," Jean said.

"Ha! No, you will not," Giordano retorted. "You, a tall Jew. In Paris. Are you mad or just a fool?"

"Both?" Jean suggested.

"I would offer to go…" Hugo began. "But I've found some ingredients for génépy, and with the war and everything, I think my service is better put to use doing that."

Eliáš stood and cleared his throat. "I will go."

"No!" his sister Eliška cried, her face still so like a child's.

Edita coughed and everyone turned to look at her. She was as quiet as the others, yet a foot taller, wider too, her face always set as if she were busy figuring out complicated mathematical equations.

"Michel will go," she said, her voice soft yet firm like a teacher's. "He is not Jewish, and he lived in Paris. He should go; it will be safer for him. If he needs someone to go with him, then Giordano is right, it should be him. He knows where Serge and Henri would go—who they may speak to. He has the right identification. None of the rest of us can risk it. Remember Anton?"

The group nodded.

"And Felix," she added. "No. It must be this way. Michel and Giordano. If they cannot find them, we wait here a little longer."

"And then?" Hugo asked.

"And then we decide what to do next."

*

Sometime after four in the morning, Michel packed a small bag and together with Giordano set out for Paris.

They picked their way down a rutted track towards the town, where Henri's servant told him to see Monsieur Gardinier, who would be taking his deliveries into the city.

"You really think we can find them?" Giordano walked quickly, clutching a small carpet bag to his chest.

"We can only try." Michel felt in his pocket once more for the address of Werner's apartment, which Serge had access to, and names of bars Frieda thought they might visit.

"They would have called the house if they were going to stay," Giordano told the early morning air. "They would have called. We are doing the right thing."

"We are."

For a few francs, Monsieur Gardinier grunted at them to sit in the back of his truck with the delivery.

"He did not tell us it was cheese." Giordano sat opposite Michel, both leaning on crates that emitted the rich, cloying scent of camembert.

"They all claim Normandy camembert is the best, but mark my words, mine is better!" Monsieur Gardinier shouted over the engine, which rattled and choked as he changed gears.

"He is crazy," Giordano whispered, as Gardinier continued his tale of how the cheese was made, and how perfect the milk was.

Michel nodded then closed his eyes, allowing the movement of the truck to soothe his nerves. *We will find them. Nothing is wrong—*

"Five minutes!" Gardinier's voice woke Michel.

"I slept," he said.

"I didn't want to wake you. I thought perhaps you needed your rest."

"Montmartre, you said. Here, be quick, and carry one of those crates back there—I need to deliver this one." Gardinier opened the rear of the truck.

Michel and Giordano awkwardly carried the crate into the fromagerie, and as soon as they placed it on the ground, they took their leave and thanked Gardinier.

"Cost you double next time." He counted out the francs Michel handed him.

Michel looked around at the streets he had known all his life and was surprised by how little they had changed. Restaurant Suzette still shone in the morning light, tables set outside even in the cold. The only difference was that her clientele all wore German army uniforms.

The cabarets still advertised their acts, the vendors still sold their wares, but the flags pinned to buildings, flying in the air, were a stark reminder that Paris was no longer their own.

"I feel like everyone is looking at me," Giordano said.

"Look straight ahead, don't meet anyone's eyes. Just keep moving."

The rattle of a truck hitting a pothole made Michel jump. Soldiers sat in the open back, the diesel engine growling. One of them stood and whistled at a woman who was crossing the street ahead.

She looked up and smiled at the soldier. Then, once the truck was out of sight, she hurried her steps, her heels click-clacking past Michel.

Werner's family apartment was on the second floor of a building on the Boulevard de Clichy, above a brasserie that had changed its name to Der Gute Deutsche, the Good German, to entice its city's newest inhabitants.

Michel led the way up the tiled staircase, his and Giordano's feet echoing with each step. He knocked on the door of apartment three: no answer. He tried the handle, but it was securely locked.

"Serge?" Giordano bent down and spoke into the keyhole. "It's us. Are you there?"

"Even if he is, he won't hear that."

"Should I shout?"

Just then, a neighbor, an elderly woman with a small dog with dainty paws, opened her front door and looked at the pair. "*Oui?*"

"Madame, I am looking for the people who live here," Michel began.

"No one lives there. That short fat man did—German, he was. Funny he's not come back since his friends arrived." She fiddled with her keys, then closed her front door and locked it. "You'll want to leave now. No one lives here anymore. Just me and Babette." She nodded at the dog, who was pulling at the leash to descend the staircase for their walk.

Michel and Giordano followed her back down the stairs and out into the street, watching as she made her way carefully towards a newspaper stand, the dog stopping to sniff at every wall.

"What now?" Giordano asked.

"We need to go to the bars, the clubs, the places where Frieda said they could be—where their friends are."

"It's nine o'clock in the morning, Michel. I doubt we will find them there now."

Michel thought for a second, then knew exactly where to wait.

Odette's café was still standing. Her morning trade sat at the scuffed wooden tables and bar, drinking their coffees and filling the air with tobacco smoke. The warbling voice of Piaf sang out from the record player as it scratched over her song, "*On danse sur ma chanson.*" Odette swayed to the music behind the bar, a red-and-white checked tea towel in her hands, her scarlet lips mouthing the words.

Michel stood for a moment, feeling as though he had been taken back in time, back to when everything was as it should be.

He spotted Bertrand's black woolen beret bent over a newspaper at the table furthest from the door, and walked towards him.

"You have not changed one bit," Michel said.

Bertrand looked up. His mouth opened and closed like a fish gasping for air, his eyes wide. Finally, he said, "Michel…"

Within seconds Bertrand was on his feet and had enveloped Michel in an embrace. When they pulled apart, Bertrand wiped at his eyes with a handkerchief. "And who is this?"

"Giordano. My friend."

Bertrand pumped his hand up and down. "Pleased to meet you. Yes, pleased. Madame Odette! Look who it is!"

"Ah, Michel!" Madame Odette stopped singing and came to Michel, kissing him on both cheeks, once, twice, then three times. "Sit. Sit. I will bring you coffee. I have croissants too. Yes?"

She did not wait for their answer and scurried about, now and again looking back at Michel to check that he really was there.

"She will drive a man crazy," Bertrand said and grinned.

"I have missed her."

"No one misses her. She's annoying."

"Michel has told me so much about you," Giordano said.

"He has? All wonderful things, I am sure."

"What else could I tell him?"

"That I made you leave your home?"

"You didn't do that. *They* did." Michel looked outside as if a German soldier would be standing, staring in at the window. "You did what you thought best."

"And here you are."

"I am only here for a day, at most. I am trying to find some friends."

"Friends? And who are they?"

Odette chose that moment to place the coffee and croissants in front of Michel, and it was a few more minutes before he could explain.

"We will go and see if we can find out anything this evening. There are a few bars, some clubs," Michel finished. "I think that's all we can do."

"And you want me to help?"

"Not necessarily, but if you wanted to . . ."

"Wanted to? I would be delighted. Anything for a bit of excitement."

"So, the Germans taking the city was not excitement enough for you?"

Bertrand sat back in his chair and lit his pipe. After a few deep puffs he got a satisfactory draw. "My dear Michel, the Boche are utterly boring. No wonder they visit our cafés and bars so much. Germany, I think, must be a dreary place indeed."

The trio spent the rest of the day in Bertrand's apartment. Giordano slept while Michel and Bertrand talked.

"Did you get my last letter?"

Bertrand stood and looked at his bookshelf before pulling out the Bible. He took out the letters from the middle, their envelopes stained.

"I thought that if the Boche ever wanted to have a look around here, they wouldn't bother with the Bible. Their souls already belong to the Devil. I wrote a reply to your last letter—it arrived yesterday. I kept it here as I had nowhere to post it now you've left Lucien's. I cannot believe you are sitting here now!"

"I cannot believe it myself."

"Read it. Not that it is as entertaining as your adventure, but it will stop me from having to tell you everything. I am going out. I will get us some food. Rationing is driving us all crazy, but I have my ways."

Once Bertrand had left, Michel opened up the new letter.

Dear Michel,

I received your letter this morning. At first I was delighted to see your familiar scrawl, yet as I read, I became fearful.

You told me of your fellow performer taken away, of your ringmaster attacked, of your escape and hiding. I sit here and do not know quite how to respond. I feel I have let you down. I should not have forced you onto that train—I did not think it would come to this.

It is worse here too. A few other familiar faces have been arrested. Monsieur Freidman and his son are gone— you remember that the Germans took his shoe shop. Madame Freidman left in the middle of the night with their daughter and her mother. She took nothing but a suitcase.

I hate to admit it, I do, but I feel safer now they have gone—not that I would wish it on anybody, but I was worried that soon they would come for me. They still could, of course.

I spoke with Arnoud the butcher the other day, and he said that he will shoot himself rather than be taken. He says he has two bullets, just in case the first does not do the trick. It is extreme, but I found myself agreeing with him. Estelle and her mother are still in the countryside, so for many months it has been just him and the dogs he feeds scraps to.

I invited him for a brandy. He said he will come, but I do not think he will. He does not leave the shop except to make what meager deliveries he has left.

There is nothing good about this war apart from one thing, Michel, and this you need to keep hold of—you and Frieda. You must tell her you love her. Tell her before it is too late. All you have is each day, so make it as wonderful as you can. Tell her you love her every hour, every minute.

I wish I had done the same, Michel. I wish it was all different.

There are things I would love to do. Travel, perhaps—I should have done that. Fall in love again—even at my age! These are regrets that lie heavy on me now. Each day, each time I hear gunshots, those blasted planes, someone else being arrested, my regrets get heavier and heavier on my shoulders, so that I feel I will soon be unable to move.

Do not be unable to move, Michel. Find a way to keep moving.

Your friend,
Bertrand

As Michel folded the letter and placed it back inside the Bible, he wiped the tears from his eyes. He looked around Bertrand's apartment and felt for the first time its hollowness, its loneliness; in the pictures of a dead wife, in the books about Africa, America, all the places he had never been and could never go.

He closed his eyes and let his mind drift as he sat in the familiar surroundings, bringing his childhood memories to the fore; of his mother who cared for him, working endlessly as a cleaner, her hands red-raw and rough to touch, just so that he could live and be happy. How many parents were out there now, worrying for their children, doing everything they could to protect them?

Michel woke to the sound of Bertrand opening the front door.

"Did I wake you?" Bertrand closed the apartment door behind him and entered the room carrying a bag. "I told Arnoud you were here. He sent some beef—a little gray, I admit, but still!"

Michel stood and enveloped Bertrand in a hug.

"Now, now, Michel. It's only beef, don't get too excited. Go and wake your friend."

When the clock on the mantelpiece gently chimed six o'clock, the trio made to leave.

They walked quickly, catching the overcrowded, sweating metro to Montmartre, Michel holding on to Giordano's shoulder as if he were a small child that could be lost in the throng.

By dark, Montmartre had transformed into a colorfully lit beast, reminding Michel of the way the circus came alive at night as if by magic.

The windmill sails of the Moulin Rouge were lit with yellow bulbs, the sign underneath in neon red. A line of uniformed men were paying their way in whilst the cabarets a few doors down churned out music and laughter that carried to the street.

"I thought it would look different," Michel said. "I thought it would be quiet, boarded-up houses—something to make it feel as though it is not ours."

"They are careful to protect it, Michel. It is Herr Hitler's prize to own Paris—full of soldiers on leave, enjoying the city as if it is their own and letting us know that we are not to partake of anything unless they permit it. Do not be fooled by the lights, Michel. They are not the real light of Paris. They are fake—all of them," Bertrand warned.

Giordano led the way down a side street, then another, to a rowdy bar that appeared too small to Michel to hold all the voices that came from inside.

The dwarf opened the door and pushed his way through, and before Michel had squeezed past two men with large tattooed arms, Giordano was back. "They were here, two days ago. No one has seen them since."

Out into the cold: Giordano led the way once more.

"Who were those people?" asked Michel.

"Performers mostly. Out-of-work actors, singers—you name it and you can find it in these streets."

"Curfew is at nine. We must be quick." Bertrand checked the time.

"Only one more place they could be," Giordano said. "But you should probably wait here." He indicated a café—small, clean and quiet.

"Why?" Michel asked.

"It is not, how do you say, *for you*, I suppose. I know how to get myself inside, but perhaps not you."

"I don't want you to go alone."

"I will be fine. Sit, sit. Order some wine. I will be back in less than the time it takes you to drink it."

"And if you are not?"

"I will be." Giordano grinned and marched away, turning down yet another darkened alley where disembodied voices drifted on the night air; the ghosts of Paris trying to reclaim their city of light.

Bertrand and Michel ordered a glass of red each and waited, expecting Giordano to return within minutes.

But when an hour had passed, Michel stood and paid the waiter. "There is something wrong. I can feel it."

Before they rounded the corner to follow in Giordano's footsteps, the voices had changed. They were no longer happy, laughing. The music had gone. The tones were harsh. German.

A crowd had gathered, and Michel and Bertrand pushed through until they could see five men, their hands on their heads, being led away by an armed soldier. An officer stood at the entrance of a small house and barked something Michel did not understand.

Two more men were led out, then a woman, and finally Giordano.

Michel moved forward once more, his heart drumming in his ears.

The German officer shouted at the crowd, who began to move away, back to their homes.

"Giordano!" Michel shouted.

But Giordano could not turn around to look. The gun was trained at his back and the soldier nudged him forward to walk quicker, away from Michel down a dark, silent alley.

"Come, Michel." Bertrand pulled Michel away.

"We have to help him! Where are they taking him?"

"Hush. Come now. Quickly."

Bertrand dropped his head down and dragged Michel by the arm.

"Quickly, quickly, Michel. Walk faster."

As they hurried along, following the shadows to Bertrand's apartment, the streets had become deserted; the only presence was German soldiers, who relaxed at the bars that were now theirs alone.

The metro had stopped for the night, so they had to walk the six miles to Bertrand's, always checking over their shoulder, neither wanting to talk.

Once they arrived, Michel slumped into the armchair he had departed in early summer and Bertrand handed him a glass of brandy, then worried at the curtains to make sure no light shone through to the outside. He lit another candle; three now cast ghostly shadows on the walls and bookcases.

"It is stupid, this curfew." Bertrand knocked his brandy back quickly.

"Where have they taken him, Bertrand?"

"If it is a round-up, I hear that those taken are questioned first—they find out if there are any resistance amongst them. Then, any Jews. Then anyone they do not like."

"We should have gone with him."

"He said himself it was not a place for us."

"What does that even mean?"

"It was a private bar, Michel, run by people Giordano knows and we do not. I expect they run many a bar in Paris without a license—they have for years. Now, I suppose, their time is coming to an end."

"They will let him go—they must. He's not part of the resistance, he's not Jewish, he's no one of interest to them."

"Unless he talks. Unless he tells them who and where your friends are." Bertrand poured the rest of the brandy into their glasses.

"He wouldn't."

"They have ways, Michel."

They both sat back and tried not to think of the ways in which they could make Giordano talk. Michel felt sick. His insides churned and his whole body ached.

"We need to let your friends know—the troupe—just in case," Bertrand said to the shadows that played on the ceiling, jumping and flickering to one another in their game.

"We?"

"Tomorrow I will take you. We will tell them and then, Michel, you will hide until the Germans get bored and go home."

"When will that be?"

"Only time will tell." With that, Bertrand leaned forward and blew out the candles. The pair sat, listening to each other breathe, until sleep finally took them away.

*

Michel woke, still sitting in the armchair, his head leaning on his left shoulder, his neck sore and stiff.

Bertrand was nowhere to be seen as Michel stood at the window and looked out at those leaving for work, going to school.

He suddenly felt nauseous. It rose up quickly, and he ran to the bathroom and vomited until there was nothing left but bile. He washed his face then looked at himself in the mirror—his eyes were red and puffy, the stubble on his face now thick.

He thought of Giordano, of his face, of what they may be doing to him. Then he thought of Jean—how could he tell him? How could he tell him his best friend might never return?

Michel sat on the bathroom floor and felt the bile rise up again. He retched until his ribs hurt, then slumped down, his head in his hands, and wept.

"I have it. She says she wants it back in a day. I say we have at least a week before she gets mad." Michel looked up and saw Bertrand, hat on his head, satchel in his hand. "What's wrong? Why are you down there?"

"I was ill."

"We need to go. We need to warn them."

"How can I tell them, Bertrand? How can I? It's my fault, I should never have brought Giordano here."

Bertrand kneeled next to him on the cool tiles. "It is not your fault. It is this war that is at fault. They will understand. Please, Michel. We must do what we can, and what we can do is let them know what happened."

Michel allowed Bertrand to help him to his feet.

"I borrowed Odette's car. She has a permit to leave the city. Her lieutenant gifted it to her. I had to give her my cognac as collateral, so I suggest we go before she sells it or worse, drinks it herself."

"What about Giordano? We can't just leave. We should look for him before we go—maybe we can find him?"

"Michel, there is nothing we can do right now. If your friend Henri is as important as you say he is, if he returns, if your ringmaster knows someone...they can help. But I am an old man. I don't know how to get the Boche to change their minds. I don't know tricks. And neither do you. The only thing we can do is leave, go to your friends and warn them. Then, let us see what happens next."

CHAPTER THIRTEEN

Ringmaster Bonnet

Beneath the darkened cloudy sky, everyone slept soundly. Michel had broken the news and they had retreated to their caravans, slowly, quietly.

Jean slept stretched out on the sofa in Henri's living room, his hand holding an empty bottle of wine. There was nothing left inside, but he had not wanted to let it go. Michel sat in a chair by the fireplace, leaning on his hand, feeling empty and exhausted.

Bertrand slept on a chaise-longue. The events of the day had worn him out quickly and he snored loudly.

"You cannot sleep?" Frieda asked Michel. She sat across from Jean with Kacper next to her, the pair stroking Gino's soft fur as he slept on Kacper's lap.

"Neither can you."

"This is not your fault, Michel."

"Then why do I feel so guilty?"

Kacper patted Frieda on the arm and made a sign with his hands.

"He says he wants you to hear his story. He says it will help you understand what is happening."

"Is he deaf?" Michel asked suddenly.

Kacper shook his head, then opened his mouth and pointed inside. Where there should have been a thick pink tongue was nothing more than a stump. Kacper made a chopping movement with his hand.

"The Germans did this to you?"

Kacper shook his head sadly, then pointed a finger to his own chest.

"You did this to yourself? Why?"

Kacper started to sign but Frieda was ahead of him—she knew his tale, she knew his words.

"I was in Poland before the war. I am Polish, of course. I was an academic in Krakow, a mathematician. I was well respected in my field and had written much on ciphers and codes. When things started to change in Poland, I was asked to leave the university. Of course, we now know why.

"I did not abandon my studies. If anything, now that I had no job I read more, wrote more. One day, one of my ex-students came to see me. He said he had been asked by the British to look at some codes—some ciphers the Germans were using. They were building a machine to try and figure them out. I wanted to help—not just because I wanted to defend my country, but because trying to figure out the code was irresistible to me.

"I went to Warsaw and helped with the codes. We worked day and night, barely eating, barely drinking. My wife and daughter came with me and stayed with an aunt of hers in the city, although I rarely saw them.

"The day came when the codes were broken, and they had to get them to England. I could not go—would not leave my family—so I stayed behind, and we decided to stay a while in Warsaw. My daughter had made friends; my wife was happy to have the company of her aunt. It was the biggest mistake we ever made.

"When the war began, the Luftwaffe dropped bombs on us so quickly it was like the whole world was going to end. We hid in an air raid shelter for three days and nights, and I did not think we would make it out alive.

"The day we left the shelter, the city was dust and gray rubble. We picked our way back to the house, but it was gone.

"As we stood there, another academic who had been working with us walked towards me.

" 'Kacper!' he said. 'You're alive!'

"We embraced. Then he said: 'They know about you—about you working with us. They don't know what you did, or what you worked on, but they have your name. Your family's names.'

"I stood there and heard the words, and my daughter grabbed my hand and asked me what the man meant.

" 'It's fine,' she told him. 'It's all right if they know my name.'

" 'What do I do?' I asked him. My legs were shaking.

" 'I'll help you. I know some friends who can help you,' he said.

"We were taken to an apartment where a skinny man with a heavy silver pocket watch spoke with my friend. Then he turned to me and said, 'We can get the woman and girl out, but not you. Too much of a risk.'

"My wife wailed and I held her. My daughter cried.

" 'It's the only way,' the pocket watch man simply said.

" 'Where will they go?' I asked.

" 'Palestine,' he said.

"My wife looked at me and shook her head. 'Not without you,' she said.

"I swallowed and looked at her, my darling wife, the only woman I had ever loved, had ever known. I said, 'My love, I will find you again.'

"I kissed her, then held my daughter tight. 'When will they leave?'

" 'Now,' the pocket watch man said. 'We go now whilst there is this mess going on. Too much confusion for anyone to notice.'

"Our goodbye was brief. Too brief. I told them I loved them. I told them I would find them soon. My friend took my arm, and led me out of the room and down the stairs to the street. I wanted to turn, go back to them, but he pulled me away. 'We have to get you out of here now!' he warned.

" 'I don't care what happens to me! Please, let me go!' I begged.

"He did not listen to me, and had to drag me away to another apartment on the outskirts of the city.

"That night was the longest of my life. I sat and smoked and drank but nothing worked; nothing numbed the pain and sent me into the oblivion I so craved.

"My friend found me tickets and papers to get to France. The idea was that I would cross over to England. I did not want to leave; how could I go? He told me I had little choice in the matter.

"So I did as he told me, and by some miracle found my way to Paris, with little money and nowhere to live. Thankfully, I had studied French, and German for that matter, and could communicate well. It was on my second day that I passed a music shop. Inside was a glorious accordion. I asked the shop owner if I could play it—he told me it was once his father's and that I could. I had learned this instrument as a boy from my own grandfather, and when I sat that day in his shop and played the songs from my childhood, I felt safe.

" 'It's yours,' the man said to me when I finished playing.

" 'I cannot pay you,' I said.

" 'I didn't ask you to. It needs an owner who will care for it,' he replied.

"It was only when I left the shop that I realized I had been crying. He had taken my tears for joy, not sorrow.

"So it was that I began to play on the streets for change, to get me lodgings for the night and a hot meal.

"I had been in France for perhaps a month when it became clear the Germans were coming here now. I called my friend in Warsaw to say I needed help to get to England. His wife answered the phone.

" 'He's dead,' she wept. 'They torture them one by one. Someone gave them his name. There are others still hiding.'

"I do not think I said anything to her. All I could think about was my own tongue—about the things that were in my head:

names, ciphers, codes. I could not let myself betray anyone, betray my country.

"That night I drank enough vodka to kill a horse. It did not kill me. When I woke in the morning, I imagined what my wife would say if she could see me now. I knew what she would say. She would tell me to be brave, to endure until the war is done, to find them, and most of all to help those who were trying to save their country and their own families.

"I took a knife and I cut at my tongue until I passed out on the bed, blood covering the sheets.

"The proprietor heard my screams and came in immediately. I knew she would—she was nosy at the best of times. I awoke in a hospital with a doctor telling me I would not be able to talk again. When he said that, I smiled at him and I think he thought I was mad!

"You may think me mad too, Michel. Perhaps I am. I did it to save others. I would do anything to protect my family, and my friends who risked their lives to save so many. I could not, would not tell the Germans what we did, what the English are continuing to do.

"Do not cry for me, Michel. It does not hurt; I do not miss it.

"Werner found me, playing on the streets. At first I did not want to work for a German, but as I found out more, I trusted him and told him my story as best I could.

"Gino was given to me when his mate died. We have been together now for a year. He is my best friend.

"Please, Michel, wipe your tears. I will get through this. We must believe we will. And then I shall find my family.

"I wanted you to hear this tale; I wanted you to understand how things are, and how they will become. I want you to be ready to do whatever you need to, to protect the ones you love. I trust you with this, Michel. Only you, Frieda and Werner know of this. Not even Henri knows. I trust you. I hope you realize it is important you know that people do. It will help you to be brave, if the time comes."

Frieda finished talking and Kacper held on to her hand.

Michel did not know what to say. Then he found the only words he thought appropriate. "Thank you," he said, and Kacper stood, shook Michel's hand and walked out of the room, Gino asleep like a baby in his arms.

"I'm going to go and rest for a while." Frieda said, standing. Michel took her in his arms and held her close so he could feel her heart beating with his.

"I'll check on Werner. Make sure he is OK."

Frieda kissed Michel and left him sitting next to the fire, his head full of Giordano, German bombs, and the vision of the stump of Kacper's tongue in his mouth.

Michel suddenly woke, his neck bent to the side. Bertrand's snoring had reached an impressive volume, and Michel sat and rubbed at his neck.

"Are you awake?" Jean asked, sitting upright.

"I am. I don't want to be."

"Me neither."

"It's cold."

Michel stirred the fire in the grate back to life, then added a couple of logs. He sat crouched next to it, warming his hands, watching the flames lick at the wood as it hissed and spat.

"It's not your fault," Jean said.

"We should try and speak to Werner about where we go next."

"I don't think there is anything he will say to help."

"So, we stay here?"

"I think we have little choice."

Michel sat back in the chair and heard the sound of footsteps. Before he could open the curtain to check who it was, Henri and

Serge barged through the door, their clothes soaked through as if they had swum from Paris.

"It was raining! Our whole walk back it was raining," Henri said, and stripped off his coat. "My car broke down. Can you imagine? It was new too."

"Where the hell have you been?" Jean was suddenly full of energy. "You know we thought you were dead? Giordano probably is! He went to Paris to find you and they took him away!"

"Quiet!" Henri's voice was harsh. "Sit."

Jean sat and Bertrand woke but did not move.

"Where are the others?" Henri asked.

"Asleep."

"Wake them. They all need to hear this."

Michel did as he was told and woke the troupe, who crammed themselves into Henri's living room, bleary eyed and disbelieving at seeing Serge and Henri.

"Where is Odélie?" Eliáš asked, his face a picture of misery.

"She is staying in Paris for now," Serge said. "She plans to join the Cirque d'Hiver."

"We are not good enough for her, never were," Madame Rosie said.

"Listen. All of you. What Serge and I tried to accomplish was not as easy as we thought. My contact—a general who is partial to bribery—is also, it seems, partial to entertainment. It is his wife's thirtieth birthday in a week, and it coincides with his promotion. The deal we have made is that we will perform for him, for his wife, a circus—right here. They have a house in town—used to belong to a musician friend of mine before he left. Now it is theirs—five storeys of beauty. I would swap my ramshackle pile with him! Anyway, I digress. He gave us a permit."

"So we dance and sing for him, and then what?" Jean spat. "He arrests us all."

"We have agreed that he will then give us papers to leave the country—all of us. Without question. But first we must do the show."

"By *we* you mean us—this tiny troupe—perform a full circus? This is a joke, surely?" Jean said.

"If you agree, I will pay to bring in more performers, singers and stagehands. I will pay for it. If we do this, it is a chance for you to leave the country safely."

The room was quiet. Then Frieda spoke. "Werner is still too ill—we will need a ringmaster." She looked at Michel.

Michel was not sure what to say. He looked at his friends, all of them tired, all of them fearful, all of them looking at him.

"What do you say, Michel?" Henri asked.

Michel thought of Giordano, of the risks he had taken. He thought of Werner, who had taken risks his whole life. He looked to Frieda.

"Where will we go?"

"America," Henri said.

Michel stood and walked to the door.

"Where are you going?" Frieda called out.

"To ask Werner's permission."

Werner slept wrapped in a sheet, his blankets thrown on the floor. Henri's servant dozed in a chair next to the bed but woke when Michel creaked open the door.

"Henri is back," Michel said.

The servant jumped as if scalded, and left to see what he could do for his master.

"Werner," Michel whispered, and sat down in the vacated chair. "Werner?"

Werner groaned. "Michel…" he said, his voice splintered like dry wood.

Michel held the glass of water from his bedside table next to Werner's lips and gently poured in a few drops. Werner swallowed, then licked his cracked lips.

"How do you feel?"

"What day is it?"

"Saturday."

"How long have we been here?"

"Almost a week."

Werner groaned once more as he tried to roll onto his side. Once he had accomplished this, he opened his eyes, red and swollen, and looked to Michel. "I have failed you all," he whispered.

Michel shook his head and smiled. "You have brought us somewhere safe. What more could you have done?"

"I shouldn't have thought I could hide everyone."

"Henri has a plan."

"Tell me."

"He says if we do a show for a general, the man will give us all papers to leave."

"All of you?"

"All of *us*."

"We will do the show." Werner's voice was firm. "When is it?"

"Next week."

"I am not sure I will be well by then. I will try..." Werner attempted to sit up and fell back against his pillows, beads of sweat on his brow.

"I have come to ask you something."

"You want to marry Frieda."

Michel was taken aback. "I do. But that was not what I was going to ask."

"You always ask the father's permission, Michel."

"I have two things to ask you then."

"Go ahead. Wait—give me some more water first."

"We will do the show. We'll hire more performers with Henri's money and then we will all leave together. But... I need to know if you will allow me to be ringmaster for one night."

Werner smiled. "I am not sure which question is worse—marry my daughter and take her away, or take my circus."

"I am not taking it. It is yours. It will always be yours, and so will she."

"No, no, Michel. It is yours now. And so is Frieda. It is time. A ringmaster must always know when it is the right time—when the band should play, when the acts should dance . . . you'll orchestrate this from now on. It is yours."

Michel watched Werner turn to stare at the ceiling.

"Werner?"

"Go and fetch me Frieda. Ask her to sit with me."

"I'm sorry, Werner," Michel said, as he opened the door to leave.

"So am I, Michel. So am I."

"Will you return to Paris?" Michel asked Bertrand, as they sat together with Hugo and Madame Rosie in Werner's caravan.

Bertrand looked up. Madame Rosie was reading his palm. "Not yet," he said. "Perhaps soon. I thought I could help?"

"It's not that I want you to leave—I just don't want to put you in danger."

"Michel, I was in danger alone in Paris. I was wasting away with no sight of a future for myself. I cannot, will not leave you. My future may still be bleak—maybe I will have to return alone—but right now I can help. I can *do* something and stay with my friend."

"You can help by taking Jean and Serge into the city to find more performers," Michel said. "Whilst you have Odette's car."

"Your wish is my command," he said, and Michel saw Madame Rosie smile softly at him.

Michel sat at Werner's small desk and began to scribble down the acts needed: magicians, dancers, more clowns.

"More clowns?" Hugo questioned, peering over his shoulder.

"A few. Just a few. You will be their leader, show them what they need to do."

Hugo nodded, then chewed at a raggedy fingernail.

Jugglers, plate spinners, contortionists, trapeze artists, unicyclists, tightrope walkers, a band.

"Animals," Michel said. "Can we get them?"

"I'll ask Jean, one minute." Hugo scurried out.

"You could get dogs and cats easily enough," Bertrand said, and Madame Rosie giggled.

"Animals," Jean said, as he entered and sat down heavily on the sofa.

"Are you all right?"

"No."

"Henri said he will try and find Giordano," Michel said. "He will try."

"Animals," Jean said again.

"Perhaps a tiger? An elephant?"

"Shall I go to the zoo and steal them?"

"Not a bad idea!" Henri burst in. "I came to see if I could be of assistance."

"I thought you were looking for Giordano?" Jean asked.

"Already asked a few of my contacts, my friend. Give it a little time. If not, I will go and see our Nazi friend in town this evening. I believe he is back with his wife after his *foray* into the city and everything it can offer a fat middle-aged man." Henri tapped the side of his nose and winked.

"OK. In that case, Jean is right—we need animals," Michel said.

"Cannot our friends at the Cirque d'Hiver perhaps help us?" Henri asked.

"Hardly friends. Werner and that ringmaster have never seen eye to eye," said Jean.

"I will speak with him."

"And what will you say? 'Can we have your wild animals and a trainer or two for an evening?'"

"I won't have to talk. Other things speak clearly, my dear Jean."

"Money!" Bertrand said, as if he had figured out a riddle.

"We also need men to help with the Big Top. We need torches and food, stalls, more tents."

"More men I can find you—there are many in need of a few francs in town. Supplies...well, I suppose I must do some more talking with other friends. Jean, I will come with you to the city. We shall go now, yes?"

Bertrand stood. "I will drive you."

"Ah, yes. Your Citroën—I am surprised it got you here, if I am honest. We can pick up my car for the journey back." Henri smirked.

They left quickly, and Madame Rosie made Michel coffee as he sketched out a plan for their performance, losing himself in the colors, the music, the magic that would come back...if only for one night.

CHAPTER FOURTEEN

Brigadeführer Diederich Wolff

Brigadeführer Diederich Wolff eyed Michel from under heavy lids. "What is the theme of the evening?" he asked.

Henri looked to Michel and smiled, as if willing him to answer. "Theme?" Michel asked.

"You know—a theme. My wife needs a theme."

"What does your wife like?" Henri asked.

Wolff heaved himself up from the desk chair in his study and went to pick up a small cigar box from the bookcase, then sat back down, his weight making the chair creak, his stomach resting on his thighs.

"What do women like?" He clipped the end of the fat brown cheroot.

"Dancing?" Michel ventured.

The brigadeführer nodded. "When she was a girl—I mean, of course, younger than she is now," he corrected himself, "she read books about Mexico, about the Maya people. Do you know them?"

Michel shook his head. *Does he mean personally?*

"Black magic," Henri said.

"Indeed. Bloody people, they were. Sacrifices of their own children, bloodletting...my dear wife Helga would tell me these gory stories in the evenings after dinner. Can you imagine? This pretty creature telling me about beheadings and stabbings and all sorts of things that would make most women faint. I believe that I fell in love with her when she told me these stories—I realized she was a woman like no other."

There was a pause as Wolff lit his cigar and sucked on it until the end glowed red. Michel looked at the portrait of Helga above Wolff's head. From a distance, she looked quite ordinary—slim, pretty, with her hair pulled up in a chignon. But as he looked closer, he saw that her smile was cunning, her eyes alert. *She has the correct surname*, he thought.

"Anyway. That's what she likes," Wolff said behind a cloud of his own smoke.

"Hanal Pixán—the Day of the Dead!" Henri clapped his hands together at his genius. "I read they believe that the dead come back to life and visit their families. They feed them to try and protect their children from evil spirits. It can be an evening of ghosts and spirits and the colors of the Maya."

"I believe she will like that." Wolff leaned forward. "Good. Make it happen. Five days."

"Thank you, Herr Brigadeführer." Henri stood. Michel followed suit.

"We look forward to seeing you and your wife in five days' time,' Henri added politely.

"And the townspeople."

"Pardon?"

"The townspeople. They have been given permission to attend. And of course, some of my comrades."

"Indeed, of course! The more the merrier, as they say." Henri smiled, and they left the five-storey house and headed for the town square.

"The whole town," Michel said.

"It will be magnificent, Michel! A full house! Can you imagine?"

"I'm ringmaster..." he said, almost to himself.

"And what a wonderful way to start your new job! A full house, people applauding. Oh, how I wish I were in your shoes."

Michel was not sure whether Henri was joking or not.

The following two days passed in a blur; men appeared as if from nowhere and staked the Big Top, using the horses to drag and pull at the large ropes, shouting encouragement when they wanted to stop. Jean and Serge made two visits to the city and brought back with them a new troupe, all of them nervous about having to perform for Germans. Henri took care of the money, and Hugo got his hands on enough ingredients to refill his stock of génépy, which kept them mellow.

"It's really happening!" Frieda was at Michel's side, her face full of excitement. "I love this part—when everyone is working together, creating something from nothing."

"I wish I could enjoy it." Michel yawned a little.

"You've barely slept. You need to rest." She kissed him on the cheek.

"How is Werner?" he asked.

"He is a little brighter. The doctor says he is recovering, but it will take time."

"I've hardly had a chance to see him, with all this going on."

"Go now; just sit with him and talk. It will give you a chance to rest, and he'd love to know how it is all coming together."

He kissed her forehead then stroked her hair. "I'll go now. If anyone wants me, tell them I have disappeared." He walked slowly away from the hustle of the camp, his legs weighted with tiredness, his mind with nerves.

Werner was sitting up in bed when Michel entered the quiet bedroom, a thick flurry of pillows propping him up, a book on his lap.

"Michel." Werner looked to him.

"Am I disturbing you?" Michel glanced at the book, unopened.

"Not at all—please."

Michel sat on the chair next to his bed, the cushion still warm under his backside.

"You just missed your friend Bertrand. A nice man—full of tales."

"He has a fair few stories, I'll grant him that."

"Henri gave me this." Werner held up the blue leather-bound book. "Poetry, of all things."

"You don't like it?"

"I cannot concentrate." Werner looked to the window as if expecting something.

"It's going well—the preparations."

Werner only nodded.

"Do you miss it?"

"What?" Werner turned to him.

"The circus, the show? I wish you could be the ringmaster."

Werner stared at him for a moment or two, and Michel wondered if he was angry.

"I'm sorry," Michel said, unsure exactly what he was sorry for.

"Bertrand spoke of his wife when he was here."

"She was a good woman."

Werner nodded. "It made me think of Éva."

"You miss her."

"More than you can imagine. I kept myself busy all those years after she left, and then when Frieda came it was almost like a part of Éva came back to me. It made me happy, but sad at the same time. She looks so much like her." Werner smiled. "Sometimes when she performs, I think it is Éva up there, ready to tumble to earth and come back to me. Sounds foolish, doesn't it?"

"I don't think so."

"I've kept her safe all these years—Frieda. But she's a woman now, isn't she?" Werner shook his head as if he had just realized.

"A woman. Almost twenty-one. Sometimes she acts like a forty-year-old, you know—bossy!"

"I wonder where she gets that from?" Michel laughed.

"Indeed! Ah, to be the boss means to be bossy, Michel. Are you making sure you are bossing them about out there? You need to keep a tight leash on them, you know? Hugo will sneak away and drink if you let him. And the triplets, they seem docile enough, but they get distracted easily. They always reminded me of puppies—how they see a stick or a fly buzzing in the air and they cannot contain themselves. They're just like that. Keep an eye on them."

Michel nodded and tried to contain a yawn.

"Tired already?" Werner chuckled. "You just wait. This is only, what—day two? When are you rehearsing?"

"Tonight. We're just waiting for the Big Top to be anchored a bit better—seems a new tear appeared at one of the seams."

"Get them to go through it at least twice tonight," Werner warned. "The first time will be like trying to herd sheep. The second will give you a better clue where you are and what needs to be done."

Werner suddenly groaned a little and Michel stood. "Can I get you anything?"

"It's just the stitches. Your handiwork, whilst it saved my life, has tightened the skin. Feels as though I am going to burst out of them."

Michel plumped the pillow behind his head and helped Werner to sit up a bit more.

"I'd better get back to them," Michel said.

"Yes. You'd better. They'll be running amok down there."

"You sure I can't get you anything?" Michel asked.

"No. I'm fine. Got this poetry to read, a nap to take."

Michel left Werner and just before he closed the door, he saw him staring out of the window once more, the book still unopened on his lap.

*

When Michel came upon the field, tents were springing up, a stern Frieda, hands on hips, directing the workers. As he approached, he heard the honk of a truck's horn behind him, followed by the trumpeting of an elephant.

Two trucks came closer, the elephant's trunk sneaking through the latticed wood of the first to sniff out her new environment. The second truck was quieter. A man jumped down, his arm in a sling, a cheroot between his teeth.

"Mind," he told the crowd, "he's in a bad mood today," and nodded at his arm.

"You're here! Voilà, Michel! Your animals." Henri appeared from his car, trailing behind the entourage.

"Two of them," the injured man said.

"Georges is an ill-tempered beast," Henri said.

"Georges is the one in the truck, I assume?" Michel said.

"Oh, heavens no! That's Bastien the lion. Georges is his trainer. He's the one you must watch out for."

"Victor says you owe him double," Georges told Henri. "He says you can afford it."

Henri's smile set in place. "We will talk later."

"I'm just the messenger. Where do you want us to set up?"

Michel pointed towards the rear of the tent.

"Stephanie, my daughter, deals with Camille. That's the elephant. So, don't get any ideas that anyone but her will be riding her. My daughter's a star."

"Where is she?" Henri asked.

"Asleep in the cab. She likes her sleep too, so don't annoy her if she's sleeping. She's worse than me."

The troupe nodded, yet none of them moved, each wanting to get a look at Camille the elephant.

"You'll see her later." Georges climbed back into the first truck and the driver took them around the back of the tent to set up.

*

By late afternoon, most of the work on the tents had ceased and Michel brought the performers into the Big Top for their first run-through. They followed him into the ring, heaped with sand. Workers were busy raking it flat whilst the trapeze and nets were being tested above. Hammering echoed around them as the men finished erecting the tiered stands, the highest seats reaching to the canopied roof.

"We have only three days to get this right," Michel told them. "I know it isn't long, but it can be done. We just have to work hard."

Michel heard someone giggle and he swallowed, his mouth dry. "I have given you all a running order. Make sure you read it. Your costumes are being completed as we speak by Madame Rosie and Bertrand, who has proven adept at sewing." Michel paused and allowed a moment for smiles all around. "After our first run-through now, we break, you eat and see Rosie about your costumes, then we do another run-through tonight.

"We will start with all of the troupe entering to the music of the band. I want it dark; one by one, the spotlight will pick out the performers. As the music swells, more lights will shed a glow on our dancers. Then, all the lights come on and the troupe have disappeared, leaving the clowns in the center, dressed in red suits and black shirts, your faces painted as skeletons."

"Like actual skeletons, so we look dead?" a small boy asked.

"Speak to Hugo. He will explain," Michel commanded, and he saw Frieda smile at that.

"After the clowns, we have our two fire eaters, one either side of Serge. Then we move to our acrobats—triplets, that's you. Then the contortionists, then our animal show. We will finish with the trapeze and the tightrope walkers. Our finale is everyone working at once, the music tense, until—boom—it goes pitch black!"

"And then?" someone asked.

"That's the end, stupid," someone else retorted.

"So, it ends in blackness?"

"Yes, because the theme is death."

"Nice theme. And I'm not stupid."

"Please! Listen. Let's begin now—just one after the other, a glimpse at the routines you have ready."

A group of slim young men and women began with a ballet routine, soft and flowing, before moving into a stilted sequence, their bodies stiffening as if growing old.

"Good, good," Michel said and clapped.

Next, Hugo and two small boys walked to the center of the ring, the trio juggling brightly colored balls.

"Can we get these painted white?" Michel asked them. "Then add some faces in black paint as if you are juggling skulls."

"Seems stupid to me," a chatty lad said. "Who'd want to see someone juggle skulls?"

"Please—get it done. Your usual tricks, Hugo, need to be darker. So no red nose, no pulling silk handkerchiefs from your sleeves."

"What am I meant to do then?" Hugo chewed on his nail.

"No need to worry. Use your imagination. What would a clown do if it came back from the dead for just one day?"

"Sounds like the stuff of nightmares," someone muttered from behind Michel.

"I don't know." Hugo cast around. "Maybe he'd walk stiffer, you know, fall over things? Maybe his leg would come off and the others would have to try and put it back on?"

"Good! Yes, a living-corpse clown! Brilliant—work on it."

Hugo grinned and blushed a little.

"Next up, Serge—where is he?" Michel looked around.

"Practicing fire eating outside. One of the others nearly burned the tent down before—see that black singe over there?" Jean muttered.

"Well—then we have the triplets."

The trio walked lethargically around the ring, backflipping now and again.

"What's all this?" Michel stopped them.

"It's not the same," Eliáš said. "We can't do it without Odélie."

"You can, and you will," Michel said.

"I'll help." Frieda came to their aid. "We need Claudette—that will help. Let's go and get her ready for the next rehearsal, eh? That way you'll feel a bit better?"

The triplets followed her, and Michel gave her a grateful nod.

"OK, so…" Michel looked down at his sheet of paper. "Contortionists? Where are they?"

"Over there." Jean pointed to three boxes in the middle of the ring.

"Where?"

"Inside." Jean smiled for the first time in days. He walked over to the boxes and lifted each lid, then tipped them gently onto their side.

The troupe could now see the three people inside, their limbs impossibly woven around their bodies. One by one they escaped from their prisons and began to crawl, spider-like, their knees and elbows bent at strange angles. Then they transformed themselves once more, this time into balls that rolled around the ring before they popped their heads out and began to crawl again.

"Brilliant! Excellent!" Michel clapped.

"There's just Bastien and Camille now," Jean said. "But they won't be ready until later."

"Thank you, Jean. We will run through the whole thing at seven p.m. sharp."

The troupe groaned.

"I know it feels rushed, but the more we practice the easier it will become. You will then break for one hour and we'll do another run-through, as this was a little thin. Tomorrow I want you here at six in the morning. Final costume fitting in the afternoon. Full run-through, makeup, band, lights. Then two more full run-throughs on our final day. You'll have one night of rest, and then we need to be up and running by six p.m."

"I thought we were just working for the show?" the little boy complained.

"The whole town and the brigadeführer's guests will be expecting food, drinks, fortune tellers, magicians, clowns, everything, right up until our show. You have been paid for it."

"Should have asked for more," the boy muttered under his breath.

"Right. Back here. Seven o'clock!" Michel left, holding the running order notes in his hand, feeling the sweat dripping down his back.

"You did beautifully." Frieda caught up with him and held his hand.

"I can't believe I did it."

"You have found your calling, Michel."

He kissed her on the cheek, then whispered, "Only if you stay by my side."

"Always."

The following day, Michel sat with Jean drinking coffee as the troupe ate breakfast in the new canteen tent—a new cook and three helpers serving hot porridge and toast.

"How did he do this?" Michel asked. "In just a few days? I'm starting to think that Henri may be a magician."

"If you have money, you can buy yourself anything—even during these times. That's Henri's magic power—money."

"Thank you for last night, Jean—the prompts and things during rehearsals."

"I have little else to do. My act is now just me—no one wants to see a tall man wander around on his own. It scares people."

"Surely that's a good thing?"

"In what way?"

"Our theme is the Day of the Dead. How about we have you dressed as Death himself? You know, we can make you look like a skeleton—a hooded figure. What do you say?"

"It doesn't seem right without Giordano."

"Henri says he is working on it. You need to have faith—he will find him and bring him home."

Jean only nodded and drank his coffee.

On the last day of rehearsals Brigadeführer Wolff came to visit.

"It looks a bit..." He cocked his head to the side as he viewed the muted colors of the Big Top, the peeling paint on the signs for the smaller tents, and the faded bunting that marked the pathways around the field.

"At night, it looks wonderful. It will come alive. We have lights to string up, torches, even fireworks," Michel reassured him.

"It'd better," Wolff said, hitching up the waistband that had slipped below his paunch.

"Herr Wolff!" Frieda appeared, her hair brushed and shining, her eyebrows shaped and rouge on her cheeks.

Suddenly the brigadeführer's face changed. A smile, then a quick wipe of the sweat from his forehead with his handkerchief.

"Mademoiselle," he purred, and kissed her hand.

"May I show you the elephant and lion we have for your darling wife's birthday surprise?"

"You may indeed." He offered his arm for her to take.

As she walked away, she turned quickly and winked at Michel. He grinned at her. The ringmaster was no one without Frieda.

*

That evening the troupe sat around a campfire, sharing stories, cups of cheap wine and bottles of beer.

Around them, workers strung up lights, attaching them to large poles so that the entire camp was soon illuminated by thousands of small white lights that gently swayed in the evening air.

Michel sat slightly apart from the group with Henri, who had brought his own bottle of Burgundy, a 1904 Clos du Roi, that he had been saving for a special occasion.

"You know, Michel, I have missed the circus," Henri said. "It had been too long."

"Why did you stay away?"

Henri drank and looked above him. "Those stars—I forget to look at them. Frieda told you about Paris. About the time Werner helped me. It was a hard time for me. It has been a hard time for me since. You see, Michel, I was in love."

"With one of the rich women?"

Henri laughed. "They were my friends, the women. My very good friends. We enjoyed each other's company. Most of them were older than me, widows with fortunes who needed some fun in their lives. I provided that for them. Ah now, Michel, don't look at me like that. We loved each other in our own ways, and we used each other. But I was not in love with them. I was in love with someone else. Someone who was part of Werner's circus, even before Werner became ringmaster. We met in Hungary. We fell in love as soon as we saw each other."

"Frieda mentioned you traveled with them."

"I did. Werner knew of my feelings, of the relationship that had developed. He saw us once and I told him the truth. As he kept my secret safe, I helped him inherit the circus, gave him money. But it was a friendship—it was not bribery at all. I would return to my wife, first in Hungary, and then when she died I married once more—a widow in Paris. She enjoyed the shows, the magic of it all. She knew I was in love with someone else, and she understood."

"Why did it have to be a secret? Was the woman married?"

"Have you finished your wine? I have one more bottle. Here, uncork it."

Michel did as he was told yet did not refill his own glass—only Henri's.

"Look who has found her way back," Henri said, nodding towards the Big Top where Odélie stood chatting to a junior soldier who had been assigned to place the names on the reserved chairs in the tent.

Michel saw her rest her hand on his arm and laugh at something he said. When he moved back inside the tent to continue his work, Odélie went over to the group, smiling and waving as if she had been away on holiday.

"Odélie," Michel said as she stopped in front of him.

"Michel! I hear you are the new ringmaster. You know, word spreads around Paris so quickly, and I just had to come back to perform—I knew you would need me."

"Not so," Henri said. "We have enough performers."

Her smile fixed in place, Odélie did not move. "Ah, Henri, you are so funny. Always telling jokes. I'll go and see my triplets, make sure they have not missed me too much."

"How quickly you make friends, Odélie," Henri said. "He's a bit young for you, don't you think?"

"Herr Weber is a courteous young man, not like *some*. He is going to take me to dinner. There's nothing wrong with that."

"Apart from the fact he's a German."

"If I remember rightly, are not Frieda and Werner both German? And yet we are friends with them. You need to stop being so small-minded, Henri. It does not suit you, makes you look old and sour."

Before Henri could retort, she stalked away towards the triplets.

"She is trouble. Always has been. She has an eye for you, Michel."

"I know."

"Ah. You do? Most men give in to her. I expect she's seething with jealousy about you and Frieda."

"She has made a few comments."

"And yet she hasn't made a scene. *Yet.*"

"This is good wine," Michel said, changing the subject. He lit a cigarette, his eyes on Odélie as she kissed Frieda on both cheeks and giggled with her. Behind them, Monsieur Bertrand and Madame Rosie held hands. Michel smiled at the pair, happy that Bertrand had found someone.

"That is nice to see," Henri said, following his gaze.

"They are well matched."

"She was not married, you know."

"Who? Madame Rosie?"

"No, not her. My love. In fact, the main problem was that she was not a *she* at all."

Michel inhaled the smoke then blew it out in front of him. Quietly, he said, "I see."

"A young tightrope walker. He was magnificent to watch."

"Where is he now?"

"Dead," Henri said simply, no trace of sadness in his voice. "Did we drink all the wine?"

"Not quite."

"Come with me to my house. We will finish it there. Perhaps get Werner to join us if he is up for it."

Michel followed Henri to the house, his head aching. He watched the count walk a few steps in front, whistling a tune. He had met men like Henri before, and had, as others did, believed it to be wrong—immoral. But looking at Henri now—his kindness for the others, his willingness to help—made Michel feel as though he himself may have been the one in the wrong.

Inside, the house was warm. Henri asked Michel to wait in the living room whilst he went to fetch Werner. The grandfather clock in the hallway ticked by five minutes before Henri appeared once more, Werner on his arm, wearing a plum dressing gown, a ruddy flush in his cheeks.

"You are looking better," Michel said.

"I wish I felt it." Werner sat heavily in an armchair by the fire and Henri placed a blanket over his legs. "Henri said we were celebrating. I told him we should wait until after the show—but as you can see, he does not listen."

"And when have I ever listened to you?" Henri sang out, as he poured the rest of the wine into crystal glasses. He handed out the drinks, then placed a record on the gramophone. The song Michel knew so well began to crackle, Fréhel's voice calling out to dance the Java with the one you love.

"La Java Bleue," Michel said.

"I thought that, as we were on the subject of love, this was the most appropriate song." Henri sat on the sofa, the orange glow from the fire casting strange shadows so that for a moment, Michel thought Henri was crying.

"I thought this was a celebration. Why are we talking about love?" Werner asked.

"It is a celebration—a celebration of love. Have you never celebrated the great loves of your lives? Éva, the circus, Frieda?"

Werner shook his head. "I have other things to do with my time than be a romantic like you!"

"Come now, Werner, I have seen you be a romantic. Michel, listen, Werner and Éva were so in love. He would bring her flowers every day, just to make sure he saw her smile at least once a day. That is romance."

"I was young," Werner said.

"And you, Michel. Are you a romantic?"

"I'm not sure. I hope I am."

"Frieda thinks you are." Henri winked, and Werner shifted in his chair.

"I hope to be everything she wants me to be." Michel was emboldened by the wine. "I hope to give her everything she wants. One day, I will have the money to buy her things, to be romantic."

"Money is not romance, Michel. It helps, of course. I have money, but I have no romance." Henri took a sip of wine, then looked above him at the painting of the man that hung above the fireplace.

"You're drunk," Werner admonished Henri. "And I'm tired."

"We are celebrating! Here, have some more, then you can fall asleep like a baby. I told Michel about my own great love."

"You did?" Werner raised his eyebrow.

"I did. His name, Michel, was Pedro, from Madrid. He could dance, you know. Oh, how we would dance together when no one was looking."

"You said he died. What happened?"

"Now, that is a sad tale. A sad, sad tale."

"Not one we need to go over," Werner told him.

"No. We must. It is romantic in its own way—just as Éva losing you and you gaining a daughter is romantic. So is the way our love ended."

"Do as you wish. You will anyway."

"Now, Michel, Frieda told you that one night in Paris, she saw me battered, beaten even worse than our friend Werner here. Well, that was the night Pedro died. You see, my wife, God rest her soul—"

"And the others," Werner interrupted.

"Yes, the others too—all my wives. God rest their souls. Anyway. She was poorly and took to bed. I told her that Pedro was in Paris whilst Werner got things organized for their next jaunt. Pedro and I spent many a day roaming Paris, buying gifts, eating and talking. We went to museums, he taught me to speak some Spanish, I painted him. In the evenings we sat, just as any couple did, and read by the fire, or listened to music. When my wife was able, she joined us, and we had dinner together. It was nothing obscene like people think. It was just love. Then, one night, we went to a bar where we could hear some singers. We ordered a bottle of wine and sat together. It was dark in the bar, very dark, so now and then we held hands under the table.

"It was about nine when things changed. The singer was taking a break, and the barman accidently flicked on the main light, illuminating the entire crowd—and Pedro and I with our arms around each other.

"It was a mere moment, a flicker of something that many would never have noticed. But to our distress, it was seen.

"A group of men behind us saw. They approached us and asked questions—*Who are you? What is your name, address?*

"We were committing no crime, so I refused to answer them. I told them it was none of their business.

"I did not know that one of the men was a gendarme. A high-ranking official at that. He did not take kindly to my refusal, so they dragged us outside. The gendarme told me he would prosecute us; some sort of law about morality. I told him once more that we were committing no crime.

"I remember that one of the men laughed. Then, before I knew it, I was on the floor, being kicked and spat on. Pedro tried to help, he screamed for others to help us, but no one came. He attacked the gendarme, who was kicking the hardest. The gendarme threw him to the ground and then Pedro was silent.

"They grew weary of their game soon enough and left us alone, bleeding into the gutter. It had started to rain, and it was as if the whole pavement ran with blood. I tried to stand and finally found

I could. I made my way to Pedro. His face was unrecognizable. His face. It was still. He did not react when I screamed, when I cried. Nothing. His face..." Suddenly Henri began to weep. Holding his head in his hands, he cried and screamed as if reliving the nightmare.

Werner tried to get up from his chair but could not, so Michel sat beside Henri and held him close, rocking him like a baby until eventually the weeping became muffled sobs.

"I told you not to talk about it," Werner said quietly.

Henri looked to Werner and smiled sadly. He wiped his tears away with the cuff of his jacket. "I know. And you were right, as always. If I would only listen to you, Werner, my life would be so different."

"Can I get you something?" Michel asked.

"A whisky. Just one, then time for a nap. Don't look at me like that, Werner, I said one more and then to bed. Thank you, dear Michel. Such a dear boy. Frieda is lucky to have you."

Michel sat and allowed Henri to drink and calm himself, the grandfather clock ticking loudly, reminding them that it was almost tomorrow—almost the day of the show.

"It is too quiet here. Too quiet. That damned clock keeps reminding me of each second of my life that is ticking away. I will leave here soon. Leave and never come back."

"It is almost tomorrow," Michel said.

"Yes. Indeed it is. You must rest. It is a big day for you, for all of us. You know Werner saved my life that day? He took me in, cleaned me up, nursed me. He went to my wife and told her what had happened. She was a powerful woman, Michel. The widow of a judge, no less. She made sure that nothing happened to me, but poor Pedro's death was classed as an accident—there was nothing she could have done to change that. Werner, he stopped me from going mad, from drinking myself to death or jumping from a bridge."

"Which you tried to do so often it kept me awake for months," Werner added.

"And yet, you persevered. You are my friend. My very best of friends. I am so glad to have met you."

"Now you are becoming maudlin. I can't have maudlin. Neither can Michel, not the night before the show."

"You are right, you are always right, Werner." Henri stood and helped him to his feet. "Michel, sleep well. I am putting Werner to bed. It is time we all had some peace."

Michel watched Henri gently half carry and half walk his friend to the stairs. The two of them leaned on each other, holding each other up.

CHAPTER FIFTEEN

La Danse Macabre

The morning of the show, the wind grew stronger with each hour; the canopy of the Big Top concaved for a moment, and then the next it filled with air and looked bulbous against the sky. Michel welcomed the wind that brought the cold and iced rain from the east, a fitting scene for their final performance—dramatic, unnerving, a last goodbye.

The horses were skittish. The wind was different here, untamed and dangerous. They wanted to be free with it, run wild across fields without the constant eye of their trainers. The wind whispered to them, made them stamp their hooves and flare their nostrils, impatient for what was going to happen next.

Under the turbulent gray-black sky, Michel waited for Frieda to come out of her costume fitting with Madame Rosie. Trees swayed and dipped as the wind bent them to its will, yet people milled about, holding down caps, grasping shut jackets, as if the wind would give up and forget about disturbing them in their final preparations. Their clothes were muted by the cold sky, making everyone seem to Michel like characters in a dream he could not control.

Frieda came to him, as wild as the wind, her hair a stream of black behind her. Her green eyes looked luminous in the dimmed light and when she kissed him, it was as though she was sealing their bond—they were going to be together forever.

"I was just going to see your father," Michel said. "Do you want to come?"

"I can't. Rosie is getting worried that she cannot do everyone's makeup in time. We are all helping. Give Papa a kiss from me. I will see you soon."

"It's almost time."

"It will be fine, Michel. Trust me. It will be fine." She kissed him again, then retreated to the caravan where he heard Rosie shouting at Bertrand for doing it wrong.

As Michel entered Henri's house, he could hear a woman sobbing, and the rise and fall of Henri's voice.

He tapped gently on the closed living room door and it swung open so quickly that Michel wondered if they had been waiting for him.

"Come in." Henri's face was tight with anger.

Michel walked into the room and saw Odélie in the corner, tears streaming down her face, her eyes puffy and red as if she had been weeping for days.

"Tell him!" Henri commanded.

"Please!" Odélie begged, then sobbed into her hands, hiding her face.

Henri approached her and grabbed her head, so she was forced to look at Michel. "Tell him!" he shouted again.

"I am sorry, Michel," she said, her voice not her own—childish, pleading. "I am so sorry." She fell from her chair and lay on the floor curled into a ball; her body racked with sobs.

Michel made to move towards her, but Henri grabbed his arm. "Don't. Leave her."

Henri walked away from her and took a bottle of whisky off a shelf, then poured two glasses. He placed one on the floor next to Odélie's head. "Drink it and pull yourself together."

Michel sat, his leg jumping with nerves, as Henri drank his whisky back and then poured another.

"She told them. She told that *fils de pute* little German officer who we all are. She told them what Werner has been doing. *Salope!* What for? What for? Some money? Some jewelry?"

"He said he would look after me, that Wolff would take care of me!" she cried. "It was a mistake—a slip of the tongue...I didn't mean it—I trusted him!"

"And now? Now he'll send you away with the others, I bet. You're no use to him anymore."

"I don't understand..." Michel said, even though he did.

"Michel, we are not getting any papers to leave. Wolff was never even going to help, so this woman says. And to make it worse—to make it worse!—she told them that Werner is hiding Jewish people here. So now, instead of just performing then not receiving papers, Wolff has plans to round us all up at the end of the show. Isn't that so?"

"I came to warn you!" Odélie sat up. "When I realized the mistake I made. I came to tell you what he is going to do! He would kill me if he knew, but I still did it. I did."

"How very noble." Henri's voice cut through the air.

"So, what do we do?" Michel asked.

"I am thinking," Henri said. "I am thinking."

Suddenly, the count stood and called for his driver. "I need to go to Paris now. I will be back. Watch her."

Michel waited until the sound of the car's engine had disappeared before he turned to look at Odélie. "Get off the floor."

She nodded and stood, picked up the glass and sat across from him, her head bowed.

"Why, Odélie?"

"It was an accident, Michel, I swear it. I was a little drunk. He said that Wolff had told him he felt there was something going on. I don't know how I said it, but I told him. He said he would tell Wolff, and then Wolff called for me and I told him, and then he said he would take care of me and I knew, Michel, I knew what I had done. I knew how horrible I have been. With you. With everyone."

"Odélie," Michel's voice was quiet, "was this all because of me and Frieda?"

"No!" She shook her head. "It was truly a mistake. I just said that everyone hides things—something like that. I didn't think he would go to Wolff—I truly didn't."

"But he did."

She nodded.

"What exactly did Wolff say?" Michel asked.

Odélie wiped her tears on her sleeve. "He asked me to tell the truth. He had three soldiers in the room. I didn't say anything at first, not a thing." She stopped and looked at the door as if expecting someone to rescue her.

Michel waited.

"He made me sit down," she continued quietly. "He put his hands on my shoulders and pushed me into a chair, and he didn't take his hands away. My legs were shaking. He spoke above me—asked me what I meant when I said people were hiding things. I think I laughed, you know, so he would think it was a joke. I said it was nothing—just something silly that everyone says."

"And then?" Michel asked.

Odélie's bottom lip quivered, her knuckles white as she grasped the glass, her legs trembling. She looked at him.

"He said he'd arrest me and . . . and . . . let his soldiers have their way with me if I didn't tell him. All the while he held me down, his hands on my shoulders. And then he kissed me, Michel. He kissed me and then ripped my dress open. He said that he would continue, then the other three soldiers would have a go. I—" She broke down and sobbed, her shoulders heaving.

Michel moved to her and despite his anger, despite his fear, he kneeled in front of her and held her close.

"You shouldn't comfort me, Michel." She pulled away. "I don't deserve your kindness, not after the way I treated you."

Michel sat back on the couch. "Odélie, you were right to be upset with me—I did not treat you as I should have."

She shook her head. "Not that."

"You didn't do anything else, Odélie. We'll explain to the others what happened—you had no choice, you had to tell him."

"Not that," she said again.

"Then what?"

"Your head," she began. "I know who did it. I didn't say anything."

"You?" he asked.

"No! Not me. But a soldier I met in Vodable. I was angry. I heard Werner tell you about Frieda, about everything. He trusted you and I knew that he wanted you to be with her. I was jealous and angry. That night when we performed in the town, I told the soldier how you had broken my heart. He—he took it badly and wanted to impress me. I didn't think he would do anything about it—you know? I just thought it was all talk. I really did. But then, when I heard what had happened, I knew it was my fault."

Michel stood abruptly.

"Where—?"

"I need to go."

"Please, Michel, I'm so sorry!" She fell to her knees and placed her hands together as if in prayer. "Please! I am so sorry."

"I need to see Werner," he said, and turned his back on her as she crouched, weeping, on the floor.

Michel opened the door slowly to find Werner sitting up in bed, reading.

"Ah, Michel! How are the preparations? Nervous? Not poetry this time," Werner waved the book in front of him, "Hergé."

"Tintin." Michel smiled. "I know his stories well." He sat on the chair next to Werner's bed.

"What's wrong? Don't tell me the elephant has escaped? It has happened before!"

Michel shook his head. He told Odélie's tale.

"Where is Henri?"

"Gone to the city."

"Then we wait. Henri knows many people. Trust me, he will sort this out for us."

Michel looked at Werner; a crease had appeared on his forehead.

"Trust him," Werner said again, and returned to his book.

The pair sat in silence, the clock on the side table ticking away the hours. It got to three, then quarter past, when the sound of wheels on gravel came from outside.

"See?" Werner said. "He's back." The crease was still deep on his forehead, and in all the time that had passed he had not turned a page.

They listened as Henri's quick footsteps climbed the stairs. Then he entered the room as breathless as if he had just run from Paris.

"Michel, things will need to change with your show tonight. You must leave here by nine." Henri was panting, his collar unbuttoned.

"The show doesn't begin until eight, we won't even be halfway through—"

"That is why it must change."

Henri passed Michel an envelope. "Everything you need is in there. You are leaving France. Tonight. It is the only way."

Michel opened the envelope. Two tickets to England, then two more on to America. Then, at the back, identification cards: one for Michel Bonnet, the other for Frieda Bonnet.

"Frieda?" Michel held up her card.

"I assumed you would want her to go with you. It will be safer for her," Henri said, his eyes not on Michel but on Werner.

"She can't leave," Michel said. "Werner—"

Werner shook his head. "Bonnet, eh? It suits her." He looked at the book again.

"But what about the others?"

"Serge and Jean will leave at the end. They know how to disappear for a night. Then, I have made provisions for them to leave too. The triplets will stay with me, in my attic if need be. Bertrand will take Madame Rosie to his home in Paris. Kacper and Hugo will travel south tomorrow. I have a lady friend with a lot of money and a large villa. She will be glad of the company."

"There are more people in the show, Henri, the others we have hired…"

"Don't worry, Michel. Fireworks inside the tent will cause a distraction. Those we have hired know how to disappear back into the shadows of Paris."

"What of Giordano?" Michel's head was spinning. "Jean will not leave until he knows he can do something to help him."

"I will have news on him soon—very soon," Henri said.

"And you? And Werner?"

"We will be OK." Henri sat on the edge of Werner's bed. "We have always been all right."

"Odélie?" Werner said.

Henri's expression changed from relief to anger.

"We must, Henri. We must help her too," Werner implored. "I know what she has done—but it was not her fault. Talk to her again, Henri. She told Michel what they did to her—what they threatened to do."

"You are kinder than you look." Henri smiled weakly. "Fine. She leaves now. Our friend in town will take her somewhere in his cheese delivery truck. I will make a call."

Henri left and Michel waited a few minutes before he spoke.

"I will take care of her," he said quietly. "I promise."

"I know you will."

"Will you really be OK?"

Werner shrugged. "Henri will. Most definitely. He has too much money and is too clever to get caught. He will disappear if he needs to."

"And you?" Michel said again.

"If I need to." Werner groaned as he tried to swing his legs out of bed. As he did, Michel saw that the side where he had been stabbed was swollen to bursting and an angry crimson.

"If I need to," Werner said again as he pulled his nightshirt down, avoiding Michel's gaze. "You'll send for Serge? I need him to help me dress. I want to see the show."

"You should rest."

"I want to see the show! It is still my circus; it still has my name on it."

"As you wish, Ringmaster."

Michel left Werner on the edge of his bed, his feet not touching the floor.

The townsfolk arrived first, just as the lights were switched on, hooked to generators that whirred and grunted. Torches were lit with kerosene, lighting the way through the maze of tents.

Serge's voice boomed from a loudspeaker, announcing the delights to come, whilst Kacper played his accordion at the entrance, the children stopping to pat Gino on his furry little head.

Michel watched the procession fill the field. After half an hour, a trail of black Mercedes pulled up, small flags waving above the headlights bearing the swastika, heralding danger.

Brigadeführer Dietrich Wolff emerged from the first car, followed by his wife, her eyes wide. She clapped her hands at what she saw, and Serge announced the arrival of the birthday girl to the crowd. The band struck up a tune and she clapped her hands again with the glee of a small child. Wolff grinned.

Michel made his way through the performers, their faces painted white, their eyes ringed with kohl, and red, yellow and green spotted designs marking their skin. The women wore peasant blouses and big skirts held up tightly with wire so they could can-can and show off their stockinged legs.

The fire eater was dressed as a groom in black, his face white, his eyes dead. His bride—a contortionist—wore a bloodied bridal gown and bent herself into painful shapes.

Skeletons danced and threw sweets at the feet of their guests and Madame Rosie sat outside her tent, decaying roses in her hair and her face painted white with black tattoo designs all over her forehead.

Michel managed to find Frieda in the throng.

"We need to talk, now," he whispered in her ear.

They went to her caravan and sat together on the bed whilst Michel told her of the changed plans.

"Does everyone know?"

"Yes. Serge has seen to it."

"So, we leave tonight?"

"Yes."

Frieda's eyes welled with tears.

"No, no, don't cry, my love. Please. It will be fine. I promise you."

"But Papa, the others—"

"It will be fine. Please. Hush." He held her to him. "I need you to be strong, my darling. I need you to help me get through this. I can't do it without you."

Frieda pulled away and wiped her eyes. "I should go and finish my makeup."

"Yes."

"And then I will perform."

"Yes."

"And then... and then we will leave."

He nodded.

"Together."

"Together." Michel kissed her deeply, then kissed her cheeks where the tears had fallen, her eyelids, the tip of her nose. "You feel warm." He placed his hand on her forehead.

"I'm OK. Just tired."

He looked at her face, pale and drawn. He placed his hand back on her forehead. "It's hot, Frieda. You're not well."

She took his hand in hers. "I'll be fine, Michel. We need to get through this. A little cold cannot stop me from performing."

"Werner always said you were bossy."

"He's right. I'm the real boss around here." She hugged him quickly.

"I'll see you soon," he said.

"You will."

Frieda left Michel siting in the caravan, his legs numb beneath him, his hands shaking. He felt sick.

Before the show began, Michel went to the stables to see the horses. The triplets sat inside, their eyes wide with fear, each of them now and again patting Beau's nose.

"You have spoken with Henri?" Michel asked them.

Edita looked at him. She pulled her shawl around her. "We have."

Michel knelt in front of them. "Don't be afraid. It will be fine. Henri will keep you safe."

"We're not scared," Edita said. "We will be OK." She turned to her brother and sister and held out her hands. Each of them took a hand and stood, walking back towards the circus, not turning to say goodbye to Michel.

Claudette nodded her head over the stable door, happy to see her master. "Hello there, my girl." He stroked her nose, her mane. "Such a beautiful girl. Keep those triplets safe tonight, eh?"

Claudette stamped her hoof.

Michel moved on to Bisou and had to open the stable door in order to see him properly. "You OK, my little friend?" Michel knelt in front of him and allowed Bisou to lower his head, resting it on his shoulder. "You giving me a hug? You always were a sweet one. Don't you worry now, Bisou. Don't you worry. Henri will keep you warm and safe here. How does that sound? No more traveling, no more getting wet and cold. He'll keep you safe."

Beau snorted above them and Michel stood, closed Bisou's stable door and went to the fine stallion.

"Now, you and I have a show to do first." Michel readjusted his bridle. "Not time to say goodbye just yet."

Finally, he visited the workhorses, all of them delighted to receive a carrot. "You have worked hard, my friends. All of you. Now it is time for you to retire. Happy days wandering the fields and eating carrots by the bucket load!" He stroked each of them. Then, just before he left, he went back one more time and hugged them, feeling a lump form in his throat.

By seven thirty the crowd had edged their way into the Big Top. First the birthday girl and Brigadeführer Wolff, followed by his entourage, which was larger than Michel had realized it would be. More than half of the audience wore a uniform; the other half were the townsfolk who, despite their obvious joy at being at a circus, kept sneaking glances at the uniforms as though they might attack at any moment.

Michel watched as the crowd filled the seats. Behind him, in a small covered area, the performers waited nervously.

Hugo bit his nails until Kacper handed him some white gloves; the little boy from rehearsals—now dressed as a clown—was still loudly complaining about his pay; and the triplets twirled their batons, every now and then betraying their fear when they dropped them.

Bertrand milled amongst them, telling them they would do fine, telling them not to look at the crowd.

"Imagine they are just normal people. Forget they are wearing uniforms."

"So, you're saying to imagine them naked?" the boy asked.

"I'm saying do whatever you need to do to perform."

"I'm not imagining no Germans naked. Maman says they have no genitals—she says they have come straight from hell and instead they have spikes down there."

"Would you hush? Please. Enough," Edita scolded.

The lad looked at her expression and acquiesced.

The orchestra began. A melancholy tune by a violin pierced the air, sending shivers down spines. Soon, another violin joined, darker, the musician quicker on the bow, as if playing an altogether different instrument. There was a rumble of thunder behind them, or perhaps the drums—either way, the volume grew, but the pace stayed the same: a slow, somber march that would soon find its end.

Then the pianist began to play. A few notes, high then low, creating waves in the narrative—no longer simply a march, but now deviating over high and low ground, searching for its end and resting place.

The lights suddenly went out, plunging the tent into a complete darkness that made the audience gasp and cry out. Then, a spotlight appeared on the ground. It was tiny—at first no bigger than a coin— but with each note, each beat of the drum, the light grew, then found its prey. There, wrapped in silks like a chrysalis, was Frieda. She hung still from the beams above, the silver silk flashing and catching the light. Suddenly another light appeared. This time it hit the faces of skeletons that had suddenly appeared around the edge of the stage. Some of the audience gasped, others laughed nervously—*Were they there all along? These people dressed in black, white bones painted on them—where have they come from? Is that really paint? Or are they real bones?*

The music stopped.

The crowd's silence deafened Michel's ears—*It will not be long now . . .*

Before the audience realized what was happening, the music changed tempo, causing the skeletons to dance and somersault in tandem. It was still an eerie song—one that warranted caution, yet one that could turn and surprise quicker than a flash of light.

Michel rode Beau out into the middle of the ring and felt the heat of the spotlight on him.

"Ladies and gentlemen, I welcome you to this night of the dead, this night of magic, of scenes you have never seen before!"

A loud bang echoed around the tent and then smoke appeared in front of Michel. The audience were silent. When the smoke dispersed, instead of Michel they were greeted with Camille the elephant, on top of whom stood Stephanie, her costume of gold sequins catching the light.

The crowd erupted with applause, and Stephanie rode Camille around the ring as a procession of performers entered the tent.

First Bastien the lion jumped through hoops, then the fire eater touched them and made them burst into flame. The crowd oohed and aahed. Then from above there was a shout, and everyone looked up to see Frieda sailing through the air, all in white, her face dotted with crystals and sequins so that she glimmered as she flew.

Below her, the acrobats had appeared; they tumbled and twirled, juggled and danced, making the crowd disoriented.

Before they could take it all in, the performers dropped to the floor, looking as though they were dead, and Frieda fell from the sky like an injured bird to be caught in the net.

Michel rode Beau back into the ring, his nerves causing Beau to jitter and step backwards, then sideways.

"As you can see, our performers have gone into the afterlife. But do not fear! Today is the day we can bring them back to us!"

With a round of applause, a figure appeared. A creature on stilts, head to toe in black, with only his deadened face and dark eyes to be seen. He asked the audience to chant words unknown to them, and as they did, the band picked up pace, the words spilling out faster and faster until there was a crash of cymbals, then all went black.

The spotlight came on, again pinpricking lights on each performer as they woke, missing out Frieda in her net.

The band struck up a Spanish tune that made the performers tumble and flip—they were alive and well! Now they moved quickly, seamlessly, and were joined by the triplets on horseback who flipped on and off Claudette. The mare rode well, her gait perfect, her nerves holding strong.

Then, just as the crowd were settling in for the show, the lights went out once more.

This time the audience clapped and jeered, for they thought they knew what was to come. Any minute now the lights would appear, and the troupe would take their bows. They clapped some more, and more... then slowly the applause stopped. There were murmurings of confusion in the crowd.

As Michel reached the back of the tent, he grabbed Frieda's hand. Then, suddenly in front of them was Herr Weber—Odélie's soldier friend.

"What is happening? Where are the lights?" he demanded.

Michel looked around. "They'll come back on."

"I'm getting Wolff," Weber said, his smile thin, barely showing his teeth.

"Wait, just wait!" Michel grabbed Weber's arm.

Weber pulled his arm away, and with a backhand slapped Michel so hard he fell to the ground.

Frieda gasped and bent down to help him.

Within seconds, two more soldiers appeared. One grabbed Frieda's arms and pulled her to her feet. Michel was scrambling to stand when the other soldier caught hold of him.

Suddenly, from inside the tent, they could hear a loud cheer as the lights reappeared and the band struck up a ditty. Laughter followed a cymbal crash—Hugo and the clowns. The show was not yet done.

"See?" Michel nodded towards the tent. "See."

"No matter. You can come and wait with us. I'm sure the brigade-führer will want to have a word with you after the show—thank you for everything." Weber smiled, this time showing his teeth.

Serge suddenly appeared and seized Weber, then punched him hard in the face. The other two soldiers let go of Michel and Frieda, and rushed to Weber's aid. Each tried to grapple with Serge, who moved quickly, first punching one, then forcing the other under his large arm, his head under his armpit.

"Go! Go now!" Serge hissed.

Michel saw Weber trying to get to his feet, the other soldier unconscious. Michel pushed Weber back down and kicked him hard in the ribs so that he yowled with pain and curled up into a ball. Serge gripped the other soldier's head so tightly he passed out, then let him flop to the ground.

"Serge, you must come with us!" Frieda pleaded. "When they see what happened..." She trailed off.

"Don't you worry about me, girl." Serge caught her in a quick embrace. "You go now. I'll hide these three. Got some nice rope back there. I'll keep them hidden—go now and be safe."

Michel looked wildly around him; the music was swelling, the acts coming to a close.

"Go! Go now!" Serge urged once more. "There's no time."

Michel took Serge's hand and shook it. "Thank you, Serge."

"Enough now—go!"

Michel lifted a flap at the back of the tent and turned quickly again to see Serge dragging one of the soldiers towards a stack of crates.

A car was waiting outside, its engine ready. Werner stood, holding on to Bertrand's arm.

"Papa…" Frieda said, tears already rolling down her face.

"Go. I love you." He kissed her.

Michel hugged Bertrand. "Quick now, Michel. Be quick."

"I can't leave you here, Bertrand—I can't," Michel said.

"You've no choice. I'll be fine—I'll pretend I was watching the show. Madame Rosie and I, we're going back to Paris. I'll be fine—it's time for me to go home."

"But Bertrand…" Michel gripped his friend's arm. "What about the others? I can't just leave them."

"You're not," Werner said. "I'm their ringmaster. I'll see them right. You keep my daughter safe, you hear? You keep her safe." His eyes filled with tears.

Frieda did not want to let go of her father, and Michel had to peel her away and place her in the car.

"Go, Michel," Werner said.

Michel climbed in after her and the driver immediately pulled away.

Both Michel and Frieda looked out of the rear window, watching Bertrand and Werner wave a sad goodbye. Then, someone else appeared—Giordano, being led by Henri towards Jean.

"Henri found him!" Frieda said, crying and laughing at the same time.

The last thing Michel saw was Jean hugging his friend next to the candy-cane canvas that dipped and blew in the wind.

PART THREE: WINTER

I've lived to bury my desires,
And see my dreams corrode with rust;
Now all that's left are fruitless fires
That burn my empty heart to dust.

Struck by the storms of cruel fate
My crown of summer bloom is sere;
Alone and sad I watch and wait
And wonder if the end is near.

As conquered by the last cold air,
When winter whistles in the wind
Alone upon a branch that's bare
A trembling leaf is left behind.

"I've Lived to Bury My Desires," Aleksandr Sergejevich Pushkin

CHAPTER SIXTEEN

New York

The air has changed once more. This air is cold—colder than I have ever known before. It blows over the Hudson River, bringing with it snow, sleet and that smell of river water—a rich, heady scent of decaying trees and ancient mud banks, a scent that to some is perhaps unfortunate, but it takes me back to my childhood, and to my home.

I wake to the cold and wrap a dressing gown around me—a worn old thing given to me by a kindly neighbor. A Polish woman, herself escaped to this strange city with little but her sick husband and a few treasures. Her husband is now dead. His skinny frame never recovered from the torment of the camp he escaped, and he died in her arms, wearing this gown. Some would think it morbid that I wear it, yet I think it an honor. He endured more than I have, even though my heart is perhaps more broken by love than his; at least he had his wife near him at the end.

I make coffee. Now I own two mugs: one blue and one white with a blue trim on the lip. I choose the white mug; it matches the color of the sky and the snow that fell last night. I fill it to the brim with a dense black coffee that I found cheap in the deli two blocks away. It smells of chestnuts and perhaps chocolate—it is harsh, bitter, and too strong for most—yet for me it is perfect.

My chair. My only chair. *My chair*—I like to say these words. It is gray and patched in places, but it is stuffed with horsehair and this is the reason I love it so—it reminds me of the chair in Bertrand's apartment in the 14th arrondissement, the chair I always wanted to own. I own it now. It cost me one dollar in a market that runs down the side of the block every Friday morning for people like me—for us who do not yet belong.

I sit, allowing the stuffing to sink and envelop my weight—not that there is much of it—and sip at my coffee whilst the snow falls, thinking as always about her; wondering where she is and if perhaps today is the day I will see her again, even though I know it's impossible. A year has passed and yet it feels as though I have just arrived; as if this is all still a dream.

Each falling flake reminds me of her—when laughter and murmurings of love whispered their way into my ears.

I try every day to shake the memory from my mind, to concentrate on the present, but the snow draws me to it, leading me into a memory that is whitewashed as a dream—which takes me back to her.

*

It was as though winter appeared the moment we drove away in that car, in October 1940. The autumn leaves littered the road and a frigid rain hit hard on the windscreen. Frieda huddled into me for warmth and I held her close, every now and then feeling her body move as she quietly cried. As we drove, I realized I had not said a proper goodbye to Beau. I had dismounted and left him with Eliáš. I had forgotten my friend.

The car ride was a blur. The driver, a man Henri said he trusted with his life, had a scar from ear to cheek on one side of his face. He didn't talk, other than to tell us to lie flat on the back seat every now and then.

He drove quickly, around bends, up hills, only stopping to fill the tank from a jerrycan he kept in the back.

Frieda cried for Werner, for the others. I held her and tried to soothe her. "They will be fine," I said. "Henri will see them all right."

Eventually she fell asleep, her head on my lap, drained from the performance, the fear, the goodbyes.

"Do you smoke?" I asked the driver.

"Doesn't everyone?"

"You want one?"

He nodded.

I tapped out two from the packet and lit one for him. He took it and didn't say thank you.

"Where are we going?"

"The coast," he said. "Where else are you going to get in a boat? Your bags are in the back, by the way."

"I didn't pack a bag."

"Someone did."

At dawn, we reached a rugged outcrop. I could smell the sea before I saw it; the salty freshness that always made me feel excited. Despite our circumstances I felt my stomach flutter at the sense of adventure.

I woke Frieda, who was pale and still so exhausted. She sluggishly came around, and our driver told us we had to get out of the car.

"It's freezing out there," I said.

"I can't stay."

"What do we do?"

"You wait."

"Where?"

"Here. You wait here. They won't be long."

"Who is they?"

"You'll know when you see them."

I was angry at this man, this stupid silent man, even though he had helped us.

Frieda and I got our bags from the trunk and huddled together like refugees. I told her what I thought we looked like.

"I guess we are now," she said, and shivered into me.

The silent man was right. Within ten minutes two men appeared from a craggy path below the lip of the cliff.

"Bonnet?" one said.

"Yes."

"Better get a move on."

We followed him down the steep path, the other man at the rear, both of them turning their heads every so often, reminding me of birds checking to see where their prey was. I supposed, though, that we were the prey.

Just as it was getting light, past the blue gray of dawn, we reached a pebbled beach and a rowing boat.

"Get in," the man at the rear said.

"We are rowing to England?"

"Don't be stupid."

I got in and held Frieda tight.

"I don't feel well," she said.

"Just put your head on my shoulder and close your eyes," I told her.

The men were impressive in their rowing and we moved quickly through the waves, leaving a silent wake. Their arms were powerful, and they moved in such synchronicity that I realized they had done this many times before.

We rowed around the edge of a longer outcrop; then, just as I thought we were heading out into open sea, I saw a large boat anchored in a tiny space between the rocks, hidden from view. They pulled the rowing boat up alongside it and we climbed up a ladder onto the deck.

No one spoke to us. No one asked to see anything but the flimsy tickets allowing our passage.

The engine started with a splutter and those of us on deck, maybe twenty or so, looked up at the cliff edge, expecting any moment to see an army of Germans firing down at us.

No one came.

The sea was as cold and hard as iron. It did not want to let the boat pass through, chaffing and tugging at the bow like a child trying to cling to its mother. But the boat did not stop, ploughing on steadily, focused on the next channel, and then perhaps the next. We sat on deck with most of the last passengers to arrive—we could not go below to the hold which was drier and perhaps safer. Instead, we sat under a balcony above; held on to each other and allowed other passengers to sit close to us, our bodies protecting one another.

I held Frieda as the boat rocked from side to side, feeling her heart beat with mine; warming her with anything that I had. Our clothes were damp, our feet frozen and wet inside our shoes. Frieda fell asleep at some stage—a sleep that made her talk of wild things, and moan and cry out. I held my palm to her forehead to check for fever, but the icy drizzle, the slap of waves on the boat and the cries of the seamen to veer left then right made me a useless doctor and I could not tell how she was.

A man with a long, wet beard came forward and told me that there was a little space in the second hold; enough perhaps for her, but not for me. At least she would be dry there.

I helped the man carry Frieda, who murmured deliriously of the triplets; that they were too young and liable to fall.

"Nieces and nephews," I told the bearded man.

He nodded.

We placed Frieda in the smallest of spaces below deck, next to an older woman and her daughter who was perhaps Frieda's age. They promised to watch her and immediately wrapped her in a blanket. I left her there with the strangers and made my way back on deck, thankful that she would be taken care of.

Southampton was the port we stopped at, an English port, and I was happy to see dry land once more. Frieda, although still sick, became brighter once she felt land underfoot.

I went to a seaman to find out where the ship to America was leaving from. He pointed to a larger ship further down the dock and we scurried there as the horn sounded.

I gave the man our tickets. "Not enough," he said. "The fares have gone up."

"How can that be?" Frieda asked.

I could see who he was, this man, making a few more coins from the desperate. I wanted to hit him, to shout at him in my exhaustion, but then Frieda grasped his wrist and looked him dead in the eye. There was something in the look she gave him; desperation perhaps—whatever it was, he related to it, and could not deny her.

"Fine," he said. "That'll do. It's enough."

*

Has it been almost one more year? Another year here in New York? The Christmas of 1942 approaching, and me with little to think of once more than Frieda.

As I sit here and watch the flakes of snow fall on another year gone, I can almost convince myself that my former life did not exist—that it was all a dream and I appeared here as if by magic.

A knock at my door moments ago disturbed me. It was my neighbor—the Polish lady. She brought me a pan of cabbage and sauerkraut with sausage. It smells dreadful but, surprisingly, tastes delightful. I am not one to dismiss free food—not with the meager wages I earn.

I work in a launderette. It is for rich people who have stains on their clothes from the wines I used to drink when I was in France, and the food my mother would cook. Now I make sure I get rid of those stains. My boss is Jewish. His name is Levi. He has a daughter, Miriam—a widow. She has a child and is not much bothered by me, but her father does not wish to leave her the business without a man in charge. I suppose he is looking to me. I am not sure that he should.

I have another chair now; it is green like new leaves on a tree in spring. And I have a rug on my floor which takes some of the stinging coldness away from those bare floorboards. I own books. Many books. Books are so cheap and at times free. It is surprising to me how many times I find an abandoned book on a park bench, in a bin or on the bus. All these books remind me of Bertrand; of his living room and shelves stacked with volumes. I take them as much for me as I do for him—I know he would want me to collect them and hoard them as my treasures. I read into the night, and on my days off, I sit outside and read once more, and this stops the loneliness, the feeling of being somewhere so foreign without a purpose.

Central Park is my favorite spot, especially at this time of year. The frozen ponds become busy with children and partners skating, holding hands, their scarves trailing behind them, their laughter hanging in the snow-covered branches of the trees that surround them. For three days, I have a break from work. Three days when families eat turkey and sing and play games. Levi invited me to their home but I said no. I now regret it.

I spend Christmas Eve walking the busy streets. My favorite is where the department stores live; all gussied up with lights, decorated trees, and red, green and gold window displays. The sewer grates here smoke and steam in the middle of the streets, and I keep thinking that at any moment they will bust open and something magical will appear.

My English is better now. I practice all the time, and I do not get asked anymore what I just said. Perhaps now I am an American?

It is Christmas Eve. I sit in my armchair. The radiator gurgles and bangs as it heats the apartment. The pipes are old, and do not like how we humans drain them in this weather.

I have no music, so I sing to myself. A tune I sang one evening in France when I was attacked, a song I sang to Frieda as we sailed to New York, and the song that takes me back to her—on those cold waves, in the middle of the ocean with no land in sight.

We had been sailing for a few days, our progress hampered by the heavy waves and restless wind, about to see out October and welcome in November.

"What does the ocean look like?" Frieda's voice had been low, crackled with dryness. I gave her some water.

"It is dark now."

"In the day—what does it look like?"

"It is blue. The deepest of blues, and then white as it is churned up by our wake. Hush now, and drink this." I passed her the water.

"Where are we going?"

"America."

"And Papa will be there, won't he? Papa and Maman?"

I felt her forehead; it burned under my palm.

"Hush now."

"It is blue... the sea?" Her eyelids fluttered.

I began to sing, softly, gently, knowing it would calm her.

*

Christmas has arrived once more. Another year gone—1943. I do not know where the time is going. It seems to be taking me so much time to write down my journey here, to America, though during the year I try to think of little else than working, existing. Yet something seems to happen to me at Christmastime—perhaps because it is the time for family and my thoughts go to Frieda, to Bertrand and the others.

This year though, I feel a little lighter—brighter somehow—as if the heavy clouds do not bother me as they used to.

I have been dancing; *mais oui*, I have. With my boss's daughter, who is kind and funny and a very charming lady; made even more so by the fact that she mourns her husband still, and sees me as a brother, or, dare I say it, a best friend.

She has shown me all of New York. From the tourist sights— Fifth Avenue, the Empire State Building and the lit-up theaters of Broadway, which remind me of Montmartre—to some of the darker bars and clubs in Brooklyn. We sometimes go to the pictures, or to a comedy club where we sit and laugh and drink and pretend that inside we are not hurting. Perhaps we are not, in those moments. Perhaps we give ourselves over to some life and fun and we actually do forget. I don't know. Forgive me; I have been reading Hemingway, which has got me worked up. My words come quicker; my thoughts and feelings seem to be tumbling from me, when, since I arrived, they have remained hidden in the depths of my soul.

Now. Here they are.

Miriam and I have decided to go Christmas shopping together. I have not been shopping much in years. She takes me by the arm to Bloomingdale's, and we look at all the things we cannot afford and pretend that we will come back for them later.

I do not buy much, as I do not have many to buy for, and money is still tight. But I manage to buy Miriam a hat pin and her daughter, Sarah, a doll. I even stretch to buying Levi a new tie and my Polish neighbor Katarzyna a tin of biscuits with a red robin on the front.

It is cold out. Every Christmas here seems colder. Miriam tells me it is because I am skinny. I ask her if she means it. She says I could put on a few pounds and then maybe the girls would look at me more. I tell her I don't want the girls to look at me. She does not ask why.

We stroll arm in arm down the busy sidewalk, every now and then stopping to hear a brass band or some such who play on the street for charity. I give a few cents to a children's hospital and Miriam says I am kind.

We say goodnight outside the launderette, which she lives above with her parents and daughter. I wish her a merry Christmas, and she reminds me that she is Jewish and does not celebrate it. I nod, but the truth is that it never occurred to me. "You like Christmas shopping though?" I ask her.

"I like the lights. The colors," she says. "That's all."

I nod again, and she goes inside to her family and I go home to my apartment, the gifts laughing at me in their brown paper bag.

When I reach my door, I decide to give Katarzyna her biscuits. She opens the tin quickly, then eyes me strangely—I have never given a gift before, so I am worried I've chosen the wrong thing.

I tell her it was just a thought, a kindness for all the food she has given me.

She tells me to come to her apartment tomorrow, Christmas Eve, and we will celebrate together with some of her friends. I agree, even though deep down I am not sure I want to.

It is Christmas Eve and I descend on Katarzyna, with nothing to give her but a pleasant smile. She opens the door and does not care that I bring no food or drink, and ushers me into her apartment, introducing me to her friends—Marta, Bartek and Tomek. They work at the university, she tells me. Bartek is small and wiry. He speaks little. They are very clever, helping the government, she says. I do not disagree with her; they look clever. They have that air—one I cannot describe properly—they can wear old clothes and make them look like regal hand-me-downs. They all wear glasses, black-rimmed, and they all smoke. Together, but especially Bartek, they remind me of Kacper. At first it gives me a pain in my chest—the pain of wondering what has become of him—but then the pain disappears and I feel a little comforted by Bartek, by this group, as if Kacper is right here with me.

They do not engage in normal pleasantries—they talk of newspapers, of politics, of what will happen next. I am by no means averse to reading the newspaper, nor a book, but I do not wish to spend my Christmas Eve knee-deep in political debate. So, I change the subject. I ask them what Christmas was like for them at home, and suddenly they soften. Marta tells us of her childhood in Warsaw. She wishes she was at home now. She says she wishes she knew where her family are. The others nod in sympathy.

Finally, Katarzyna breaks the maudlin atmosphere with a mulled alcohol that breathes cinnamon from its cup. She has small pastries too. "American," she says, "or at least, that's what I thought."

Next, she brings out her Polish specialities and this is when the party begins. The politics and all our memories of happier times fall away as our nostrils engage with the smells of rich food.

"This arthritis is really slowing me down," Katarzyna says, as she places the tray on the table.

"You have done a wonderful job," I tell her.

"I know some people and I must feed them. They like my food."

The people who like her food eat quickly, as if there might be no more food tomorrow.

Someone puts on a record. It is Frank Sinatra. I tell them I like it, and someone starts to sing along. There is more food and more drink, and Katarzyna sits and tells us that her family are all in Poland and she does not know who is alive and who is dead.

Everyone goes quiet again, but then Bartek says we shouldn't be like this. It is Christmas, and Tomek tells a joke and everyone laughs.

The doorbell rings and more people come to the party. There is a singer from one of the jazz clubs I visited with Miriam, and his girlfriend. I am impressed at Katarzyna's social circle. She says it is easy to make friends if you try. So, I talk to the man and his girlfriend. She is coffee-colored and his skin is darker, reminding me of the African traders I so often saw in Paris. His voice is light when he talks, almost as if he is singing. We drink and then everyone sits down and there is that lull again, when everyone is scared to talk in case their fears or their sorrows fall from their mouths and we all drown in them.

The singer, Freddie, says, "Tell us, Michel—tell us how you came here."

I am drunk on the two glasses of whatever I have been served, and I like the way he sang my name even when he wasn't singing. "OK," I say. "I'll tell you."

One of the Poles fills my glass, and Katarzyna complains that her arthritis is stopping her from bringing out the rest of the food, and I begin.

*

We were into November 1940, and Frieda was sick day and night. I could not get her to eat. We shared bunks with an Italian woman and her husband; both were as sick as she. The Italian woman tried to read the Bible for Frieda, to calm her. She only stopped when she herself grew too sick, instead talking deliriously in Italian, her husband, pale as snow, trying to tend to her.

I did not leave Frieda's side other than to fetch things or use the toilet, which overflowed. I was surprised that more of us weren't sick.

One of the crew told me that we were a mere two hours away from docking. I went back to the bunk room and told Frieda to hold on—we were nearly there. Her face and body were flaming with fever, and a rabbi's wife had come to sit with her. She told me to leave for a while as she was going to undress her and cool her.

I stood on deck, and it was as though all of the ship's passengers were there too—all waiting for a glimpse of their new home. But the weather was not kind and the sky was dark even at midday, a thick gray that reminded me of how smoke looked rushing out of chimney pots on a cold day. Perhaps New York was a very cold place, and everyone had fires lit.

The ship slowed and even more people came on deck. Before I could turn to go back below there were so many people emerging—children crying, women weeping with relief—that I could not move.

I was pinned against the rail, and it took all my strength not to allow the swell of people to push me overboard into the murky water.

As the Statue of Liberty appeared, her hand reaching to the sky, a calm and reverent silence overcame us all. Tugboats churned through the water noisily, turning up the sea, making it green and gray at the same time. The city came into view; buildings that reached the sky, the tops of some hidden in the low-hanging storm clouds that held a belching of snow.

The wind whipped about us, making us hold on to our coats, our hats. I blew warm air into my cupped hands, which were raw and red.

And as we docked, it felt almost magical. Chains jangled and men shouted at each other on the quayside as they secured the ship. Horns blared from other vessels, causing soot from their chimneys to fill the air, dirtying the overcast city.

Mothers told their children to get off the railings as they perched, waving their hats, their chubby hands and even their kerchiefs in the air at the people that waited. Some waved back, shouted to their family and friends. Most were smiling, relieved to have made the crossing; relieved to have found safety.

The gangplank was lowered and hit the concrete of the port with a loud thud and shudder. Within moments, everyone had gotten themselves into lines to disembark as soon as possible, their papers clutched in their hands. Those without the proper authority stood aside smoking, worried looks on their faces that they would be sent back.

I weaved through the crowds and finally reached our cabin. Frieda was gone.

"The medics took her," the rabbi's wife said, and gathered her things. She put her hand on my forearm. "It does not look good." She squeezed my arm.

The Italian couple were gone too. "They all have the same thing, I think," the rabbi's wife said, holding a scented handkerchief to her nose.

I collected my belongings quickly and took our papers out. We shouldn't be detained long; we had the right papers, I was sure. Henri would not have given us the wrong things. I opened mine and saw a stamp, the approval of a U.S. consul and my name. Frieda's were the same. But where had they taken her without any papers?

I raced back on deck and asked one of the crew where she would be. He said there was a hospital and told me to get off the ship.

There were queues everywhere, waiting to get inside the gray stone building.

"Over there." Someone shoved me towards the back of a queue.

I had to wait. I had to queue like the rest of them, my hands holding the papers, my heart almost in my mouth.

As we waited, a woman gave her children a stale biscuit. They were tired, hungry, and looked as though they could fall asleep at any minute.

Soon we were inside, and families were taken together to be questioned, stamped, checked by a doctor. I stood with the other men, those from the deck who had looked worried.

I asked a security guard where the hospital was. He told me a doctor would see me soon. I tried to tell him it was not for me, not about me, but he pointed to the line, to the worried men, and told me to wait.

Hours passed. It was warm inside, and all I could smell was the sweat and grime from our journey that clung to our tired skin. Now and then the smell of saltwater wafted through the air, and I welcomed it.

Someone behind me asked if there was any water to drink and someone else told him to shut up, all of them eyeing the security guard in his dark blue suit with shining brass buttons.

It was my turn at last.

"Where is she?" I asked the man as he stamped my papers.

"Next," he said.

"No, please—look," I said, my English muddled. I pointed at her name. "Sick." I mimed being ill as best I could, and he pointed to a desk in the corner.

"Missing persons over there."

I was not sure she was missing, but I did as he said.

There was a woman there with two children; she had misplaced her third. The man behind the desk wore small rimmed glasses. He called over a woman who spoke gently to the frazzled mother, led her to some chairs and gave her some tea.

"Yes?" the man asked me.

"Frieda. Frieda Bonnet?" I said. Her name on the papers was no longer German. My fake wife. "She is sick. She was taken away."

The man picked up the phone and dialed a number, the dial turning slowly and making me angry with its sluggishness.

He spoke. I heard her name. He nodded, then looked at me, then at the woman who was now reuniting the mother with her young son, who looked suitably abashed at having run off and given her such a fright.

The man nodded into the phone, once, twice. The he put the phone in its cradle and smiled at me for the first time.

"One minute," he said. He stood and went to talk to his female colleague, who nodded a lot and looked at me with sadness in her face.

I felt my whole body go cold. I felt sick. She walked towards me, smoothing down her jacket as she did.

My legs fell from beneath me before she reached me, and the man with the glasses fetched me a chair.

"I am so sorry," the woman said. "She died."

CHAPTER SEVENTEEN

Le Jour de la Libération

Five years away from France, five years away from Frieda.

1945: the first winter of freedom, Miriam has called it. Even though the German army never reached America, she is right; there is a change in the air, the exhilaration of knowing that maybe soon, things can go back to normal.

Miriam asks me over coffee and a bagel in the diner next to the launderette if I will go back to France. Her father has died; she is worried that she cannot manage the business alone.

"I don't have a reason to return," I say.

"You have a reason to stay though, to help me?"

"I cannot marry you, Miriam," I tell her. I know this is what her father wanted, but we are like brother and sister.

She laughs. I like it when she laughs, as she so rarely does. She shakes her head. "I don't want to marry you, Michel. But that does not mean we can't be partners, right?"

I smile and we shake hands. We are partners—business partners, and the best of friends.

This year she is breaking with her traditions and coming to Katarzyna's for Christmas Eve. I told her about the fun from the last couple of years, and she thought she would like to try it.

She will get a babysitter; she tells me the next day at work.

"Will the jazz singer be there again?" she asks, her eyes alight.

"Perhaps."

"I do hope he is."

That afternoon, I come home to receive a letter with a familiar scrawl—Bertrand.

I have sent him letters over the years, but I have never received a reply. A part of me resigned myself to the fact that he was dead—the bombs that fell in 1943 and '44 decimated such large parts of Paris and Europe that it would have been a miracle if he survived.

I sit in my chair by the window, the condensation making it hard to see the street below. Yet I do not need to see the street—I have something more precious in my hand.

My dearest Michel,

Before I begin, with so much that I have to tell you, I must first offer my sincerest apologies that you have not heard from me sooner. It is not for want—that I can say, at least. It is because I have only just returned home to Paris, and I have only just now been able to read the letters which you have so dearly sent to me, and see the address to which I can reply.

I am so sorry to hear of what happened to Frieda. I cannot imagine the pain that you endured. I wish I was with you, my friend, to ease the pain. But time will heal you, Michel. It has been five years already, and I am sure that whilst the ache still lives on inside you, it has become easier for you to get out of bed each day, to eat, to smile without feeling guilt that you are here and she is not.

Be strong, my friend. We all must be.

This war has taken so much from us all, and I am amazed that I am still here. You must be wondering what happened that night you left, and here I will tell you—but prepare yourself, Michel, we have lost much.

When the car pulled away with you and dear Frieda inside, loud fireworks were set off so that the crowd would come outside the tent and watch them.

Henri took the triplets and the horses back to his house and stashed the triplets away in the attic as he promised he would.

Serge hid those soldiers well, Michel. When he told me of what he had done, I must admit I laughed—it was rather comical to me to think of those Boche all tied up with rags in their mouths!

The speed at which our performers vanished was a sight. Jean, Giordano, Hugo and Kacper were smuggled into the cheese van the next day, and driven south to a woman—a former wife (?)—of Henri's.

Serge, Madame Rosie and I made for Paris in Henri's car, leaving behind a small bunch of workers who were of no interest to the brigadeführer and his men.

At first, it all looked as though it had gone to plan.

It was only when we reached our street that we realized all was not well. The brigadeführer had sent two armed men who stood outside the door to the apartment block—right there on the street. Serge drove past them quickly, muttering under his breath—realizing that Herr Wolff had known exactly who we all were.

We had only one place left to go. We abandoned Henri's car on the outskirts of Paris, and walked and hitched rides to your friend Lucien. I knew his address, and we hoped we had a chance to hide there.

He welcomed us—of course he did—but we knew once we entered his farmhouse, we could not leave again, and Lucien knew the same.

We stayed there for four years, Michel. Four long years Madame Rosie and I lived in Lucien's cellar. We left, sometimes early in the morning, to walk a little around the farm, but never for long and we dared not venture into the town. I could write a book about it, Michel—about the air raids, the Germans who came to Lucien's house for money, for food, and how each time we resigned ourselves that this was the end. But each time, we were given a stay of execution and stayed in that cellar—no longer a prison for us, but a fortress.

Serge, as you can imagine, could not stay cooped up like that and left Lucien's within a week. He was heading to England. Said he would swim if necessary.

We did not hear from Serge for over a year, but one day a letter arrived, with a London postmark—Serge had made it.

He was working in a pub in the East End, happily engaged to the landlord's daughter. He said he was ready for a quiet life and I did not blame him.

He told us of Werner—that he had lasted two more days at Henri's until Wolff found him and took him away for hiding Jews. He had no evidence, and Henri thought he would have been able to help him—but before anyone could help or harm him, he died from infection. Serge believed it was his last revenge on the Boche, for what they had taken from him—dying before they could take pleasure in killing or torturing him.

Henri left for Switzerland soon after Werner's death, taking the triplets with him. The last postcard Serge had received from him showed a photograph of Henri and the triplets, all smiling in a field full of wildflowers. Serge thought the triplets looked the happiest he had ever seen them.

Odélie left for Paris, and no one has heard from her since. But you know her, I'm sure she is fine, she always could take care of herself.

As for Kacper, Hugo, Jean and Giordano. I can tell you that Hugo died—the drink took him in the end. Jean and Giordano—my friend, they left for the south and were taken on their way to Italy. As of now, no one knows where they are, but we fear the worst—we have heard of experiments in the camps on twins, little people and the like. Madame Rosie says we will see them again one day—she has not seen their death in the cards…and so, we hope.

Kacper is still in the south. He wrote to Madame Rosie at my address and his letter was in amongst yours when we came home. He was going to try to get to Palestine to see his family—I will write to see if he has succeeded, whether there is any word of Jean and Giordano.

Madame Rosie is in the kitchen as I write to you now, cleaning and scurrying about to make this our home. Odette saw us arrive and is feverish with rage at the sight of her competition! I wager the next few days or weeks will be full of cat fighting between the two!

That is all my news for now, Michel. I will write again soon. I will write to Henri, Serge and the others, and give them your address. We will all keep in touch with each other from now on and let each other know of any news from our missing friends.

I am so happy to know that you are not amongst the missing.

We shall speak soon, Michel.

All my love,
Bertrand

*

I close the letter and wipe the condensation from the window, looking out into the busy street of yellow taxis, women pushing prams, and am amazed at how the world is continuing to spin, when everything has fallen apart so badly.

Miriam comes to my apartment on Christmas Eve at five o'clock. She is early. Too early.

"You are early," I say, letting her in.

"It is much nicer now, Michel." I see her looking around approvingly.

I have decorated, bought rugs, cushions, pictures. All from flea markets. I want it to look like Frieda's caravan—full of color and life.

There is a charcoal drawing that hangs in a gilded frame that you can see as soon as you walk into the room.

"That is her?" Miriam asks.

"Yes. I asked one of the Poles who is an artist to do it from my memory. It took us almost a month to get it right."

"She is beautiful."

"She is."

In the drawing, Frieda is staring at the viewer, her long hair trailing over her shoulder, her lips parted as if at any moment she is going to laugh or speak.

Miriam sits in a chair and I get her a drink.

"Do you think you will fall in love again?" she asks.

"Maybe. But not like with Frieda."

"That's what I think too. It won't be the same again. It can never be the same, can it?"

"Maybe that's OK, for it to be different."

"Maybe," she says, then throws her wine back in one go.

I pour more.

"Do you think that jazz singer will be there tonight? Do you?"

PART FOUR: SPRING

Nothing will die;
All things will change
[...]
A spring rich and strange,
Shall make the winds blow
Round and round,
Thro' and thro',
Here and there,
Till the air
And the ground
Shall be fill'd with life anew.

"Nothing Will Die," Alfred Lord Tennyson

FIN

Spring has arrived. It's 1946 and there is a promise of warmth from the very first opening of a daffodil in the park. I have just enjoyed my twenty-eighth birthday and there is a lightness in my step that I have not felt in years.

The grass is full of picnickers at lunch, enjoying the thaw and the brightness of colors that the park has to offer. Birds flit, seeking worms and taking crumbs from leftovers. I sit on a bench and watch ducks swim on the pond; now and again I throw a chunk of rye bread to them. If Miriam were here, she would scold me and tell me I was wasting food.

Bertrand talks of coming to visit me and perhaps staying. Paris, he says, is not the same after the war; he cannot look about him without feeling fear. New York might be right for him. I would, of course, enjoy his company; a piece of my old life that could fit into this one.

Miriam asks me why I took such a long lunch break and if I will go and watch Freddie sing tonight. Ever since she met him, she cannot stop mentioning him, and if I am honest, I have seen that giddy light in his eyes too. I wonder if they will ever admit it to themselves. I do hope they find a way.

In the meantime, I dry-clean the suits and dresses of the rich Upper East-siders who have been loyal customers for years. By three o'clock, Miriam's daughter Sarah is back from school and asks me if she can play in my workshop. I tell her she can't, not without me. She pouts and I laugh at her. We go to the back room, my workshop. It is nothing but chunks of wood, some chisels, and a few knives I keep locked away. On one shelf sits a collection of horses carved from driftwood, which I found on the banks of the Hudson. On another shelf are miniature people; one taller than the others, one shorter, one with bulging muscles and a sword in his hand, one wearing a top hat.

Sarah likes the man with the top hat the most, and makes him direct the horses in a show for us. Whilst she plays, I work on another figure, one with her arms outstretched ready to grasp the trapeze that flies towards her. This piece has taken me so long. It is never right, never finished.

"You are done for the day then?" Miriam stands at the doorway. She is smiling, so I know she is joking with me.

"I'll close up," I say. "Go home."

"Are you sure?"

"I'm sure."

Miriam takes Sarah's hand and she waves goodbye to me. I wave back, already looking forward to seeing her face tomorrow.

Once Miriam leaves, the shop is quiet. I switch between cleaning and my carvings and running to the counter when the bell over the door rings to alert me to a new customer.

We close at five. At a quarter to, the bell rings as I am carving the curve of Frieda's back. It makes me jump and I take a wedge out of it. I throw it on the floor—it will never be finished.

The customer is already piling a jacket on the counter and bending down to fetch something else.

"It's got a stain. From ice cream, of all things. Ice cream on wool! Can you get it out?"

Her voice is rich and accented. I like it.

"I can."

I bend down myself to find a new slip, and when I stand up again to fill it in, she is standing straight, staring at me, her mouth open.

Then: "Michel."

My heart is beating so fast I think I am going to pass out. There is no air left in the shop, in the entire city.

"Maman!" A voice breaks the spell. A small girl is at her heel, tugging on her coat. "Maman!" she says again.

"Frieda," I say, as if I was expecting this very moment for years.

"Michel," she says again.

"*Mamannnn*." The child is irritable.

"I thought—" we both say at the same time, then smile, then shake our heads—mirror images of each other, confused, happy, scared.

She bends down to the child and says something to her. The child goes to the green plastic chairs we have for people to wait on, and she climbs up, her pudgy legs swinging as she turns her head to look out of the window.

"They told me you were dead," I whisper. It sounds wrong to say it in English. I say it again in French. "But you are here."

"They told me the same about you!" Her eyes are filling with tears.

"But…why?" Then I think of the poor Italian couple in our bunk—the same illness.

"Is this really happening?" she asks.

I lean over and stroke her cheek to check she is real. "I thought I saw you everywhere—all the time. In the street, in the supermarket."

"I saw you too."

She leans away from me and looks at the child. "They took me to the hospital," she says. "I didn't wake for a week." Then she turns back to me, a tear rolling down her cheek. "They told me that my husband had died."

"Where did you go? After the hospital?" I ask, still wanting to touch her, to make sure this is not one of my mad dreams.

"I had no papers, and because of my situation a convent in New Jersey took me in."

"Your situation?"

Frieda looks to the little girl on the chair once more, and my heart soars.

"You have been here, in this city, the whole time?"

"In Brooklyn."

"And now you are here."

"And now I am here."

The bell rings above the door again and one of our elderly customers, Mrs. Gregson, comes in.

"Michel," she starts, "I have a banquet and I must, *just must*, wear this one." She hands me a red velvet dress. "It is a mess. Smells of mothballs. Tomorrow?"

I don't answer and she looks at Frieda, then at me.

"Tomorrow?" she says again.

I nod.

"A ticket?" she reminds me.

I scribble down the basics, not caring what it says.

She shakes her head at me and leaves.

The child gets up from her chair. "Who is he?" She points her finger at me, her eyes narrowed.

"This is my friend, Michel," Frieda tells her.

"I don't like him." She takes Frieda's hand and tugs at it.

"She wants to go?" I say; the girl is struggling to pull Frieda to the door.

"She's meant to be going to a ballet class," Frieda says, looking at the child, then at me.

"*Mamaaann!*" the child wails at her, then shoots me a look and sticks her tongue out at me like Kacper's monkey, Gino.

"I have to..." Frieda says reluctantly.

"That's OK," I say, but I don't mean it.

"But I'll be back—tomorrow," she says, and looks at the jacket.

"Yes. For the jacket. Of course."

Frieda's smile drops and I don't know what to say.

"Goodbye, Michel," she says, and the door opens and closes, the bell tinkling in her wake.

I go to the door and turn the sign around to say we are closed. As soon as I do, I begin to weep.

I go to see Miriam and tell her what happened.

"Why did you let her leave?" she asks me.

"I don't know!" I say. "The child had a class. And, I don't know. I didn't know what to say. She didn't either. She wanted to go... I don't know." I put my head in my hands.

"She'll be back tomorrow?"

I nod.

"Well, then. Sort yourself out. Tomorrow your life starts again."

"And what about you?" I ask, my eyes filling with tears—of joy, of regret, of absolute wonderment.

"What about me? I have an even bigger family now. The girls can play together. Really, Michel, you do think too much." She kisses me on my cheek and tells me to go home and rest.

I do not rest. I stay awake all night, listening as the swish-swish of traffic on wet tarmac becomes quieter and quieter.

At around 3 a.m. there is little to be heard but the spatter of rain on the window and the knocking of the radiator as it wakes up.

I get to the launderette by 6 a.m. and two hours later Miriam arrives. She fusses all morning—nothing is right, the bookkeeping is shoddy—she is nervous too.

Every time the bell rings, we jump and my heart stops. By late afternoon, I think that if the bell rings again I might have a heart attack, and I listen out, but no noise comes.

"It is almost five," Miriam says quietly to me.

I am in the back, putting the final touches to a horse I wanted to give to my daughter. "She'll come," I say, and I don't look up.

It seems to me that it is hours later—but Miriam tells me it is only minutes—when the bell chimes at last.

I know without looking that she is here, and I walk straight out to see her. She is standing near the door and our daughter is peeking out behind Frieda's legs. I can see that Frieda is as nervous as the child—I am too.

"I came back," she says and smiles. But the smile does not reach her eyes as it used to.

I want to take her in my arms, to spin her around and pretend that we had never been parted, but I do not. So much has changed, we have changed, and I don't know if we can love each other like we once did, but I know we will try—if only for our daughter.

Instead, I bend down to the child. "Hello," I say to her.

"Her name is Michelle," Frieda says.

"Michelle, this is for you." I take the wooden horse from my pocket and hand it to her.

"A pony?" Her eyes widen.

"A pony."

"I like ponies."

"Me too."

She smiles.

"And I like clowns," I tell her.

"Me too!" she says. "Maman says we can go to the circus. Maman says that there are people who can fly in the sky and magic people who can make things appear from nowhere."

"Like this?" I say, and pull a nickel from her ear.

"You're magic!" she says. "Like real magic."

"No," I tell her. "That's your maman. She makes everything better—just like magic."

The child looks to Frieda and then to me.

"Do you like the circus too?" the little girl asks me, her eyebrows raised in question.

"I do," I say. "It's one of my favorite things."

YOUR BOOK CLUB RESOURCE

READING GROUP GUIDE

DISCUSSION QUESTIONS

1. The opening of *The Ringmaster's Daughter* begins with Michel and Bertrand showing their friendship and bond. What did you feel when you read their scenes together? Did you think that they would one day see one another again?

2. Bertrand is almost a surrogate father to Michel. What lessons do you think Bertrand was able to impart to him? How did Michel draw on these lessons throughout his journey?

3. The novel is set in rural France in 1940. Were you surprised to learn how few battles were happening at the time? Did you still get a sense of dread, however, knowing how close the war was to all the characters?

4. When you met Werner, what was your initial impression of him?

5. A major theme of the book is the revelation of the characters' stories—how they each came to the circus and what their lives were like prior to the war. These are based loosely on real-life accounts from this time. Did you feel that they were authentic? Did you learn anything new from them about WWII?

6. The title "The Ringmaster's Daughter" points to the revelation that Frieda is the daughter, but it is not just a reference to a plot point in the novel—it also highlights how Frieda is a different kind of ringmaster to have brought together this ragtag bunch of players, and how her daughter with Michel was her hope of a better life. And it is about Michel as the

ringmaster, too. Just as Werner finally found his daughter, so did Michel. Did you feel that these interpretations were clear in the novel? How did you interpret Frieda? Was she a conduit that brought them all together?

7. The narrative switches from third to first person toward the end of the novel. This shows that Michel is the only one left and brings insight into his personal feelings after the fact. What did you take away from this switch in narrative perspective? Did you feel closer to Michel and get a sense of the loneliness that envelops him?

8. The novel explores many themes—of loss, friendship, religion, and sexuality. What theme stood out most to you and why?

Q&A WITH CARLY SCHABOWSKI

How did you first get the inspiration to write a historical fiction about World War II with a circus as the backdrop?

The story was inspired by the moving true story of Adolf Althoff, an Austrian circus owner during World War II who bravely hid four members of the Jewish Danner family in his circus. I love looking through history and finding those hidden stories that have yet to be told, and this story in particular was one which really stood out to me.

The Ringmaster's Daughter has a unique cast of characters. Do you have a favorite character? Why him or her?

I think my favorite character has to be Giordano. Mostly because he is a little grumpy, a little vain, yet he loves everyone and is a true best friend to Jean. I loved writing his character and he made me laugh!

Michel is shocked to find himself on a circus train as he flees Paris. Why do you think a circus was such a strong cover for trying to save Jewish performers from the war?

I am not sure whether a circus was a particularly strong cover for saving Jewish performers during the war, as it still posed certain risks, especially if German soldiers would come to performances. However, I suppose there was some form of anonymity within the circus, too, in that they could dress up, wear a mask, and hide behind it.

The Ringmaster's Daughter **unveils an unlikely and hidden hero from World War II history. Are there other individuals and groups that you can recommend to readers that they look up to find more instances of heroism during those dark times?**
There are so many to note. A specific group that has always interested me are the so-called *Sewer Rats of Warsaw*. These were resistance fighters in Poland who smuggled people and food in and out of ghettos and fought for their freedom, all from the underground sewerage system of the city.

Frieda is such a strong woman in the story. What was the inspiration for her character?
Frieda was an amalgamation of many strong women I have known. She embodies love, courage, strength in such a way that makes Michel fall in love with her the instant he sees her. She is the one who persuades her father to help others, and it is she who propels the story forward with her courage in the face of adversity.

The circus travels widely throughout France. Is there a specific reason for your location choices?
The French locations were chosen due to the research I did about what was happening in France during this time and where there could be towns where they may find safety. Each one conjures up a beautiful image of the French countryside and old villages, which I particularly love.

All of the circus performers come together to create a new family, one they can rely on no matter what. Which is why when they are betrayed by one of their own, it's devastating. Why did you

have Odélie betray them and was it pure jealousy that drove
her to it?

Odélie is a flawed individual—as we all are. Although she betrayed
them, it was through desperation rather than jealousy—of fear for
herself, of what could happen to her. Of course, there is an aspect
of vanity with Odélie, and she has always known that she can
get what she wants through her looks. But she shows a strength
despite what she did, in that she perhaps felt like an outsider and
that she only had herself to rely on.

**Michel is quite gifted with the animals in the circus. What do
you think that says about his character?**

Michel's love of animals shows how he feels more comfortable
with them—they are loyal, loving, and it juxtaposes what was
happening around him, where humanity was seemingly disappearing before his eyes. I think there are many of us who get
comfort from animals during difficult times in our lives too,
and his love of them shows how he is going through inner
turmoil—of fear, desperation, sadness—and he can find solace
with his animal friends.

**Historical fiction is incredibly popular right now. Why do you
think that is?**

Recent years have seen a boom in what's referred to as the
"memory industry"—more historical records online, more
tangible links with anyone worldwide through varying modes
of communication. Genealogy advertisements, websites and
home-kit DNA tests have propelled the rapid growth in society's
preoccupation with the past as a means for self-identity. These
personal, familial historical endeavors convey what I see as
an irresistible longing for the past to speak personally to the
present—we want our ghosts not just to speak, but to speak *to*

us. Thus, historical fiction can reflect that search for self-identity that we crave and gives us insight into our shared pasts.

Do you like going to circuses in your personal life? What's your favorite act at a circus?

I have never been to a circus! Not once. Partly due to the fact that the use of animals always bothered me. I have been to many a fair, however, where acts such as jugglers, clowns and fire eaters entertain the crowds. If I were to choose a particular act from these fairs, I would say that the magician always captivated me, and although I knew they were tricks, I desperately wanted to believe in magic.

What's one thing you want all of your readers to know about you?

I write at night—late at night, usually around 11 p.m. until 4 a.m.! This is mostly due to the fact that I am easily distracted, and during the day this happens a lot! It doesn't have to be much—a leaf blowing in the wind, and I stop what I am doing to watch said leaf.

It is better for me to write at night when all chores are done, there is nothing to watch on TV, and it is quiet. Then, I can be completely creative.

HOW WE CHOOSE TO
WRITE ABOUT THE PAST

When we think about historical fiction it is a strange beast. It is a compilation not just of historical fact but of fiction, of reimagining what the past could have been, and for an author of historical fiction it becomes a balancing act of when to utilize fact and when to reimagine the past.

This balancing act is something that I have been very curious about. Indeed, it inspired me to complete a doctorate about such a topic—about how we, as authors, enter into the historical debate, and how we view our responsibility in the lenses we choose to portray the past to our readers. Are we responsible to our reader, to fact, to fiction, or to our characters?

Of course, the subject is academically arduous, but also is one that I believe a reader should be invited to engage with, as my choices as a writer have an effect on how you read this book and how you perceive the history contained therein. It also affects the type of historical fiction you are reading. Is it a historical memory novel, or is it a fictive history?

The Ringmaster's Daughter, whilst inspired by a true story, has not assigned itself to telling the whole truth about what happened to a particular man and those within his actual circus. Rather, as I sought the more obscure corners of historical record, I found that objective fact was as unavailable, limited, and distorted to me as it often is to a historian, and yet I had tools at my disposal—imaginative and fictive ones—that might broaden and deepen the historical narrative rather than detract from it.

As such, I approached the telling of this story through multiple personal accounts of that time—of memories of experiences—merging them together into fictional characters to give a glimpse of the lives lived and of those persecuted. I wanted to show a story that was deeply rooted not only in the characters' memories of their lives prior to the war, but of the interactions and friendships that can be born from this time—in essence, becoming a collage of backstories, of secrets held within.

These "secretive" stories of each character really called out to me during the writing of this book; begging me to tell how they came to be in the circus and giving insight into human nature and experience. Each character's secret life was drawn from research on real-life stories during World War II, allowing me to merge fact and fiction to create a realistic picture of the past.

This realistic past that I wanted to re-create for my reader was one that aimed to connect them to the authentic multiple stories set in the backdrop of a circus, allowing perhaps a theme of magical realism to become apparent, all of which underpinned the main theme of hope: hope of life after the war, hope of love, of friendship, and hope of the ending of persecution.

Frieda is the conduit for hope in this narrative. She draws all the characters together through the empathy she feels for them, through the kindness that she shows, and through her love for Michel. Indeed, the title of the book itself draws on this fact—that the story begins with the ringmaster's daughter, of how her birth changed her father, of how she created the circus we read about, and ultimately, how she has her own daughter with Michel (the new ringmaster), showing new life, and of course, new hope for them all.

A LETTER FROM CARLY

Hello,

Firstly and most importantly, a huge thank-you for reading *The Ringmaster's Daughter*. I hope you enjoyed reading it as much as I enjoyed writing it.

The Ringmaster's Daughter was inspired by the moving true story of Adolf Althoff, an Austrian circus owner during World War II who bravely hid four members of the Jewish Danner family in his circus. On 2 January 1995, Yad Vashem recognized Adolf and his wife Maria as Righteous Among the Nations. "We circus people see no difference between races or religions," said Adolf when he received the honor.

This selflessness in the face of persecution called out to me as a story which needed to be explored. Whilst the inspiration was drawn from Althoff, the characters and their journey are based on my imagination, coupled with a historical understanding of that time. I do not pretend to be a historian; instead, I hope I have widened the scope of historical reality through my characters' lives and personal experiences, their loves and losses. In this vein, any historical inaccuracies are entirely mine.

My interest in World War II history stemmed from the stories I was told as a child by my Polish grandfather, who had been forced into the Wehrmacht at a young age, then escaped to England to join the Polish army in exile. The stories handed to me begged to be explored, to breathe life into those ghostly voices of the past, to let them speak and tell their own tales.

These are characters who have come to mean a lot to me, so thank you for spending your time with them—I hope you have found it worthwhile. If you have a moment, and if you enjoyed the book, a review would be much appreciated. I'd dearly love to hear what you thought, and reviews always help us writers to get our stories out to more people.

I hope too that you will let me share my next novel with you when it's ready.

It's always fabulous to hear from my readers—please feel free to get in touch directly on my Facebook page, or through Twitter, Goodreads or my website.

Thank you again for your time,
Carly Schabowski

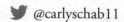 @carlyschab11

ACKNOWLEDGMENTS

I'd like to thank my wonderful agent Jo Bell, who has never stopped believing in my writing and is always on hand to cheer me on! My editor, Kathryn Taussig, has been great—encouraging me every step of the way and spotting my errors with a keen eye!

My family and friends also deserve a huge thank-you for putting up with me during the writing of this book, through my writerly tantrums and my constant need to talk over the plot and characters. I could not have done this without your support.

Also, a thank-you to Alison, who helped with the French translations! And a big thanks to my US editor, Kirsiah, who has been wonderful throughout!

Lastly, I want to thank Rebecca, who took me to my first circus—all I can say is that it was not what we expected!